Rowan Blaize and the Starbane Exile

Brightbourne Media

rowanblaize.com
brightbournemedia.wordpress.com
facebook.com/rowanblaize

Library of Congress Cataloguing in Publication Data applied for
ISBN 13: 9780615708768
ISBN 10: 0615708765

Rowan Blaize and the Starbane Exile

Enchanted Heritage Chronicles:
Book III

Jonathan Kieran

2012

Contents

Prologue

"I am at war, boy. Ha! Oh, you look at me with derision and revulsion, and I don't blame you. I do not look like a warrior, caught as I am in such grim circumstances, but I am at war, all the same. We are both at war, now."

A filthy hand erupted, striking like a serpent between the corroded iron bars of a cell in the dungeon gloom, grabbing the arm of a boy being dragged in chains, dragged by guards who loomed above like obsidian towers.

"Who are you? What do you want with me?"

"I'll tell you who I am," croaked the far more ancient voice.

It was a voice like small stones being crushed with violence, over and over, in the palm of someone's hand, a voice that even the murderous soldiers were reluctant to silence amid such darkness, at this strange and unexpected moment. Against orders and their own judgment, the sweating brutes paused in the dank corridor, seemingly captured beneath the veil of some thin and final spell.

"I am a beast that is no longer free, and rather quite soon I shall no longer *be!*" rasped the caged attacker, spewing flecks of saliva and breath foul enough to wither the senses. "We are fellow captives, you and I, but my heart tells me that *you* have a chance to escape, boy. You, who are nothing but mortal dust compared to the splendor that I once was, a glory not so long ago diminished."

"Let go of my arm!"

The boy's face was a muddy remnant of shadow and his eyes no more than a swift flash of moisture in the black. He wanted to get away from this vile interruption, yet he did *not* want to get away, for there was no place where one might hope to go. Not anymore. His jailors, those who pulled taut his shackles even now, were hardly to be invoked for assistance in the best of times, much less in the subterranean prison against this new and stinking foe.

"I've done nothing to you, old one. I do not know you and have troubles of my own. Can you not see this?"

"See? Did I not say that we are fellow victims, impertinent little whelp? *See?* I see my doom and your flight. Yes, I see that. Flight like a desperate sparrow, seeking to outrace the winter wind. But you'll do it, I think. The wretch who's got us likes to collect certain valuables to increase her status, you see. I expect you know that much, already. I am just one piece in a particular 'set' she's been after. But she must not get all the pieces. And when your flight has begun, I'll ask that you bring a message to a certain crucial piece, one of my associates, when you can manage."

"Leave me to my own misery! I don't know you or your associates. I cannot help myself, far less an unfamiliar voice coming at me in the stench of this tomb."

"You *will* help me."

Another hand shot out between the rusted bars, this one balled into a fist and bearing a signet ring that had, by some manner of trickery, been hitherto concealed from prying eyes—sequestered in places where even torturers' implements were not inclined to probe. The little ring gave off a weary glow and then sparked a bright, fleeting red in the murk. The fist pressed it hard into the flesh of the boy's forearm, where it burned its brand. The boy screamed, more in surprise than in pain, for he had been suffering worse than *this* kind of treatment, of late. The guards emerged from whatever little mind-storm had clouded their progress, their momentary trance evaporated, and they snarled like a pack of hunting dogs suddenly attuned to a ripe scent. Rattling chains and spears against the bars, they kicked the Old One back into the rather shallow depths of his cell.

"Away!" they hissed. "This is *her* property, not yours. She will hear about your tricks. Oh, you can believe us. She will hear."

They began to haul the boy up the passage and toward the faintest whisker of light quivering above. The Old One laughed and muttered under his breath as they scraped and clanked and clamored along. Then he cried out a final time.

"Yes, do indeed take him! I shall have no chance, whereas he shall out-chance us all. Go! Go to the South, boy, when your opportunity comes, and find one of my peers. His name is Rowan Blaize, and I have seen the edges of the future, even from this cesspit. You, boy, shall cross his path. Show him the scar on your arm—for my stinging ring shall leave this scar forever on your flesh—and tell him how you got it! He'll know *who* gave it to you," the Old One screeched. "You see, I struck a little bargain with him during a rather harrowing predicament when he first stumbled upon these lands, long ago. He is bound by an old spell, and by his own interests, to aid you on my behalf, if you demand it, and if you show him the sign. And believe me, boy ... you shall need aid. I have been subtly taunting *her* in regard to Rowan Blaize for quite some time, too. Oh, she will appreciate my little trickery ... perhaps my final trickery."

"Who are you?" squawked the boy as he was yanked, breathless, across a floor of rough and jagged stone.

"Just show him the scar when you see him," muttered the Thing in the Dark. "And you can tell her something, too, when you are granted an audience."

"I will tell her nothing, for I do not speak to her!"

"Be silent," barked one of the guards, cuffing the boy on his mouth.

"Tell her *this*," floated hoarse words through musk and filth and dust. "A wizard came from Worlds-within, as ancient legends say. 'When I am dead,' a captive said, 'then *he* must guide the way.'

"Now you go, boy, and you *tell* her."

෫৵ৡৌ

PART ONE
A SPARROW OUTRACING THE WIND

I

Cackle-at-the-Moon Stuff

Her boots were made from elf-skin, laced with whiskers she had pulled from the snout of the dragon, Blixtus, after she killed it. She could have plucked them, boldly, one by one, while the great wyrm was still alive, had she wanted to do so. On her head rested a crown fashioned from the skull of one of the redoubtable beast's hatchlings, carefully hollowed-out and washed—as recommended by discriminating sorcerers—in the enchanted waters of the Hespera Springs. Beneath the gruesome headpiece, her face was a mottled gray even in the candlelight, and pale like the chalky Cliffs of Senu. Once upon a time, her skin had been whiter than the snowy mountaintops of Meryx, which she could still see, in the twilight distance, from the rock-hewn window of her tower's spell chamber.

Now, however, Oblixta's flesh reflected death and reeked of malice. The pupils of her eyes glowed onyx, and not even the most impenetrable night sky could compare to them. The cloak she wore had been wrought from the silvery hide of an Eskanthian werewolf she had happened to catch lurking around the castle moat one summer evening. It had only been hoping for a drink, but got much, much more.

Oblixta was, in a word, *bad*.

On the long table in her Room of Incantations, books were stacked in haphazard piles, some open to pertinent and arcane texts while others remained shut—locked and opened only by the proper charm or intentionally misshapen key. All of these tomes were rather ancient and most were covered in precious metals or studded with jewels. A few were even bound in the flesh of various beings that had once walked or crawled, alive in bliss or malevolence, upon the land. Some skins had come from things that once soared above in the heavens.

There were also utensils upon her worktable; mortars and their pestles rested in various stages of postponed grinding and pulverizing. At least a dozen flasks and phials, filled with liquids or powders of myriad color, occupied one side of the bench. The noonday sun-bleached bones of small animals, mingled with unholy stones, were spread in meaningful disarray on the other side. Sigils and runes engraved upon these items were only visible in the sputtering flicker of a taper that Oblixta had made from the lard of a particularly useless Servant-Goblin's belly. At the moment, however, the most curious item upon the table was a small wickerwork cage fashioned from willow twigs and a few dried vines of deadly Caltressian Ivy. Trapped within this cage was a living person. The dragon hatchling's skull-crown lowered and loomed. Oblixta the Sorceress brandished between her fingers four miniscule wings, much like those of a dragonfly, wings that emitted sparkles of iridescence even in the gloom.

"You're quite the catch, Tramayda."

Oblixta wiggled the wings a bit, taunting her captive.

"One of my best acquisitions ever, in fact. Though, I must admit, you're not nearly as valuable to me as *these* are." She twitted the wings again for good measure. "Even *I* was beginning to lose hope that I would ever ensnare the most powerful Fey Empress in the land."

The wispy figure in the cage moved closer to the edge of the wickerwork prison. Though her own face, normally quite fair, began to flush red and then a sudden, sapphire blue with anger, her delicate features remained awash with at least *some* measure of dignity, simmering below a full-fledged boil.

"You're absolutely vile. But I suppose you know that already," said Tramayda, Empress of the Fey.

"Thank you," replied Oblixta, her every sigh a toxic fume. "For your information, I do know it. Some fool once wrote that it is good to 'know one's self,' and though I'd surely skewer and eat such a blithering ninny, if I had him in hand today, I might also give him a prize for navel-gazing, before the roast."

"Vulgar as ever, Oblixta," noted Tramayda. "Again, that's no surprise. Nor are your goals. Those goals have never been a secret to me, or to anyone in any kingdom of this entire world, I suspect, or even in the Places Unseen, the worlds within. But I've thwarted your plans before and I'll do so again. Count on it."

Oblixta rose to her full height and removed the hatchling skull-crown. She placed it on a warped shelf, next to a nest of squirming, starving pinkie-rats that had recently lost a mother when she'd required entrails for a quick scry of current gossip among the castle's servants. Then she patted the top of the wicker cage with an almost gentle appreciation. The talons that served as her fingernails lingered for an instant upon the weave-work of the enchanted little prison.

"Don't look so smug up there. I *will* find a way to finish you," promised the captured Tramayda.

Oblixta yawned. "Lovely display of bravery, my pet, but we both know you're in trouble. Really, Tramayda, do you think you're still dealing with an amateur, like in the old days? Even as an amateur I was a handful, wasn't I? And even the most louse-ridden village hag knows that a fey loses three-fourths of her magic when her wings are, shall we say, *clipped*. The Empress of the Fey knows that part best of all."

Tramayda considered this for a moment, trying not to fold and unfold her translucent arms with obvious nervousness.

"No doubt you took great pleasure in plucking my wings off," she sneered, "but that's so 'cheap sorceress,' isn't it, Oblixta? Rather cackle-at-the-moon stuff, don't you think? Maybe you're still more of an amateur than you'd guess. I can't speak to the current crop of witches in Kelnia, mind you, but in *my* day, wicked sorceresses had a great deal more nuance and artistry. You seem a bit of a hack."

Oblixta held up an index finger and raised a brow, casually dropping the fluttery wings into a nearby chalice. "You're quite correct about the pleasurable aspect of the plucking," she admitted. "Tell me. Did it hurt? You didn't actually scream when I yanked them off your back, so I wasn't certain."

Tramayda glared at her foe with a scrabbled aura of helplessness and condescension. "So this is how low you've fallen?" she said. "Plucking wings? Why, you're no better than a cruel mortal child that amuses itself by torturing a housefly. That alone speaks volumes about your quality. No worthy witch would let herself be comparable to a silly child."

Oblixta laughed a little at this remark. "Perhaps, but we don't mind houseflies, which can often be put to good use in magic. In this case, Tramayda, the analogy is superb, for you are *my* housefly. By the by, please know that this great work of mine was not done merely for pleasure." She began to add a variety of odiferous potions, powders, and elixirs to the chalice containing the wings. "That being said, I'll admit to a sliver—just a sliver—of delight when I ripped these appendages from your body, and to a certain bit of satisfaction that comes only with revenge."

"A *bit* of satistfaction?" chortled Tramayda. "Chance would be a fine thing! What's more, you've had revenge in mind for years, you obsessed, scrawny old broom-handle. Ever since my spells stopped you from sending that pack of Eskanthian werewolves across the Bibb River to terrorize innocents in Ombos, you've had quite the wasp in your skull-crown over me."

Oblixta turned to face her captive with a frown, slamming one fist hard upon the worktable. The resulting tremor caused Tramayda to stumble and fall within the cage.

"That river incident was none of your affair," Oblixta said evenly. "Besides, I got over that unwarranted intrusion long ago. I have other reasons for our current meeting. Incidentally, those ingrates in Ombos had refused to render the homage—and taxes—due to me. They live in *my* fiefdom and I had every right to exact punishment, seeing as you brought it up."

"Your fiefdom? Hah! You've no legitimate claim to power over any kingdom, Oblixta. Everyone knows it. Not by birth, and certainly not by virtue of the dark arts you practice, much less the vicious acts you've committed. But selfishness has poisoned you from the beginning of your lovely career, hasn't it? I hardly feel the need to remind you that such arrogance has been the downfall of many a sorcerer. Sorcerers greater than you."

Oblixta dropped a pinch of Purple Dung Beetle dust into the chalice. "Perhaps you think you are right, Tramayda," she said with a shrug.

"All the same, I have changed the rules, whatever the rules may have been at one time. After all, my powers were honed through hard work and study. Hard work is always rewarded as it deserves, whether that reward is freely given ... or taken. Moreover, you forget that I am now greater than any sorcerer who has ever lived."

"*I* am greater," countered Tramayda, inspecting her fingernails with as much nonchalance as she could muster.

"No," said Oblixta, holding up one terrible talon of her own for emphasis. "You *were* just one of the greats, sweetmeat. Now, I'd say that even your former greatness is called into question, given the circumstances."

"Talk, talk, talk," sniffed Tramayda. "How soon you forget that it was *my* power that instantly froze the waters of the Bibb River as your werebeasts swam toward their mission of murder."

Oblixta smiled. "A clever trick, I'll give you that much. But that village is still around, as you well know, and no spell of yours can protect it now."

Tramayda stamped a tiny foot. "Remember, too, that it was *I* who brought you low when you attempted to transform King Rigel of Gurda into a salamander!"

"Another good one," Oblixta conceded. "Again, I'll give you some credit for originality. Encasing the old dotard in quartz before my spell had a chance to enshroud him was a keen preemptive strike." Oblixta began to hum and chant as she searched for specific odds and ends among her vast paraphernalia. She procured an oblong crystal phial from the grim assemblage of artifacts, grimmoires, and magical bric-a-brac. For a moment, she held the phial close to the candlelight. Its contents seemed to pulsate with a robin's egg shade of blue.

"What's that for?" asked Tramayda.

Oblixta emptied the contents of the phial into the chalice. "This, my little hobbled mosquito, is the blood of a freshly killed bat from the caves of Ta-Kensesh. It's for my potion."

"Ta-Kensetian bats?" shrieked Tramayda. "That species is of unmitigated evil stock."

"Well, what else would you expect from the likes of me?" said Oblixta. "In any event," she continued to explain, "it's the catalyst for the spell I'm preparing to work."

"No doubt you're going to tell me *all* about it, too."

"Of course I will." Oblixta tapped the last of the blue bat-blood into the vessel, where it congealed atop Tramayda's shorn wings and the other ingredients. "You might as well know. After all, it's the spell that'll seal your doom and my latest, greatest triumph."

"Don't be so certain about that," puffed the fey, though her show of confidence wasn't making much of an impression.

"This spell will do many things," instructed Oblixta. "Among them, it will enable me to extract the truth from your miserable little soul, which is a thing very difficult to obtain from faeries at the best of times. I've had a spy in the castle lately, and I think *you've* been helping that spy, whoever it is. This kind of subterfuge interferes with my ability to plan for war and manage my other captives. Yes, someone's been helping my prisoners make little plans with each other, and my guess is that you and some of your miserable handmaidens are the culprits."

"If you're referring to the wizard that everyone knows you've got cooped-up here, then I know nothing about any 'plans.' Neither do I have a care for your war schemes, or any spy that might be sneaking around these foul hallways. I *do* wish them luck, however."

Oblixta shot the fey a withering look. "Stop that squeaking or I swear I'll lose patience and sew your lips shut with spider silk," she muttered. "Your wishes for luck are as good as spells, in my estimation, so I guarantee you'll tell me everything I want to know before we're finished."

Tramayda regarded the witch with a glower that normally would have melted the most formidable Ice Daemon lurking in any Meryx Mountaintop crag. Oblixta, unaffected, gingerly wiped one hand against another, making certain that every possible particle on her fingertips fell into the chalice.

"You see, O Wingless One, I've accomplished quite a great deal over the years, and I don't want to mar my excellent record, just as the best is yet to come. Why, in my career to date, I've forced nobles to grovel at my feet. I've set entire cities ablaze with a wave of my hand, a few choice words, and a mere twitch of thought. I've enchanted the waters of the Klykoff Pools until even the trolls that drink there are obliged to do my bidding. I've changed form and prowled the woodlands of Brayl by nightfall, unafraid of any foe. I've conjured mazes that even the smartest of Queen Leebo's pet ferrets have failed to navigate."

"Big deal," said Tramayda, yawning.

"I have walked unscathed across the rivers of molten rock that drool from the top of Ypax volcano," continued Oblixta. "I've nearly finished raising an unconquerable army. What else? Oh, yes. I've bested dragons and the Creeping Imps of Kasha. As you likewise know, several great wizards have wet their knickers in my presence. Now, even Fey Empresses tremble before me. And yet, for all of that, I remain curiously unfulfilled. Why do you think this is so?" Tramayda snorted. "For one thing, I'm not trembling," she said. "For another, I'm not interested in any of your so-called 'accomplishments,' you desiccated hag. And for posterity, I'm not remotely concerned with issues of your personal fulfillment."

"Right," said Oblixta out of the corner of her mouth. "But you *will* be interested when I tell you that I am planning to smash the Southern wizard, Rowan Blaize, under my thumb and capture all of the lands beyond the Pyr Mida Mountains." She began humming a morbid and discordant tune while she stirred the chalice with a rib-bone. The bone had been culled from a lesser warlock named Crablus, whom she had conquered four years earlier in a pithy battle.

"So you're going after Rowan Blaize," sniffed Tramayda from the cage. "The one the Gragan has been needling you about. Making you feel frightened, obviously. Just another scalp for your collection, I suppose?

"This isn't about a matter as tawdry as mere collection," informed Oblixta. "It is about conquest. And *you* stand in my way with your spying, here in my own castle. Believe me, I won't have you warning the wizard before I make my move against him. I simply *won't* have it."

"I already told you—I don't know anything about any spy in this dump, and I have no concern for Rowan Blaize or your designs upon him.

Your efforts to rattle me will be wasted, I guarantee. You don't frighten me, Oblixta, even with all your pestling and chanting."

"Feign indifference while you can, Tramayda," cooed Oblixta. "But you *will* be frightened. And you *will* tremble, before it's over. Now look at me, going-on about my wonderful deeds! You haven't even let me tell you of the other portion of this spell I have yet to master, the one bit of magic that has eluded me thus far."

"And what might that be?"

"*That* would be the power of flight," answered Oblixta.

"Oh, please, you cracked conjurer! Every creature from this hell-hole to the borders of Valnogoth, be it mortal or immortal, dweller in town or in forest, castle or hovel, has had the misfortune of seeing your bony silhouette streak against the full moon of nights. Yes indeed, every-one's seen you flit about on that scab-riddled familiar of yours."

"Perhaps, but I no longer wish to ride a flying goat," hissed Ob-lixta. "Besides, Rundl can only bear me at night. I want to fly by my own power. You know—course the heavens by day and by darkness, unaided by enchanted props."

"Impossible," Tramayda huffed. "Even *you* cannot acquire that gift. Rowan Blaize hasn't even been able to do it, if you believe the legend. It is quite simply and intrinsically beyond your nature."

"So I had thought ... for the longest time."

Oblixta finished stirring her potion and placed the now smolder-ing, smoking chalice very close to Tramayda's wickerwork cage. "How-ever, some years ago, as you may have heard, I dueled with the sorcerer Calphur, near the Pillars of Lamentation. Of course, I triumphed."

"I heard about it," Tramayda admitted.

"Good," noted Oblixta, raising another talon. "What you didn't hear about, perhaps, is that the idiot's entire library came into my pos-session, after the victory. That's correct. All of Calphur's lore. All of his secrets. All of his *books.*"

"And what startling revelations, pray, did you discover amid the spoils?"

"For one, I discovered the spell I am now crafting, one that will also grant me the unlimited power of flight ..."

"Rubbish!" snapped Tramayda.

"... if only I were able to procure four tiny-but-crucial ingredients."

Tramayda's eyes widened to the size of peas. "My *wings?*"

"Clever girl! You see, in Calphur's most precious book of spells, I happened upon a procedure—a very ancient and monstrous incantation—that would guarantee me the gift of flight *if* I were able to capture a living Fey Empress and yank, one-by-one, each wing from her back to use in the appropriate potion."

Tramayda began to visibly shudder for the first time.

"The small matter of the wings has already been accomplished," added Oblixta, "as you can attest."

Tramayda wrapped her arms about herself in an attempt to stay her quaking form. The bloody nubs on her back, where her wings had been amputated, were now swollen and aching.

"As *you* can attest, witch, taking my wings was no 'small matter' in the least," countered the Fey.

Oblixta pursed her lips and regarded her captive with a half-lidded, baleful stare.

"You put up a commendable fight. That much is true." She tapped a talon to her dry-as parchment lips, drawing a tiny bead of blood as she reflected upon her victory. "I believe the turning point came when I blasted you with a Spell of Immobilization and you chose to parry with a Curse of Ecstasy. Fatal mistake, on your part."

Tramayda shook her head in regret. "I should never have been lured from the protection of my forest by your crass imitation of one of my handmaidens ... pretending to cry out that she was caught in the web of a Prithian Spider, of all things!"

"Yet, you couldn't help yourself," reasoned Oblixta. "Your fluttering fey heart is filled with such goodness, and I, being an excellent mimic, left you with no choice but to follow your instincts and leave the safety of your glade. Prithian Spiders can't be managed by just any of the Fair Folk, after all. They're rather beastly. No, it requires the power of a fey *empress* to rescue one of her subjects from such a snafu. Still, once you discovered the ruse and the battle commenced, you should have guessed that a Curse of Ecstasy would backfire. Normally, of course, such a curse—leveled by a being of your stature—would send a lesser magician into complete giddiness and lack of control, unable to focus upon the magic at hand. Luckily, I have long since embraced the fact that I'm most ecstatic when I'm doing evil. Your curse actually *empowered* me, Tramayda! That's when I knew I had you."

Tramayda paced back and forth in her cage. "So let's say you've won, Oblixta. Perhaps you *do* possess a spell that will enable you to fly."

"There's no 'perhaps' about it. This rubric is solid, and no mistake."

The Empress rushed to the willow-twig bars and thrust her head out as far as she could. "Even if you do work such a spell, I hope you crash head-first into the jagged cliffs of Aleegis and that the Ghoul-Yaks of Bijma lick your splattered brains right off the rocks!"

"My, my," muttered Oblixta. "What sour sentiments from a good-ly sprite."

"Look," said Tramayda. "Let's strike some kind of deal here. You have my wings. Presumably, you'll use them to help you zigzag through the clouds at leisure. Fine. Just let me go and return me to my people. There'll be no hard feelings and I promise not to interfere with your future machinations in any capacity. My people need their leader, even if I *am* incapacitated. You've got what you want. Set me free and we'll call you the all-time winner."

"Good grief," Oblixta sighed. "I must say it's a pity to see a once-great Lady affecting such transparent desperation."

"Whatever do you mean?"

"What do you think I mean? You're taking me for a fool, though I daresay you're left with no other recourse. Don't you understand that I, of all people, know that only a Fey Empress, alone among her kind, has the ability to *grow back* her wings once they have been lost?"

Tramayda cast an angry gaze at her own bare feet.

"If I let you go," continued Oblixta, "you'd have a brand new set grown in—what?—*ten* days at the most? Your powers would be restored to their former strength, and then some."

"Well, you won't get much use out of the wings you've already plucked," seethed the faery. Clapping her miniscule hands, she formed a crackling green ball of energy that beamed from the little cage and hit Oblixta's chalice at full force. The chalice, pestled fairy wings and all, exploded in the witch's hand.

"You miserable insect!" wailed Oblixta as pieces of the unholy goblet and globs of its contents clattered and oozed onto the flagstones. "My flight potion! How have you managed this treachery? That wicker-work cage was surrounded by the most powerful wards possible. I wove it myself. You were entirely under my control in there!"

"And a fine piece of work it is," retorted Tramayda. "But every great construction has its little flaws in design. Yours was here, between this wedge of willow-bark and this bit of Caltressian Ivy. See for yourself. You didn't make the proper knot for the spell. I couldn't escape the cage, but because of your mistake, just enough of my magic *could.*"

"Interfering wretch," growled Oblixta, drumming her talons atop the worktable.

"That's as may be," piped Tramayda with a smirk, "but the fact is, you've no longer got the ingredients for your flight-spell, and no means of getting me to spill the beans about any potential spies in your castle. You've lost my wings, wonderworker."

Oblixta grabbed the entire wickerwork cage from the table and, with one dismissive grunt, flung it into the roaring flame of the chamber's hearth. There ensued a terrible crackling and one dramatic squeal of pain, a wail of doom that quickly faded to a mere sizzle.

"I also don't have ten more days to wait until you grow a *brand new* set," murmured Oblixta.

The sorceress sat down, somewhat weary now, in a chair uphol-stered with the tanned skin of Spersax, the mightiest warrior in the army of Baron Zerkul, another of her many defeated foes. This had not been the best of days, by any means. Dealing with fey empresses was always fraught with difficulty, but she realized she should have stopped gloating and paid a little more attention to how she had built the wickerwork cage. There was nothing to do about it now, except vow never to repeat such a haughty mistake. Flying powers would have to wait.

A spy in her castle—and the problem of Rowan Blaize—could not.

ॐॐ

The Gragan Wizard of Drothgad Mountain had not suffered the thing called Fear for the greater part of his three hundred and twenty-three years. Wars had erupted and cooled. Kings and their campaigns had risen and fallen. Lords and barons who had once feted him with wine and bribed him with damsels had long since become dust and rot. Famine and pestilence—a few cases of which he had conjured himself—emerged, struck, and faded into the recollections of history. Throughout all of that grand epoch, Gragan had never been afraid of anything.

Worry?

Yes, he had felt his share of *that,* but it was never tinged with the singular and mortal terror of something he could not control. Or escape from. Or demolish. Now, he could hear a stone door crack open at the end of the corridor, and the sound was a blade of ice jabbing, frost on flesh, at the base of his brain. Voices rumbled, and he listened to them as he would listen to a conference of thunderclouds in the distance, envying their power to threaten. Night and swamp and stench were eternal things within his cell. Trapped in this dismal realm he leaned against layers of slime on the wall, placed two hands across his brow and suffered Fear.

Familiar footsteps began to echo, and Gragan hissed at the sound, remembering the kind of shoes that made such awful noises. They were *her* shoes, all tanned and fashioned from elf-skin, laced up the middle with the whiskers of that dead dragon she never stopped bragging about killing. He gave his head a good shake, mumbled a spell, and let his fingernails slice into the skin around his ears, trying to banish the possibility of her approach. But his magic was gone, truly gone, and a moment later he sensed her figure before him, shrouded by a midnight he could not dispel, beyond the row of rugged bars he could no longer melt with a few choice words and a little concentration. A halo of lantern light began to wax through the dark, and he took advantage of the glow to turn his hands back and forth before his face, making certain they were as filthy as the rest of his body. It was a strange comfort to be sure of such a thing.

Wit and cunning, he thought. *These will be the keys to survival once again. If time can no longer be controlled, then* perhaps *it can be persuaded.*

Gragan had always fancied himself an expert at persuasive maneuvers, with or without magic. Despite the gravity of his predicament, he could not help chuckling in the gloom.

Wouldn't the Galwyn Crone envy my wit? And wouldn't the miserable old hag try to steal it from me!

Then another voice flooded his mind.

"I see that you're still alive."

Beyond the bars, the lantern was held aloft and looking at its light was, for Gragan, like looking straight into the mid-day sun with the eyes of a mere mortal. He shrieked a little from the pain and shielded his face with a spindly forearm. When he dared to look again, he could see that his captor was swaddled in black, as usual, and attended by two, perhaps three, of her bronze-clad warriors. As he peeked at her between spread fingers, eyes blinking a rheumy drip, draining in a stream down to his chin, he imagined catching a glimpse of *her* eyes. Those black pools were as harsh a beacon in his memory as was the lantern in the dungeon.

"There's something I need to know, old man. I advise you to answer me without delay or detour."

Poison, thought Gragan, and he pulled his tattered robe-rags around tight with a shiver. *The voice is still dipped in poison.*

He wanted more than anything to spit in her face, but after clearing ten days' worth of cobwebs from his own voice he barely had enough spittle with which to speak.

"I am your servant," he muttered, smoothing his louse-ridden beard. "What can I teach you today, pray tell?"

There came the sound of another door, this one closing somewhere in the expansive labyrinth far below. A few screams rose up from the spiraling tunnel of cells, betraying tortures more grim than any Gragan had yet suffered. Though such things were indeed a pleasant distraction to his ears, the voice beyond the iron bars snagged his attention on a sharp and unyielding fishhook.

"I need to locate someone who has, quite unexpectedly, become lost. I expect *that one* has become lost partly on your account, as well. I heard about the scar you burned into his arm. Now give me the proper spell."

Gragan was a fish, indeed. Caught by the mouth and ripped from his world of foul water and waves to thrash, helpless, at her feet.

So the little brat escaped, after all, and she needs to find him!

Gragan was mildly thrilled, of course, but he also cursed, to his very soul, the mere boy who had managed to elude her clutches. Even if he secretly celebrated it, how could such a thing be true? It was impossible to believe some fool had slipped away while he, master of three centuries' worth of power and wisdom, ate cockroaches in the dark and licked condensation from the moldy rocks for a drink. His mind spun, faster than a straw windmill in some Dyridian farmer's barnyard. She didn't like to wait for her answers. Would she ask him about Rowan Blaize and their prior association? Had she actually *seen* the scar on the boy's arm, or had she just heard about it?

"The one you seek—is this one loved or despised?" he queried, laughing bitterly within all the while; she could love no one, and the whole world would know it soon enough.

"Of what importance is love to the spell?"

Her tone was colder than the last dryad Gragan had bothered to kiss.

"It is of grave importance for the working of the proper incantation." Rousing himself, he struggled to make eye contact with his adversary through the mud-puddle of air between them. "Disposition determines which materials to collect, not to mention the attitude with which you must address the elemental powers. If you were to make a mistake in delivering the—"

"Insolent idiot!" she snapped and, to fortify this statement, one of her warriors growled and slammed the iron bars with his spear. "Don't imply that I'm going to make mistakes." She leaned a bit closer and Gragan fought the urge to reach out and rake her face with his fingernails. "How soon you forget the skills of your conqueror, old one. And you have the nerve to speak of mistakes," she scoffed. "Keep in mind that *your* mistakes have left you without the power to extinguish a mere candle's flame. Now simply do as you're told and reveal the spell."

Gragan flinched. For the perceived insult she might not send him bits of rancid, maggoty bread for days. Luckily, a cockroach scurried across his toes just then in the darkness.

"You need only some personal articles belonging to the subject and a rather complicated incantation belonging to the Aktonnite Tradition," he instructed, snagging the cockroach between his thumb and forefinger. Already his taste buds were beginning to tingle. "Keep in mind that a response may take several hours and, even then, the spell may only reveal a place your subject has recently visited, especially if great distances are involved." He sighed, tiny legs tickling the bottom of his palm.

"The main problem lies in whether or not your quarry *wishes* to be located. In dealing with a lost companion or a war prisoner on one's own side, the spell's response can be quick and accurate. Otherwise, if you're looking for someone who wishes to elude you, the results tend to be a bit more unreliable. That is simply the nature of this vein of sorcery. No one knows quite why."

Oblixta exhaled a musty cloud of contempt and Gragan knew she would never look for any one desirous of rescue, at least not rescue by her. He popped the roach into his mouth and, after two good crunches, dinner was over.

"Just tell me the articles I'll need. And the incantation. Tell me quickly, before I heave due to the smell of your flesh."

Gragan scratched his bald, scabby head. The personal things were rather standard for a location spell—a scrap of clothing, a feather from the subject's pillow, a drop from a drinking cup—but he had to rack his brain a bit longer to come up with the actual incantation. He hadn't used it since one of his favorite kitchen-wenches was carried off by a mob of trolls while she hunted mushrooms in the woods, fifty years prior. After a moment's thought, however, the words were escaping his lips and entering the knowledge of his captor.

"*Wedgewynn. Heflixx. ShynnBane. Snod. Zoo-loo-Aga. Flixxwynn. Scrod.*"

She made him repeat it again, and he was about to suggest she write it down before prudence warned against insulting her sensibilities another time. Besides, he knew her retentive powers were up to the task. Indeed, they were the most formidable he had ever the misfortune of encountering.

"You are certain that this is the correct spell?"

"Of course, dear Lady."

"I have warned you before of trickery. If any of your instructions should cause me harm, the guards have orders to slowly peel the flesh from your bones."

Gragan winced, and he began to caress the grimy skin on his arms.

"My words are free of trickery. At least *now* they are. Simply take care to use full concentration and stay within the rubric of the Aktonnite Tradition. This, of course, you already know."

Now that she had the information, he expected her to vanish until she needed more, a span that could last hours, days, or even entire months. His hope for survival and escape rested in the knowledge that she was adept only in certain vengeful realms of High Sorcery, and he relished the fact that there were still many pathways she had not yet explored. These less-developed regions of her talent would leave her hungry for some time to come, and perhaps vulnerable to the proper, carefully orchestrated attack. He had already planned, rune for rune, what he would do to her once he regained his powers.

At that time he would inflict her with boils from head to toe, and a thousand lice for every strand of hair on her head! When at last she had itched her way to the edge of insanity, he would transform her into the rat she really was, beneath all the spider-silk finery, and then drop her on a treadmill with a couple of walnuts placed forever out of her reach.

But now, seated as he was in a pile of rubbish featuring his own feces, and trapped in a dungeon cell a league beneath her castle, frustration sunk its fangs to the soul, flooding his veins with the venom of regret. He turned from her stare, cursing the day he had let his infatuations get the better of him.

If only he had discerned her motives long before the moment of deception! Her raw power, her Gift, was strong, indeed. Yet, she was still dependent upon his greater knowledge, and that meant he still had time.

"While I'm here, I have a bit of news for you, Gragan."

The lantern light sputtered, threatening to die, so meager was the fuel of prison air. Though the wizard wished the lungs of his nemesis were equally desperate for breath, it was a surprise to hear her call him by his proper name—*the name at which the elements themselves had once trembled!*—and offer, perhaps, a hint of intrigue from the outside world.

"I have found your Book of Confoundments and Convolutions," she whispered, and as she spoke, he could barely see the corners of her mouth rise upward in a smile. A whimper churned at the bottom of the wizard's wrinkled bag of a throat, and would have pried its way through his lips had he not summoned strength to stifle the sound. She had more to tell.

"I've been ransacking your castle for nearly three months, as you know. I turned the place inside out and had it razed to the ground so my men could sort through the rubble, stone by stone. One of my seers confirmed the discovery two days ago. As of yesterday, their caravan had descended as far as the Galpern Valley. The Aktonnite Tome will be in my hands at dawn." She leaned close to the bars once more. "Now tell me, old captive one: how valuable are you to me *now?*"

The hobbled wizard could only shudder; his spirit had deflated in resolve and ballooned just as swiftly again with terror. As far as he knew, the Tome was still sequestered behind the most secret of stone panels in his castle. This panel was designed to open only at the behest of a rather difficult incantation and was located in one of his lair's most inconspicuous chambers. Indeed, nothing short of tearing the place down could have uncovered the secret. But Gragan remembered: when he lost his powers, the wards he had weaved around his home evaporated with them.

Perhaps she is lying, he thought as panic started to munch its way around his heart. *Perhaps she wants nothing more than to torture me at this moment, to see me beg for my life.*

If the Aktonnite Tome was truly in her grasp, his days of "usefulness" were indeed finished.

"I will be honored to help you fathom the mysteries of the ancient volume," he offered, shifting on his haunches in the cramped space. "Aktonnite magic is most treacherous, but with me at your side to guide you—"

"Save your pleas for mercy," she interrupted. "I didn't bother to get any from that annoying Fey Empress before I tossed *her* into the fire a few days ago, and I'm not interested in yours."

"You may find the boy, but you won't defeat Rowan Blaize," Gragan croaked. "Fate will see to that, somehow."

"And what would you know of it?" she asked. "Is that where you sent my newly branded little ingrate, as I expect? To your old friend in the South? Are *you* the spy that's been troubling my castle of late?" She laughed. "No, I think not."

Gragan gulped. Beads of sweat began to fill the furrows above his brow. He saw a flash of her hand, milk-white as she raised the lantern and hung it on an iron spike jutting out above the cell. There was a shuffling of the warriors behind her in the dark, and the sound of armor scraping against the rock-hewn walls. The lantern wobbled and Gragan's vision began to reel. A collection of keys rattled and one of the guards turned the lock of his cell door. After this, the bars were opened wide and she moved upon him, silent and gliding as if she were some spectral figure in a dream. He imagined certain things when she stood above him at last: a devilish whisper flying from the top of her black tower; a flash of gray fire; and laughter, like the tinkling of the daintiest bells. He gasped and fell back against the wall, feet sliding in the muck, his ears hearing the first words of her incantation.

"Vax. Halmah. Vag. Tromah…"

He knew she was going to change. He knew it even before her spider-silk robes melted away and her feet emerged from the elf-skin boots as limbs of razor-claw, flexing toward his throat. The lantern swung, there was a rush of heat that singed the hair of his beard, and a cry of pain was knocked from his lungs as he slammed to the floor. His urine pooled. The face of the beast she had become was soon pressed against his own, nostrils as great and wet as a bull's, nuzzling and snorting for his neck. Fangs dug deep, slicing into the wizened muscles. There came a swift suck upon arteries now open and spewing. Talons ripped in one mad pass after another upon his belly. Gragan's mind grappled for the words of his most powerful Spell of Revenge, but memory evaded him, slipping here and floating there like so many feathers tossed upon the wind.

He was on his mountain.

He was holding a glass of wine at some grand dinner table.

He was bending down to pick up a snail.

He looked about, and a nymph came to him from out of a cluster of ferns, bowed sweetly, and said, "Good night."

Then he was dead.

II

There's No Face Like Gnome

Fearsome storms battered the heartland of Kelnia that winter, and most inhabitants believed that the sky itself had come to detest the world of mortals. It was as if a great mouth had opened in the vault of the heavens, speaking for all of the gods in their fury and leveling constant condemnation by way of blizzard and gale. From the northern foothills of the Galpern to the vast reaches of Pyr Mida Mountain farmland in the south, a luminous white blanket had been cast upon the terrain by one maelstrom after another, allowing towns and villages mere token room to exist.

In almost every place, bare forest trees poked skyward from the deep of the cover, their branches reaching for salvation, clutching the air like the hands of people suddenly buried alive. Streams and rivers that had babbled or roared through a maze of sweltering valleys and hollows in summer were now frozen veins, each one a meandering passage through land hidden beneath layers of unbreakable ice. It was a time of anxiety; every Kelnian farmer harbored a fear that Spring would never come, and every Kelnian chimney for a hundred miles in any direction spewed a smoky sacrifice to Dryndym, the god of the season, but mercy from him was unknown.

These were days of malicious visions, when things that should never be seen with mortal eyes held sway to prowl in the distance among the trees, watching and waiting one instant and then vanishing in the next. This was a winter of winds that howled, crying out—most believers said—like the children of Mandulis the Dwarf King ... a million souls of the Forest forever doomed to heartbreak because the Galwyn Crone had long ago robbed their father of his magic wand. Safe inside homes where bread baked and broth bubbled, mortals often laughed at visions and legends, raising cups of beer in vindictive toasts to all woeful sprites. But, when necessity forced the same people to venture out of doors for firewood or tend to shivering livestock, it was a different tale, indeed.

Then, faces turned grim and eyes glazed with fret should they catch a glimpse of something that might only be the quicksilver reflection of sun on snow, or something that might *not* be. Hearts missed a beat when, out of the most unsuspecting corner of an eye, there came the fluttering of a crystal wing, or the dash of unholy feet from one creaking tree to the next. Mortal steps hastened in alarm should a strange tangle of breezes suddenly chatter across an otherwise tranquil glen, or whip around the corner of a barn. When such things happened, people bundled cloaks tighter, pulled warm fur hoods lower, and finished their chores as quickly as they could. People with a pinch of sense knew that souls caught outdoors when the Children of Mandulis started to scream might just find themselves mad in the blink of an eye, or possessed with the desire to wander off into the woodlands, never to be heard from again.

One boy wandered such a woodland, and though the Children of Mandulis left him well alone, the winter was his intimate companion. He would have cursed this constant and fellow traveler, but he knew too well how lucky he was to be alive and feeling the relentless chill. It did not matter that he had been weaving his way in secret through forest and remote countryside for nearly six days, or that ice had captured the sweat of his brow, hindering sight of what lay ahead. He did not care that the lush Bog Bear fur of his boots and hooded coat failed to keep the elements from accosting him, and he was not bothered at all by the dwindling food reserves in his leather satchel. None of these things mattered, for the lingering exhilaration of recent escape made the brutality of white-bearded Dryndym quite tolerable. Escape was the one thing that drove him onward. Escape ... along with the breath of magic.

His name was Starbane, he was fifteen years and three months young, and he knew—as well as he would know his own hazel-eyed, raven-haired reflection in a mirror—that escape was far from complete. Bounding along in a kingdom of frost and bramble, he breathed the air of sudden freedom with a vengeance, even if the breath entering his lungs with every gasp was so cold that it burned, and his nose seemed useful only for the production of snotty icicles. More disturbingly, the strange scar that had been scorched upon his forearm stung as if covered with nettles. Despite the harrowing conditions, however, he managed to keep one snowshoe moving in front of the other at an astonishing pace. During the past five, frantic days he had stumbled upon the environs of at least a dozen villages, always knowing he approached one by sight of the roiling strands of chimney smoke that wafted upward beyond the distant trees.

Though sorely tempted, he did not enter any of these seemingly benign places to seek warmth and shelter. Knowing that his pursuers were likewise on the move, he realized that civilization was a thing far too dangerous, and far too apt to be *un*civilized. This was nothing new, in Kelnia. Thus, he did as he had been told, following the instructions and keeping to the loneliness of pathways that snaked through grove after grove of deep forest, where the tree trunks were closest together and their crowning limbs dense enough to create a partial ceiling. Here, even the most pristine patches of snowfall were dominated by gloom, and the shadows were so gray that dowdy Bog Bear fur seemed luminous in comparison. Strange sounds of the wood filled the hours from morning until dusk and, trapped in such solitude, he often felt compelled to holler at the top of his lungs, desperate to break the monotonous effects of the otherwise protective spell that had been cast around him. Fear and several tightly-sewn threads of sorcery combined to prevent him from doing anything which might draw the attention of those already on the hunt, or of the meddlesome creatures he knew to inhabit every forest of his homeland.

Despite the driving force of a magic that seemed to keep his legs as strong as those of a deer and his determination more badger-like than boyish, Starbane could still find himself paralyzed with fright. If some tree limb broke from the weight of a recent snowfall and went crashing to the ground, he would go wild, extracting the small but whistle-sharp dagger hidden within his coat. Then he would freeze, arms outstretched and wide eyes scanning the wood for any sign of the enemy. So far, no hint of real danger had materialized, and he was swift to mutter prayers of gratitude to Dryndym and to Blood Thistle Maggie, the benevolent sprite whose duty it was to warn mortals in the forest of approaching harm. Strange, how he remembered prayers he had never used before in his life.

Onward he trudged, aware of nothing but the need to keep heading south to save his very life. Hunger gnawed, but he paused only once a day to nibble on the cured meats and cloth-wrapped cheeses in the satchel he had been given for the journey. Over and over, his mind played the words of advice that had likewise been entrusted to him:

Travel to the south. Go to Pyr Mida. Look for the sentinel. Keep to the shadows.

Like the sing-song melody of some childhood game, this chant propelled his every footstep in the snow. He had been given a tattered map for good measure, but it rarely left the safety of his pack, because the strange creature his rescuer had provided as a "guide" proved to be most reliable.

Only at dusk would the sentinel appear, emerging from the places where daylight made its final stand against darkness, rising up where shadows began to lose form and blend into the slow creep of night. As to what manner of creature the sentinel was, Starbane had no idea; it said nothing when it appeared, and never came very close. Sometimes it would simply stand, solemn and aloof, near a riverside or a particular spot of trees, beckoning him hither only to disappear and reemerge someplace else a bit farther away in the wood. He knew the child-like figure was blazing a trail for him, pointing the way toward safe, overnight shelter in secluded thickets or hillside caves, but he half-wished for its companionship throughout the day, or at least some word of assurance that he was getting closer to his destination.

It was nearing dusk on the sixth day of his journey, right around the time the sentinel usually appeared, that Starbane decided to take a moment's rest atop a rotted-out stump in the middle of a clearing. The winds had blown most of the snow off to one side of the glade in a massive drift, obscuring the black-speckled trunks of an encircling row of Falthurn trees up to their lowest branches. The boy buried his nose in the crook of an elbow as he lingered, enjoying the warmth of Bog Bear fur and listening to the screech of what he hoped was only a harmless bird in the distant forest. Above and over a jagged ridge to the south, the sky was the same wall of gray it had been on every afternoon since his escape. Indeed, he had counted only four times thus far that the sun had been allowed to get so much as a peek at the world below. Worries about the approach of darkness engulfed him and he tried, for a moment, to guess the fading disk's position in the heavens before a familiar rustling reached his ears from the opposite end of the glade. He whirled around on the stump just in time to see the dreamy figure of the sentinel emerge from a gangling patch of Butter Berry scrub.

"Thank the gods," muttered Starbane, his lips numb from exposure to the cold. "I was beginning to wonder if you were going to show up."

The sentinel's arrival sent an instant wave of relief through the boy's soul, even though the other-worldliness of its appearance always left him a trifle dazed. The thing had certainly never appeared pleased to see *him;* even now its comely face was wrought with a drooping expression that reminded him of a child suffering the first pangs of a stomach ache.

All the same, it waved and, most unusually, came straight toward him, still garbed in nothing but a loincloth that looked like a collection of autumn leaves strung haphazardly together with bright green grapevines. The leaves made a dry crackling noise as their wearer tip-toed, barefoot, across the glade without leaving the faintest trail upon the snow. The skin of the sentinel's form was the same tint of blue one might see in a mortal body dredged up from the bottom of an icy pond, and its short, spiky hair was as moist black as the belly of any raven that coursed the skies. Though its ears were nonexistent, leading the youth to conclude that it was not a member of the elfin tribes, its eyes were light hazel, like his own, and sparkled with a crystal-on-fire brilliance. In its hand was a small staff—really nothing more than a branch broken from the limb of a Falthurn tree—and around its neck hung a twisted leather cord. Upon this cord dangled a clay tobacco pipe, a goose-feather, and a tiny glass bottle filled with silver pins. Surrounding its entire figure was a mild aura that glowed like a flurry of dust trapped in a panel of sunlight.

"Don't be so glad to see me, mortal boy. I come this time with a warning."

Starbane's ears pricked at the sound of the sentinel's piping voice and his heart started to race. The shimmering creature stopped in the snow, no more than ten feet from where Starbane sat on the stump. The "mortal boy" realized he wasn't at all comfortable having the thing *that* close to him.

"So you can speak," noted the mesmerized youth, who started edging away, sliding his rear toward the opposite end of the stump. "I thought you were good only for pointing out hidey-holes."

"Of course I can speak. *Our* kind are not born mute." The sentinel blinked at him once and then seemed to relax, one hand on a hip amid loincloth leaves and the other resting atop the Falthurn staff.

"How come you haven't said a word to me before now?"

This time the sentinel simply shrugged and unleashed a cat-like yawn, glancing away toward the forest with obvious disinterest.

"Let's just say that talking to you was *not* part of my original job description."

Starbane was unsettled by the resentment that simmered below the sentinel's words. Even worse, the normally golden aura around its body was beginning to pulse a moody red.

"I ... I ... don't know what your name is or even what you are," stammered the youth. "But I want to thank you for leading me to safety these past several nights. I wouldn't have made it without you."

The sentinel snickered. "Believe me, it wasn't done out of the goodness of my heart!"

"Excuse me?"

"Your sorceress friend arranged all this," the creature said in a huff. It made a mocking swirl-of-a-gesture with a blue hand. "She's the one who bound me to this thankless job. I don't know who gave that old lady my name, but believe me, I *intend* to find out. These witches! The country's full of them and they're always thinking they can snag any Forest Dweller to do their bidding. Well, I've got news for them—Sentinel-gnomes have lives to lead, too!"

"Sentinel-gnomes?" said Starbane. "So that's what you are. I've never heard of your kind before."

"That, my wiry little ferret, is no surprise. Your kind barely knows what's going on in its own decaying world. Particularly with the Queen of All Hags running the show these days. I guess I don't blame you for being such idiots, what with a monster like that as ruler."

"Please, it's not safe to mention her." Starbane felt his blood begin to boil in anger, but he also felt a deepening fear. He knew the Shadow Peoples could be tempestuous, but this particular sprite seemed a trifle harsh, considering it was supposed to be at his service. For an instant he was tempted to give the "Sentinel-gnome" a piece of his own mind but wisely thought the better of it.

"I have no wish to discuss the demerits of mortal lifestyle or of this kingdom," he said as diplomatically as he could. The gnome rolled its green eyes in reproach, as if to say *I should hope not!* "But it *is* getting dark and I tend to get a little concerned about that, seeing as I'm running for my life and haven't the slightest real clue about where I am. Perhaps you could kindly show me the way to the nearest shelter, as usual, and then be off about your own affairs."

The gnome bristled. "La-di-dah. You've got quite an attitude for such a young and vulnerable whelp. Still, your words do remind me why I've stopped to have this little chat."

Starbane closed his eyes and tried to remain calm. "As I recall, you said something about a warning."

"Yes, indeed!" The gnome snapped its tiny fingers. "I've come to tell you that I *won't* be around to help anymore. Ha! Your sorceress friend's powers are weakening and I'm afraid she won't be able to afford my services after tonight."

Starbane's heart fell and he jumped to his feet in the snow. "Oh, no! She said something like this might happen, but I didn't expect it to be so soon. What am I supposed to do? This journey's not nearly over and *I* couldn't find some of these caves you point out if my life depended on it."

"That's not my concern," sniffed the gnome. "And don't be such a baby. You'll do fine. In fact, there's a wonderful little cave for you to sleep in this evening, just over that hill before us." It pointed toward the south. "On the other side of the hill is a ravine. The cave is at the very bottom, behind a hedge of Moab briars."

"Oh, wonderful." Starbane slapped his hands against his sides in frustration and glared off toward the tree-topped hill.

"You're not that far from your destination," mumbled the sprite. "And besides, you have the map, don't you?"

"Of course I've got it."

"Good. Then, the safest cave for you to sleep in tonight is the one I just mentioned. Others ought to be marked for you on the map. You'll be on your own."

Starbane drew his satchel closer. He had placed it next to the stump when he sat down to rest. "What's happened to Celintha, the old lady who set me free back at the castle?" he demanded. "How come her powers are weakening? Are my enemies after me? Have they managed to find my trail? Are they closing in?"

"Hold on!" protested the gnome. "It's not my job to know such things. I was hired to find you a place to sleep at night and, like I said, *that* magical coin is now spent. As for your witch-friend's powers, I'm sure I don't know about those. I only know that the spell she cast to bind me is losing its grip and I am obliged, under the law of this particular enchantment, to let you know that *you'll be on your own*. Perhaps you should have secured the favor of a stronger sorceress to get you out of whatever mess you were in."

Starbane kicked the snow in front of him. "I didn't exactly arrange this whole escape myself, you know! Not that I'm ungrateful, but let's face it," he lamented, "I've been pulled from years of captivity and sent off into the wilds with nothing but the clothes you now see on my back and a bit of cheese and … *Hey!* Where are you, sprite?"

Where the sentinel had stood only an instant before there was nothing but a furious little cyclone of snow that caught a ride on a sudden gust of wind and stung Starbane's face. The youth sighed and sat back down on the stump, glowering as the realization that he was now totally alone began to grip at his spirit. Never had the cold of the previous five days seemed more powerful than at this moment. The silence of the vast wood seemed more threatening, too, as the light waned and a purplish darkness swelled at the edges of the sky. His mind began to turn vicious circles in its mounting anxiety and backtracked to seize upon the gnome's final words about the cave. Where had it said the cave would be? Over the ridge before him, to the south? On the other side, or in the clutch of trees along the base of the ridge? He was finding it suddenly difficult to remember.

A branch snapped somewhere in the haze of forest. There was a thud and another crashing of limbs followed by the calling of several disgruntled birds. This noise drove Starbane from his seat and sent him traipsing in his snowshoes to the edge of the glade. Which way should he go? Back into the wood where there might be danger? Toward the ridge? He couldn't think, so he leaned against the trunk of a Falthurn, closed his eyes and forced himself to catch his breath. Panic wouldn't do him a bit of good at this moment and his mind fought to make his body believe everything was okay, even as it struggled to arrest the mounting wave of distress. He took a final, cautious glance toward that section of the woodland where he had heard the prior commotion. Certainly it was just another tree limb breaking from the weight of snow, he assured himself. Even so, as the sky grew darker by the moment he pushed away from the tree and headed toward the ridge.

He cursed under his breath when a wayward piece of Moab-scrub managed to entangle itself in the netting of his left snowshoe, nearly causing him to fall, face-first, into the drift. He stooped to rip the offensive branch out of the ground and, in a few moments, had crossed the clutch of trees and made it to the slippery incline of rocks that formed the base of the tiny ridge. He took one final look back at the surrounding forest. It was void of malevolence, as far as he could surmise. Still, his mind was ever prepared for the sight of whoever—or whatever—was doubtlessly on his trail.

For a desperate instant he felt like crying out to the weird gnome who had so blithely abandoned him. He felt like begging it to return and personally guide him one last time, at least to the spot where the cave was hidden. *That would be an exercise in futility,* he grumbled inwardly. Leaning against a boulder, he removed his snowshoes and began to make his way up the snow and ice-encrusted remainder of the hill. After only a few steps he paused to look upward, his face meeting the onset of yet another snowfall. He was sick of it.

The resumed effort of ascent made his lungs heave and a cascade of snowflakes swirled and evaporated in the warm wake of his breath. Above the top of the little cliff, a black fringe of nighttime sky seemed like the frown of some disdainful god, and he wanted only to find the safe haven and forget the horror of what was happening to him for at least one more evening, secluded in the temporary oblivion of dreams.

"This Blaize wizard I'm supposed to find had better know his business," Starbane muttered. "He'd just bloody well better!"

The scar that had been burned into his forearm began to throb.

Time was running out. He could feel it.

࿐࿔

Oblixta looked out over the moon-washed kingdom and the frown that had been fixed upon her face degenerated into a snarl. There was a sudden, scurrying movement in the dark chamber behind her, but she did not turn around. She knew who it was, already, and far preferred to maintain her gaze over the night.

"Majesty, I have returned." The voice was ethereal in its sinister cadence.

"Then I trust that you have found the boy?"

Only now did Oblixta's face edge slightly back toward the interior of her watchtower, and the thing behind her saw how the glow of the moon caressed her visage, revealing a distasteful expression. The servant was duly afraid.

"No, Majesty," it whispered in the same burbling tone. "But rest assured that every effort is still being made, even as we speak."

Oblixta sighed. "If you don't find him soon, you'll be destroyed. You *do* realize that?"

Her stark promise elicited more movement. It was the unmistakable sound of groveling.

"I beseech you, Great One," came the quavering plea. "It was three days before we even discovered his absence and, by the time our search was underway, a fresh snow had fallen. The trail was lost, though temporarily. *Just* temporarily. Even so, we searched and alerted. We warned and we punished. Every town and outpost between here and the Pyr Mida Mountains has been given notice of our undertaking. I ask you to be merciful, for I am your faithful servant, who has never failed you before."

Outside, the moon waxed, indifferent to servants faithful and treacherous.

"I'm tired of your excuses," said Oblixta, tapping her scimitar fingers on the stone of the window's ledge. Tapping ledges seemed to be her favored habit these days. "You have three more days in which to find him. If you fail, I'll kill you and all those in your company." She paused as a particularly fond memory brought a bitter smile to her lips. "Yes. That's what I'll do. I'll kill you. Just as I killed the faery empress and just as I killed the old bag who aided the boy's intolerable escape. With as much pain. More, if such a thing is possible—and trust me when I tell you that I believe it to be *quite* possible."

"Majesty, do not forget that the old lady you destroyed this morning was a sorceress. She was the castle spy you have been seeking for so long. She may have covered the boy with some kind of trickery that is beyond my skill to discern. I am no magician! Perhaps I am dealing with matters beyond my realm. Perhaps I am not able to—"

"Fool!" spat Oblixta. "Any power that may have covered that boy vanished, along with its source, at today's execution in the courtyard. Do you presume to second-guess my knowledge? Believe me, the brat is vulnerable now. Perfectly vulnerable. This will make your failure to find him all the more insufferable."

Oblixta scanned the countryside beyond her fortress, her gaze lingering for no reason upon a flicker of candle or lantern light in some distant dwelling. "Besides," she added, "he is a pathetic weakling, ill-suited to such a grand escape, no matter *who* planned it. He is uncertain of his actions, uncertain of himself. I can sense it. Given all of this, I don't see why you're having such a difficult time. Find him and bring him back to me alive, mindful of your fate, should you fail."

Her breath erupted as a steaming cloud in the frozen air and, with an eye equally as chilling, she turned to regard her servant. "You'd do well to reinstate the search immediately, Xerbex. I'll see to it that you're not impeded by the elements this time. Now go, before I change my mind and slay you where you stand. This task can easily be handed over to others, though I've no desire to waste further time in doing so. For the moment."

The spindly rat-troll departed her presence and, once alone, Oblixta stood again surveying her kingdom from the tower window. For an instant, she thought she could make out the jagged skyline of the distant mountain peaks through a billowing mass of winter storm clouds, so many miles to the south.

The Pyr Mida Mountains.

Of course, she seethed. *That's exactly where the little wretch is headed. And beyond that, to the miserable King of Corydia and his no-good warlock, Rowan Blaize!*

In truth, Oblixta could not really see the mountains. The blizzards in the distance were now too thick in their midnight fury, the peaks too far away. Still, she knew that they stood at the boundaries of her realm, menacing her and mocking her in the silence. More than anything, she desired what lay beyond those mountains, even more than she wanted the boy, who was out there, she knew, somewhere in-between. There were problems, though. Even she had to admit as much. It would do her no good for the Corydian king or the Blaize sorcerer to receive a timely warning about the nature of her plans. It would be even worse for them to see the mark which the Gragan wizard had apparently burned onto the boy's arm.

"He *will* be found," she muttered to the monolithic banks of boiling cloud above her tower. As if in defiant response, those clouds began to release another blinding sheet of their snowy cargo. It was then that the constant disgust of her facial expression returned and she retreated from the window, weary at last of the cold and determined to see that the winter did not interfere with her plans again.

It was time to consult the Gragan's Tome.

III

By The Blood of the Fire Salamander!

At twilight on the seventh day of his frantic flight, and without the aid of the long-gone sentinel, Starbane somehow managed to find shelter in yet another cave, this one being little more than a burrow wedged at the bottom of a craggy gulch. The entrance to the place was partially hidden by the icy limbs and bramble of a briar thicket, along with some fallen tree branches. It was there, blessedly there, just as the map (he was finally forced to use it) indicated. Just as he had been promised:

"...and you shall find many smaller places of refuge along the way, child. Within such shelter no harm should befall you, if you are wise enough to remember the value of silence. But do not linger in the assurance of temporary safety. Move on! Always, the sentinel I have summoned shall guide you. And you have, of course, the map, if things should not go well for me in this foul place you left behind."

Since the first encounters with the gnome, Starbane knew that sheer desperation was hardly responsible for his success in navigation thus far. He was bright enough to know that he had been *unnaturally* impervious to the cold, and to the gnashing winds that had dogged him since the beginning. The kindly but decrepit old witch had told him that he would be guided in a southerly direction by forces far more substantial that what his own, meager mettle could ever provide. Celintha—she who had called herself a "spy," she who had saved him—had also said, ruefully, that there would be no longstanding guarantees. For a time, however, even with the sentinel's help and the map in his clutches,

Starbane had felt himself almost magnetically drawn to the appointed landmarks. He had been quite content not to be left at the mercy of his own thinking, especially as the gray skies made it all but impossible to follow the course of the sun, which was the only real traveling skill he possessed. Even that talent was tenuous.

Before reaching the cave on this particular evening, however, what little strength and guidance that had seemed so innately part of his being completely vanished, just as the sentinel had vanished the night before in its whirlwind of slush. In fact, the boy could pinpoint the exact instant he felt something different within himself. After the harsh warning of the gnome, he had not been surprised, but that did not mean he was pre-pared for the harrowing shift. Things had taken a turn for the worse as he walked along the banks of a frozen brook at mid-day. Quite suddenly, he had been stricken with a violent attack of apprehension, a sensation of absolute vulnerability that made him feel as if he had been stripped of the very clothing he wore. This anxiety began in his lower extremities and fingered a snaking pathway up his spine and into his brain, causing him to experience, for the first time, the wrenching bitterness of the weather.

At that particular moment, Starbane had stopped in his tracks and, after several fearful looks into the forest depths, the sensation had finally dulled to some semblance of manageable suffering. Then, the greatest difference he experienced rested in his inability to perceive everything or anything around him with even the slightest shred of confidence. He was gripped with hunger and exhaustion. His body ached from head to toe, and what miniscule sense of direction he had possessed was now ut-terly slipshod. For the remainder of that day's expedition he had plodded along in fretful disorientation, relying as best he could upon the map to find various landmarks and pathways. He believed it was only by virtue of frantic prayer to Dryndym, the Winter Lord, that he'd been able to find this seventh night's cave at all, with not a moment to spare.

Shadows were descending like so many curtains dropped around the world. At last, before making his way inside the little cave, he wea-rily gathered an armful of firewood by breaking off the lower limbs of a dying Falthurn tree nearby. Once he had cleared away the bramble and crawled within the narrow crevice, he winced at the cave's musty, ancient odor, though it was very much like the other caves he had inhabited, and this putrid scent had not bothered him before. As darkness began to overwhelm the landscape, however, he reminded himself that *this* was the scent of welcome. The interior of the hole was only wider than his body by half and too cluttered with debris for him to make his way any more than five or six paces past the entrance. With frustrating discomfort he removed his snowshoes and squeezed around to pull as much of the tangle of outer brush over the entrance as possible. The last tendrils of dusk had retreated entirely and he could see nothing in the black outside. Cramped but somewhat situated, he removed the burdensome satchel from his back and began to fumble among its contents for the most precious gift given at his departure.

"That miserable sentinel-gnome can end-up in an ice ogre's stew, for all I care," he whispered. "I've still got *this* stuff."

"This stuff" consisted of a small flask, corked with an ornate stopper carved from some sort of bone. In daylight, the flask's liquid contents appeared thickly green, like the muck covering a particularly stagnant Kelnian swamp at summer's height. In the blindness of the cave, however, Starbane could only feel the smoothness of the vessel and its unusual, ever-present warmth, filtering even through the glass, even through the thickness of Bog-Bear gloves. His teeth were chattering a bit as he pulled a bare hand free of one glove and tossed it upon the rocky floor of the cave. Once he had enough room to work, he assembled the array of sticks and limbs yanked from the Falthurn into a pile near his feet. Gently easing the stopper from the flask, he grimaced and coughed as the dank air was filled with a familiarly pungent, smoky fragrance. He aimed the flask with a shaking hand toward the pile of dead branches and tried, in the gloom, to let a few drops of its contents spill out onto the wood.

A faint hissing sound was followed by silence. In a few seconds, wispy licks of soft green flame materialized to illuminate the burrow. Moments later, the dingy niche was permeated by an aromatic and comforting heat. The boy sighed, leaning back against the curvature of the cave wall. He allowed himself some time to close his eyes and rest before replacing the stopper in the flask and reburying it among the items in his satchel. The making of this mystical fire had been a nightly ritual since his escape and he was certain that its presence meant more to him now than at any other moment. Again, the bracing sense of isolation that had manifested itself earlier in the day reared up from abysmal pools and clutched at his soul. He was utterly on his own now, and knew it. He let his mind drift, too tired to worry. On this hypnotic wave of despair his thoughts coursed back to the first day of his emancipation, and to the promises and instructions given to him by Celintha.

"Your journey is one that might cause the strongest of men to crumble, but fear not, boy, for I shall cover you with the necessary assistance. I have given you the map, but your need of it shall be cursory, so long as the sentinel I have conjured remains empowered. Like the flock that journeys to its winter refuge without command, so you shall travel. Like the mouse in a field which, pursued, can find the smallest and most secret of hideaways, so shall you move onward to your destination, though you know not the pathways you traverse.

"The hunger a man feels shall be but a trifle, and weariness a mere dream. Neither the cold nor the elements shall affect you, mortally. For your comfort, I give you this elixir, made with the blood of the Fire Salamander of Zerheroun. Its drops shall instantly ignite whatever manner of wood it may touch, burning its fuel slowly and leaving no billows of smoke to betray your hiding places. Use it sparingly, and its warmth at night will heal that portion of sorrow and exhaustion you do not perceive. After your departure, I shall raise a storm fit to hide all trace of your escape from those who will surely pursue you. If I can do this, the delay may strike our enemies with confusion … for a time. Would that I could travel with you, child, but such a journey cannot happen for one as old as I am. Hopefully, my spells will prove swift and strong enough to protect you, guiding you to the necessary end. I shall work them daily on your behalf.

"Know that there is a real danger that I, too, may be detected and apprehended. I am a spy in this horrid place, after all, and there are other magicks far more potent than my own. I do not wish to worry you about such matters, but you *must realize that, while working the pertinent charms to guard you from afar, the ability to guard myself will diminish. If I should perish, so will my blessing. Then, only the mercy of the gods will offer hope for your survival … and some gods are sparing with their favors in these fateful days. Even so, take heart, for this dilemma is only a possibility. I am confident that no harm shall befall you on your trek and that you will eventually find the Corydian king, alert Rowan Blaize according to the Gragan's Pact, and soon you will be safe in the midst of—"*

Starbane woke up with a start.

The sound of a sharp hissing in the cave had so rattled him from sleep that he knocked the back of his head against the rock. He had no idea how long he had been dozing, but it was obviously long enough for the magical fire to have dwindled and died. As he cupped a hand around the throbbing lump that rose on his skull, he wondered whether a gust of wind, like the one now whistling through the debris at the aperture of the cave, had extinguished the flame. The sound reverberated through the burrow, conjuring memories of a distant past when his father had halted with him while on a hunt in the countryside, listening to a similar, mournful sound. His father had told him, then, that it was the sound of an ogre in the Harsperu hill country, playing a dirge upon its hideous shin-bone flute. This remembrance made Starbane shiver with fright, even as the rising chill of the wind outside began to quake his body even more.

He felt aimlessly in the dark for the satchel with one hand and with the other discovered a few scraps of wood that had not been consumed by the enchanted elixir. He removed the stopper once again and, in his haste, dribbled a drop of the potion upon one of his huge, fur-trimmed leather boots. The faint hiss was followed by ignition and he cried out at the sight and smell of burning fur and tanned hide. Leaping as much as he could in such close quarters, he grabbed the satchel and pounded its weight upon his foot to squelch the flames before they waxed any higher. After quelling the potential disaster, he took another aching breath and forced himself to relax. The hand still holding the flask would not stop trembling, so he quickly gathered the bits of remaining firewood and used the elixir—far more carefully this time—to kindle some proper light and warmth. The effort produced just enough illumination for him to put on his snowshoes and head out for more fuel.

Pushing his way past the makeshift thicket at the cave entrance, he peered with a lump in his throat in all directions before crawling into the whistling gusts of wind. He listened for any sign of possible danger, knowing that it could come at any instant, from any direction. Hearing nothing to frighten him, he glanced up and perceived that the night sky was as overcast as ever. The underbelly of the roiling clouds was laden with snow, with just the faintest hint of moonlight reigning above them. The ravine was dimly visible due to the snow-glowing cover of its steep flanks, so he had little difficulty detecting the cluster of dead Falthurn trees from which he had secured his first batch of wood.

Loneliness pressed long and penetrating fingers into his very soul and seemed to clutch at his heart. He guessed, but was afraid to conclude, that his rescuer, his salvific Celintha, was dead. The mental effort he made to suppress this thought only succeeded in doubling its potency. He trudged over to the eerie grove of trees and broke several limbs in succession from the listing trunks. Within minutes he had acquired enough wood to last well until the morning, mindful that he had been told how sparingly the mystical green flame was designed to consume wooden fuel, even though it could incinerate most other materials in an instant, if used in hazardous fashion. The accident with his boot had driven that lesson home.

A mere shadow across the slate-gray expanse, Starbane scuttled and wormed his way back into the tiny cave, pulled the concealing bramble close to the entrance after him, and vowed only to make enough heat to let him sleep, free of nightmares, until dawn. The demons of worry and terror could beset him at that time, if they so desired. Now, however, as he determined to snatch rest from whatever god might prove generous enough to parcel it out, worry and terror were exiled by the unyielding weight of a terrified refugee's exhaustion.

≈◆≈

"I think it's unfair, Xerbex. You're poorly compensated for your leadership and she's always putting *you* to her most thankless, difficult, and filthiest tasks."

"Oh, keep your mouth shut," warned Xerbex as rivulets of a soup made from grave-robbed bones and rancid cabbages ran down through the bristles of his chin, leaving bits and chunks everywhere. "She's got eyes and ears throughout this land, Oblixta does. She could be watching us from within the bit of gleam on that rusted sword, up against the tent-pole, there. Or she could be listening to us out of that bubbling pot of swill you've made for our supper. It's never safe to criticize the queen, even when miles away. That mistress of devils has powers to eavesdrop that'd make the very spies of King Sye green with envy!"

"If that's true, then why'd you call her a 'mistress of devils' just now?"

Xerbex hurled his now-empty bowl of soup at the clawed feet of his companion. It shattered on frozen earth as the target hopped out of the way. "Don't be smart with me, Vuzbahg! You're quick to try and get on my good side by saying the queen's mistreating me, but everyone at Castle Cadrach knows what a two-faced little insect you are. Thankless, difficult, and filthy our tasks may be, but we're only a couple of rat-trolls in the service of Oblixta. What do you expect? That we be appointed her personal wine stewards?"

"I was only voicing an opinion," grumbled Vuzbahg, hunched and shamed, flicking shards of greasy pottery out of his way.

"An opinion that'll get us both incinerated," hissed Xerbex. "Like I said, keep your trap shut and focus on the work at hand. It's your job to set up this moth-eaten tent when we need shelter, build the fire when we need to cook a meal, and do exactly as I say, *when* I say it. We've got to get a whiff of that awful boy very soon, or it's the end for us—secret insults against the queen or not."

"Then the outlook is as grim as your mother's reflection in a cesspool, Xerbex. It's been another long day of snooping about and we've found not a hint of that Starbane brat. Nothing. Normally I'd be able to detect the foul stench of a mortal child from leagues away. Even if the blizzard *hadn't* let-up this morning."

"And you can thank Her Majesty for that break in the weather," snorted Xerbex. "But you'd better get a stick and scrape the snot and rot out of your dripping nose, my friend. Tomorrow is the day we're going to catch him. I feel it in my spleen."

"You've got a new idea?"

"Ha! The queen says that the magic protecting Starbane is gone. She's broken it. Killed the old cow who helped him in the first place. But that doesn't mean we can't use magical sources of our own to locate him in this miserable wood."

"Magical? Us? Have you been sneaking a peek at her spell-books, then?" gasped Vuzbahg.

"No, idiot. Use your head to *think*, for once, or else I'll crack your blistered skull open and scramble your brains with some ravens' eggs for breakfast in the morning. Haven't you smelled the magic in this forest?"

"What are you talking about?"

"Dryads, you bungler! Dryads by the score."

Vuzbahg frowned, exposing rotted yellow fangs. "Oh. Them things. Yes, I've smelled them. But what good will they do for us? Their kind don't stoop to speak with the likes of trolls."

"They do when the troll has bait!" sneered Xerbex, removing a small pouch from the folds of his rank and tattered cloak. "Look in here. See what I had the good sense to bring with us."

"A stinky old red briar?" croaked Vuzbahg after peeking into the pouch.

"Not just *any* 'stinky old briar,' you dimwitted piece of ogre-fodder. This is a Blood Thistle. Dryads' most favorite food in all the world, and it doesn't grow in winter. They hunger for it during the cold months, you see, and by this time of year their own stocked-up supplies of it have run out. Yes, it's this time of year when dryads get especially restless and leave the safety of sleep in hollowed-out trees to wander about, working mischief and watching what passes beneath the boughs of the woods."

"You think one of them has seen the boy?"

"I'd bet my dead grandmother's knuckle-dice on it!" said Xerbex. "And with this," he added, clutching the pouch close to his chest, "we can lure one of those forest faeries into our midst for a bit of interrogation. A hungry dryad can smell a prize like a Blood Thistle from anywhere."

"Then I must say I'm impressed," admitted Vuzbagh. "It's a plan, at the very least. But how do you know so much about dryads, and how did you manage to get hold of one of their choice snacks when they themselves apparently can't find them out-of-season?"

Xerbex smiled and then wiggled his lanky frame beneath a blanket made from quilted toad skins. The inside of the tent had grown steamy from the fire and the ever-putrid breath of cantankerous troll conversation.

"Watch and learn, Vuzbagh, my pet. You'll soon discover that I've forgotten more about the proper ways to track a fugitive than you'll ever know. Watch and learn."

☜❦☞

In the morning, Starbane woke up amazed to feel a scattered spray of sunbeams playing upon his brow. Through the tangle of vines and briar-clusters he had shoved into the cave's entrance, golden rays managed to penetrate to where he had collapsed, supine and snoring, the night before. The startling and unexpected brightness seemed a foreign thing, for he had not seen the sun at all since the beginning of his journey. Rousing his various aches and pains into some form of functional attention within the crevice, he was astonished at the change, hoping that it was a favorable omen. The air remained murderously cold, but the good night's sleep combined nicely with the newborn light to fill his spirit with a thread of rejuvenated purpose. That was all well and good, but it only took another moment's self-assessment to prove that his previous directional instincts were still utterly evaporated.

A few green flames continued to burn in faint licks atop the remnants of his wood pile. Now, the onset of this seemingly magical dawn prompted him to gather his things and extinguish the fire. It was time to move on. He pushed his way out of the cave and into the ravine. Blinking furiously, his eyes were accosted by the lively glow of the jagged and whitewashed landscape. Though he had beheld many such days during the course of his young life, he judged this one to be the most breathtaking. The armies of gnarled and leafless trees no longer appeared drenched with menace and he gloried all the more to hear the call of birds coming from nearly every direction. For a moment in the vast stillness, he imagined that he could even hear the distinct *drip, drip, drip* of ice as it melted from the tips of branches and struck the earth in myriad places. He took several deep breaths of the frigid air and whispered a brief prayer to Asbethell, Goddess of Morning, grateful that the Dawn Maiden had somehow seen fit to smile upon him. From the satchel he retrieved his scroll-map, cautiously optimistic about his abilities to ascertain the necessary course of travel on a day like this, even without the long gone and touchy sentinel-gnome.

Since yesterday's loss of all supernatural guidance, he had discovered that he was not much of a map-reader, and this proved true again, even in the renewed hope of the day. He had little idea what he was looking at on the weathered parchment, or where he should even begin to look. His buoyed mood began to fade, but not to the point of despair. The Fire Elixir, at least, had still proved valuable to his well-being. He resolved to make the best of it. The last marker he had fought to discover on the map had been a crumbling stone footbridge spanning the first stream west of the Sahlorn Hills, which he had been fortunate enough to always keep in sight above the distant treetops throughout the previous day's trek. This rocky cluster of hills had been directly *behind* the place from which he had originally escaped and, for all he knew, might remain his only point of reference until, as the scroll indicated, the Pyr Midan Mountain range would rise before him at last. The footbridge was not far from where he now stood in the ravine, perhaps a half hour's walk through the forest.

He knew he had been lucky to find any sort of landmark before nightfall, and wasn't at all certain such luck would continue even in the best conditions. Teeth beginning to chatter again, he strained to comprehend the crudely drawn guide. According to his best interpretation, the parchment indicated that he must now double-back to the footbridge and then continue westward until reaching a large market roadway called "Old Keeper." Then, he would have to follow Old Keeper south, staying in the shadows as much as possible, never coming into plain view, meandering discreetly around the various towns and villages the roadway traversed.

How easy!

The boy shook his head in dismay. When the road itself came to an abrupt end at the gates of the city of Pyr Mida, at the very foot of the mountains, he was to find the "First One" to whom he had been sent. Only then would safety, or some semblance of it, be within his grasp.

Starbane's belly yowled in hunger and he sighed, plumes of steaming breath erupting from his lips and nostrils. By the look of it, this route alone would take several days to complete and he began to sorely regret that he could not travel at night. He dared not. Though daybreak seemed friendly enough for the moment, and the surroundings benign, travel by even a few moments of darkness would increase the odds of encountering any number of troubles.

Like anyone in Kelnia, he knew that these forests harbored an almost mindboggling array of potentially sinister and supernatural beings that held sway when the sun vanished and moonlight shrouded the land. Even if he was lucky enough to avoid a meeting with a two-tusked Eskanthian werewolf or an ogre, there were still plenty of crylvanes, shadwocks, night imps, hedge-hags, ice pixies, dryads, and possibly even a troll or two waiting to do him harm. And that was to say nothing of the common wolves, wild dogs, badgers, and great cats that might happen across his path. Goaded by the realization that every step would bring him closer to his destination, he scampered out of the ravine and headed for the cover of the surrounding forest. Beyond that, he would make for the stone bridge.

Starbane prayed again, this time that the day would carry him far from the doom that gripped all of Kelnia with fingers more icy than those of the Blizzard Lord, Ashkivul, brother of the kindly god, Dryndym.

A small flicker of resolve filled his being, and though this determination was not anywhere near as potent as the magical forces that had earlier energized his progress, he took some measure of comfort in the fact that he didn't feel quite as vulnerable as before. Overhead, a pair of swallows flitted and swooped as if to express their own approval of his newfound mettle, flimsy though his mettle was. He stopped to watch them for a moment. As his breath continued to emerge in billowing clouds, he even managed a weak smile before entering the fringe of thick forest. The birds dived and dodged him before rising to disappear in an arc of flight that carried them up and over the sturdy Falthurn trees, southward to the peaks of the Pyr Mida Mountains that only *they* could see in the impossible distance.

ॐॐ

The book was a sacred relic, placed with solemnity upon Oblixta's Primary Ritual Altar. Its binding was cracked and tattered, and the faded brown patina of the cover was mottled and spotted with a creeping collection of fungi accrued over devious centuries, but Oblixta could not have revered the volume more than if it were bound in gold and embossed with gemstones. She had no need or much use for jewels, but she craved *this* book.

At last, she thought. *I have the Gragan's Tome of Confoundments and Convolutions.*

The queen touched the tip of a long index finger to the surface of the book, as if to reassure the reality of its presence, and then she placed the same finger against the tip of her tongue, savoring the taste. Subtly, beneath the tang of the decomposing leather, she detected the flavor of power, and of long-forgotten ages. She hadn't fully perused the book, yet ... knowing well that the legendary acquisition was hardly a thing to be casually riffled-through. There were possibly even a few dangers inherent in reading the tome. Bitter old wizards were always booby-trapping their written works with spells. Even so, Oblixta was mighty in terms of innate power, and such dangers could be neutralized with the proper time and in a carefully orchestrated setting.

When she had tackled other matters at hand and strengthened her grip upon the newly assimilated provinces in her kingdom of Kelnia, she would have ample opportunity for more thorough study of the tome now in her possession. Then, the inconvenient sorcerer of the Corydian realm, Rowan Blaize, could be ousted and Oblixta's ultimate goal—mastery of the glorious Southern realm itself—could be realized. Rowan Blaize's dead body would be the perfect welcome-mat. In that moment she blushed red with sheer longing for a time when the ebb and flow of life *everywhere* might course solely according to her whim and design. She paced around the altar, staring at the book, knowing that, in many places already, the existence of her people was permeated by deference to and awareness of her extraordinary power. Around her own capital city of Grohal and its rose-granite fortress, the very forces of nature rarely made a move without her consent. It no longer mattered that the withered Gragan wizard was now dead. His usefulness had dwindled steadily as her own strengths had continued to blossom, fueled by her goals and her frightful talent for self-discovery.

Oblixta's fingers drifted, as they often did, to the tresses of her shoulder-length hair. At long last it had grown back and was beginning to reclaim former signs of its raven brilliance. Cutting all of it off two years prior had been a curious blow to her vanity, even if it *was* for the purpose of the spell required to defeat the Gragan. Next, she caressed her face in the gloom of her ritual sanctum, wondering if the soft skin was still a tad on the pallid side. That had been another consequence of doing such extended magical battle against the old sorcerer, this deterioration of her looks. She had jettisoned every mirror and reflective surface in the fortress in those days, so there would be little opportunity to assess her current visage.

Mirrors might suit other witches, but she did not aspire to the mere chance that *she* might get attached to them, especially in a weary moment.

If she looked weary now, it was due mostly to unavoidable hours of strategic planning with various military leaders, late into every evening. Above and beyond such fleeting worries about her physical appearance,

Oblixta knew that the frightful aspects of her bearing commanded far more respect and trepidation from her underlings. This was a thing to be utilized in times such as these. Besides, if she wished, she could easily construct an illusion of former beauty at any time and for any reason. Still, there were no reasons for comeliness, at the moment, and none she could foresee in the immediate future. All unproductive forms of vanity had been eradicated in her soul, so she thought, replaced by an efficient arrogance far more pertinent to the sheer scope of her developing abilities.

Finally, the eyes of the witch moved to a stack of maps, scrolls, and other books occupying a large table in the corner of the chamber. These were updates and other materials given to her by her Supreme Warlord, General Kerrion, in his daily briefings. Three days ago, the news had been rather typical. Several towns north of the old Sistram Fortress of Hibisha had been assimilated with only token resistance. Oblixta knew that the winter had finally drained the fight out of the few, independent Northern provinces that remained untaken. Even the factions she had expected to cause the most trouble—the hearty Spersenes and Braxtu clans—had barely caused her troops to break a sweat. Basically, with the exception of a few scattered outposts, everything in the realm of Kelnia was hers, now. Oblixta grinned at the thought of such utter conquest, but before the expression came full to her face, it crumbled into a frown.

Corydia.

Always, Corydia hovered, just beyond her range of success, beyond the majestic Pyr Mida Mountains, taunting her and magnifying the incompleteness of her dominion. She clenched both of her fists until every knuckle was bone-white. Only Corydia, the mighty Southern realm, remained to be conquered, and Oblixta's anxiety for this domination made all of her other accomplishments seem to be little more than practice. The forging of her plan to capture Corydia was now three years in the making and would be the sole agenda of her military conferences for some time to come. First, however, she had to remove the magical obstacle—the obstacle of Rowan Blaize, who had emerged, it was said, from some mysterious "Other Universe" centuries ago. For that mission, she would turn to the arcane writings and powers culled from Blaize's own, defeated peers ... the Gragan wizard being the most recent of these.

Simultaneously, however, forces were being steadily recruited and trained for the great siege of Corydia, once Blaize was out of the way. In her relentless drive to usurp all things, Oblixta had already marshaled thousands of new slaves into service from the battered eastern provinces of her own kingdom. Those from the lately crushed Northern reaches were soon to follow. It would be an invincible army that marched out of Kelnia in the future to cut the throat of Sye, the churlish, idiotic Corydian king, and devastate his legions. She would see to that.

Tomorrow, potential battalion commanders would be interviewed from a horde of nominees and, though tedious, it would be interesting to see exactly what stock of warrior her chieftains had molded out of the conscripted men. General Kerrion had been viciously effective in testing the prospects. He had no other choice, and knew it well. Yes, tomorrow would be a long day, and she would have to retire to her apartments as soon as possible. Dealing with the Gragan wizard, with the annoying Fey Empress, Tramayda, and most of all with the vile traitor, Celintha, had weakened her magical reserves. Sleep was crucial to the restoration of supernatural strength.

Of course, there was still the matter of the boy.

His potential to interfere with the elimination of Rowan Blaize was weighing most heavily upon Oblixta's mind. Kerrion had assured her that the search was a domestic priority. Starbane would be rooted out, and soon. Warnings and notices of reward had been posted in every known fiefdom and village on the way to Corydia. All of the loyalist barons and governors of South Kelnia had put their troops and scattered mercenary groups on immediate alert. For added measure, the general populace had been notified by mandatory public assemblies rife with terrific threats. Because of all this, General Kerrion was quite convinced that the youth would not escape detection, were he to reach any civilized post—if he even managed to survive long enough to reach any worthwhile place at all. Yet, with each passing day that left Starbane's location undetermined, Oblixta's vexation burgeoned in intensity. Not solely confident in the General's methods, she had, of course, employed her own means—and her own, special minions—to the cause. Thus far, her impish envoys had discovered nothing, but with the sweeping blizzard conjured by Celintha now neutralized by Oblixta's far greater craft, there was every reason to be optimistic.

It *did* bother the queen that a few other magical methods had proved unproductive thus far. The Gragan's final instructions before death had yielded exactly the results he had predicted: hazy and incoherent images. It was frustrating to be reminded that not everything still moving about in Kelnia was currently within the framework of her control. If the boy was dead from exposure—and this Obixta hoped to be true; it was the cleanest solution—then she had nothing left at all to worry about. Yet, if Starbane was being assisted by the spies of King Sye, as she suspected, there could be trouble. The Corydian's ruler's emissaries were a plague upon Oblixta's ruthless path of conquest. With stealth and cunning they continually sought to unseat her in her own territory. While these fools plotted her downfall in pitiful yet disconcerting ways, she would not rest.

The mighty sorceress sighed. With any luck, the boy was dead by now, but killing him herself would prove to be a most delicate matter, for a variety of reasons. This was why she had not attempted it while he had remained a captive. If the sinister gods she often invoked were on the move, then the boy had been frozen by cruel weather into some comical block of ice that her scouts would discover in the upcoming spring thaw. After all, the frail youth was no outdoorsman and he had quite obviously dashed straight for the forests upon his escape. Had Oblixta not discovered, a bit too late, that it was the spying witch, Celintha, who had helped him with some sort of spell, her guards might have caught the little rat on the first day. As it was, the stubborn old woman had opted to perish in agony rather than reveal a thing.

So be it.

Gazing toward the sole window of the tower room, Oblixta pondered the idea of conjuring-up another clue before retiring for the night.

The moon was now a curvy yellow jewel at its apex in the firmament; it seemed to reflect her nervously jagged, scimitar mood.

No one will dare to shelter him, she thought. *He must not get to Corydia and show that scar to King Sye or—worse—to Rowan Blaize himself!*

Again, her disseminated instructions had been most explicit: magnificent reward for the one who turned him over to the castle, and excruciating destruction for anyone found to have aided his emancipation. Mindful of tomorrow's military affairs, Oblixta decided against any more magic for the evening and hoisted the Gragan's Tome from the altar, tucking it under one arm as she made for her apartments. Starbane, if alive, could wait another day for her immediate attention. From now on, the hallowed book of spells would never be far from her sight or reach. Perhaps tonight, if sleep were slow in arrival, she would sit up in bed and read a bit—provided she felt like stringing together the protective spells necessary before opening the deadly book once again. It was all becoming such a bother.

Outside the Chamber of Rites, two sentries waited faithfully in their positions on each side of the entrance, bowing low as she locked the door behind her with a massive iron key. She instructed a nearby maidservant, one of her Blinded Ones, to go ahead and prepare her rooms and then she followed alone, sweeping along to cast an imposing shadow across the circuitous torch-lit corridor. Within moments she had reached the end of the tower hall and veered off, like some gliding night-bird, for the portion of Cadrach Castle reserved for her inviolable suite of rooms. Oblixta blended cleanly into the swell of darkness, as if she and the shadows were somehow made of one and the same substance.

III

Of Things That Go Hunting at Dusk

Old Keeper Road did not look as impressive to Starbane as it appeared on the map, which was becoming about as weathered and shredded at the edges as his nerves. No wider than the length of a tall man, this slushy lane seemed to lead toward hopeless Nowhere in both directions as he peered from the cover of dense roadside brush and tiers of icy branches. As far as could be surmised, someone had traveled the highway not long before, since there were fresh horse and wagon tracks in the porridge of mud and snow, all coming from the north. The sight of these made him duly apprehensive about crossing the road and only when certain that the surrounding region was deserted—even of the most gently fluttering bird, if he could detect one—did he scramble up from the little ditch to make his way into the looming forest on the other side.

Finally, away from the throngs of trees that normally obstructed his view of the horizon, Starbane could see the peaks of the Pyr Mida Mountains, looking somewhat closer than he had dared hope from his questionable consultations of the parchment. He judged the foothills of the mountains to be perhaps two full days away, if he felt confident about gauging anything correctly at all in his state of mind. Even so, this was the judgment he preferred. Hours earlier, he had eaten the remainder of his cured meats and the last crust of bread he had been given, washing them down with a handful of snow. He vowed not to waste any more time returning to travel with such strength as he still possessed, for his hunting skills were non-existent. Moreover, he had no tools with which to hunt, save for the tiny bronze dagger Celintha had given him at his initial departure. Risk of discovery notwithstanding, a venture into the next town or settlement he chanced to encounter would be necessary.

For the next six hours, he tramped southward through the dense woodland, staying as close to the road as possible without coming near enough to be potentially seen or heard. The sun continued to lend some measure of comfort and token warmth upon his face and, during his steady trek, he did indeed come upon the outskirts of a few small villages. The sight of a Castle Cadrach soldier on horseback, riding into the first of these towns, was more than enough to stir fear. He circled around this village and then, his resolve dwindling, avoided all of the others in order to stay out of trouble. His stomach seemed to gnaw upon itself, but he stayed his course, venturing even deeper into the growth in mounting disorientation. Near dusk, it was an exhausted and famished youth who came upon the outskirts of what appeared to be yet another small township. A quick look at the map revealed that it was possibly, but not at all certainly, to be identified with a place called "Lugarne."

There was a cluster of other town-names and dots in roughly the same region of the map, so proper identification didn't matter much to him at such an hour. Judging from the wraith-like billows of smoke rising over the treetops ahead, Starbane figured he was a half hour's walk from the place, *whatever* it was called. For the moment, he decided to lean against a Falthurn tree and rest. Shadows were beginning to creep again across the sylvan terrain and, despite the closeness of this upcoming village, he castigated himself for being hopelessly behind schedule. He cursed the deficiency of his progress aloud, knowing that he should be safe by now in the city of Pyr Mida. With his stomach surging from a constant churn to a gurgling yowl, he had to find some way to get food for the night, even if he had to sneak into the yonder town and beg, or perhaps even steal.

He had no other choice; beyond this portion of the map, there were no towns or villages other than the ones already marked, and certainly no other "safe haven" caves designated for his use as darkness hovered in its inevitable descent. Still, the freezing lad stared with grave suspicion at the plumes of chimney smoke beyond the groves, watching as their ends vanished into the lowering tips of the evening. He would have to be insane to enter any town, he realized woefully, and did not *want* to realize that he had no idea how to approach the strangers that awaited him. Worse, he had a nagging suspicion that, during the past several hours, he had strayed somehow farther from the parallel with Old Keeper Road than he had intended. He could not see the highway now at all.

The need to find a safe strategy for entering the town pulled at every fiber of his frantic mindset, even as reason fought against the horror of potential discovery. Discovery would seal for him the same doom suffered by so many others … or worse. He tried to trick himself into believing that an approach under cover of complete nightfall might improve his chances for stealth, but the illusion was dashed when he heard a sudden, sharp sound in the cluster of Falthurn trees behind him. All thoughts about going anywhere or doing anything were swiftly dismissed.

The relatively brief time spent thus far in the forests had accustomed his ears to the typical sounds of nature, enough so that he was not as often startled by the occasional crashing limb or calling animal. But this sound had been much different in tone. Starbane's deepest instincts warned of danger. Steadying himself against the huge Falthurn, the boy froze in a posture of wary rigidity, gently cocking his ear from beneath the hooded Bog Bear cloak to discern the exact direction from which the sound had come. He heard it again, an ominous crunching.

Something was not only out there, but quite close, in an adjacent thicket, hidden from view. Again he heard a swift snapping, but this time the sound emanated from *across* the tiny clearing. His heart began to race and he whirled to face a cluster of saplings, behind which the sun was just now beginning to vanish. Again he heard noise, this time two sounds, coming from either direction, behind *and* at his side. With shaking fingers, he drew the little dagger slowly from a pocket of his coat.

"Who goes?" he called into the growing murk of the forest. "Show yourself."

He was struck from behind with a force so massive that the breath was knocked from his lungs even before his body slammed face-first into the snow. Struggling and moving his jaws for air like a beached fish, he became aware of a heavy presence clinging to his back and shoulders. Turning his head in panic, it took only an instant to realize that a massive Eskanthian werebeast was trying to sink its double-tusks and fangs through the thickness of his coat and into his shoulder blades, creeping and slavering upward to find some sort of hold on the back of his neck.

Now, the air had come alive with the sounds of ravenous snarling as blood and adrenalin pounded in the boy's brain. The beast had pinned him helplessly into the deep drift. Letting out a frightful scream, Starbane tensed his shoulders as best he could in an attempt to protect his neck, but the beast merely moved from its frenzied jabbing at his neck to raking the back of his skull with its maw. Then it tried once again to nuzzle its nose into the crevice between head and shoulders, desperate to snap the victim's spine. In the crushing grip of such terror and the agony of his struggle for breath, Starbane realized that he was still holding the dagger in his right fist. He gathered every ounce of his strength and thrust his arm backward desperately, onto the creature's body. The wolf emitted a feral howl of pain and surprise, yelping once as it rolled off the boy and hit the ground. Terror flooding through his system, the gasping boy scrambled to his feet and came face-to-face with the thing, holding the now-bloodied weapon well out in front of him. The wounded monster crouched in the snow with a chilling growl, blood spurting from a wound in its ribcage.

Praise the gods, thought Starbane, his lungs burning as he gulped icy air. *The first strike had been true!*

The foe was about three-fourths his own size, the largest he had ever seen or imagined. Everyone in Kelnia knew and feared these were-creatures, descended from a stock bred in secret and set loose upon the wilds by an Eskanthian king and his coterie of magicians in ancient days, created to accost unwelcome travelers and bandits that plagued the outlying regions of the kingdom. They were thought be shape-shifters, taking the forms of benign forest creatures during the hours when sunlight ruled the countryside, but transforming into murderous wolf-beings at the onset of darkness. Covered with thick black fur and snarling in misery, the present specimen appeared to be nothing but a set of awesome fangs, the notorious tusks and gray eyes swirling like vortexes of ash. The long ears were now pushed rigid against its head in warning as great columns of breath erupted from its maw in blood-flecked clouds.

The thing crouched, haunches tense, and charged again. But the beast was more hesitant in attack this time, and Starbane sensed a gossamer strand of opportunity. He yelled as he drove the dagger deep into the side of the onrushing head, below the left ear. Then he screamed, barely evading one of the horrid tusks, and twisted the razor-sharp blade for good measure. The screeching denizen flailed backward, convulsing quickly toward death. Mad with fear, the youth collapsed to one knee beside it in the reddening snow, tears beginning to sting as they gathered in the corners of his eyes. The panting sounds he made were almost as grotesque as those of the fading attacker.

Alas, the fugitive had barely caught his breath and his wits when he was suddenly sent flying forward again! In another, awful flicker of despair he remembered that he had heard *two* sounds in the forest before the first attack, sounds coming from opposite directions. Now he floundered sideways, managing to knock the second Eskanthian wolf temporarily away from him with another fortunate slash of the dagger. When Starbane also hit the snowdrift with a muted thud, the dagger flew from his grasp to disappear in the white cover of the forest floor. He had no time to plan any sort of new defense before the stunned second beast resumed its onslaught. Feebly, the shaken victim tried to get to his feet, but the snowshoes had become mangled traps shackled to his limbs and he stumbled forward even as the wolf's jaws found and bit deeply into his left forearm—the one he had had enough sense to raise at the last instant to protect his face. As the fangs shook and tore into his flesh, he wailed, kicking off the snowshoes now to try and gain some measure of foothold in this rapidly spinning world of pain. The stubborn demon-wolf held its ground, rearing up on its own hind legs to start clawing with paws at the torso of its prey. Then it wrestled him down to deliver the decisive bite.

Starbane did not feel the blood coursing from his arm and shoulder as it flowed beneath his coat, but in astonishment he watched it spill in great crimson drops and streaks, melting little chasms into the snow as the wolf continued to shake him without mercy. In the midst of this confrontation, he felt little tangible pain, only the inborn instinct that somehow pulsed toward the need to survive, to find a way to live! He knew, with an almost dreamlike quality, that if this attack was not repelled soon, he would certainly die. Thus, with a last summoning of his strength, he jumped as best he could from the forced crouch and brought both of his feet forward and onto the ribcage of the scrambling devil. He managed to deliver such an inspired kick that a few of the animal's fangs remained embedded in the bone and flesh of his arm while its body buckled and flew some distance away. The Eskanthian horror was dumped into yet another snow-drift, howling in anger and more than a little surprise. Starbane, bleeding and pale, bolted as best he could through a shallow drift of snow toward the nearest Falthurn tree, hoping to find some branch that he might scale toward refuge. Once there, he discovered that the lowest limbs were massive and beyond his reach or strength to grasp. In misery, he collapsed at the base of the tree, one hand falling upon his satchel, which had been tossed away during the fray.

Only a sliver of daylight remained in the wood as the youth's breath rose in a furious crescendo of pace and pitch. Eyes wide, he watched the beast compose itself and turn to charge him hungrily once again. A bitter snarl drove all other sounds from the approaching dusk. The fallen youth began to scream and clenched his fist, helpless, as it moved into the open satchel. There, among the jumble of articles, his hand closed by chance upon the small flask.

The Blood of the Fire Salamander.

The werebeast hurtled toward him, jaws agape and tongue lolling. As it leapt, Starbane flicked the bone-stopper from the phial and somehow managed to shove the entire thing into the deadly maw. Though his fingers and the back of his hand were shredded by the wolf's canines, he wedged the vessel deep into his adversary's gullet and the onslaught came to a sudden halt as the creature began to shake its head in agony and claw at its own face. Choking and barking as it tried to dislodge the object, the wolf's confusion lasted mere seconds for, suddenly, its entire head and neck burst into a fearsome ball of explosive green flame. There was no time for it to cry out again, nor even to fall into a series of convulsions, like its companion. The monster perished immediately and collapsed in a heap, stunning the frantic boy, who had not in his wildest hopes counted upon such a potent reaction. He did not even know how he had managed to think of such a counterattack; in the instant before his own death, it seemed as if his body had done all the thinking for him. Still gasping, he slid upward slowly and leaned with a measure of bewilderment against the Falthurn tree. Moments earlier, he had stood in the same spot unmolested, seeking but a moment of rest, and now his entire being seemed distorted and listing toward some imminent submergence in a torrent of pain. He sensed death lurking very near, a grasping shadow at the edge of his perception.

A terrible weakness began to spread from his stomach and down into his legs, even as strange tendrils of comfort and relief teased and tickled his mind like swift, clinging vines. He surveyed the scene. Two dead Eskanthian werewolves lay within feet of each other, and though Starbane now began to cringe at the pulsations of agony coming from his wounds, he found it hard to believe that he had escaped with his life. He felt the steady, sticky flow of his own blood, now, coming from injuries on his hands and beneath his torn fur coat, oozing from a number of ravaged spots. He accepted the idea that he may not have "escaped" at all, and would bleed to death in such a forlorn place. Looking above the trees, he coughed up a bit of blood, ignoring it, barely able to detect the chimney smoke still wafting upward in the distant town. Was it really a plume of smoke, or just the snaking tentacles of some twilight cloud? Evening fell like the smothering wings of a celestial, predatory bird and the bodies of the wolves became insubstantial specters, fading and formless.

Forgetting to retrieve his satchel where it lay near the Falthurn, Starbane stumbled forward into the bracing chill of the forest. A silvery tip of the moon's crescent had now come into view through a tattered streak of cloud above the western treetops. Stars were beginning to glimmer across an obsidian layer of sky in the East. Although it could not be seen in the darkness, the trail left by the boy as he forced himself onward was increasingly dotted and splotched with blood-drops of varying size. These dripped onto the snow and sunk, forming crater after crater with their life-warmth. He had no immediate realization of the severity of his wounds, but was filled with the distinct impression that time was running out. He had to get to the nearby town, whatever town it was, however he could manage. Discovery by enemies was now far from his thought, as was the fact that he had left what little money he possessed behind in the satchel.

Past ancient trees and enshrouded by gloom, he thought he could see a few pinpoints of light and judged them, with a dangerously quickening heart, to be signs of his destination. These lights comforted him and soon inspired weird visions of warm hearth fires, tables laden with food, and steaming baths. He became quite calm. The walk might not take so long, after all, he mused. He heard voices, then. At first, these sounded almost like the voices of his parents, calling him by name. Though he was vaguely tempted to stop and better discern the source of these echoed mutterings, he was unable to do so. In fact, his feet seemed to be almost skating across the top of the snowy terrain, rather than plowing awkwardly through it, even without his now-ruined and discarded snowshoes.

The whole forest assumed a surreal aura; everything was becoming incoherent, yet oddly focused at the same time. The distant lights he watched began to swirl a bit, first coming together to form one glistening ball and then exploding outward to occupy separate orbits. Starbane staggered on in this state for some time before everything went black and he fell down against something hard, his very soul seeming to spin and tumble toward a serene and quiet world, one void of pain and the constant crush of anxiety. In the few seconds before he no longer sensed anything at all, he knew only that he wanted to sleep, to allow this new landscape to enfold him forever, if necessary. He had never felt better in his entire life, or at least since he could remember. Soon, he could remember nothing.

In the deadening embrace of this comfort-realm he allowed himself to become irrevocably lost.

꿍ᕽ

Ona bundled herself methodically with the animal-skin wraps and furs hanging from various hooks by the front door of her hovel. She sneered, tired of the dressing ritual required to simply walk outside in such a godforsaken winter. Ona was also mildly peeved that it took so many cloaks and wraps to cover *her* body, which was a body particularly hefty around the midsection. She glanced, not without a mixture of spite and envy, at the large and luxurious stag-skin coat hanging in its place of honor on the other side of the door. She entertained the notion of putting it on, but only in the most obscure recess of her mind. The stag-skin was sacred and reserved only for her husband, Rufthar, who had "earned" it during one of the Hunts, just as all the men of the camp had earned theirs, if they had yet earned one at all. To even touch the coat with a woman's hands would render the thing immediately unclean and bring some form of misfortune upon the family.

They had enough of *that* already.

The burly woman bent to pick up one of the torches that lay in a pile near the hearth. Nearby, her husband sat in a massive burl-wood chair that Ona herself had made. Rufthar was snoring and grunting and unconsciously enjoying the warmth that radiated from the fire that Ona had built and stirred. Her husband's belly was visibly full of the supper of venison stew Ona had cooked. Ona grumbled a little more. It was her only luxury. Though her husband didn't appear to have a worry in the world, at the moment, she knew that he, like everyone else in Kelnia, was inwardly very much concerned with the scourge of oppression that had infiltrated their lands and homes. Though it was comparatively idyllic living in the remote isolation of their hunting encampment, deep in the woods where Cadrach Castle soldiers did not bother to venture, life back home in their native city of Pyr Mida had never seemed so wracked with doom.

Let him sleep peacefully while he can, Ona thought. *Come spring, we shall all have to go back to the real world.*

Opening the ramshackle door, the woman was hit with a blast of icy air and a dusting of snow that fell, as if in sarcastic greeting, from the thatched eaves. She moved out into the night, having lit the rag-swathed and oil-soaked end of her torch by the fireside. She was somewhat pleased to discover that the evening was neither as cold nor as dark as she had expected. Perhaps such relative mildness was a faint sign of the impending thaw; she could only hope that this was the case. All the same, the air was still cold enough to "freeze a dragon's breath as it burns," which she often liked to aver in winters such as this one. A fine crescent moon was peeking through several slender fingers of cloud and the pleasant light from the heavenly jewel made her efforts almost worth the while. Stooping once again, she gathered the ropes attached to a small sleigh that the family used to transport firewood from pile to hovel. The rest of the encampment, where tiny shacks and cabins like her own were spaced but a fallen Falthurn's length apart, seemed quite settled for the night. Ona could see a few of her neighbors dragging firewood of their own indoors, torches glistening. Everyone in the camp was responsible for their firewood and fuel and generally kept it against the front walls of their homes for easy picking.

Tonight, however, there was nothing but a few twisted branches and pitiful bark casings left in the snow near Ona's front door. The community pile was further down a pathway where her man (like all the others) had spent the day chopping and splitting to replenish the supply for another full moon's span. Her husband would haul a significant amount up to the house tomorrow, but for the moment Ona would have to trudge the path by herself, chiding her husband for not bringing at least enough back from his day's work to get through the night. Down the path she trundled, sleigh in tow, her eyes soon catching sight of the great woodpile, axe, and table-sized splitting-stump in the glow of torchlight that preceded her. On both sides, gnarly frozen bushes and dense thickets gave way to full-blown forest further on. Indeed, not far ahead, she could just about see the line of taller trees that marked the expanse of the Pyr Midan woodland. The sight of the forest made her shiver and she lifted the torch a bit higher and more out in front as she ambled, knowing that beasts and bogies of all sorts feared firelight, if they had any sense at all.

Reaching the woodpile, which was now three times as long as her hovel and half her own height, Ona began to fill the sleigh's little bin.

One trip's worth would keep the fire going until dawn and start things off nicely at breakfast. She paused to take the axe and chop a few pieces of kindling, of which there was none to be had save for her work. Just as she prepared to throw the last few pieces of wood into the sleigh, however, she heard a noise that stopped her where she stood, hunched over her load. The breath sucked silently into her lungs as she fought to suppress a gasp of surprise. There was an eerie, dismal moaning, coming from behind the massive woodpile. It was surely the most horrible sound she thought her forest-attuned ears had ever encountered, and despite her woodland hardiness, Ona instinctively began to scream.

Though her mouth prepared the way for a quavering bellow, however, nothing emerged from her lips save for a falsetto squeal. Even her feet would not obey when, somewhere deep in the brain, an order was given to dash away. Then, the same mind began to conjure a flurry of grotesque images. Perhaps the sound had come from an Eskanthian werebeast, or a crylvane that was even now crouching, making ready to spring for her throat. Worse, she envisioned a rogue troll, famished by the winter (as was often the case with trolls), lurking and waiting to knock her senseless with a bone club, drag her through drifts of snow to some fetid cave, and there roast her on a spit for the drooling, slobbering satisfaction of its brood. Ona's feet were finally ready to obey her head when she detected the unmistakable sound of words coming from the frosty gloom.

"M-mother. Mother ... help me ..."

The quavering words were a striking counterpoint to the baleful croak that had first chilled her very heart, a faint invocation that rang different bells of instinct in Ona's being. She listened, moist clouds billowing from her nostrils. There were more words, and these more clear:

"Help me, mother. Please ... I can't move. Something's happened and I ... I can't see."

Ona's eyes widened. This was obviously a wounded child—perhaps a child of the camp, though she did not recognize the voice—calling for its mother! She clamored awkwardly around the mighty pile, through slush and snow and chunks of bark, nearly falling headlong as her feet caught on scattered blocks and logs. Once on the other side, she pointed the crackling torch far out in front of her ample body, still half afraid that the moans and pleas for help were a ruse by some malicious forest sprite eager to ensnare her. For a moment she saw nothing but the hodgepodge side of the pile and its drift-blown environs. As her eyes narrowed and strained to penetrate the murk, she soon ascertained a form, sprawled against a discarded stump and nearly buried in the snow. She could not tell whether the shadow was man or beast and in her uncertainty dared not move toward closer inspection.

"Who goes there?" she trumpeted as best she could, but no reply came from the supine figure. Instead, she heard another soft murmur, again almost child-like. With new courage she ploughed a few steps closer, the torchlight soon revealing what lay at her boots. At first, Ona reeled with terror, for the thing was covered top-to-bottom with a layer of thick, dark, fur. Before the prior vision of Eskanthian wolves and were-beasts flooded back, however, she noticed a very human face poking from the hood of what was obviously a coat. Bringing the torchlight closer to this face, she saw eyelids flicker briefly and bluish lips moving without sound. Stooping to peer so that her own head was mere inches away, Ona noticed that the face was covered by a dark shadow, yet one that glistened in the moonlight as if moist. The air tasted suddenly unwholesome, like copper on the tongue. She gasped, knowing well the sight and scent of blood.

"Muh … mother?"

The face lolled to one side, muttering groggily. Now the eyes opened, full but unfocused in the torch-glare, to behold big Ona. The irises were gray and glassy, and Ona noticed how the pupils shifted wildly from orbs to mere pinpoints and back again.

"Mother you came … you're here. I knew. I called for you."

"Hush, whoever ye may be!" breathed Ona, pressing a finger to the cold lips below. "Don't move. Not that ye *can* move," she added, surveying the rest of the rather crumpled figure. "I'll fetch my husband to help." She stood erect as a bare hand rose to grasp at the hem of her skirts.

"Don't worry," she urged. "I'll be back very soon."

With speed that would have surprised anyone who had ever known the normally lumbering woman, Ona scrambled up and over the woodpile like a monstrous rabbit and was soon bustling up the narrow path toward camp. She flung open the door of her house and barreled within, snow falling and quickly melting in the oppressive heat of the little cabin. Her husband snorted once in his sleep and then jolted awake at the sudden racket.

"What in the name of Dryndym's Ninth Concubine is the matter with ye, woman?" he barked. "Ye look as if the Galwyn Crone herself just asked ye to supper." Ona said nothing as she took in great gulps of the warm air and stared at him. Her spouse peered behind her at the open doorway.

"Don't *stand* there looking daft!" he said. "Half the winter's coming in behind, intent to spend the night. Shut the door, already. I can only hope ye fetched enough wood to last till morning, seeing as how you're letting what heat we've got go outside to play!"

Ona stalked across the rough stone floor and placed a heavy hand upon his shoulder.

"You must come, husband."

"Come? Come where, by the gods?" he yawned in irritated fashion and settled back into his chair. "Shut that murderous winter out of doors and leave me be, woman!"

Ona shook him now, perhaps a bit too roughly, for he flinched and pushed her hand away with a snort. Ona backed up against the hearthside table and glowered at him with obvious worry.

"What's gotten into you?" demanded Rufthar, her devoted mate. His brow arched as it dawned upon him that something might indeed be amiss. "What would possess you to disturb my sleep?"

"To the woodpile, and quick!" burst Ona. "There's a … a … man, or a boy. Yes, I think it's a boy. Out there by the woodpile. Dying in the snow!"

With that blunt revelation she turned in a cyclone of heavy skirts and made for the door, slamming it shut behind her as she reentered the night. Her husband grumbled and snorted some more, wobbling slowly out of the comfortable chair and to his feet. He fumed about the delusions of women even as he stomped across the floor and snatched at his gargantuan boots and bearskin coat.

"Foolishness! Dying boys indeed."

He put one massive foot in a boot and clutched the coat around himself at the neck.

"That old battleax fell asleep and took to dreaming out on the woodpile, as like as not," he grouched. "It's lucky she didn't die out there herself, frozen like a heap of the same butter that's betwixt her ears."

"Father, what is it? What's happening?"

Wylla, his daughter and only child, had risen from the niche-like corner where she, too, had been asleep, on her bed. She rubbed her eyes in the flicker of firelight, her haystack of blonde hair tousled out of its usual braids.

"Eh? Go back to sleep, child."

Wylla watched dreamily as her father opened the door and peered into the swirling chill. "I'll be back in a hen's breath, I've no doubt. If ye hear your parents clubbing each other with fire-logs in the night, let it be a lesson not to drive your own true love mad some day."

He winked at her from beneath the intimidating bear-skull hood of his coat. Wylla could not stifle a giggle, for she knew that the threat of war-with-wood was far from imminent. Her parents were dedicated to each other, despite their constant bickering. She blinked sleepily as her father bounded outside and heard him call to her mother, who was Dryndym-knew-where. The last cold rush of winter wind whistled in as the door was slammed, tickling Wylla's nose even as she nestled in the tiny bed and pulled the down cover up to her eyeballs. Warm again, she wondered what sort of drama could possibly be going on between the two of them *this* time. It was always something, especially when they were all stuck together in the seemingly endless grip of camp and cruel winter. Sinking with a sigh into her lumpy, rag-filled pillow, Wylla was certain of one thing as she drifted off again to sleep.

Whatever her mother had come up with *this* time would probably keep everyone entertained for days.

☙❧

As usual, the twinge of apprehension struck suddenly, surging from the base of Oblixta's brain and inundating a typically arid region that circumnavigated her heart. There, it massed into a dull but painfully solid shape, and lingered. Oblixta placed both palms upon the surface of the stone table and tilted her head back, taking a succession of breaths in order to regain control of her emotions. Within seconds, the distress began to fade, along with the tremulous uncertainty that always seemed to ride upon its heavy cloak. She pursed her lips, grim for a moment, her eyes closed. These attacks came less frequently these days—perhaps two or three times in the span of a month—but they remained harsh enough to make her wary of the risks she was continually undertaking. These occasional agonies stemmed from such risks, in one way or another, and she accepted it.

This evening's panic had been amplified by recent lack of sleep and proper nourishment, though as Oblixta's powers grew in scope and complexity, her need for the trivialities of sleep and food waned. This was to be expected, but she was walking the edge of a knife until she managed to reach the fullness of her strength. Perspective and caution were therefore crucial in the interim. She had tossed and turned throughout the previous night and this happenstance had rendered her most irritable during the morning's interviews of prospective legion commanders. Overall, however, the day had been a success.

She was pleased by the progress her warlords had been making, particularly with the Eastern recruits. The nominees for command had demonstrated a vicious zeal and standard of depravity that surpassed much of what she had seen in her core battalions. Inwardly, she reveled in the wisdom with which she had played her hand in the matter. The plan had been deviously simple from the start. Her Supreme Warlord, Kerrion, had expressed as much doubt as he dared three years ago, when she had initiated the strategy, but she had held firm in her conviction that the policy would pay handsome dividends in the end, and when they needed it most.

"Conquer and subdue all of the Eastern provinces," she had said. "Crush them without mercy, but leave enough of the strong alive. Then, we'll befriend them. Stuff their cities, towns, and homes with the fat of the other Kelnian fiefdoms we've taken. Show the common wretches prosperity such as they have never seen."

"When they become strong again," Kerrion had warned, "they will remember their fall and turn against you."

"Not if they are made constantly aware of the source of their prosperity," she had countered. "Not if they know it comes at a dear cost, and that it can be taken away in one fell breath that will leave them begging for mercy."

Oblixta's idea was to train the best of the conquered Easterners in accordance with her unique military vision, making these soldiers "citizens of honor" and paying them relatively generous salaries.

"They'll go back to their homes and families singing the praises of the queen of Castle Cadrach. 'We never had it so good,' they'll say. 'Money, food, beer, security.' Yes, the East will come to prosper and grow strong and their allegiance will be fixed upon *me*."

It had long been Oblixta's belief that a full belly and a warm home were the keys to procuring the blind loyalty she needed to fulfill her plans. General Kerrion had again dared to gently question her tactics.

"Will not this bolstering of the East come at our own cost?" he had said. "Will not your own reserves be depleted?"

Oblixta had brushed his concern away like so many cobwebs. "You needn't worry about the state of my resources, General. I have more riches at my disposal than you guess. They have been acquired with much pain and effort of craft, and I plan not to disperse them frivolously. Besides, we'll milk the other, weaker provinces of everything they've got, make them sweat and slave for the Eastern peoples, who are more barbaric and inclined to cruelty on the battlefield. They are the ones we need, and a sufficient balance of power can be wielded over slaves and warriors alike. Yes, we shall channel all of our efforts into the East."

"And what of the Northerners?" pressed Kerrion.

"The North!" she had spat in response. "Ramshackle cities like Holofern and its stinking, weathered people. All useless to me, militarily. Too far away to bother with, and too mild tempered. They've got the whale-oil, though, and the salt. That much we can buy from them at an insulting bargain, and what we don't feel like buying we'll take. Leave that to me. And before you ask, General, the Western farmers of Colstra are in my thoughts, as well. Their young men will make fine reservists, but we need to keep their fathers' heads on exports, not battle maneuvers. It shall all be accomplished."

So it came to pass that Oblixta's armies, led by Kerrion, had crushed the East, and her plan to reconfigure their fortunes and loyalties was set into motion even as the last outposts and strongholds of resistance were razed to the ground. The success had proved overwhelming, stunning even her most skeptical strategists.

Always in the back of Oblixta's mind, however, writhed the ultimate goal and challenge: the legendary Southern kingdom of Corydia and its king with *his* legions—Corydia and Rowan Blaize, its shadowy sorcerer for whom even Oblixta harbored a certain measure of fear. Lately she had been carrying out her campaigns in Kelnia without qualm, even smashing a number of barons that were once known to be on good terms with the distant Corydian monarch. But she knew that the formidable King Sye would not make a move to help his Northern acquaintances, just as he had not bothered to aid those he knew in beaten districts like Demas and Tarsuris. Yes, Sye had made vehement, though token, protest via diplomatic channels, but with his kingdom surrounded in a mighty crescent by the vast and dangerous Pyr Midan Mountain range and the protective wizard, Rowan Blaize of the Forest of Shadnai, in the deepest south, any military involvement on Sye's part was pointless.

Oblixta knew he was laughing at her; to him, she was plotting and "playing" at war games, moving men around like pieces on a board with nowhere to go. Moreover, Corydia was self-sufficient in its lavish wealth and Sye himself an isolationist if ever one existed. He cared little, if at all, for the troubles of nations beyond his encircled domain, and little more for news of their tribulations. Sye and his precious Corydia were wealthier and more potent than Oblixta and all that her dark craft had managed to procure for Kelnia. She coveted Corydia more than she had coveted the Gragan's Tome, with its power and lore. King Sye, safe with his great army and under the mythical legend of Rowan Blaize's power, behind his dagger-like mountains, seemed to treat her with an indifference that boiled her blood. So, she had plundered her own land and its neighbors for four straight years while he flung occasional, vaguely worded chastisements her way by letter. It was almost as if he mocked her. Of course, in these letters there had been more than one grim assurance that his own armies were ever alert and primed for battle, should Oblixta entertain the foolhardy notion to move her efforts southward. He had warned her against magical interference and, indeed, she did not have the power to do much in Corydian lands.

Not yet.

As if dancing a sinister waltz, Oblixta took measures to portray herself to King Sye as an ultimately harmless, salvific sovereign with the unification and betterment of her realm—and its "needful" neighbors— at heart. As for magic, she reminded Sye via her ambassadors that many monarchs and great leaders of the past had been falsely accused of the same machinations. Thus, he should have no cause for concern on any level, safe and superior behind his various bastions. It had been a gamble, perhaps, against the well-known volatility of the aged ruler, but Oblixta took an almost obscene pleasure in her obsequious diplomacy with the Southern Realm.

All of that was now on the brink of change. The hunger for war against Corydia was gnawing ominously at her thoughts, threatening to shred not only the eventual object of her aggression, but her own efforts to put certain finishing touches upon the plan of attack. Rowan Blaize, above all other things, must be handled first. Even a façade of diplomacy could not be maintained if she continued to marshal Kelnia's forces in so obvious and manic a fashion. Surely King Sye's maddening network of Kashizma spies—spies that always seemed to elude Oblixta—would report on the new acceleration of military endeavors along the cities and towns of the Pyr Midan valley, north of the stern mountains. Surely the eyes of the dreaded, iron gray peaks themselves were blistering at the sight of burgeoning encampments far below. Wreathed in billowing winter storm-clouds, they seemed already to howl at the proliferation of garrisons, and the steady influx of supplies coming closer, ever closer, to the few navigable passes that led into treacherous depths and scaled the very heights of peril.

But King Sye's current thoughts about the issue, if any, no longer mattered to Oblixta. This was a war she finally felt prepared to win. This at last was the ultimate prize in her struggle for mastery, and all the more inevitable due to the rapid swelling of all legions and the ever-waxing potency of her spell-craft. Only last night the mad, demonic General Kerrion had told Oblixta in tones approaching awe that her longsuffering plans had been wiser and more effective than even *he* could have predicted. Though loyal and fearful of her, Kerrion was not a commander given to hyperbole of any kind, much less expressions of wonder. She had enthralled him with results, as had been the intention. *Her* Kelnia would be ready to go over the mountains, crush King Sye and capture his bountiful Corydia … as soon as Rowan Blaize was destroyed. Oblixta now envisioned the fall of her rival with grim satisfaction. She ruminated upon plans to be set in motion when General Kerrion entered the conference chamber of the castle's central tower and bowed low, helmet in hand. With one glance, the queen could tell from the sweat in his hair and the redness of his face that her behemoth had been outside in the grip of winter's fury, tending to his duties. She motioned him, with a gnarled claw, to a chair at the narrow table in the middle of the circular room.

"I'm pleased with the candidates," she said as he sat down. "You've done well, Kerrion. Everything seems to have gone according to my direction."

The General bowed his head once more in deference. "Thank you, Majesty. We have finished for the day and I've already drawn a preliminary list of my own choices. There are twelve, as you requested. I thought you'd like to see them."

"Yes, I would, but not at the moment," said Oblixta, leaning her now-crownless head slightly into one hand, her elbow resting atop the table as she passed Kerrion a parchment scroll of her own. "Here. Compare your list with mine and, where we agree, make the appropriate selections. We'll put the finalists to the test at dawn."

Kerrion sensed her fatigue and decided that it would be wise to keep the meeting brief. He had seen her this way before and knew that in such moments she could be especially unpredictable, as if to compensate for weariness.

"Our messengers from Holofern have just arrived, Majesty. They report that all has been taken in hand, without incident or interruption. The largest of three salt shipments should reach Colstra by tomorrow. Midday, it is expected."

"Good. And what news have we got from the West?"

Kerrion averted his eyes for a worrisome instant, and then thought better of it. "Captain Marcincus reports a marked increase in espionage activity and the stirring of resistance this past month."

Oblixta rose smoothly from her chair and began to glide away from him, a raven swelling toward some dismal midnight sky. She turned to frown at Kerrion from across the room. "Kashizma resistance?" she asked, knowing already the answer. The Kashizma was King Sye's cult-like network of masterful spies, and they had been sowing the seeds of discord and insurrection for years as she rose to power. The General nodded as she resumed pacing.

"There is no doubt of it."

"I thought we were through with their worst at Tarsuris," she spat, regarding Kerrion now with an accusing eye. "You assured me that we crushed most of their chief operatives."

"I thought we had, Majesty, but I was mistaken."

"Obviously. What happened this time?"

"You know that Sye always has more rats to replace those who fall beneath our wrath. How they keep getting over the mountains and past our people is still a mystery, but we're doubling the watch all along the Pyr Mida, in every conceivable place. Just the same," sighed the General, "there were a series of fires in the winter granaries at Lystil. Fires with their undeniable ... *signature*. Also, two assassinations. Mere guards, no one in administration. No one of consequence. Most significantly, our men intercepted a large cachet of weapons being smuggled into Bhrogetha, not far from the Colstra Pass. Captain Orus was also personally in the contingent that stumbled upon one of their little meetings in Lystil."

"And what passed at this little meeting?" said Oblixta.

"Their usual planning and propaganda," replied Kerrion, clenching and unclenching a mammoth fist. "They traded accounts of mass-starvation in Tarsuris, enslavement of women and children. They know that Tarsuris is being used to fatten the other provinces for war. There was some talk of the wizard, Rowan Blaize, too."

Oblixta returned to her chair, her agitation visible in the further whitening of already bloodless lips. "How many were present?"

"Orus reported little more than a dozen, but we have reason to believe that this was a conference of local Kashizma sympathizers only. There were likely many more of the spies and those rebels they stir-up undetected in Bhrogetha, judging from what we already know about their structure and hierarchy. Orus questioned the men at the meeting, but to no avail, as usual. They were killed and the entire town was burned to the last child in its cradle, as a warning to other Tarsurian communities. Tarsurians who are already inclined to mistrust the Kashizma rats will perhaps be more apt to expose the filth when future opportunities arise."

"Kerrion, I want no more opportunities to arise. I want Sye's Watchers rooted-out and destroyed once and for all," ordered Oblixta, cold as the night. "Do you understand me? Find every last one of them, in Tarsuris and elsewhere. I don't care if you have to burn every village and outpost. Obviously, it's better if you and your men acquire the wit to find their leaders. We don't need smoldering bones and ruins in the place of slaves and resources, after all. Focus on their operatives and make their deaths exemplary."

"It will be done, but with much difficulty, Majesty. I don't need to tell you that their bases of operations are elusive and change at need. They clearly seek to confuse us," added Kerrion with contempt, hoping to communicate his own anger unmistakably to the sorceress-queen.

"Then don't allow yourselves to be confused!" She pounded a fist hard on the stone table. The General blinked; it was as much of a flinch as he dared. "Kill every one of them you can find, without ruining the investment of our efforts in Tarsuris. Skewer their bodies on poles in the squares. Terrorize the townspeople who may be hosting these insects. The men. Their wives. Children. This is a primary order." Oblixta glared at Kerrion with barely controlled fury. "I want nothing—especially this Kashizma obstacle—to jeopardize my plans for Corydia and taking down their wizard, Rowan Blaize. Is that clear?"

"Of course, Majesty. I share your concern."

"That means nothing to me, General. I want results instead of assurances and shared concerns."

Kerrion quailed in his being; he knew she would dwell upon the problem of the Kashizma spies like a rotten oyster polishing a grain of sand. His life would be heaped with extra misery until *he* produced some pearl of success in the matter, and Kerrion did not need extra misery. The stress of building an army strong enough to daunt King Sye of Corydia was enough of a burden, much less any worries about that nation's magician. Magic was Oblixta's domain, and hers alone. He didn't want it any other way.

"You may begin tending to these matters *now,* Kerrion." She leaned well over the table to stare at him, nodding her head toward the door. It was the dismissal he had been craving and he rose to make for the exit.

"Just a moment, General."

Her sharp call stopped him at the door.

"Yes, Majesty?"

"Tell me how goes the search for my *brother?*"

Kerrion now feared her glare as he would the strike of a lightning bolt. Imposing warrior that he was, he shifted his feet like a nervous child amid the tension that seemed to overwhelm the chamber. Still, there was no sense in obfuscating, not with Oblixta.

"The boy eludes us. I do not know how. My finest scouts and woodsmen have discovered his trail only to lose it, time and again."

Oblixta held up a suppressive palm. "I already know this much on my own, Kerrion. Such is my misfortune to have an army incapable of handling such a small matter."

"I feel confident, Majesty, that if we are given enough time …"

"You must leave me, now," she interrupted. "I understand. Your methods are clearly inadequate."

Oblixta grinned, a talon-finger tracing strange signs atop the table. "With the Gragan wizard's tome at last in my grasp, General, nothing will remain hidden from *me* for long. But my brother must not get to the sorcerer of Corydia before we do. Rowan Blaize must not know that I have the Gragan's Book of Convolutions and Confoundments." She glared at Kerrion beneath lowered eyelids, pleased to detect a fleeting look of raw terror beneath the trained, iron gaze of her greatest general. She guessed, correctly, that he feared to think of her as more powerful than he already knew her to be.

"In time, Lord Kerrion, I'll perhaps have no need for an army, or of servants to do my bidding. You may become obsolete, my old friend. But until then …"

The General could think of no reply, of no assurance or promise that he would always be of value to her. Why was she so worried that the boy knew of her possession of the dead wizard's book of magic? How *could* the boy know such a thing—he had been imprisoned quite apart from the stinking old conjurer, most of the time. Magic and its ways he would never fathom. Spells and incantations sickened him. He swallowed hard, and let his eyes travel to the flagstones. Oblixta's tone of voice softened, but her whisper was still laced with enough bitterness to taint an entire ocean.

"Don't worry, Kerrion. I'm not ready to send you to the mines, yet. Go. Prepare tomorrow's finalists and set your lapdogs on the Kashizma, as I commanded. We'll meet at dawn."

Kerrion bowed his way out of the chamber and, in retreat, his thoughts drifted to the boy.

Long dead.

That was his opinion. Dead in the cruel grasp of winter, or dissolving in the belly of some wild beast or fell creature. He knew enough of the boy to know the youth had little in the way of mettle. Certainly not enough to survive the obvious hurdles, much less the rabid, fear-driven suspicion that had been aroused about him among the Kelnian people since his escape. But Kerrion guessed at Oblixta's ultimate worry, too—or at least he believed he guessed it. She worried that the old wart-charmer, the witch-spy, Celintha, who had set the boy free in the first place, had done so at the behest of Kashizma spies. It was rumored that he had been loosed with some sort of message for the Corydian wizard, a message from the now-murdered Gragan. Perhaps Oblixta worried that the boy might even now be in the midst of their enemies, a royal icon to be propped-up and used for some new, resilient insurrection.

But it was the queen who had let him slip away. She had miscalculated, not only by refusing to kill her brother, Starbane, as everyone thought she would, but by failing to discern a traitor among the castle staff in the person of the old witch, Celintha. It was the only major mistake Kerrion had ever seen Oblixta make in his many years of service, and he knew it rattled her to the very soul, if she indeed possessed one. For all of this, he also believed that his scouts would, at best, produce a frozen carcass or some mangled bones to drop at the feet of the queen, despite her insistence that Starbane be brought back alive, if possible. For the moment, however, the General was simply glad to be out of his Lady's presence, bound for the barracks and the vulgar but deferential company of his fellows. All of Kelnia had come to fear Oblixta's moods, and Kerrion, above all, knew that a severe "episode" was likely on the way. It was indeed going to be a devilish season. And a long, treacherous war to come, no matter how potent Oblixta fancied herself to be, and no matter *if* she managed to bring down the fabled Rowan Blaize, this enchanter who was supposedly guarding the Southern realm with spells of his own. Corydia would not be taken lightly, even by an army of sorcerers, he guessed.

With this potential war in mind, General Kerrion crossed the keep's vast torch-lit Reception Hall. No one was received in this place anymore, and the expanse had long since been stripped of its former splendor. Now, only shadows flickered with menace in the dank corners and seemed to streak and flow between the high arches and columns. Kerrion did not dare to pause and look about, knowing that Oblixta's own spies were rife in the castle, and that *her* kinds of spies dwelt most comfortably in shadow. He exited through a ruined but hidden door behind the marble dais and its smashed pair of thrones, disappearing into a jagged shard of night beyond.

Nutmeg!

The scent filled Starbane's nostrils and suddenly he found himself safe in the warmth of the castle kitchens. Dozens of servants worked the fires, tables, churns, and the breweries, and all around was the scent of nutmeg and how he loved the smell of it.

His mother was near. He could see her supervising the preparations for a feast, so he ran to her and it seemed then that he was little more than a toddler. She turned and saw him running and she smiled, leaving behind the tables, the servants, the world itself. Her eyes gleamed and her laughter was like the sound of delicate green leaves rustled by a breeze. Milk-white arms opened wide to receive him and he knew he could leap and fly and she would catch him from all the way across the cavernous room. Into those arms he fell, laughing, and together they continued to fall, swirling and plunging against some gently uplifting darkness, and she smelled of nutmeg and home and—

Starbane awoke with a gasp.

His eyes were seared with pain from some brilliant burst of light and though he could see his surroundings but vaguely, at first, he soon realized that he was indeed not in the castle kitchens and most assuredly *not* in the arms of his mother. Once his vision began to clear, he stared upward at a smoke-stained ceiling of cracked daub and protruding bits of thatch. Nearby, a whitewashed wall was sprayed with sunlight coming from some unseen opening behind. Shielding his eyes with the back of his hand, he struggled to reposition his body in the small bed upon which he lay, trying at once to sit up straight and swing completely around. His hand brushed against some sort of soft material on the rear of his head and, feeling about, he discovered that whatever it was extended around both of his shoulders, part of his neck, and down his back across the ribcage. He tried to concentrate and his thoughts began to drift. Bandaging, and lots of it. Then, the drift of his mind became a wild flood and his head was deluged with horrifying memories of the Eskanthian wolves and their attack.

Where am I?

In pain that grew with every breath, Starbane did his best to get his bearings. He looked around the place, trying to align the sequence of events that could possibly have led him to this moment. He had survived—that much was apparent—but the attempt to fully remember *how* produced only a dull, stony ache behind his forehead. He sat up fully on the straw mattress and gazed at the drab coverlets bunched near his chest and then at the crudely woven tunic in which he was dressed.

These aren't my clothes.

Looking about, he saw that the little bed was just one of many rough furnishings in a large, one-room hovel. A few feet from the end of his bed and in the center of the dwelling stood a table. Its base was fashioned from a gnarled tree stump. A roundish slab of slate had been placed, somewhat lopsided, atop the stump. The surface was littered with wooden bowls, cups, and a few twine-tied bags of brown animal-skin. Beyond this was a foul-smelling and crusty old hearth jammed with all manner of implements, most of which hung from a simple plank mantelpiece of redwood Falthurn. In the fireplace hummed and wheezed a mound of glowing coals. Even across the room, he could feel the warmth on his cheeks. Against one of the misshapen walls, he spied two other beds; one was quite big and positioned in a niche-like portion of the abode, behind a pulled curtain of sewn rags. Another bed, small as his own, was wedged into a corner niche.

Throughout the rest of the somewhat oblong interior, Starbane saw poverty: dilapidated cupboards; a sad-looking loom and spindle; various bins filled with logs or mere scraps of wood crawling with cutter-bugs. A pair of tiny windows boasted thick glazes of frost on the outside and were too high, anyhow, to see directly out of while still in the bed. Sitting up had fatigued the youth and, feeling dizzy, he dropped back into a recumbent position. He was certain he was alone, at least for the moment, but how he had come to be in this place—wherever it was—still eluded him. The notion that he had been captured crept icily into his mind, but this place betrayed no hint of malice, much less the appointments of a jail. On the contrary, all seemed snug and domestic, if decidedly primitive. Perhaps some kind stranger had taken him in? But if he had been rescued, where were his rescuers? More frighteningly, what was the extent of his obvious injury? What was the source of the throbbing jolts of pain that gripped his torso, his forearm, and which coursed along his skull? The last thing he could recall was walking at the brink of nightfall toward the mapped-out town of Lugarne. Then ... the awful attacks. Perhaps his final steps had taken him into the village after all, whereupon he collapsed. That scenario, at least, would not be as surprising as his present surroundings.

Summoning another burst of strength (and a dim burst at that), Starbane slid his feet from beneath the rough woolen coverlet. The present uncertainty called for some form of action, no matter how awful he felt. He managed to stand on legs that seemed as heavy and as flexible as tree trunks. Palming a shabby, sawed-off bedpost for support, he began to hobble a few steps toward the stone table and braced himself against it. Again he scanned the untidy space for some clue about the gravity of his current predicament. In the midst of his disorientation, a door flew open to his left, banging against the wall and startling him enough to disrupt what little sense of balance he possessed. Down to the filthy floor he crashed. Huddled in agony and clutching the legs of a burl-wood chair, he lifted a hand to block the overwhelming blast of sunlight coming from outside. He winced, heart pounding a fearful tattoo, and tried to discern who owned the slight silhouette visible in the doorway.

"Now *you're* a sight, there on the floor! Yes, that's what you are," said a sharp but not unfriendly voice. "A sight and then some."

Indeed, the voice was young and lilting, with a thick accent he could not place. As the form moved closer into the shadows of the dwelling, shutting the door behind, it revealed itself to be a girl of perhaps twelve or thirteen. She kept her wide eyes fixed upon the crumpled youth as she dropped a pile of firewood into a bin nearby.

"Did I scare you?" she piped. "Sorry if I did, but then you shouldn't be out of bed in the first place. What were you thinking, trying to get up and wander about like that?"

Starbane could only stare back at her in astonishment, bereft of words. He dared not speak until he knew with certainty whether he was sprawled before friend or foe.

"Are you hurt?" questioned the girl, pulling off her coat of silver fur and tossing it onto the table, where it knocked a few wooden cups to the floor. "I mean more hurt than you already are? Let's have a look at that. You've probably broken a leg, and that'll never do, on top of what's already brought you low."

She moved closer to him with obvious concern. Kneeling down, the girl supported his unresisting torso in her arms and placed his head squarely amid the thick skirts on her lap. Looking up, he saw that she was a rather pretty thing, with large chestnut eyes and a healthy, if unkempt, head of straw-blonde hair to match. Her robust face was white, save for a dash of winsome freckles, and her tiny pink mouth smiled as he made his silent study.

"Is that all you can do? Stare at me like you've never seen a girl before?" The freckled cheeks turned crimson and Starbane tried his best to speak, but only a hoarse, broken moan escaped his lips. The maiden silenced him with a finger to her own lips.

"You needn't talk just yet, if you can't. Mum wouldn't like it, I suspect. We'll have to get you into bed again before she comes back. If she sees you flat on the floor she'll switch me up one side and down the other for not minding you proper. Anything broken, do you think? Anything *new* broken?"

Cold sweat was beading on his brow, but he managed to shake his head, being fairly certain he had done no serious damage to himself in the collapse.

"W—where ... am I?" he croaked as best he could croak.

The voice didn't sound remotely like his own and, for an odd instant, he realized that the last time he had actually conversed with someone remotely *human* had been before his frantic escape. Celintha, the kindly old witch, was the last person with whom he had spoken, and after that only the wretched sentinel-gnome had favored him with its cryptic sarcasm. The girl was visibly surprised to hear him speak at all and eyed him with curiosity as she labored to lift him onto the bed and tuck the covers around his bandaged shoulders.

"How ... how long have I been in Lugarne?" he said before breath deserted him.

The maiden cocked her head sideways.

"Lugarne?" she said. "You're in Rufthar's encampment, sir. Lugarne's way on the other side of Feru Forest, a good ten miles from here. Probably more."

Starbane was confused now. He remembered being certain that the town of Lugarne had been quite near where the werewolves "happened" to him. *Rufthar's Encampment?* He had certainly never heard of such a place and did not remember seeing it on the parchment map. As he lay back, he was suddenly forced to wonder about his scant possessions, where they might be, and how he might get some answers.

"What town did you say this is?" he whispered.

"Town? It's not a town. It's an encampment, like I told you. A hunting post. This is where we come in the winter."

"This ... this camp. It wasn't on the map."

"And what map would *that* be, sir?" The girl stood slightly away from the bed, looking down upon him, her hands fumbling with the sides of her ratty dress.

"Oh, it's nothing," rasped the patient, his head against a blessedly soft pillow. "Who are you, girl? What is your name?"

"I'm Wylla," she answered politely. "You are in the house of Rufthar—that's my father. He owns this whole encampment, if you like, along with a few of the other men. My mum's been looking after you," added Wylla, eyeing the bandages. "I've been helping her, of course. Tending those wounds."

Starbane sat up with a sudden gusto that surprised them both. He grabbed Wylla by the sleeve. "How did I come to be here?" he demanded. "I don't remember a thing about getting to this place after the Eskanthian devils came. Please, you must tell me at once!"

Wylla's face clouded with fright, but she did not pull away. "My mum, sir … she found you in the thick of night, lying by the big wood-pile, yonder. Moaning something terrible, she said. The werebeasties had been at you pretty bad. Don't you recall *that* much, at least? I guess I wouldn't blame you if you didn't. My father helped bring you inside. You were pretty chewed up."

"Of course I remember the attack. I just said so. But how did I get *here*? And who else knows I'm here?" Starbane was wild-eyed.

"My mum and dad brought you to the house and only the other folk in camp know. Everyone's been talking about it, but we're out in the middle of nowhere, if it worries you. Some might wonder how and why you yourself came to be in these parts, traipsing alone in the deep woods."

The strength drained from him as if someone had pulled a plug at the very bottom of his soul. He flopped back onto the bed with a thud and closed his eyes. Wylla began to nibble on a dirty fingernail and, after a moment's reflection, dashed to a small wooden cupboard near the hearth. Finding a cloth atop a shelf, she dampened it in a bucket of water and came back to place the rag on Starbane's forehead. He was bathed in sweat, breathing heavily as he teetered on the edge of losing consciousness.

"Please … Wylla," he gasped, fighting the swoon. "I don't mean to frighten you, but I need to—"

"You'd best not speak right now, Mister," interrupted the girl. "I think you're gettin' weaker."

"How severe are my injuries? Do you know? Don't be afraid to tell me."

"I'm not afraid to tell," asserted Wylla a bit testily, turning to wring the damp cloth into a bowl on the slate table. "You were close to meeting the gods, up front and center. That's what my mum said. And close enough to get a good whiff of the ogre's breath. That's what my dad said. But at least *one* of the gods was looking after you. My mum knows everything there is to know about nursing sick folk. All the right herbs and ointments and teas to give them. That sort of thing. You couldn't have gotten yourself into worse trouble in a *better* spot." Wylla grinned with a measure of pride and brought a small cup to his lips. "Mum thinks you're going to be fine soon enough. A little rest is all you need. Drink a drop or two of this."

The slightly brackish water went down in small sips, but each drop felt salvific.

"That's better, isn't it?" said Wylla. "I must say, it's good to see you wide awake after fifteen days."

Starbane nearly choked. He pushed the cup away and glared at Wylla. "Fifteen *days?*" he groaned. "That can't be. Half a month and I remember nothing about being here? I've been out all this time? I don't believe it!"

Wylla began to chew her fingernails again, bothered by her charge's agitation. She could kick herself for always managing to say something wrong when things were otherwise going quite well.

"Most of the time you were deep in sleep," she said. "Mum had to keep you a bit *under,* else the pain would've been too much. Plus, she couldn't risk infection setting in if you were moving about." She pointed to all of the bandaged areas: head; right shoulder; left forearm; hand. Pulling the covers down a bit, she pressed lightly on his tunic. There was even a bandage on his stomach. The boy could not recall sustaining many of these wounds during his confrontation with the beasts.

"Mum kept you full of her best teas," explained Wylla. "That's what made you sleep so much. It's likely what made you forget, too. Mum *has* mentioned that her teas can do that, sometimes. These past few days, though, you really started coming up a bit. Speaking strange names in the night. Crying out. Even laughing, if you can believe that."

"I guess I'll have to believe anything at this point, won't I?" snapped the invalid. He shook his head in woe and tried to find a comfortable place for it upon the sweat-soaked pillow. Wylla went rigid, remembering her overall duties, and bustled over to the wood she had left near the door. He watched her, weak as a boned fish, as she made for the hearthside.

"I've gone and let the fire nearly die away," said Wylla. "It'll get wicked cold in here if I keep prattling on with you."

The spell of frustration was beginning to pass slowly as he watched Wylla rebuild the fire atop pulsating embers. He was determined to get as many details as he could before sleep might ensnare him—Dryndym forbid—for another fifteen days!

"Where are your mother and father now?" he asked.

"Dad is hunting with the other men and mother's in the frish with the women of the camp. They've been out since dawn."

"The frish? What in the world is that?"

Wylla turned from her work and shot him a disbelieving glance. "You're *not* from around here, are you?" she said, raising a brow. "I guessed as much from your way of talking. The frish is in the middle of camp, where meats are cured. It's women's work, down in the frish." She placed a dry, crooked log atop the burgeoning flames. "Like I said before, the men are hunting. That's what they do here. That's why we're in this place."

"Yes ... of course, a hunt," nodded the boy. "I've been on many." The girl obviously expected him to know something about the things she related to him, and his wits told him to feign a certain degree of familiarity.

"I didn't have to go to the frish today," continued Wylla. "After all, you can't be left alone, yet, and Mum said she'd be able to get more done by herself, anyhow."

"I see."

"Tomorrow *I'll* go and Mum will stay with you. We've been taking turns like that. Sort of. I suppose I ought to have run down to the frish and told her you've come to your senses, but she figured that'd happen any day now, and the women are not to be interrupted in their work. Not when we'd practically starve, if it weren't for this camp."

"Does your family live here all the time? I mean, are you from somewhere else? Lugarne, perhaps?"

"No, we come here only in winter," said Wylla with a slight smile. She was now pleased to be a font of information for her strange guest. It made her feel more useful than she was to her own parents, who loved her but hardly ever asked her even the slightest thing about herself. "The rest of the year we live in Pyr Mida. Everyone here is from *there*. Wait, no, that's not exactly true. A few are from Nancour. That would be Master Turl and his family. But otherwise we all leave our homes in Pyr Mida in the autumn and travel through the forest to this camp. Been doing it ever since I can recall. This is Rufthar's camp and Rufthar's hunting guild, you know."

"And Rufthar is your father, right? You said he owns this place."

"Yeah. Now you're remembering things! His father—my grandfather—left it to him when he died. The other families pay a bit every season to hunt here and use the houses and the frish, but father doesn't ask for very much at all, especially in these times."

"And how many other families are here in the camp?"

Wylla shrugged. "Twenty or so, this year. Most of the same families have been coming every year, though not all." She ambled back to the bed and sat, prim and proper, at its foot, staring at Starbane until he began to feel most uncomfortable.

"So, now you're awake and asking what you want," said Wylla. "But I think it's only fair to ask a little thing myself."

"Like what?"

"Like who *you* are and where *you're* from."

"You mean I didn't tell you that already?"

"Uh uh."

Wylla leaned forward in glowing, childish anticipation as Starbane's head whirled to think of a ruse.

"My name is ... uh ... it's ... Gremm," he sputtered. "Gremm from ... Tythnia. Yeah, that's it."

Wylla smiled, delighted to have pried such intimate information from the youth before anyone else. "Tythnia, eh? I know where that is. Well, I know where it's supposed to be, anyhow. Never been there, mind you, but isn't it to the east, across the Wridwren swamps?"

"Yes," nodded the boy, relieved. "That the place, alright."

"Tythnia's a lot farther away than Lugarne," said Wylla, puzzling over distances in her mind. "You *did* mention Lugarne first. What were you doing so far from home in a forest like this?"

"Some men of my city had also been on the hunt," Starbane lied. "In a snowstorm, I was separated from my own father and the rest of the party. I ... I just wandered, lost in the wood for days until beasts fell upon me. Somehow I managed to get close to this camp, though I don't know how. A kind wood-spirit, perhaps, took pity upon me."

"It was no wood-spirit," said Wylla. "The spirits in these parts haven't got much in the way of pity, though they keep well to themselves by day. There's iron scraps strewn all about the encampment to hold them off in the night, too. No, Gremm of Tythnia, my own mum found you and my dad brought you in. What a mess you were, too! Poor fellow."

He began to entertain the hope that he wasn't in any immediate danger, stuck with this girl and her people, deep in the woodland at some hunting commune. But he had to be certain.

"How often do the people of this camp make contact with Pyr Mida or Nancour, Wylla?"

"Usually just once or twice, I guess. Never thought about it until you asked. Some of the men head back if extra supplies are needed. That sort of thing."

"And when was the last time someone went back to the city?"

"About a month and a half ago. Why do you ask, Gremm?"

Starbane breathed a sigh of relief. That had been before his initial escape and before any possible alert could have been raised toward his capture. "So the rest of the camp knows I'm here but no one's been back to Pyr Mida in a while?"

Wylla frowned, unsettled by this questioning. "Like I told you, Gremm, this is a small camp. Everyone here knows about you. But why should you care? And why care about Pyr Mida? You said you come from Tythnia."

"I just ... well, I suppose it's all due to the shock of waking up in a strange place and being unable to remember much. That's what makes me ask silly questions. Don't mind me. I'm obviously enough bother as it is."

Wylla smiled at him the way a girl does when attempting to be maternal beyond her years.

"Don't you worry about being a bother," she said. "It's not your fault you were lost in a storm and almost eaten by werebeasties. Eskanthian ones, too! Eww—what awful tusks they've got, or so I've heard. Glad I've never seen any for myself. Besides, people here in the camp are decent folk and they care about what happens to you. It's been a little exciting for them, if you want to know the truth. Every day someone asks about the 'young-man-from-the-woodpile.' I'm sure someone'll be helping you find your way home as soon as you're up to it, Gremm. Your own folks must be worried sick!"

Starbane swallowed hard, bitterness getting the better of his thoughts.

Home indeed. If she only knew.

He watched as Wylla uncovered a woven basket and rummaged through its contents. Presently, she withdrew a small red box. "This will help what ails you," said the girl. "Inside are leaves for a special tea that Mum gave you every day to take away the pain and help your body heal." She opened the receptacle and extracted a few small, bark-like slivers of the stuff. "When I grind this up and put it in some hot water, it makes a powerful drink. Calms your nerves, too."

He knew the girl sensed his pain and uneasiness, but hoped she could not discern his deepest fear, the one that could bring destruction upon him and likely anyone found with him. Then and there, he resolved to escape to his appointed destination of Pyr Mida as soon as he was able, no matter how he had to manage it, though werewolves and wood-spirits might bar his way.

A few moments later, Wylla returned to his bedside with a steaming cup and bid him to drink. The contents were bitter to the taste, but the effect was immediate and soothing. She had not ground the substance, whatever it was, very well, for little bits of it stuck to his tongue and lips. Even so, he soon emptied the cup and sighed. Already his toes were starting to tingle and, seconds later, his knees went completely numb. At the opposite end, he began to feel his head swell, or so he thought, to the point of bursting. It was not an altogether unpleasant sensation. Looking at Wylla, he perceived a knowing stare on the girl's face; it wasn't long before the room began to rock and spin, as if he were a child's toy boat in the midst of a whirlpool. Bright colors and shapes merged and swirled before his eyes until everything else was distended and blocked from view. Bits of what looked like cloud whipped about in cyclones as he sank into delirium and, at last, unconsciousness.

As Wylla watched, it appeared to her that "Gremm" was merely easing into a peaceful nap, eyes narrowing and drooping until they fluttered shut. She watched him for a moment longer and then went back to tidying and other tasks at hand. As she went about her work, she stole occasional glances at the stranger.

Real handsome, she mused, supposing he wasn't terribly much older than her. Perhaps fifteen or sixteen and so ...

... *uppity,* she concluded. Perhaps it was his accent, bold and yet polished like a gemstone. She wondered if all the young men from Tythnia, across the Wridwren Swamps, were like this one. There was plenty of time to find out. This boy wasn't fit to travel more than a snail's crawl away from his bed, not yet. Wylla resolved that, in the coming days, as he regained his strength, she would find out much more about the mysterious Gremm, even if Mum did not approve.

IV
A Camp for Recovering Wolf-Slayers

The drill field erupted with violence. Men bludgeoned and wrestled each other to the mud and blood-soaked ground and tore each other apart with bare hands on one end of the expanse. On the other, soldiers used spiked clubs and chains to shatter and hammer the brains from their pitifully armed targets, the castle prisoners. Shrieks and pleas for mercy rose upon the air in eerie dissonance, accosting gods as heartless as the murderers below. One by one, the practicing warriors of Kelnia's First Regiment felled their hapless victims.

As she cast baleful survey upon the proceedings from a nearby balcony, Oblixta found the noises of death and rage very much to her taste. This was a veritable symphony. The soldiers knew she would be watching today and thus took great pains to be more demonic than usual in their onslaughts. That, too, was satisfying. After all, these were her front-line men, feared throughout Kelnia and all of its satellite realms, dependencies, and conquered territories for their notorious lack of conscience. In the vanquished northern fiefdom of Ballustrok, for example, the men of Oblixta's primary legion were the specters of tales that could still make local men—hardened by years of their own internecine wars—quake with fright. In that place, her legions were called the *chium ludisi,* or "morning devils," by those few survivors who recalled looking across fortifications to see the surreal horde approach like shimmering tongues of fire from the gaping maw of dawn.

Everywhere the prized legion cut a ruinous swath, lamentations were made in the unleashing of a bloodlust that could emanate only from those believed to be in league with Perdition itself. The epithets of Oblixta's men in all places were similar and equally well-deserved, for it was their mandate to daunt enemies by such savage acts of initial cruelty that entire towns, villages, and cities would freely surrender to mass-execution or slavery, rather than endure the torture. Even so, the men of this awful horde used their fury only at need. Spells of cruelty were upon them, yes, but so were spells of preservation; they slept like bitter vampires in the silent chill of their barracks when not training or in the midst of battle.

Oblixta scrutinized their current maneuvers, careful to search for any sign of weakness or hesitation in a particular individual. There was no place for *that* deficiency in her army, especially with the harrowing front lines of Corydia that loomed on the horizon. The queen savored the brutality of the men she called her "wolves-at-heel" when she had them lined-up for inspection. Most of them she had handpicked, and she took an active interest in the regimen through which they were controlled physically, psychologically, and supernaturally. The past few days of observation and accelerated training were just the balm for her lingering fears about taking on King Sye, a victory she would be able to claim only after she had managed Rowan Blaize, of course. Curse even the thought of the sorcerer that so haunted her thoughts! Looking at her men now, however, she knew they would fill Corydia with mountains of torn flesh once all magical matters were firmly in hand.

The last living castle prisoners allotted for this day's exercise were being slaughtered as the two training groups prepared to switch routines on the grisly terrain; soon one faction would move to the hand-combat arena while the other entered the weapons zone. During a break in the skirmish, a contingent of slaves comprised of filthy, worm-infested humans and a few rat-trolls swarmed the field and methodically began to clean away the dozens of corpses and parts of corpses. Behind, in a penned cage off to one side, could be heard the whimpering and praying of strong men of various conquered provinces that would soon have the "honor" of dying in the combat drills. They, at least, would have a chance to fight back, for a moment or two. More pasty and malnourished prisoners were on the way up from the castle dungeons, as well. These were mere targets for steel, iron, and absolute bloodlust. It did not matter that they could not fight back—dying without mercy was enough. Such gruesome display, in itself, afforded no obsessive thrill to Oblixta. Rather, the prospects of power and dominion that these methods could procure were objects of intense interest. After over an hour's supervision, she had seen all she needed to see. The men looked ready. She was about to withdraw from her balcony into the tower when General Kerrion approached from the shadows, bowing in his perfunctory but flawless manner.

"A word, Your Majesty?"

"What is it?"

Kerrion paused, looking out across the scattered remnants of doom beneath them. "I assume you are pleased with the morning's exercises," he growled and then half-grinned, the only facial expression of pleasure of which he had ever been capable. "The men are in prime condition, as you can see."

Oblixta nodded, nonchalant. "I'm satisfied. For today. Now, if you'll get on with whatever business brings you here, I'm late for a trade meeting with my regent from Colstra."

Kerrion held out a deferential hand. "Of course, my Lady. There is good news coming from the task force we sent to Lystil. They arrived only an hour ago."

"Oh?" Oblixta looked with interest behind the General, down toward the courtyard in front of the great barracks. Developments from the West, at last.

A shame such "good news" couldn't be about Starbane, she thought.

"Your servants have apprehended a man said to be a key leader in King Sye's Kashizma spy ring," said Kerrion, his dark eyes glinting.

Oblixta's own eyes smoldered with a sudden, expectant flame. "From Lystil? Is he here now, in the castle?"

"Yes. At the far end of the courtyard. I thought, perhaps, that you would like a word with him before he's taken for further interrogation."

Oblixta gathered her sigil-embroidered robes and pushed Kerrion brusquely out of the way as she stalked into the tower and down its winding stairs to the courtyard, her warlord soon apace.

"Has he revealed anything yet?" she muttered as they passed beneath the flicker of torchlight.

"Nothing" replied Kerrion. "But the usual, preliminary means of persuasion have been employed, I assure you."

Oblixta huffed, knowing well that King Sye's Kashizma spies were chosen for their astonishing ability to withstand torture. Their secrets were powerfully guarded, and this state of affairs was most vexing to the queen, for she had not yet discerned the source of whatever power or skill kept them so silent when pressed for information. She had dealt with the Kashizma rabble before and was aware—not without some respect—that they could sometimes withstand the wiles of torture as coolly as her experts could administer the agony. Even before seeing this latest captive, she realized with a twinge of disappointment that they would likely get nothing out of him at all. Only the slight possibility of finding a weak link drove her onward.

A circle of guards awaited them at the edge of the main courtyard, two of the biggest men supporting the disheveled prisoner. He was a tall and handsomely bearded specimen, with thundercloud-gray eyes that stared in disgust as Oblixta approached. From his scars and the unsteadiness of his feet, it was obvious that he had been tortured, but he lifted his chin with resolve to confront the queen. She raised a brow as the circle of men parted to make way for her, and stared back. Though despising all who sought to thwart her plans, Oblixta was nonetheless intrigued by courage and bravado wherever it might be found.

"What is your name?" she said quietly, a cobra smirking at the cornered rodent.

The captive returned only a broad smile, revealing a bloodied maw that was now void of several front teeth. *Persuasion.* Then he spat at her, the phlegm landing mere inches from the hem of her garment on the stone terrace. Kerrion signaled and the guards delivered a blow to the man's stomach, one potent enough to make him double-over and vomit blood and bile in agony. Oblixta gestured with a twitch of her fingers to stay further punishment, for the moment.

"Who are you and whom do you represent?" she questioned.

The man continued to choke and hack, gasping pitifully for air. Oblixta spoke to another guard, one whom she recognized as the leader of the Lystilan task force.

"Where, exactly, did you find him?"

"He dwells in Lystil, but we apprehended him in Ochaea, your Highness."

"Under what circumstances, pray?"

"Our spies had warned us that a few Kashizma rebels were planning to gather in the cellar of a certain inn in Ochaea. We hoped to be ready for them when they did. Some thirty or more were to be at this meeting, but by the time word reached our contingent about the exact hour, they'd gotten wind of us and fled." The guard pointed a chain mail glove at the man. "We managed to catch this one, though. Our own watchers tell us he was the leader of the lot of them, and that he spoke of impending assassination plots against your provincial regents and a number of the Colstran barons. His name is Emodacus. That much we were able to get from him, but they all give their names as a matter of point, when captured. He and his family operate a farm midway between Lystil and Ochaea. We killed his wife and children and burned the place to the ground, in addition to the inn."

Oblixta sighed, knowing that further questioning was useless. The guards would momentarily kill this rebel at her order. "So you've obtained nothing pertinent from him through force?" she said.

"No. He is like the others."

"Then he's good only for extermination. Soon our forces will uncover and fully crush King Sye's Kashizma network, anyway."

"There are more of us than you think, demon-witch. We know that your brother has escaped and is heading to Rowan Blaize, and to King Sye." The man could barely breathe now; gobs of blood and saliva trickled from his lips. The captive's bold interruption raised brows and the arm of a guard to strike, but Oblixta halted the blow with a gesture.

"So it speaks to us, after all," she scowled, taking a step closer. "Do tell me all about your great numbers, if you dare. But whether you do or not, know that I *shall* crush your brotherhood of interlopers and every member that we take will become fodder for the war games of my army. None of you, no matter your number or your strange powers of defiance, can challenge *me.*"

Emodacus raised his fading vision to face her with as much contempt as he could summon. "Your time will come," he hissed through bubbles of the blood and vomit. "I won't live to see the day, but you won't go on butchering and starving the provinces forever. You can put no spell upon me to make me speak, witch. Would that I were free now, I'd run you through myself and feed your vile carcass to stray dogs."

He struggled for a moment in vain, reeling in frustration and pain. Oblixta had listened to him, calmly, and then glanced around at her men.

"By all means," she announced. "Let this hero have his opportunity! Give me your sword, General Kerrion. Now."

He drew the gleaming blade from its scabbard and offered it to the queen across his forearm, uncertain of her plans, as were the others. She always managed to surprise them, and always in ways they did not appreciate. Oblixta took the weapon in her bone-white hands and weighed it thoughtfully for an instant. She nodded toward the guards.

"Let him go and do not hinder him, on pain of your own deaths," she said. After a hint of hesitation, they looked at each other and obeyed, releasing the broken man and stepping well away from him across the flagstones. Emodacus himself was suddenly perplexed at what manner of scene this was to become, standing alone a mere ten paces from the terrible Mistress of Kelnia.

"So, Kashizma spy. You would run me through? Behold, I give you the chance. Be quick and be merciful. Take the sword!"

Kerrion looked on, incredulous, as Oblixta tossed the blade to the captive, who managed to catch it with some measure of stirring expertise. The queen closed her eyes and stretched out her arms on either side of her body, beckoning.

"Come on, my good man. Do your best. These guards will not stop you. They will not dare disobey my order."

Time seemed to halt across the very universe. Emodacus looked at the sword, then at the queen, then back at the sword. At last, with all his remaining might, he raised it high and, emitting a fearsome howl, charged Oblixta. In a magnificent arc the blade swung and hurled downward toward her neck.

"*Lo trogothen,*" said the queen softly in that instant, as if whispering from the recesses of a dark, echoing forest. "*Stygia adrocath mogreb.*"

All of the surrounding guards felt it—there was a strange thickening of Existence, a sucking inrush of unseen power as Oblixta's incantation lifted the rebel at once into the air, the sword frozen in his grip. He remained suspended many feet above them, screaming and treading like a dog in water.

"*Lamac bachabe,*" said Oblixta, making a slight pushing gesture with her palm, and this time the man whipped around and flew toward the rugged stone wall of the Great Barracks, hitting it with such force that his body split in two at the hips upon contact. Pieces of Emodacus oozed and then slid into a gory pile below as Kerrion's sword bounced off the wall with a terrible clang. It spun to the flagstones, chipped and irreparably destroyed. Oblixta turned to regard her men, who had not the courage to meet her gaze in the stupor of their horrified reverence.

"That's one spell I *could* put on him," she said with a short, chilling laugh. "Now get the rat-trolls to clean up this mess. They can eat what's left, if it suits them. General Kerrion?"

"Majesty?"

"Send this accomplished task force back to Lystil as soon as possible. I admire their work. I want the rest of those fools rooted-out and destroyed. Give them whatever extra resources they require."

"At once, my Queen."

"Good. Then meet me at dusk in the ancient Hall of Welcome. We have other matters to discuss."

With that, Oblixta turned in almost dainty fashion, lifting the hem of her enchantment-laced robes and stalking away toward the castle keep. A few of her handmaidens, young virgin girls now bewitched and bereft of memories—and eyes—slid between the columned shadows like phantoms, closing round to engulf her. Kerrion barked orders at a few soldiers who were shuffling nearby, trying to see what had happened, and sent them scurrying as well.

The General walked to the spot where his sword lay broken on the stones. He picked it up as several rat-trolls descended from an adjacent tower in chattering glee upon the remains of Emodacus. The blade had been Kerrion's favorite, a valiant and reliable weapon in countless battles. Now, it was of no further use. He turned it reflectively in his grip and hazarded a swift but angry glance at Oblixta, who was just entering the castle keep with her entourage. There was a fleeting temptation to curse her under his breath, but the idea never achieved full thought in his mind. He feared Oblixta more than he feared any army or pack of wild, wicked beasts, and it was this fear that moved him to merely fling the ruined weapon high over the wall and into the moat beyond as he lumbered off in the wake of morning toward his own quarters.

The sword sank into the fetid waters, spiraling down until it became, like so many other objects and secrets, a prisoner of the muck and decay on the bottom.

❧❦

After sunset on the day he met Wylla, Starbane awoke from his drugged repose. Sitting up in bed, he drew the attention of careworn Ona, who had been darning an ogre-sized woolen sock at the table. Wylla was seated by the hearth in her father's chair, mending a garment of her own with needle and rough black thread. Ona put her work aside and approached the groggy youth, her eyes twinkling with excitement.

"My girl told me you'd regained your senses and I can see that it's true, by the gods."

Starbane tried to focus on the plain, rotund woman who seemed to be sizing him up like a toothsome shank of ham.

"You ... you must be——"

"Ona, wife of Rufthar," came the eager interruption. "I'm Wylla's mum."

The boy smiled, weakly. "Then you're the one who—"

"Saved you from the freezin' night and nursed you back to health!" burbled Ona. "How vexed you must be, separated from your kin and stuck among strangers like us," she went on. "Yes, yes, Wylla told me *everything* while you slept today, the whole tale of you getting lost in the storm. Imagine!"

Starbane shook his head, an effort that made him dizzy. "That tea you two brew really packs a punch. But I have to admit, I feel five times better than I did this morning."

Ona grinned, proud of her healing skills and of her daughter's nursing nature. "Oh, it's a potent medicine, I can promise you that, young Gremm of Tythnia."

He blinked stupidly for a moment at mention of the name, and then remembered his stab-in-the-dark alias. It was fitting, for the night was black as pitch beyond the windows and the interior of the hovel seemed saturated with shadow. Ona mopped his brow with a damp cloth as Wylla had done that morning in glaring sunshine. Firelight danced in the corners of the hovel as the logs snapped and whistled in the hearth.

"I fed you my special tea every morning and every night, though I don't expect you remember it, boy."

"Indeed I don't."

"That's right," said Ona, pulling back the bedcovers to examine his bare legs. "I've kept you full of soft curd, too. You've lost some weight, but not as much as I worried you'd lose. Wylla, bring me a bowl of that broth, girl."

Starbane blushed when he saw that Wylla was looking at his legs. Wylla suppressed a blush of her own and turned to ladle a helping of hot broth into a cup. Ona pinched her patient firmly on the thigh.

"Ouch," he said, not very convincingly.

"You'll live," concluded Ona with a wink. He gratefully accepted the bowl from Wylla. It smelled delicious and he sipped the hot liquid and its bobbing globules of fat with some measure of greed, even though it burned his tongue and throat.

"So, Ma'am, do you always make teas strong enough to stop a king's regiment in its tracks?"

Ona laughed, the most delightful, round, and homey noise he had the pleasure of hearing in years. "Perhaps I do, my boy. But you ran a mighty fever for days on end, and my tea helped keep it down. Eskanthian werewolves have poison in their tusks, did you know that? But I've had to tangle with their handiwork before. Lucky for you." She began to gently unwrap a section of bandaging on his head and neck. "I also have a salve that was perfect for preventing foul infection in these sorts of wounds. It's looking much better tonight," she judged after a careful survey. "Ah, yes. Girl, come over and have a gander at this."

Wylla came to have a peek and the bedridden one began to feel rather like an exhibit.

"What is it?" he asked. "What are you both looking at?"

Wylla put a dainty hand of comfort upon his shoulder. "It's alright, Gremm. Mum just wanted me to see how well your wounds have healed and how clean the stitching has become. So I can learn."

"It's all due to my salve," averred Ona, wandering off to fetch soap and water with which to bathe her charge anew. "Though, I don't know *what* I could've done about that burn scar on your arm. Strange looking thing, if you ask me. Almost like a branding."

Starbane turned his forearm inward, hiding the bright red scar left by the Gragan wizard's ring.

"Childhood accident," he muttered. "It looks odd, I know."

"Hmph!" grunted Ona with a swift side-glance, and she said nothing more about it.

The rest of the evening saw his injuries being gently cleansed by the rustic nursemaids, who chattered and fussed all the while. As they worked, he learned that Rufthar, the man of the hovel, would be away for at least another two days on the hunt. When he and the other men returned, however, there would be a great celebration in the frish. At one point, as the fire dimmed, Wylla asked "Gremm" if he would be willing to deliver the full details of his horrendous attack, but her mother immediately protested. Starbane, sensing a curiosity about his true identity, particularly in Ona, decided to distract attention from potentially more damaging questions by regaling them with an account of his adventure. Balancing an odd mixture of revulsion and relief, he told the story of the Eskanthian wolves and their ambush. He soon had them mesmerized with his recollection of the creeping sounds at dusk in the wood, the charging beasts, the pain and terror. As he spoke, he found himself wishing that the tale were merely some awful morsel of the imagination, that the scene unraveling in his mind like a spool of Wylla's sewing-thread was only a dream. But it wasn't, and his audience of two was cheering each swipe of the now long-lost dagger.

"Ayieee!" crowed Ona, wide-eyed and flinching. "That was a good one. A perfect strike no doubt guided by the hand of some kindly god or goddess. I'll bet it was Nemty or even Blood Thistle Maggie—she's very good for looking after strangers lost in storms. I've got a little statue of her somewhere in this mess of a house. Just a charm my grandmother gave me ... I wonder where I might've put it."

"You're probably right," said Starbane, trying to smile. "There was certainly some sort of divine intervention."

He opted, wisely, not to tell them anything about the Blood of the Salamander elixir and its strange, fiery magic. He sensed that a tale like *that* would not rest well in the curiosities of such simple hosts. In his experience, magic made everyone—save those few who practiced it—most uncomfortable and suspicious. Thus, he finished the story with a sigh and an assertion that he had likewise stabbed the second slobbering beast with the dagger, before all the world began to spin toward darkness for him. Timidly, he mentioned the pack of supplies—but not the map—left behind, and expressed his desire to perhaps retrieve it. Had Ona seen it when she found him mangled and moaning by the woodpile?

The kindly woman laughed anew.

"Packs and satchels!" she said. "That's not likely, now, is it?"

"I suppose it's long buried and lost for good in the snowdrifts."

"I don't know about snowdrifts," added Ona. "Hasn't snowed all that much, come to think of it, since I found you. But you must have forests like this near your own place in Tythnia, Gremm. Forest Folk or those blasted Ice-Dryads have got hold of your pack by now. You can mark my words."

"Of course," said the boy, a subtle arch of worry snaking across his brow. "I hadn't thought about that. Ice faeries will take anything they can get hold of, won't they."

Ona nodded and went on, then, with several mundane tales of pixie thievery and mischief to which she had fallen victim over the years. He listened, growing drowsier by the moment. Fretfulness, however, kept him from sleep. His mind stayed fixed upon the satchel and the grim possibility that it might well have been found by some unwholesome spirit, and that it would make its way into the wrong hands, as everything decent and secret seemed to do in these foul days.

The fire was stoked by Ona, sending a gale of sparks wafting up the crude chimney. The darkness outside seemed to thicken and pause, as if waiting. Wylla was sent off to her little bed, across the room. She went obediently to nestle beneath the thick blankets but continued to watch and listen as her mother resumed her darning and conversed with "Gremm" a bit more. Evening continued to enshroud in the most comfortable and lavish way it could for the poor, nestled as they were in rough but warm environs, hungry flames casting a glow on rough-hewn walls and snapping, hypnotically, in the ears. It was the hush of safety. Starbane closed his eyes and asked them about their lives, asked if they liked spending winters in a hunting camp so far from their home in the city.

"It's not an easy life," Ona admitted, "and things are a bit more comfortable in Pyr Mida. You know, markets and friends and wells in every square, not to mention the river. But it's good to get away every season, too." A curious shadow flitted across Ona's face, perhaps only a pall cast by the flickering hearth-light, but Starbane thought it signified more. Much more. From her bed, Wylla sat up, indignant.

"Wells, markets, friends, and rivers," she spat. "I *hate* Pyr Mida!"

They turned to look at her. Starbane was surprised by her tone, but the mother did not appear to be.

"And why do you hate it, Wylla?" asked the guest.

"Because I can't *do* anything in Pyr Mida anymore." She began to pick irritably at a feather sticking out from her down quilt. "I used to be able to play with my friends, stroll down to the river when I pleased. Then, just like that," she snapped two fingers, "the Kelnian army says we must all keep to ourselves, indoors, except for necessity. That, or go to prison."

Starbane cast his eyes downward across his own blankets as Ona sewed away, silent for the first time that evening.

"That awful army!" continued Wylla. "Filthy, greasy soldiers everywhere. They're like monsters. Some people even say that they are related to the old troll warriors that died out long ago, in the more western parts of the world. As it is, though, you can't even stray very far from your house or they see you and scream at you. Give you their strange looks. Oh, I know what happens. Some girls—ones older than me— have to ... have to *go* with them."

Ona finally put her work down and gazed with quiet concern at her child.

"Go with them?" said the boy. "What do you mean?"

"To cook for them at their bases and garrisons, and in the field, and to ... do whatever else they need done."

Ona broke in at last. "Child, your father and I have promised that *you* will never have to do anything like that. Haven't we told you time and again? Now hush and go to sleep. It's not good to trouble our sick lad with these matters."

Ona turned to Starbane, unable to conceal the aura of doubt that now clouded her features. "Some girls, it's true, are taken and set aside for the army, and even for the politicians, but it's only ones of marriageable age that haven't yet found husbands," she added, glancing protectively back at Wylla. "Her father and me, well ... we've already started making plans for her marriage. There's a fine man in Pyr Mida whose family we know rather well and—"

"He's forty-three, has no teeth in his head, and I don't even *know* him, Mum!"

Wylla's cheeks were flushed red; even Starbane could see the shame in the gloom of her little corner.

"Hush now, child!" snapped Ona. "You'll not raise your voice like that again."

Wylla fell back and flung the covers over her head, embarrassed.

"You must forgive her, Gremm," said Ona. "But it *is* hard on her. On all of us, these days. We've got to marry her off, to save her from the army's clutches, and there are few choices for husbands in these times, when so many stronger young men are forced into the service of the castle, or find themselves at the mercy of the wretched army itself. And marrying a man with no teeth is a sight better than ending-up a military wench." Ona blinked, sad and unconvinced by her own speech. "But surely, Gremm, you know all about it. Such things are no doubt the same in Tythnia, among your own people."

Starbane frowned. "Isn't there anything you can do?" he asked, feeling suddenly ill at the thought of sweet Wylla marrying a much older man, not to mention a toothless one, even if it *was* to spare her a far worse fate.

"Do?" repeated Ona. "What would we *do?* Son, you must know the state of things as much as I, a simple hunter's wife. I lost a son, not much older than you, in a battle three years ago that our people had no business fighting. But the will of the castle is not to be thwarted."

The hobbled guest winced. He had not meant to arouse the kind woman's emotions.

"I'm sorry. I obviously didn't know about your son. What was his name?"

Ona set her jaw against any possibility of tears and ignored the question. "We've come to accept the changes," she replied instead. "To deal with them as best we can. What choice have we got, after all? Treated like cattle and taxed to the point of starvation, with husbands having to work five times as hard for five times less the wages, breaking their backs to feed families. It's either that or the old knock-at-the-door in the middle of the night." She shuddered, chasing away the cheery comfort that had pervaded the place only moments ago. "Yes, the knock. That's when a woman'll find herself without any husband at all. Without a son. Without even a daughter."

Starbane heard Wylla weeping softly, her eyes poking just over the edge of the quilt. A steady stream of tears reflected the hearth's twisting flames on her face.

"They say the queen's a witch and that she killed her own family," muttered Wylla, drying her eyes with a nightshirt sleeve.

Starbane looked away from the women, staring at the wall lest they catch sight of his own dismal expression.

"That's enough from all of us, now, child." Ona sat up straight in her chair and summoned her resolve. "Let's not have any more talk about this wicked world tonight. Things are the way they are, and we face them. We're lucky that your father has this place for us to come to, even if it *is* in the merciless winter. There's much heartache I'm sure we avoid several months out of the rest of the year by virtue of the camp." She rose and gathered three more logs for the fire. Looking back at her patient, Ona tried to be as motherly as before.

"Pity you—listening to the complaints of women. Our wounded guest and captive audience, no less. But you know how it is with women-folk, Gremm. Always complaining about something."

"It's quite alright," said Starbane, his own mind ablaze with memories. "It's been hard for all of us, everywhere."

Ona poured some water into a kettle that hung from a spit across the hearth. "I'll make your nightly cup of tea and send you into a fine sleep, Gremm. How would you like that?"

"No, if you please. Tonight I think I'd like to sleep of my own ability, if it's all the same to you. I'm grateful for the tea, and it's helped ever so much, but I think I'll be fine." In truth, the tea, though it sent him diving into a painless oblivion, was unsettling. He did not like the idea of being sedated and out of control, not in his predicament.

Ona scrutinized him with the gaze of a seasoned country doctor. "Alright," she concluded. "We'll compromise. You'll have just a small sip, then? I promise it won't be enough to send you out, but like I said, it *does* have great power to help a body heal, and your body still requires some healing, my boy."

He nodded, trusting her judgment.

Outside, the wind howled around the hovel and he could also hear, in the frigid distance, the distinct cry of some baleful creature. Ona heard it as well, her eyes moving instinctively to the rusted sword that was propped among some crude fishing rods in a corner.

"The wind can sound very strange, coming out of the forest at night," she said with a yawn.

"As soon as I'm able, I want to head for Pyr Mida," Starbane blurted as Ona prepared to pestle the right amount of herb for his bit of tea. The woman was genuinely surprised.

"Pyr Mida? But I thought you'd be off the other way, son. Towards your own town of Tythnia. That *is* where you said you were from, right?"

"Yes, however, I ... I know some people in Pyr Mida, believe it or not, and it's my thought that they could possibly help me get back home without any inconvenience or danger to anyone."

"Relations of yours in Pyr Mida?" said Ona, now quite curious.

"No, just friends that I know."

"Well, Pyr Mida's certainly closer than Tythnia, there's no denying that," reasoned Ona. "Who is it that you know in Pyr Mida, Gremm? It's a big city, but I might know them, too. Wouldn't that be a thing?"

Starbane hesitated. He didn't want to get himself into a bind. He dared not, despite the trust he had come to place in his hosts.

"I'd be looking for a man named Rakahr," he said. "Telvyn Rakahr, to be exact."

Ona thought intently for an instant. "Don't know him. Sorry."

"He runs an inn and a drinking hall with his wife on ... oh, by the gods, let me remember! Yes, on Genora road. That's it."

"I know where Genora road is," answered Ona. "But not the place you speak of. You'd do well to ask my husband about it when he returns," she added. "A drinking hall is right up his tree, it is."

"Thank you, I will ask him," said Starbane, eager to change the subject now that it had been broached. A moment later, the kettle began to whistle and Ona brought him a fresh but much weaker version of his nightly tonic.

"Drink a sip or two, Gremm of Tythnia, or you won't be fit to walk across a room. You lost a lot of blood in your calamity with those devil-wolves and blood takes a body some time to replace."

She took the cup from him when he was done and patted one of his hands gently before moving to the table and blowing out the little oil lamp on its surface. Though he did not spiral into deadening sleep as usual, he felt the room grow deliciously dark and warmer. He snuggled under the blankets as the noise of the wind continued to whir and hum around the exterior of the slovenly house. The fire sang a soothing lullaby of pops, cracks, and little hisses, eventually cajoling them all toward a sleep that, at least for this night, would be peaceful and free of worry.

I will *not* go!"

The girl, auburn hair a mess and blue eyes aflame like living, vengeful jewels, slammed a fist hard upon the table, knocking three earthenware cups from that evening's dinner to the crude stone floor. They shattered, along with her hopes. She knew that this expression of defiance would be as ineffectual as all of the others had been. Her father looked at her, scowling with his typical, odd mixture of pity and determination aroused by healthy intake of beer. Her mother sat in a corner, near the sputtering hearth fire, weeping into the upturned palms of her hands.

"We been through this every night for a month, girl, and I'm telling you again that you *will* go," said the man, who wavered crazily between a desire to slap his daughter across the face or embrace her. "There's nothing that any of us can do about it now. You know it to be true."

"You would give your own child to a beast? To a murderer?" stammered the girl. Her lips trembled, accusing her father of the thing they all knew he had every intention of doing. The man folded his arms across his ample gut and moved closer to the table where his only child stood, alone and helpless. Sweat beaded on his forehead and his eyes seemed to bulge as he took her firmly by the shoulders.

"He wants *you*—and you alone!"

From the hearthside, her mother's weeping reached a furious crescendo.

"If you don't go with him, child, if you try to give him any trouble, he'll punish your poor mother and me. Probably kill us. Is that something you want on your soul forever? Do you, Ilyssa?" He began to shake her as if she were one of the toys she had long ago ceased to play with, in days far more innocent and untroubled. "Speak up! Is that what you want for us?"

Ilyssa's mother erupted in an almost bovine wail that punctuated the grim standoff. The girl collapsed in a sobbing heap to the floor, clutching at a gnarled leg of the table as her father began to pace around her, watching her with eyes that betrayed no hint of mercy. The man turned to his wife, satisfied that he had conquered the moment, even as a stream of searing acid rose in his throat. Finally, he sighed and went to his woman, placing a hand of comfort upon her heaving shoulders.

"She'll accept it, Nayda. You'll see. No harm'll come to us. Ilyssa has a few more days to see things our way and then everything will be much better. Why, all the girls everywhere are doing this kind of thing. For their families they're doing it." He glared accusingly at Ilyssa, who had not the strength to meet his gaze, not this time. "We may even be rewarded, if she can come to terms with this simple thing." Fear forced his brain to entertain a sliver of contempt for the child. "It's just the way things are, in these days, in these perilous times. We must do as we are bidden. As a family."

Ilyssa's mother looked down at her daughter through red, swollen eyes. She could not bear the thought of what was going to happen even more than she could bear the sight of her child, shivering in a crumpled ball on the cold floor. Sensing her look, Ilyssa lifted her face from the puddle of tears upon her own hands and their eyes met, communicating in a way that they had mastered through years of loving interaction.

"Now, you see?" growled her father, sensing nothing of their deeper, unspoken solidarity, feeling justified with his latest display of household authority. "Cease this moaning, you two, and reset the table for my second helping of supper."

Do not be afraid, said the eyes of Ilyssa's mother. *We'll think of something. There is still time.*

To her, the invocation in her child's frightened eyes was also very clear.

Promise me, Mother, those eyes pleaded.

If only you'll promise me.

࿇

Within five days, due to the constant care of Ona and Wylla, Starbane began to regain his former strength and motivation. The thread-stitched bite-wounds and gashes were healing with astonishing speed and he was now walking about the hovel and shoveling mouthfuls of the cured meats, cheeses, and porridge concoctions that were forced upon him. During this time, he had finally managed to meet the redoubtable Rufthar, who had returned from his hunting expedition with the other men, elated to have caught so many deer, rabbit, pheasant and wild turkey. Their encampment would not need another foray into the woodlands for the rest of the winter, at least not for meat.

Rufthar, as the recovering guest discovered, was a robust and jovial behemoth who had been genuinely pleased to see his family's improbable boarder coming along so well. During the day, while Ona and Wylla went to the frish with the other women to cure the bounty of the hunt, Rufthar and Starbane would nap, eat, and converse, though the youth found the black-bearded man to be even simpler in mind than his wife and daughter. Still, he could not help but like the gruff hunter for his honest and forthright nature, to say nothing of his unselfish hospitality. He need not have rendered Starbane the grace of caring at all, in such tenuous circumstances, and the boy was well aware of this. Thus it was that, between those naps of great snoring and hunting-dreams, Rufthar drank beer, along with plenty of wine from an ancient and rickety looking cask. He gorged on every kind of preserved food available from the tiny cellar beneath the house and related one boisterous story after another to his audience of one.

Every tale was about hunting, in some form or another, but Starbane—still under the alias of "Gremm," by all means—listened dutifully and was grateful for the company. On the evening of the seventh day since Ruftar's return, he was feeling especially rejuvenated and joined his hosts in a celebration of the hunt, the party Ona and Wylla had foretold. The gathering was held at the smoky, circular mud-brick building the women had called the "frish," and it was Starbane's first opportunity to meet the other denizens of the surprisingly large camp. He was not at all astonished to discover that they were very much like Rufthar and his family, unsophisticated and blunt, but quite decent. Music was played on simple instruments and folksy dances were staged, though the stranger in their midst recognized none of the songs or rituals. Dozens feasted on tables strewn with the same foodstuffs to which the boy had become accustomed in Rufthar's house. People stared with a measure of nervous curiosity, before and after being formally introduced. Such an improbable werebeast-killer, such a willowy wolf-slayer, was an extraordinary attraction, indeed.

All were by now familiar with his mishap; there were no secrets in this place. Each of those who greeted him asked politely after his aches and pains and wished him the speediest of recoveries. No one asked nosy questions about his battle with the Eskanthians—the gory details had reached their ears, too—and not a thing was mentioned about his place of origin or other circumstances. This was all well and good for Starbane, who hated to lie, even when survival demanded that he do so. Rufthar and Ona encouraged him to join in the festivities as much as he felt able, assuring him that the people of the camp were not bothered by the presence of an outsider, so long as he was under Rufthar's patronage, and he most certainly was.

The banged-up but bolstered youth used the time wisely. He listened and watched, and laughed, when appropriate, at various party shenanigans. Everyone was lighthearted and in the mood for fun. Very quickly he learned that most of the people gathered were longtime residents of the city of Pyr Mida, when not encamped. He made it a casual point to ask some of the more attentive guests if they knew anything about a man named Telvyn Rakahr and his drinking establishment on Genora Road. Rufthar himself had not known about Rakahr when asked days earlier, which was much to the hunter's surprise, since he boasted of many nights in Pyr Midan drinking halls. The fifth person queried that evening, however, knew something useful. A scrawny and scarred hunter named Myrk was quite familiar with Rakahr and his inn.

"Tel? You mean old Tel Rakahr?" sputtered Myrk over great suds of ale. "Why, yes, I know him. Heh! I've darkened the door of his place many times. It's just a small spot, mind ye, way on the other side of the city, but he's got a fine old dog that hangs round the hearth and his wife is a good woman, though she's a Corydian by birth. Telvyn himself is a decent enough man. How do you know him, lad, if you've never been to Pyr Mida?"

Starbane was reluctant to divulge anything more specific, particularly since he was lying. Lies were like Caltressian spider webs—the more they are spun, the stickier and more inescapable they become.

"Oh … well, Telvyn Rakahr is an old friend of my family in Tythnia, and I haven't had the pleasure of meeting him, yet," he answered. "But I've heard *so* much about him."

"If that's the case, Gremm, you're lucky to have spoken to me," said the odd-looking Myrk, stuffing his face with venison sausage even as grease dripped from his wiry mustache. "When you're fit to travel and you've a mind to venture into the city, all you have to do is find the Marketplace Road that runs right through the heart of Pyr Mida. It's long, but eventually it takes you to the central marketplace itself—imagine that!—and there, just past the Hall of Meeting on the left, you'll find the Harkhenu Footbridge. The Dir Mida River runs underneath it, and right through the center of the city, so you can't miss that, at least. You'd want to cross the footbridge and keep right on Candler's Road till you find Genora on the left, all the way to the very end. Rakahr's inn is at the very end of that, also on the left."

Starbane breathed a subtle sigh of relief and bowed his head in gratitude. "I don't think I'd ever remember as well as you, Myrk, but I can't thank you enough for the information. I'm sure I'll be able to find the place."

Myrk merely grunted and turned his attention back to the mug of ale in his hand, but the youth fought to etch every shred of the man's directions upon his mind, which was the only map he had left. Yet, remembering details seemed the least of his worries. How in the name of all the gods would he ever *make it* to Pyr Mida in the first place, alone and in his condition? Despite the past days' health improvements, he was hardly up to another ill-fated romp through the woodlands. His heart drummed a despondent beat, as if reminding him that time was just about to run out. Pondering his options, the boy gazed across the merriment of the busy frish when Wylla approached from behind. She had been chatting with two other girls, all of them discussing the merits of his bandaged yet handsome features. He started a little when she put a hand upon his shoulder.

"I've got some good news for you, Gremm."

Shyly, she handed him a mug of ale. "Mum asked me to bring this to you. You've hardly had anything to eat and drink tonight. We don't want to have to put you back in bed for another month."

He took the mug and sipped the bitter but refreshing ale, smiling at Wylla's mild teasing. "So what's this 'good news' you're talking about, Wylla? Come on, I can see you're dying to tell me. There's no need to blush."

Wylla was indeed blushing, not so much because of her news, but rather due to her growing crush on Gremm, the heroic houseguest. "Well," she whispered, leaning in close as the music for a new dance began to swell in the center of the building. "I overheard my mum and dad talking about the supply problem in the camp, so it seems that some of the men will be heading off to Pyr Mida in a few days' time."

"To Pyr Mida already? But I thought the hunt was successful and Rufthar said they wouldn't need more supplies for the rest of the winter."

"And that much is true," nodded Wylla. "We've got plenty of meat now, but there's such a thing as grain, you know. Are we to go without bread for a few months, Gremm? And we'll be needing more beer by the look of things tonight. Anyhow, it's not odd for some of the men to go back into the city for dry goods during a hard winter, and Mum said that, if you felt fit enough, you could go along with them and perhaps find this friend of yours."

The refugee was thrilled to the core of his being, but tried not to let too much of his enthusiasm show. He didn't want anyone taking more interest in *his* perilous interests than necessary. Still, what a timely stroke of good fortune, he thought.

"Wylla, this is excellent news. I'm certain I'll be ready to make the trip." He patted her gently on the arm and saw that she couldn't help the delighted little sigh that escaped her lips.

"I'll be a bit sad to see you go, of course," mumbled the girl, her creamy, freckled cheeks flushing red once again. "But I know you need to get back to the folks who care about you. They must be worried out of their minds, if they haven't given you up for dead. If this friend in the city can help you get home to Tythnia, that would be a fine thing. It's a shame *we* couldn't get some sort of message to your kinfolk, at the very least, before now. But you've seen how stubborn this winter can be. You've seen it more than any of us, Gremm."

"You may be right about that. And I'll miss you, as well, Wylla. You've been very sweet to take such fine care of me, along with your parents. Maybe someday I'll be able to repay all of you as you deserve."

Wylla wrinkled her nose and looked back over her shoulder, no longer blushing as she returned to her circle of friends. "People like us don't want anything from you in return, Gremm. Just your safety." There was an almost womanly gleam of wisdom in her eyes, a solemn maturity upon her words that belied younger years, and he knew she spoke from the heart.

Late that night, it began to snow again, large, powdery flakes taking enjoyable ages to descend, it seemed, and the festivities ended. Starbane stayed behind to help the women clean up the detritus of festivity in the frish, much to the inebriated chuckling of the men. He paid no attention to the gentle jibes as formidable hunters wandered off to their respective hovels, laughing and singing. Despite Ona's insistence that he return to her own dwelling, "Gremm" was determined to contribute in some form. The tediousness of being a virtual prisoner because of his wounds—along with news that he would be going to Pyr Mida in mere days—had energized him. He doubted he would be able to sleep at all, for the pace with which his mind was racing.

As he strained to help move tables and benches back to their places against the walls of the curing-hall, Ona confirmed what Wylla had told him earlier, echoing her daughter's sentiments about missing their "lucky young wolf-slayer" once he was gone. She added that the men selected for the trip to Pyr Mida were going to be spending the first night of their city-visit in the home of Rufthar's sister, Wyrnie. Gremm, she assured, would be welcome to do the same until he felt rested enough to find his friend, Telvyn Rakahr. The trip through the forest would be draining, she warned. Starbane thanked her profusely, even as he began to fret about the dangers of entering a city like Pyr Mida under any circumstance. What if Rufthar's sister had heard something about him, some report from the castle (there was certain to be one), and she was not as kind-hearted as her relations?

When at last the frish was locked for the night and everyone had gone to bed full of food and drink, the boy's mind began to plot and ponder the various actions he might need to take upon reaching Pyr Mida, regardless of hunting down Rakahr. For one thing, he had some idea of the forces that were already searching for him, but little sense of what the general populace might know about things that transpired back in the castle before, during, and after his escape. All he could do was thank the gods for thwarting whatever odds had been stacked against him, by Fate or by magic, and for guiding him to a refuge so conveniently isolated from whatever perils awaited in the kingdom at large.

In the dark, tossing and turning upon his pillow, he remembered the old witch Celintha's most explicit instructions: he *must* find a way to reach Pyr Mida and Telvyn Rakahr. This, he had been told with grim certainty, was the only way of accomplishing what he had been sent to do, and what he was meant to do. As for the "meant" part of things, he had no idea what was expected of him, but as sleep at last drifted near, he was fairly certain he would find out, and soon.

☙❧

Four days after the celebration in the frish, it was time to bid farewell to Rufthar's Camp. In just over a month, "Gremm's" wounds had healed well enough, due to Ona's potent balm and obsessive nursing, and required only two token bandages now, both for the most severe bites he had sustained on the back of his neck and left forearm. Ona's cooking had been as successful as her healing skills; the patient had regained much of the weight lost since the first days of his escape, and indeed much of what he had lost under pitiful conditions long before that.

It was a clear and sunny morning that convinced six designated camp hunters and their accompanying wolf-slayer that Dryndym, that most capricious of winter gods, was at last ready to ponder ceding some territory to his springtime peers. The men carefully prepared their packs and gear for the expected two days' travel through the forest between camp and city. Ona had mended the torn Bog Bear coat and Rufthar provided their new friend with a spacious new satchel fashioned of stag-skin. Both gifts were accepted gratefully by the boy, who was more than a little relieved to see that the satchel was stuffed full of more cured meats, cheeses, nuts, and dried berries than even Celintha had provided at the start of his bizarre adventure. Young Wylla, for her part, gave him something quite different and unexpected.

"Hold out your hand, Gremm," she said as the chill reddened her face outside the family's hovel.

He lifted his palm close to hers and into it she dropped three small, jagged white objects, strung together with an artful and complex binding on a cord of durable rawhide leather. He stared at the simple necklace for a confused instant, and then into Wylla's smile.

"We didn't tell you before, but those teeth were taken from your wounds when Mum first brought you in and cleaned you up," said Wylla, now a bit uncertain about the appropriateness of her gift. "I don't know if you take offense to having them, but I … well, I thought a young man like you would want such a souvenir. It's quite a thing at your age, surviving not one but *two* werebeasts. To say nothing of killing them."

Starbane normally went a bit pale at the mere thought of the now surreal ambush in the forest, but as he fingered the smooth, dagger-like teeth that had broken off into his bones during the fray, he felt an exhilarating chill. The attack may have been the most horrific in a series of terrifying events that had lately overtaken his life, but he had lived through it, and things seemed different now. He was still as uncertain of what awaited in the dark days ahead, but perhaps not quite as fearful. The gift was appropriate.

"I don't know what to say, Wylla. I hadn't expected anything like this. Never imagined I'd have a chance to wear such a necklace."

"Mum helped me bind them with the cord," said the girl, more bashful than ever. "They were certainly big enough. We think you should be proud to wear them."

"I will be," he said, reaching to tie the leather cord behind the wavy, flowing hair around his neck. The fearsome teeth were soon buried in the thick fur collar of his repaired coat. "I'll never take it off, and I'll think about you and your family whenever I look at it. When anyone asks me about it, I'll tell them how good you all were to have rescued me."

Ona smiled approvingly as the wives of the five other men accompanying Rufthar and the boy arrived and walked with the little group to the very edge of the encampment, where the bare trees seemed to patrol the earth in thick clusters and the snow piled in windblown drifts amid streaks of gray gloom beyond. Everyone was nervous but tried to hide it by making unnecessary last-minute checks of their supplies and traveling gear as they approached the forest. The wives clucked hearty farewells and terse warnings; Ona felt especially useful, having both huge Rufthar and "Gremm" to see off.

"You two should have just a bit more than you'll need for the long walk, so I'm not worried," she said, referring to their ample foodstuffs. "Mind you watch out for wayward Ice-Dryads, though. This is their time of year, when Winter first starts to toy with the notion of slipping away. They don't like it and it puts them in a mind for mischief," added Ona, self-appointed faery authority.

Rufthar simply growled somewhere beneath his bushy black beard and summoned the party at last to its course. The previously fair dawn was beginning to attract a swarm of wispy clouds. Ona and Wylla hugged Rufthar first, and then their now somewhat stalwart patient, who returned the embrace with all his strength, hoping to dispel the lump growing in his throat.

"My word, Gremm!" said Ona proudly. "You *have* got your strength back."

"Thanks only to you. I don't know how I'll ever repay you, but if I'm able in the future, you can be certain I'll do it."

"Stuff and nonsense, lad! It was nothing that any decent soul in this land—yes, even such as it is these days—wouldn't have done for someone in the kind of trouble you were in. If you wish to repay me, just make sure that my husband doesn't give his sister, Wyrnie, a rough time when you get to town. Those two squawk at each other like magpies whenever they get together."

Rufthar growled again. Starbane laughed. "I'll do my best, but no promises of success, Ona."

With that, and with final assurances that prayers to all winter gods, major and minor, would be sent skyward, the traveling party moved into the forest, warm in their furs and boots, their snowshoes kicking up the powder until it glistened in the stray panels of sunlight like specks of crystal.

It was to be a tedious journey, but not a perilous one. The day's building clouds portended bad weather, worrying the men, but no snow descended into the gnarled woodlands. Twice the group halted so a hunter named Gillar could nab roosting pheasants with his bow, and everyone agreed these would make fine "gifts" for Rufthar's sister, which in fact meant supper for their own bellies. The only other stop provided them with a chance to eat and rest for a bit, though Rufthar was especially suspicious of the surroundings and watchful as he stood eating his lunch against a tree.

A true hunter, thought Starbane and, as he chewed some venison jerky, he wondered how he himself would have fared as a hunter, had he been able to learn the art from his father.

Probably not very well, he concluded, looking sadly away from the others, *since father was more of a poet than a killer.*

At nightfall, the men camped without comfort or incident in a glade. It was nearly sundown of the following day before the weary host saw the distant billows of chimney smoke that assured them they were approaching the city. The sight produced an eerie feeling in Starbane's heart, for it was precisely at this time of day that he had seen what he believed to be smoky signs of the village of Lugarne, over a month ago, when the beasts had fallen upon him. He clutched absently at his toothy necklace as the group began to extract itself from the woods, seeing other vague indications of civilization through the encircling wall of brush and trees. Houses and buildings of all sorts were soon visible after that, and they all heard the sounds of voices carried on the frosty edge of a breeze, along with the barking of dogs and the neighing of any number of horses. Rufthar turned to his companions as they finally reached the outskirts of Pyr Mida proper.

"If we swing a bit to the south, I know a way we can enter the city close to my sister's place without any of us being seen," he said.

Starbane questioned him immediately, feeling a rush of anxiety at the prospect of entering a large community with a conspicuous group of hunters who did not wish to be noticed. "Why are we worried about being seen, Rufthar?"

"There's no problem, Gremm. It's only that, if we walk through the main streets right away, dressed as we are and straight outta the woods, we're bound to be stopped and questioned by soldiers from Cadrach Castle. They'd give us no trouble in the end, I expect, but it would be a nuisance and I can't stand the sight of the devils. The day's been long enough as it is. Right, men?"

The rest muttered in agreement and then they veered finally to the south, behind Rufthar's stomping leadership, moving along the visible edge of the city, quite close to some sort of frozen irrigation canal but still deep enough in the woodland border to be discreet. As dusk fell with all of its oppressive stillness, Starbane began to think irrationally of werewolves once again, but forced himself not to worry while in such intimidating company. By nightfall, when it was growing difficult to see the fur-clad men walking around and in front of him, they all seemed to spill, suddenly, from a narrow gulch that lay behind a large cobblestone flour-mill. Torches blazing farther on in the streets made footsteps easier to place as everyone removed their snowshoes and then trudged up a rocky channel. Thus they entered the great city of Pyr Mida, snaking between the mill and one of its smaller dependencies, coming out upon a slushy avenue that sported dozens of smoke-spewing houses and shanties on either side.

"Wyrnie's place is two streets over," Rufthar said with a nod to Starbane, who was trying to work his way as much into the middle of the ambling group as possible. His pale green eyes darted nervously in all directions. There was no one else about on the streets, it seemed, but he couldn't wait to get inside the house of Rufthar's sister and away from what he felt to be total and excruciating exposure. So heaped were the boy's fears that he half-expected a mob of soldiers and citizenry to come barreling around a corner in pursuit. *There he is!* they would shout. *That's the one we've been looking for. Seize him!*

"How much farther?" he gasped at Rufthar.

"It's only around the corner, Gremm. What's wrong? You feeling sick or something?"

"No, I … I'm ready for this day to end, that's all."

"I daresay the rest of us are, too."

They turned a corner of crammed houses onto another bleak avenue, their breath exhaling in steamy clouds almost as thick as the surrounding chimney smoke. The long rows of dwellings on this street were more than twice the size of those on the first, though not much more well-built. At the great wooden door of the third house on their left,

Rufthar walked up and pounded with gusto. After a moment and some audible griping from within, a tiny, sour-faced woman with equally irritated eyes opened the door and stuck her head out. It took her only an instant to recognize the identity of her visitors and she struck a hand to her forehead, cackling in dismay.

"Not the *lot* of you?" she wailed.

"Well, don't just stand there griping, Wyrnie," said Rufthar. "Open the door and let us hungry men inside." Rufthar didn't wait for his older sister to react; he flung open the door and bounded past her with the others waddling behind like ducklings.

"Ah, Rufthar, you horse's hinder! I wasn't expecting you for another month, at least."

Wyrnie wrung her hands as she watched them all track snow and slush onto the wooden floor of her warm, spacious kitchen. She moaned a little, knowing she now had a great deal of work ahead of her this evening. The day had already been exhausting enough. "A woman never gets a chance to rest her weary bones," she said with a short, sharp gnash of the few teeth left in her head.

"Sundries ran low at camp sooner than expected, sister." Rufthar settled with a thud onto one of the great benches at Wyrnie's long kitchen table. "And you know we have to travel in packs, like wolves, through the woods … when we *must* travel." He winked at the others. "Now, what've you got for starving men to eat around here, after our hard day's journey?"

Starbane and the men shuffled shyly off into a dim corner at one end of Wyrnie's sizeable dwelling, the front half of which was dominated by the huge kitchen and its table, built from rough but sturdy Falthurn planks. A fire of considerable ambition flared upward in a gigantic hearth made of smooth, round river-stones. Rufthar pointed to a large stewpot nearby.

"What's in there?" he demanded.

The diminutive but feisty Wyrnie wrung her hands again and flew like a nervous bird to her pot, shooing Rufthar's monstrous paws out of her away.

"Don't open that, I've got a pudding in there. Save it for later." She looked around at the rest of the crew, fretting profusely. "Alright, all of you!" she admonished. "Get them snowshoes outside my door, along with any sacks dripping wet across my floor. Rufthar! Show these men to their bunks in the back when they're done. By the gods, you've all come at a rotten time. I've got my hands full."

No sooner had she spoken when, from a door at the other end of the kitchen, three small children came running. Starbane guessed them to be from four to seven years of age as they chased each other, playfully oblivious to the presence of the men now intruding in the domain. The tallest of the trio—a girl with a shock of hair as wild as a briar patch— slammed right into Wyrnie. She nearly knocked the old woman to the floor. Rufthar leaped from the bench to scoop up the other two giggling imps, holding one under each arm as he jostled them gently.

"I see you're looking after the niece and nephews again, Wyrnie. What was it this time? Did Berga toss Rubel out on his behind for drinking, or are they about to have *another* of these little brats. It's got to be one or the other."

"Oh, put those little monsters down," muttered Wyrnie with no small amount of misery. "Berga's mother has some silly ague, so she's moved temporarily into their house to be cared for. The brittle old baggage! This isn't the first time she's been the cause of grief for me. Your brother brought these trolls over yesterday, so they wouldn't catch whatever the hag has got."

"I'm not a troll," wheezed one of the children, a flaxen-haired boy with a comically dirty face, now clinging to one of Rufthar's tree-like legs.

"You are *so* a troll!" snapped Wyrnie. "Now hush, or it's out into the woods with the lot of you for the night, and we'll soon see how little trolls fare against winter wolves and ice goblins."

The children merely laughed, to Wyrnie's increasing discontent.

"That's what you get for being so mean that no man would marry you … and so bighearted that no one would ever believe your threats," joked Rufthar, who finally elicited a smile from his wizened sister. She cuffed him on a shoulder.

"You can hush as well," she said, "or share the fate of these urchins." Wyrnie then screeched at the youngsters with the rueful authority that only an exhausted, routinely put-upon aunt could affect. "Off to your beds this instant, children. I want no lip or I'll rip what lip I can strip! You've all been fed and I'll have no more whining and games tonight. Cirana, see that your brothers get tucked in or I'll whip the tar out of you!"

As quickly as the little ones had entered, they burst into a new round of braying laughter and dashed out of sight through the same door into the recesses of the house, one after the other. Wyrnie gestured at last for the men of the encampment, who had finished stacking most of their snowshoes and non-essential equipment outside, to hang up their furry cloaks and mittens, come closer to the fire, and seat themselves at the formidable table. "On such short notice I haven't near enough in the larder to feed so many men," said Wyrnie to Rufthar as she began placing large wooden mugs taken from one of her many ancient-looking cupboards before the guests.

"Not to worry, old girl," answered Rufthar, motioning to Gillar, the man who had killed the pheasants on the trip. "We brought something to stretch all our bellies. Fetch the birdies, Gil."

Gillar jumped up and stomped outside, where he had put the plump, dead fowl before entering. When he came back in and handed them to old Wyrnie, she received them with a weak croak of exhaustion and tossed the things onto the floor by the hearth. She next procured an enormous jug from one of her ramshackle cupboards and placed it between the men and their mugs on the table.

"Help yourselves to some of last year's applejack, boys. There'll be beer with supper as soon as I've cleaned these fine birds and can climb down to the cellar and heave the cask up on my broken old back."

Wyrnie was clearly not amused. The gathered men, for their part, didn't bother with vessels, opting to guzzle from the great jug itself, passing the thing from one to the next. The liquid was tart and powerful but warming after such a frigid journey. Rufthar enjoyed a particularly ample sip and sighed as he began to remove more of his furs in the stifling kitchen.

"Wyrnie's quite an old scout," he said of his sister to Starbane. "She puts us up whenever the men of the camp come back to the city for supplies."

"Like I've got any choice," muttered Wyrnie, yanking feathers in a huff.

Rufthar ignored her, gesturing proudly about the dwelling. "This was my folks' house, you know. The place where I was born. I suppose it should have been mine, but when Father died he left it to Wyrnie, seeing as she never married. Didn't matter, though, as I got the encampment."

Wyrnie, meanwhile, had thrown on a cloak and was now out in a woodshed annex to the kitchen. Through the open door, Starbane could see her struggling to gather more logs for the fireplace. It seemed to him that his time in such company was increasingly pointless; he served no purpose among them, now that he was finally in the city. He resolved then and there to find the mysterious Telvyn Rakahr, as soon as morning showed its face, and he mentioned this plan to Rufthar.

"Yes, by all means," rumbled his friend in agreement. "The sooner you get some message to your friends or family, the better."

The boy nodded, taking his own quick turn at the jug of apple brandy. The fiery drink relaxed him almost at once and he felt a little more comfortable with the idea of this one final night of uncertainty.

In what seemed little time at all, most of the men became slightly inebriated, pheasants were stripped to the dimpled skin and skewered on spits, and a cask of beer from the cellar was procured by two unsteady volunteers. Rufthar hummed discordant tunes to pass the time as men kept drinking, smoking cob-pipes, or watching idly as the old woman slaved over various kettles and pots around her hearth. The fare was soon starting to smell delicious, which caused stomachs to grumble and roar. A pervasive, lazy silence was broken by happy bellowing when Wyrnie heaved a stack of bowls and the first piping tureen of pheasant stew onto the table in their midst.

"Excellent sister!" praised Ruftar, nudging Starbane on the arm at the same time. "Take your fill, boy. You're still more of a guest here than the rest."

Starbane rallied from his sleepy, pensive haze and helped himself. Rufthar was next and soon gravy was coating thick beards all around the table. Wyrnie, tending to the hearth and holding her lower back in pain from her efforts, began to scrutinize the young stranger, as if she had not really taken notice of him heretofore. He chewed his food respectfully and met her gaze, unblinking. Wyrnie looked away at his glance, wiping sweat from her brow with the back of a hand.

"Never seen *you* before," she said over the din of feasting men.

Starbane nibbled a hunk of bread, reluctant to answer.

"You don't talk like you were born in Pyr Mida, either," Wyrnie continued. "Leastways not from what little I've heard you speak."

Her tone seemed innocent enough, but the boy had a dull suspicion that she spoke with a measure of guarded curiosity. Luckily, Rufthar answered for him, lowing like a typical woodsman with his moose-like voice.

"His name's Gremm, sister." Slop went another ladle of stew into his mouth. "He's not one of the lads of the camp. Fell in with us after meeting up with a couple of Eskanthian werewolves in the forest. You oughtta get a look at his scars. Especially the one burned on his arm. Never knew Eskanthians could burn as well as bite," he kidded, gesturing to the mortified youth. "Show her the teeth we strung for you, Gremm."

Rufthar's sister was suitably interested at this revelation, her mouth forming a pitiable 'O' and her head twisting to scan the scrawl of pink scar tissue on his forearm as she approached. But she also scrutinized his face. "You poor young man," she murmured. Starbane slowly covered the Gragan's scar with his sleeve, but not before she had gotten a glimpse of *that,* as well. Her brow furrowed, as if her mind sought to recall something from impenetrable depths.

"I would have died, if not for the kindness of Rufthar and his family," Starbane quickly interjected as he burned beneath her lingering gaze. He looked hopefully at the other men, who said nothing as they eyed their stew-plates and mopped pools of pheasant gravy with heels of bread. Wyrnie took him gently by the chin and inspected a small bit of bandaging he still wore on one cheek.

"Ona's a fine nurse," she pronounced with authority. "That I've seen before with my own eyes, when Wylla was sick, and once when I came down with a nasty bug myself. She cares for a body as if she were its own mother, that's what."

"Without a doubt," the boy agreed. "She tended me constantly, and made me feel like I was in my own bed, in my own house."

"That's right," said Wyrnie, tapping him on a shoulder and remembering to be nosy. "Where *is* your home? You didn't say. That accent doesn't hail from these parts, and what in the name of Dryndym were you doing, tangling with werewolves in that frigid old forest?"

Again, Rufthar answered, though this time it was to Starbane's suppressed annoyance. "He's from Tythnia, sister. Now stop bothering the lad and let him eat his fill."

The unsettled young guest could tell from Wyrnie's uncertain expression that she did not quite picture him as a Tythnian, either.

"Hmm …" she mused. "I would've guessed you was from a bit farther north, the way you speak, but then again I've known only two or three people from Tythnia in my day."

Starbane felt it best to add nothing to this assertion, but Rufthar proceeded to explain the boy's entire tale of wolf-wrangling and, furthermore, his intention to seek Telvyn Rakahr the very next morning. "Gremm" began to sweat, though not from the heat of the stuffy room. Wyrnie listened to everything and wished him well—if a bit too suspiciously, for his sensitivities—and bid him eat as much as he liked. He was welcome to get a good night's sleep in *her* house, at any rate.

"Now, Wyrnie," blustered Rufthar. "What's the latest news from Castle Cadrach? Answer me that! I'm half-surprised there's still a city *left* after being away for three months."

"Aye, and the woods is a far better place to be in these days," replied the old woman with an ominous rasp. The men at table laughed, soft yet nervous. This angered Wyrnie as she prepared to lift another steaming tureen onto the table. "You laugh now, boys, but that's because you spend your winters deep in the wood, where you're ruled by none but yourselves. You weren't laughing three years ago when you first saw this city invaded and some of your neighbors killed!"

The men grew sullen and Rufthar tried to calm his sister. "Ah, Wyrnie, don't let your feathers get ruffled. We're just asking for the latest news, not one of your bony fingers wagging in our direction. We all know how things are."

Starbane sat like a stone, wishing he could fade into the coarse knots of the thick wooden wall behind him.

Wyrnie clutched at her tattered brown apron. "Then you'll not be surprised to learn that nothing has changed," she hissed. "There's still a solider on every corner, it seems, and the city square is still a barracks. And all of them are still being paid with *our* hard work, in addition to our tax money."

"That won't change any time soon," puffed Rufthar.

"There's also more talk of war than ever," mumbled Wyrnie, and once again the men took up their odd chuckle, a browbeaten sound that Starbane guessed to mask a long-shared apprehension.

Rufthar slammed his mug down hard upon the table in a gesture for refill. "There's been talk of war for two years now, woman." As Wyrnie scurried for another jug of something alcoholic, the leader of the encampment turned to look at his cohorts. "Oblixta may have beaten down all of Kelnia's provinces, but she'll never attack old King Sye," he said with confidence. "She knows—like Sye knows and we *all* know—that he's got a wizard in his country too powerful even for her. Not to mention an army bigger than any in all the realms. Nah, Corydia's too safe behind those mountains above us and this mysterious magician of theirs farther on."

Rufthar waved a massive hand toward the South and the other men nodded, murmuring in agreement among themselves. Starbane looked at his knees and shook his head when Wyrnie offered to refill his own mug. He wished he were anywhere but in her kitchen at the moment.

"They say Oblixta's been building a bigger, stronger army, brother. In Colstra," Wyrnie added. "They say she's just biding her time for the right moment to strike and it wouldn't surprise me at all if it were true."

"Is that what you women discuss when you get together at the markets and in your sewing circles?" snorted Rufthar in dismissal. "Trust me, sister. These matters are best left to the worries of men."

"That's as may be," pressed Wyrnie. "But this is what folks are thinking and whispering about all the same. Everyone feels that something's going to happen soon. I'm not one to believe everything I hear, but I *do* like to keep abreast of what news manages to get passed about. And besides, you asked me."

"That I did, sister." He patted Wyrnie on her back, but she yanked away, tired of being patronized. Rufthar smiled at his friends. "Well, men, I guess the wives will be both disappointed and happy. The meaningless gossip hasn't changed at all since we left."

The others laughed and even Wyrnie cracked a wry smile. Then her eyes grew wide, as if she had forgotten to mention something of grave importance. This turned out to be the case.

"By the gods, I forgot about the biggest stir of all, a month or so ago," she exclaimed, pointing a finger at the now half-reclining and besotted Rufthar. "There was quite a to-do about some prisoner who escaped from the castle. Someone—let me see—yes, *someone* they said was guilty of crimes against the new regime."

"Ha! Crimes? What crimes could possibly be done against the new regime? The new regime is already a crime," averred one of the men.

"There weren't many details, as I recall," said Wyrnie. "But I'll tell you, someone at Castle Cadrach was fit to be tied. There was a city-wide search in Pyr Mida, and if they're searching here, you know they're searching everywhere. Soldiers knocking at doors, the whole lot."

"You don't say," said Rufthar.

"I *do* say. They knocked at my own door one night and I thought I'd drop dead of fear when I opened up and saw those Cadrach devils."

"What did they want?"

Wyrnie shuddered at the memory. "They showed me some decree from Castle Cadrach about this escapee, and then they described the one they were looking for. I was so scared I couldn't tell you now what the man is supposed to look like, though I think they said he was quite young.

All I could do was clutch my poor heart and nod and pray they'd go away. As I recall, they did put some sort of likeness of this man on posts in the marketplace, but they kept getting ripped down before I had a chance to see. That was another stink. Rumor had it that those Kashizma spies of the Corydian king were behind the whole thing—this young man's escape from the castle *and* the disappearance of the likenesses. Rumor says it's one of those Kashizma men that the castle is looking for."

"Well, then, I wonder who he is and what he did," sniffed Rufthar, rolling his eyes.

"It must have been no small matter," chattered Wyrnie. "The army is offering a huge reward for his capture—alive, it was made clear—and they threaten death upon any man, woman, child, or family that might be caught hiding him."

"Why would anyone want to hide a criminal in these days?" wondered Rufthar aloud. He soon recognized the irony of his words. "By Dryndym, in Castle Cadrach's all-seeing eyes, anyone who hates Oblixta is a criminal, so I know that *I'm* a guilty man!"

Starbane tried to laugh along with the others, but found that he felt like choking on his suddenly dry tongue. He dared not throw his gaze anywhere near Wyrnie, for fear she would somehow recall in his face the image of "the man" the soldiers had described.

"How much was the reward?" Rufthar asked his sister.

"Five thousand kriel," Wyrnie replied. "That much I won't forget. Though I hate the castle as much as any of you, I can say that part of me wishes this escapee had knocked at my own door looking for shelter. But I shouldn't say such a thing. One can't trust Castle Cadrach to honor its word, even if one were tempted by twice the money."

"Five thousand, though," said Rufthar, whistling once between his teeth. "That's a fancy sum. They *do* want this fellow, whoever he is. But any man in his right mind wouldn't enter the city knowing that Oblixta's army was after him, along with whatever else gets sent out of that foul place. Anyhow, if he's one of the Kashizma spies, I half hope they do catch him," continued Rufthar, though sheepishness laced his gaze as he uttered these words. "I know they're looking to guard their own king's interests and maybe stir us up to fight for freedom, but what they end-up doing is making things more difficult for the rest of us, don't they? They don't realize that the fight has been taken *out* of us. Unless King Sye's army or his warlock or whatever comes over the mountains to help, we're out of luck. No, this escaped fellow would be be wiser to keep to the woods and head south to the mountains as fast as his feet can carry him. Ha! If I were him I'd rather take my chances with the trolls and the Eskanthian were—"

Just as Starbane knew, in the mounting dread of his heart, that Rufthar was about to say "werewolves," there came a frantic rapping at the front door. Everyone froze, transfixed by the sound. Wyrnie's fingertips flew to her mouth. The knocking ceased and they all listened in the silence. Once again the rapping commenced. Rufthar dragged himself to his feet, not without some effort, and pounded over to the door, a grimace fixed upon his imposing face. He leaned his head close to the wood.

"Who's there?" he demanded.

From where they sat or stood, the rest could only hear a muffled reply, but Rufthar had obviously heard more. He lifted the latch and flung open the door. In flew a young girl dressed in a thin buckskin coat and white shift, sobbing and soon clutching at Rufthar's shirt. Starbane was reminded first of Wylla, for the girl seemed to be about the same size and age, but he soon saw that this young lady, with her cascades of wavy auburn hair and glistening blue eyes, was much more beautiful and delicate than the hunter's daughter.

"Why, Ilyssa!" said Rufthar to the crying waif. Wyrnie bustled to his side.

"What is it, child?" she asked. "Tell us what's wrong. My goodness, you're barely dressed for a night like this! Where are your parents?"

There was a frightful urgency in Wyrnie's voice, one that only seemed to intensify Ilyssa's sobs. Rufthar moved her, very gently, close to the warmth of the hearth as Starbane stood and offered his own seat on the long bench. There Rufthar lowered her while Wyrnie slammed and locked the door after a suspicious look deep into the untrustworthy night outside. The girl glowered at them all through her tears and Starbane, struck by her simple beauty as well as by her distress, was moved beyond his own current troubles. Wyrnie took the edge of her apron and began to wipe the girl's cheeks that were reddened by cold and the sting of salt.

"There, there, child, you must tell me what's happened to make you cry so."

"Please don't let them take me!" begged the girl, bursting into a new round of frightful sobs and little gasps. She bent low on the bench and clutched the old woman's skirts, glancing back and forth from Rufthar to his sister, pleading as much with her great sapphire eyes as with her words.

"They don't care about me," she choked. "They're going to just let me go with him. They decided a month ago." She dabbed at her nose with a sleeve of coarse linen as the rest listened with confusion.

"But I told them ..." she went on, her eyes narrowing in anger, "... I told them if they made me go I'd kill myself. I'd open my own veins and I *swear* I'll do it!"

Wyrnie began to caress Ilyssa's back, a defeated look soon clouding her own face in the flickering shadows cast by the firelight.

"Child, you mustn't speak of such things," she said, weakly.

All of the men from the encampment had instantly become stone-faced, their pity transformed. Rufthar was the most iron-jawed of all. Several of them had daughters of their own and these seethed inside at what they knew would be Ilyssa's fate. Yet, theirs was an impotent anger, all the more poisonous for its inability to produce action, or inspire some sort of resolution. They had all encountered this feeling before. So they sat, grim and ashamed even to look at one another. Starbane spoke-up first, well aware of the situation from his conversations with Ona and Wylla back at camp.

"We can't let this happen!" he said with a resolve that stunned the rest of those gathered. His eyes met Ilyssa's and, in hers, there shone a strange instant of hope through the tears. It was a desperate hope that someone—anyone, even this stranger boy—might dare to offer an answer, some secret pathway winding its way out of her nightmare.

Rufthar shot Starbane a contemptuous look and turned at once to his sister. "Wyrnie, take the girl to your room and let her bed down for a bit while we discuss this matter."

Wyrnie bowed her head in recognition of her brother's obvious anger and pulled the forlorn Ilyssa from her seat, leading her off to some adjacent chamber in the rambling house. She put her arm about Ilyssa's waist and filled her ears with comforting little words and noises. Starbane's eyes followed them, unable to look away from the vanishing girl. When they had gone, Rufthar put a hand on the boy's shoulder and firmly swung him around. Face to face, the hunter's words were as cold and hard as stone in the midst of a blizzard.

"You oughtta think before you speak-up like that, *boy.*"

Starbane looked at his friend, his rescuer, and his face contorted with misunderstanding.

"What do you mean?"

"Don't you think *we'd* like to be able to haul-off and say such things?" growled Rufthar under his wine and beer-soaked breath. "And we're men who know this girl! Who *live* in this city. Unlike you, Gremm. The truth is, we're helpless, and we have been for a long time." His expression toward the youth now bordered on revulsion. "I don't know what it's like in Tythnia, where you say you come from, but this city is under the yoke of Cadrach Castle, like any other place in Kelnia that I know about. If we interfere with Oblixta's laws and plans, it means death."

Starbane went crimson to the ears, even though he was old enough and smart enough to realize that Rufthar was more ashamed than contemptuous—ashamed that "Gremm," a mere buck and stranger, had been the one to speak in protest and not he.

"Interference can mean death to entire families," informed one of the men at table, a ragged hunter named Volnar. "The Cadrach army has been known to butcher whole villages, just to set an example, and in cases exactly like this, where the girl doesn't *want* to go. That's why we keep our mouths shut, little wolf-wrestler." Volnar took a healthy slug of beer from his cup and slammed a fist atop the table for emphasis. Rufthar nodded his agreement.

"I happen to know this girl's parents, Gremm. They're old friends of the family and hard-working folk. Law-abiding. It's up to them to make the decision to let their daughter go, or, if they wish, to suffer death in refusal. No one here—except perhaps you—would fault them for making either choice. We don't condemn those who want to live."

Starbane shook his head, deaf to such cold reasoning, particularly when he remembered all that he had endured and how Ona had promised Wylla that no such fate would befall *her*, safe in their distant encampment.

As if sensing the boy's disdain, Rufthar's muscular jaw began to work in consternation and he added, "I, for one, am ready to die if the need should ever arise." He said this to the rest of the men, most of whom lowered their gazes, not wishing to reveal their own buried doubts or already-fixed opinions. Wyrnie entered the kitchen, dejected.

"You know we've got to fetch her parents," Rufthar whispered to his sister. His voice sounded like ice sliding across the smooth stones of a lifeless riverbed. She nodded, reluctantly.

"Ilyssa said her mother had come up with a plan to send her off to her Auntie's home in Galarue," she muttered. "But her father got wind of it and threatened to send the army after her if the Prefect came for Ilyssa and found her missing. And it *is* the Prefect himself who wants her, as I have just learned!"

Despite themselves, the men at the table grunted in disgust at this revelation.

"Damn that Garn! He's always been a coward," spat one of the men in reference to Ilyssa's father. The Prefect was known by one and all in Pyr Mida for his unmitigated cruelty.

"If Garn can live with the decision, then that's a curse on his own head," warned Rufthar. "We do not get involved, other than to see that Ilyssa is returned to her people. I won't risk the security of my camp, and any man that disagrees had better be ready to deal with *me*. Sister, throw on your cloak and go fetch the girl's parents. They live just down the road from here and, besides, it'll look bad for us, too, if the Prefect should come early and find out she's in this house. She's safe in your bedroom, I take it?"

Wyrnie's eyes widened in horror. "Yes, she's resting. I locked the door from the outside!" The old hag dropped her apron and forgot about her own meager tears, scrambling to the front door and snatching a pitch-soaked torch, along with the thick woolen cloak that hung beside it. In a moment she had lit her craggy stick and disappeared into the frosty night.

"As for the rest of you," Rufthar ordered, "I think it wise to move to the bunkhouse and get some sleep. We get our supplies tomorrow and are out of the city by noon. Forget this matter and go on as if nothing has happened. Is that understood?"

Slowly, the men began to rise and shuffle away from the table, moving to a doorway that opened onto an even larger room behind Wyrnie's hearth, lowing like cattle in their ebbing dismay.

"It's even wiser that *you* forget this, Gremm," said Rufthar.

Starbane looked to the door through which Wyrnie had just vanished, torch in hand, to betray Ilyssa. In his mind, this girl's parents couldn't be true parents at all. What he thought of the selective cowardice of Rufthar and the others he hadn't enough ill words in his vocabulary to describe. Still, he felt as helpless as any of them on this night, caught between the certainty that he must soon resume his own perilous mission and the powerful desire boiling within his soul to somehow rescue the doomed girl.

"Follow the men, boy," said Rufthar. "The bunkhouse is through that door. Find a bed and get some rest. Tomorrow at dawn you can be about your own affairs."

Starbane's mind whirled in a kaleidoscope of emotion and frantic thought that suddenly formed two salvific words: *Telvyn Rakahr!*

The vile Gragan wizard had scarred him and sent him to find another magician, but perhaps the *man* that old Celintha had sent him to find first would have an idea to save this girl. It was worth a try; after all, finding Telvyn Rakahr had been the initial point of his escape and the possible redemption of his subsequent misery. He knew that if he spent one night in a bunkhouse with the hunters, tossing and turning and hearing the screams of Ilyssa in his thoughts, he would go mad. He glanced up at mighty Rufthar with all the dignity he could summon, all that he could remember possessing from more noble times long eradicated.

"I think I'm going to take my leave of you tonight, Rufthar," he said. "I want to seek my friend before dawn comes."

Rufthar reached for a cup of beer, his face impassive. "If you wish, Gremm. I must warn you, though, that the city is not safe to travel after dark. There are Cadrach soldiers about and they don't mind questioning anyone, just for the fun of it. Wyrnie is lucky she has only a few houses to sneak past before she gets to that girl's place. But, if your friend owns this inn you spoke of, perhaps he'll be able to receive you at this hour. It's up to you. I'm not throwing you out. Not until morning."

Starbane swallowed hard. "Yes, I think I'll go now."

Rufthar sauntered over and held out a massive hand to the youth.

"Then I guess it's goodbye. I wish you well, lad. I know, at least, that my wife and child would want me to give their blessing."

He shook Rufthar's hand unwillingly but firmly. Moreover, his final thanks were sincere. He owed Rufthar that much, and there was no getting around it.

"For all you've done, Rufthar, I am indebted to you and to Ona and Wylla. If one day I can repay—"

Rufthar silenced the lad with a terrifying frown. "Don't speak of payment. There's no need," he growled. "Well, do you think you know the way to your friend's inn, Gremm? At night?"

"Yes, one of the men told me back at the encampment. The directions seemed easy enough to recall. If you'd be so kind, you might get me started by at least pointing the way to the Pyr Mida marketplace. The big one, in the middle of the city. I think I can find my way from there."

Rufthar bowed his head a little. "If I were you, I'd keep to the smaller streets as much as possible. Like I said, the Cadrach army prowls about at night, even in winter. If you get stopped, you're on your own. Don't you *dare* lead anyone back here."

"I wouldn't," retorted Starbane, coolly. He could hear Ilyssa crying in some distant room.

"They're liable to play rough with a boy like you, if they catch you," added Rufthar. "But perhaps that's the worse that would happen."

That's what you *think,* thought the boy.

Moments later, he was snow-shoed, dressed, and ready to go, new satchel in hand. Rufthar gave him a few small coins as he opened the door. Starbane was momentarily distracted from his simmering anger.

"It's not much, but it might buy a meal, or a night's stay at another inn, should things not work out with your friend," said Rufthar. "My wife wanted to you to have it," he was careful to add.

"Then please give her my deepest thanks." Starbane took the money and tramped out into the darkness in the direction Rufthar had indicated a moment earlier.

"The gods be with you," muttered Rufthar before slamming the door harder than necessary. The boy was alone once again, and the starkness of the fact was like a jolt of lightning through his body. In his mind, he played and replayed the directions to Telvyn Rakahr's drinking hall as he trudged away, panting for breath even now, past rows of sprawling shanties and lopsided homes much like Wyrnie's. In anguish he thought once again of the girl.

We do not get involved, Rufthar had said.

Even Starbane had not realized the depths to which despair had plunged Kelnia in the aftermath of what everyone decent called "Oblixta's Great Treachery." If this man, Telvyn Rakahr, knew of a way to save Ilyssa, he vowed he would ask the man to do it, if he was still in any position to ask for anything. This remained to be seen; far too many questions were still left unanswered. Moreover, there was much-needed trust yet to be built! The boy felt exhausted merely thinking about trust. Though he had only seen her for a few, bewildered moments, he felt a kinship and empathy toward this fair girl, knowing all too well the sorrow of living in the oppressive shadow of impending doom.

He didn't have any idea where he was. Not really. The frosty, wind-whipped streets were meaningless to him. He closed his eyes and decided not to care, for just a few moments. Then he turned left and disappeared down a dismal avenue, hoping it might eventually lead to the marketplace. Hope was all he truly had, and even this seemed like the most useless of all gifts as the night clutched fingers about him and drew him heartlessly into its depths.

V
Tales Told by Tavern-Light

Alone in old Wyrnie's dank bedroom, Ilyssa sat up on the down-stuffed mattress and wiped the tears from her eyes, trying to gather her wits. If there was any time left at all, she knew that the need for a radical decision had arrived. Coming to Wyrnie's house had been a fateful mistake; she had no doubt that her parents were even now being summoned. Worse, their impending arrival would rob her of what courage she currently possessed. Then, they would watch her like a hawk until morning, when the repulsive Prefect would come and she would be led away, broken and betrayed by family and friend alike. Taking a deep breath of the chilly air, she rose and tip-toed to the bedroom door.

Finding it locked, she stifled a small gasp of outrage and instead pressed her ear close to the wood. She heard snoring. Loud snoring. It was only Rufthar—the hunter and father of her friend, Wylla—no doubt sitting at the long table, muttering within the depths of drunken sleep and his enormous beard. Ilyssa ground her teeth in disgust. She had grown up with Wylla, knowing well the whole family and their annual sojourns to the hunting encampment. Heretofore Ilyssa had looked upon Rufthar as a man of strength and virtue. Old Wyrnie was nervous and cranky, but just as virtuous, she had thought. She had been so certain, upon seeing Rufthar at the door this very evening, that he, of all people, would be willing to help her in some fashion. Indeed, his presence was, at first, a welcome surprise despite her tears, for she had come initially to beg refuge only from Wyrnie. Why was Rufthar back in the city, so far away from his camp in the distant woodlands?

She had no time to ponder such questions now. None of them mattered. It was obvious that she had been mistaken about them all. Wiping her face with her hands, she forced herself to stand straight and think of the disaster to come. Sniffling but wide-eyed in the dark, she moved to the only window in the little bedchamber and tried to open the shutters. She was able to do so only with some difficulty; the clasp seemed frozen, at first—*As icy as Wyrnie's heart*, she thought in misery. With a loud *thwang* the clasp suddenly popped open and Ilyssa threw her back against the wall for fear that Rufthar would come running in an instant to investigate.

With no apparent reaction from outside the room, she resumed her work and pushed the shutters fully outward, her teeth beginning to chatter in the wild rush of frigid evening air. She stepped softly to a large chest at the foot of Wyrnie's rickety bed and opened it, fumbling for an extra cloak or shawl with which to shield herself from the elements. Thank the gods she had thought enough to wear her best fur-lined boots before her mad dash from home! Finding a tattered but luxuriously thick woolen mantle in the musty chest, she wrapped it around her own hooded coat and went back to the window. There she climbed as quietly as possible, up and over the sill, landing safely on her feet in the ankle-deep slush outside. She shuddered and glanced around the vicinity of the house. Which direction could she take? Did it matter? All of her other friends and their families were useless. These routes had already been tried and found as wanting as the one she picked on this penultimate night of ruin.

She paused a final time, steeling her resolve. There was no way she would allow herself to be taken. They could all burn to cinder: the Prefect; Rufthar; Wyrnie; her parents ... the whole town. She knew what would likely happen, at least to her parents, if and when she was discovered missing by the vile man and his underlings. She tested herself for the feeling of heartache, standing there in a sudden updraft, but found she was numb to that particular emotion. She was numb and empty now from all the worrying and thinking and suffering endured in the pit of her soul for well over a month. She turned on her heels and began to run for the roadway that she knew led straight out of Pyr Mida and upward, into the mountain passes beyond, weaving between houses in the darkest patches of night she could discern.

If I'm going to die, she vowed as she ran, *better it be in the arms of Winter than those of the Prefect. For I'd surely die the moment he touched me.*

As for her parents—the father who had been willing all along to give her up without protest and the mother who finally bowed to his wishes—Ilyssa no longer worried.

Let people fend for themselves. That's what we all *must do in times such as these.*

Her father himself lived by this philosophy. For all she cared now, he could die by it as well.

Ilyssa ran onward, her breath steaming and Wyrnie's warming, layered mantle flying out behind her. The only friend she had now was the oblivion of nightfall in the city and, as Starbane had done before her, she vanished swiftly into its welcoming clutches.

ॐॐ

Starbane crossed the massive central marketplace of Pyr Mida, with its seemingly endless rows of now-empty stalls, and passed over the stone bridge that spanned the Dir Mida River. Throughout his new trek he had managed to elude the half-dozen or so soldiers he had spotted along the maze of streets, every one of his senses heightened as adrenalin pulsed steadily through his body. Rufthar had once told him that Pyr Mida was home to more than ten thousand people, and the youth could now believe it. The place was impressive, with far more stately buildings and monuments at its center than the crude but spacious dwellings found on Wyrnie's outlying street and its environs.

Safe in shadows that blended like one substance with the dark fur of his clothing, he passed two more side-streets after the bridge and another small city square before reaching what he hoped was Genaro, the road he had been told to seek. It was narrow and packed with buildings of wood and mud-brick, but at the far end he noticed a rather bright light coming from a taller edifice on the left. There were perhaps five or six people milling about in torchlight before the place and he guessed that this activity signaled the presence of a drinking hall. Could his luck be turning around so quickly? Having discarded the clumsy snowshoes in a ditch several streets back, he made his way with stealth down the well-cleared road, careful to keep his eyes moving in all directions.

The door of the inn was slightly ajar and, on both sides of the portal, as well as hanging across a second-story balcony, oil lanterns flickered and seemed to pulsate in the surrounding gloom. Two fur-clad men stood talking and laughing just without, but they didn't even notice as the young interloper approached and peered within. The others he had seen moments earlier on the dilapidated porch of the place had already straggled off for the evening. There were no Kelnian soldiers—Starbane had been able to recognize their shiny black leather uniforms all too well for several years now—but he hardly felt safe entering the inn. He wasn't even certain he had the right place to begin with. Inside he glimpsed a cavernous hearth, bigger than some of the caves he had sheltered within after first escaping the castle dungeons! A veritable bonfire roared and snapped in a swirling column up the magnificent chimney. At least two dozen men and a few women were seated at long tables or upon various benches inside, all drinking from huge mugs and conversing in the merry warmth.

Starbane pulled his hood tight about his head, until little save stray locks of sweat-curled hair and his cold, red nose were apparent. As casually as he could, he walked into the place and was pleased not to feel the instant scrutiny of the other patrons, who continued their mild revelries, unconcerned with the new guest. Making his way past a number of tables, trying to keep his satchel from knocking anything over, the boy gasped when he nearly tripped across a large, unkempt dog sprawled near the hearth.

"Sorry, girl," he mumbled as he extended his hands toward the blazing fire. The animal barely stirred its body but looked up and cocked a quizzical eye at the inn's newest arrival.

"Mind you look out for my dog there, lad."

A woman was standing behind him. She had just slammed down two foam-dripping mugs at a nearby table and was giving him the sternest look she could summon. Even so, the surprised youth saw that she was rather pretty, with thick hair that flowed out over delicately boned shoulders and then curled in wild, golden tufts above her breasts. He shrugged and smiled apologetically but the woman maintained her skeptical gaze and gave the dog a gentle kick on its hindquarters.

"Get out of the way, Feebee, before you break someone's leg. Or someone breaks yours."

The plump, motley beast rose, scratched itself with a hind paw, and stretched with a brilliant yawn before shuffling off to another spot even nearer the hearth. Starbane yawned compulsively after seeing the dog yawn and tried to stifle his embarrassment with a little chuckle. The woman's stare grew even more oppressive.

"You look a bit young to be in a place like this," she said, raising a brow.

"Are you the … um … how do they say … *bar wench*?" squawked Starbane.

"Wench is it, now? You've got a smart tongue, you little stoat. I serve the drinks, if that's what you mean, and I *happen* to own the place as well. This establishment is for grown-ups, not wandering brats, which is what *you* are, if my eyes don't deceive. Now get out of here, before I call my husband and have you tossed into the cold on your backside. You're blocking the fire for my paying customers!"

Starbane was mortified. The last thing he had expected was a question about his age in a drinking hall, much less a possible scene with a barmaid who happened to own it! He had come so far and had obviously walked into the wrong establishment. His mind raced for a quick and inconspicuous way out of the situation.

"Look, I'm sorry, Ma'am. I'm in the wrong spot altogether and didn't mean to trouble you, or your nice dog. I was looking for someone named Telvyn Rakahr, who owns a similar inn. I'll just be on my way and out of your hair, begging your pardon."

"Just what do you want with Rakahr?" asked the woman, putting one palm flat on a table and massaging the small of her aching back with the other hand.

"You … you *know* him?" gasped Starbane.

"Know him? He's my husband, boy. I own this joint with him. Now speak up and answer my question. What do you want with Telvyn Rakahr? You ain't here to ask for money, I hope. Or perhaps you're here because you *owe* some? Ha! What am I thinking? I must be drunk like the rest of this sorry lot. That'd be the day—when someone who owes *us* money bothers to darken our door."

Starbane's eyes widened and his heart began to race. "No, no. I don't owe him any money and I'm not here to ask for some," he whispered, waving both of his fur gloves with discretion, hoping this woman would manage to keep her voice down as well. "I just want to talk to him, if possible. I *need* to talk to him."

"About what?" snapped the woman.

"Er. I can't say."

"Well, if you can't 'say,' then how do you expect to talk to him in the first place?"

"I meant that I can't say right here and now," muttered Starbane, losing his patience, even as a few of the patrons were beginning to peer with curiosity at the bickering twosome. "If he's here, can you get him for me? Or get a message to him? I was *sent* to see him."

"Sent?" said the woman, a slightly altered gleam in her eye. "By whom? And what's your name, boy?"

Starbane shook his head almost imperceptibly. "I can't tell you right now. But you can tell Rakahr that Celintha sent me, with a little souvenir from Gragan. That much I was told I *could* say, when the time was right."

The woman looked at him with renewed interest, but didn't seem quite ready to budge. She did, however, lower her own voice to a hurried whisper.

"I've never heard of anyone by those names," she said. "What else have you got?"

"I've got nothing else," said Starbane. "Only those names and the name of your husband. You're going to have to trust me, or I'm going to have to leave, and if I have to leave, some questions that deserve answering will probably never get answered."

"I see," said the tavern-wife, her eyes beginning to sparkle with a mixture of skepticism and suppressed excitement. "In that case, I think it's best if you sit down, over there, away from prying eyes." She motioned to a tiny table in a corner, not far from where her dog had ambled and thrown itself in a snoring heap. "I'll get my husband and pass along these names you've given. This Gragan person and this Celintha. If he comes back into this hall *with* me, I'll make you both a nice cup of hot spiced cider, perfect for a wretched winter's night and frozen bones. But, if you see me walk back in here alone, then you'll want to be up and away as quick as you can. That's the way things work around here, when people show up unannounced, with little *messages*. Understand?"

Starbane gulped and nodded as the woman motioned again to the corner table, this time with a stern jerk of her chin. There in the shadows he soon sat and watched as she moved to an alcove behind her bar and opened a door that revealed a narrow, ramshackle stairway flying up into the darkness. She called out at the foot of the stairs, though Starbane could not hear what she said because the chatter of the patrons had grown louder once he sat down. A moment later, a stocky old man with a gray moustache that dipped like two tornado funnels on either side of his mouth descended the stairs. His brows, boasting the bushiest growth the boy had ever seen on any man, furrowed as he stooped and listened to the woman, who whispered and gestured, pointing first at the visitor, then at the door, and then finally, inexplicably, at the ceiling of the little hall. At last, some form of recognition must have struck, for Starbane saw the great eyebrow tufts flare upward and a bearded jaw drop in astonishment.

If that's her husband, Telvyn Rakahr, thought the nervous boy, *they are definitely a strange couple.*

The old man stared at him for a moment, blinked twice, and then spoke rapidly into the woman's ear. As she began to nod, he glanced around the drinking hall with piercing suspicion, but none of the patrons seemed to notice or care about his sudden presence. Then he turned and ran back up the stairwell, out of sight. Starbane's heart fell in dismay. Would the woman now walk back to him alone, prompting his immediate ejection from the place as promised? Had he come so far only to have the mysterious Telvyn Rakahr refuse to speak with him at all? Nothing made sense—as if it *had* from the beginning!—but as Rakahr's wife glided swiftly toward the corner table, a strange look upon her face, Starbane was prepared for the worst. He rose slowly to flee.

"Don't leave!" she murmured, bending low to the boy's ear. "See that stairway over there?"

"Yes. What's happening?"

"You'll find out once you go up those stairs. My husband, the man you saw, is waiting for you in the hallway above. It's dark on the way up, so you must be careful, and please try not to make yourself any more obvious than you already are. You must do as I say. Quickly, but not *too* quickly!"

Rakahr's wife had no sooner uttered these words when she spun around with a great whirl of her skirts to resume tending to the guests, several of whom were now grunting for refills. Starbane moved from his chair, gloves shoved in his Bog Bear coat-pockets, stepped over the sleeping dog more carefully this time, and sauntered toward the alcove behind the bar. He looked back once to make sure no one had noticed him, but attention in the hall was fixed upon Rakahr's buxom wife as she went about her work. He ascended the creaking stair and, just as he had been told, Telvyn Rakahr stood waiting for him beside a small window in a long hallway at the very top. In his left hand he held a lantern that sputtered and cast eerie shadows in the unfamiliar place. Through its flickering aura he peered in awe at the young arrival. Starbane stopped in his tracks and gulped.

"Telvyn Rakahr?" he whispered. "Is it really you?"

The old man put a finger to his lips, which were lost in the billowing moustache. Below, they heard the low chatter of the drinkers and a few saucy wisecracks made by Rakahr's wife. Then Starbane was taken gently by the arm.

"I am indeed Telvyn Rakahr," the old one whispered, looking ghostly in the lantern light. "Is it true what my wife told me, that you have been sent by Celintha, and the Gragan himself?"

"Yes!" Starbane replied, elated to finally be dealing with someone to whom he could be truthful. "Celintha set me free after that weird old wizard burned my arm in the dungeons and then she sent me here to find you. I'm sorry it's taken me so long to get to Pyr Mida, but if you knew all that's happened to me since—"

"Then you really *are* the Prince Starbane Cadrach of Kelnia?" interrupted Rakahr in quavering tones.

Starbane felt his body go weak with relief. "I'm afraid so. Son of King Adraeus Cadrach himself. But how did you know? Did Celintha tell you that I was coming, even as she told me to flee to you?"

Telvyn Rakahr shook his head in wonder and switched the lantern to his other hand. "Come with me, Your Highness. It isn't safe to converse in the open like this. There are a few others staying in our rooms tonight. No one dangerous, I think, but we must be careful. Let's get out of this hallway, at least for a minute, until I can think of how best to make things ready for you this evening."

He led his new charge across the moaning floorboards of a corridor that boasted numerous doors on either side; this was the "inn" portion of Rakahr's establishment, Starbane guessed. When the two came to the last door in the row on the right, Rakahr fumbled for a key among the many dangling at his belt and unlocked the way for both of them to enter a small room. Once inside, he shut the door quietly and hung the lantern on a large spike jutting from the wall. He motioned, with a humble bow, for the guest to be seated on a bed in the corner of the musty chamber.

"These are dour accommodations for one of your dignity," said Rakahr, "but the room will afford us privacy, just for the moment."

Starbane frowned. "Don't worry about accommodations. If you'd been through what I've been through this past month, you might be happy to see the very walls of a dungeon cell again, believe me! But don't keep me in the dark any longer, though darkness is all about us. Tell me how you knew that I am the Prince Starbane of Kelnia, and about Celintha. What's been going on since I escaped from the castle? By all the gods, I can't believe that I'm here, at last. It seems like I'm living in some unending dream world."

Rakahr pulled up a small footstool and sat close, whispering. "There are many stories to be told, Your Highness, but I've no time to tell them right now. Suffice it to say that I—that *we*—have been awaiting your arrival with much anticipation and lost hope, especially in the past few weeks. Tonight, you will sleep in my own apartments, which are on the third floor of the inn. They are likewise humble surroundings, but you'll be comfortable and well-fed. You also look like you could use some sleep, so sleep you shall have. In the morning I'll explain everything, and I trust that you will do the same for me."

"But I want to know what's happening *now*."

"There's no time, as I said. I shall be awake for the rest of this night, contacting several of my men here in the city to let them know of your presence."

The Prince of Kelnia sat bolt upright. "Men? What men? Who else is going to know that I'm here? I demand that you answer."

"Please, Your Highness," answered Rakahr, holding up a strong but wrinkled hand to calm the youth's fears. "I realize that this has all been a nightmare for you, but there is no time to waste with explanations. Not tonight! You must trust both me and the word of she who sent you into our midst. How she managed to protect you across this bitter landscape, I don't know, but she's been capable of great things, and I do intend to find out more in due time. Meanwhile, know only that you are safe and among friends!"

Before Starbane had the chance to query further, Telvyn Rakahr was up from the stool and at the door with surprising agility. He took the lantern and left the room, motioning for the Prince to follow. Down the same corridor they went, but this time they bypassed the stair leading to the bar below and passed through another door at the end of the hallway and up an even narrower flight.

"I didn't see a third story from outside."

"You can't see it from the street in the dark," said Rakahr, trudging slowly ahead. "It's set a ways back, atop the second floor, but this is where the wife and I dwell."

At the top of the stairwell, Rakahr grunted with effort as he unlocked and then threw open the door upon a tidy and attractive living area. A merry fire crackled upon its mouthful of logs in a hearth much smaller than the one downstairs. Two handsome chairs covered with plush bearskin and assorted furs were drawn close to the blaze, but there would be no sitting down. Rakahr dragged him, by the forearm, across the room and through yet another door.

Things are happening much too quickly now for my taste, thought the boy. *I know nothing of this situation!*

Within this final room, Rakahr used a sliver of wood to light an oil-lamp sconce from the flame in his lantern and the Prince sighed to behold another cramped and cold bedchamber, much like the one they had entered briefly below.

"Make yourself as comfortable as you can, Prince Starbane. But do one thing for me first."

"Whatever you ask," said the Prince, bewildered.

"Show me your forearm."

"The scar?"

"Yes, the Gragan Wizard's mark, his seal. Celintha sent word that you bear it."

The Prince rolled up his Bog Bear coat and underlying sleeve, brandishing his flesh. Rakahr's eyes grew wide at the sight of sigils scorched into the boy' skin. He nodded.

"I must take my leave of you now," said Rakahr, somewhat out of breath due to excitement and exertion. "I'll help my wife, Telize, to close this place for the night and then I'll be in contact with my men. Tomorrow we shall have much to share … and to do."

The repeated reference to unidentified men left the boy unsettled, but he found himself so overwhelmed and exhausted by now that he could only shrug. His eyes were growing heavy.

"Ah, yes! You're ready for sleep," noted Rakahr. "That's to be expected. Everything you need is here—blankets, nice down pillow, night pot. Leave the door open to catch the fire's warmth from the main room. I'll throw some more logs on and the wife will be up soon. Are you hungry at all?"

"No," croaked Starbane, sitting heavily on the bed. "I've eaten tonight. Just worn out. That's all."

"Again, that's as it should be, brave Prince. But you'll be safe in this place. That I guarantee."

With that, the newly met and decidedly strange Telvyn Rakahr shook his head in disbelief once more and scurried out of the room, leaving the boy more stunned and disoriented than he had been in days. Part of his body fought its own weariness even as an excitement ran through his veins, making for a debilitating state of mind. He felt like passing-out on his back and leaping madly through a window at the same time! What manner of odd place had he stumbled upon now, and how trustworthy were its inhabitants? In an instant of panic, he felt the impulse to get up and run away, indeed—to run as fast as he could, perhaps back to Wyrnie's house where he could beg refuge again from the grumpy Rufthar. Then his head began to reel as he faced the absurdity of the idea and Telvyn Rakahr's words came drifting into his mind.

Tomorrow we shall have much to share, and to do.

There was nothing for it. This was the place to which he had been sent, the reason for his perilous flight. No matter how apprehensive he felt now, he resolved to be patient and demand answers only in the full light of dawn, when the world might seem more willing to give up its secrets.

The Prince Starbane Cadrach of Kelnia looked at the room and the little bed and then laid himself, agitation passing, upon the lumpy mattress. He made up his mind not to sleep at all, but to wait for either Rakahr or his wife to come back up the maze of stairwells and at least *be* nearby, for he felt as alone as he had ever felt during his grim woodland trek. He didn't even bother to take his boots and gloves off, instead burying his head in the wonderful pillow and fixing his eyes on the door by the stairs in the outer room. Soon, however, those eyes drifted lazily to the dancing fire in the hearth and, once there, they were mesmerized. Eyes closed completely a moment later, however, and all new worries were forgotten in the gentle spiral of sleep's irresistible descent.

❧◈❧

Ilyssa heard them calling her, but dared not move a muscle from her hidden spot, up under the rafters of the abandoned mill. After walking just to the edge of the city, where the Kurda Road wound its slippery way through the surrounding forest and then soared to Troll's Fall Pass, she had been overwhelmed with second thoughts about her spontaneous escape. The night weather was beyond bitter—had she expected anything less?—and the sight of the lonely, snow-swirled road stretching out before her into miserable patches of forest filled her with terror. Too afraid of what she might encounter in the darkness, she vowed to make good on her intentions in the morning and had turned back to the city, weaving her way in retreat the same way she had come. It was easy to keep to the shadows, for shadows reigned supreme over everything. Dull slivers of moonlight here and there showed that the night sky was filled with low clouds, like upturned cauldrons of boiling iron.

Coming upon the ancient and dilapidated mill, which was only a few streets away from her own house, Ilyssa had at last been forced to seek shelter from the elements. This spot would not be such a bad option; for years she and other Pyr Midan children had ignored parental warnings and played in the mill at leisure. It had been deserted for as long as anyone could recall. Knowing every nook and cranny of the place well, even in the frigid evening, Ilyssa had crawled through a jagged crack in one of the mill's rear walls and climbed up to a ledge that ran along the border where roof and wall met. There was plenty of room to stretch out flat on this ledge and enough space to peer out under the deteriorating eaves to see and hear what might be going on outside. In fact, she had a slight view of her parents' house, which stood jutting out from a corner some distance away on the end of an avenue. So far, Ilyssa had stayed on the ledge for two hours, shivering beneath her thick layers of clothing yet confident that no one would find her, at least not until morning. By then she would be gone, no matter how great her fear of the grasping woodland or the mist-wrapped mountains that loomed above.

At one point, she had been able to see her frantic parents as they dashed in and out of their house several times, calling desperately for her in the empty streets, rousing reluctant and grumbling neighbors by knocking on almost every door. Ilyssa could make out the pathetic figure of her mother, swathed in a heap of woolen shawls, looking helplessly up and down alleyways and streets that would reveal nothing. Twice the girl had been sorely tempted to jump down from her roost and run to her mother's arms, but she forced her mind to conjure images of the Prefect, with his beaked nose, filthy beard, and crooked brown teeth. Most of all she could remember his eyes, as beady and vile as those of a weasel. The memory of his lustful glances made her shudder, and her body became as heavy upon the mill's hidden ledge as if she were made of rock, too.

Going back was impossible, now. Her father would only beat her without mercy and she was as tired of *that* constant fear as she was of her imminent fate in the Prefect's clutches. As much as she loved her mother, deep down, she knew that the woman—like most in these confused and dangerous times—was far more loyal to spouse than to offspring. Husbands could protect against the evils that were ever-rising like a foul tide all around the city and the kingdom ... or at least women *thought* their husbands could protect them. Unfortunately, Ilyssa's mother had never been one to think too much on her own, even before the Days of Dread had been thrown like a smothering cloak across the land and its people. She rarely questioned and never confronted her husband concerning even the smallest of matters.

Flimsy and uncertain plots, like squirreling Ilyssa away to an aunt in another town, were the best her mother could manage, and even these would never find fulfillment. No, Ilyssa's parents were lost to her, forever and always. Somehow—and this was a cold comfort indeed, though it touched her mind often—she knew that she had been uniquely blessed by the gods. They had deigned to give her the grace to *know* better, to recognize the flawed existence of her own family, even amid the much more daunting flaws of a ruined kingdom. These gods, whoever they were, had given her the bravery to walk away and hope against all sense (and perhaps sanity) for a better life. But where would that be found? In death?

It would certainly not be in the bedroom of the Prefect.

True, Ilyssa had witnessed some girls go off with the Kelnian army, the corrupt magistrates, and a few slovenly nobles without a tear. She had heard the whispered stories told by women in their kitchens, stories of how these girls became the slaves and playthings of men that had been allegedly ruined by the power of the ruling witch in Cadrach Castle. She had heard the tales of how these girls became soulless, walking as if dead within, serving their new masters and adapting so completely to their new world that they, too, became as evil and as insensitive as their captors. She herself had been accosted by two of the "Army's Girls" less than a month ago, in the Great Pyr Mida marketplace as she bought a few eggs. The girls were only a little older than she, with their painted-up cheeks and lips reminding her of malevolent cats that had just eaten their own kittens. Yet, for all their tinkling laughter and colorful trappings, their eyes were hollow, their spirits ruined. The girls had snickered as they sized her up, nodding and whispering.

No, not long. Not long till she's one of us.

She had tried to ignore them, but such efforts had proved useless.

One so fair has already been promised, surely. Have you been promised, blue eyes?

Ilyssa had grabbed her basket of eggs from the vendor and dashed away.

Are you ready, blue eyes? Why bother to run? There's nowhere to go!

From that day, Ilyssa had promised herself another fate, one far removed from the designs of those who would only use her, destroy her, and inevitably toss her away. Even now she cringed at the realization that her only alternative might indeed be death. Rigid on the drafty ledge, she shoved a hand up into the thickest portion of her hair gathered beneath wretched old Wyrnie's shawl. That was a little warmer, for her auburn tresses were thick and heavy. She sighed, a small flower of cloud blooming from her lips in the wintry air. It had never helped matters that she was beautiful. When the sorceress of Cadrach had first given the army permission to randomly apprehend young women of Kelnia, some parents made the heart-wrenching decision to disfigure their daughters' faces, in an attempt to make them repulsive to the lecherous devils.

Those parents—and their daughters—were invariably punished for the ruse, adding horror to something already beyond terrible.

Ilyssa's parents weren't brave enough to try such a stunt, but only for fear of reprisal, not out of warped protectiveness for their child. After seeing some of the blinded or burned girls over the months, she was glad that her parents were cowards in *this* sense, at least. It was two months ago when the Prefect of Pyr Mida had noticed Ilyssa while she was at the crowded marketplace with her mother. They had tried to avoid his stares, but it had not been long before an underling was dispatched to demand a meeting. The rest was a nightmare from which the girl had not yet been able to awaken. Her parents had been notified, with an order that they relinquish custody of Ilyssa within three days, to "serve the needs of the Kelnian Cause" at the Prefect's lavish new compound on the edge of the city. Her mother had made an initial, feeble protest, informing the messengers that her daughter had not yet experienced her first "womanly affliction" and would they not reconsider?

The useless goose, thought Ilyssa now with a derisive snort. That particular bit of information had only served to heighten interest in her "services."

Even so, the Prefect had agreed to wait an entire month before summoning Ilyssa; news spread throughout the city that he had been called to Castle Cadrach by the Queen on important matters of state. More messengers were sent in the meantime, reminding Ilyssa's family that she would be taken as soon as the monster returned from his conference.

Don't get any ideas, they had said. *The Prefect hasn't forgotten you, not in the least.*

Now, as Ilyssa huddled to conserve what little warmth remained in her body atop the mill ledge, she sensed calmly that dawn was only a few hours away. The Prefect would be riding into the city to claim her, along with any other unfortunate girls who might have been the objects of his desire. She thought again of the promised punishment her parents would suffer if she was found unwilling to go, or if she turned up missing—her father had taken great care to remind her of this constantly, even to the point of locking her inside the house during the day. But he had not counted on her being bold enough to flee at night, in the throes of winter. Again, she cast all visions of her parents' punishment aside. Her choice had been made, even to the point of suicide, and she accepted it. If her mother and father were unprepared to follow, then she had enough wisdom to know that such was *their* choice, and theirs alone. Their fate, too, would be uniquely their own.

A sudden gust of wind caught a particularly high crest of some snowdrift and found its way under the eaves, stinging the skin of her face like a thousand frozen needles. Yes, she planned to be on her way well before the Filthy One came to call. She would have to stay awake until she could leave in an hour, or perhaps two, at the most. That would give her an hour or so to get out of the city under slight cover of dark-ness, before the sun actually emerged and, with it, those who would certainly be on the hunt for her. There was no use hoping that she might have enough time to freeze to death where she was, and some clarion voice deep within her being railed against the very idea of dying ... yet. Perhaps there was hope in simply slowing her mind and going forward without expectation of anything whatsoever.

Ilyssa's parents had stopped calling for her in the night. She turned her face away from the crack in the wall beneath the eaves and pulled her body into a ball on the ledge, snuggling within the cloak she had stolen from Wyrnie. Sleep was tempting, but resolve would keep it at bay. In the gloom she prayed to the gods and determined to run for her life—or death—before the first muted rays of morning snaked across the cruel Kelnian sky.

"Prince Starbane, wake up!"

The startled royal sat up, eyes still half-shut and head spinning away from the remnants of a dream. In the dream, someone had been slowly piercing his flesh with pins, one after the other. He gasped.

Sunlight beamed through cracks in the shuttered window near the bed and Telvyn Rakahr was beside him, shaking his shoulder gently and proffering a cup of cider that steamed in the chilly room.

"I can't believe it's morning already," said the Prince, sipping at the delicious drink. "I swear I only went to sleep a few minutes ago. Gods, this has been a bizarre circumstance!"

"I'm sure it *has* been," said Rakahr, smiling between the great wings of his moustache.

"But I'm glad you got a few hours of rest, for all the trouble. You needed it, and it's more rest than I've had the long night through."

Rakahr definitely looked tired to Starbane, who tried not to stare at the huge, wrinkled bags of flesh sagging beneath the old man's otherwise lively brown eyes. Telvyn Rakahr appeared even older, now that the youth was seeing him in daylight for the first time.

"We haven't too much time or too little, for that matter," continued Rakahr. "I've been seeing to all the preparations, Your Highness, and we'll be taking you as swiftly as possible over the mountains into the realm of Corydia."

"So that is the plan, after all? Celintha told me as much. Or at least that she *hoped* you'd be able to get me there. To find this Rowan Blaize sorcerer the old Gragan was so insistent about."

"Yes, that is part of the plan. You're going to see King Sye, too. The journey will begin after mid-day."

Starbane finished his cider and swung his legs off the bed, rubbing his eyes and trying to process this latest news. "Did Celintha plan all of this with you? With the Gragan wizard, too? I cannot possibly imagine all three of you in collusion, but then again I haven't had time to wonder about it much, due to all the running-for-my-life."

Telvyn Rakahr bowed slightly and gestured through the open door toward the main room and adjacent kitchen of the apartments, where Rakahr's wife, the barmaid, could be seen bustling about, setting a table for breakfast.

"I arranged everything for your upcoming trip between the time I left you last night and this morning," said Rakahr as they moved into the inviting space. "Come and have some breakfast and we'll discuss every-thing that's happened up until now, Majesty."

Near the table, Rakahr's wife stopped her preparations and turned, skirts twirling once more, to face their intrepid visitor. She fell at once to her knees and kissed his hand in reverence. The guest was duly stunned, not expecting this sort of treatment from the woman who had so badgered him the previous night. Moreover, he had not been treated like a prince in a very long time, and wasn't feeling particularly royal, bedraggled as he was. The woman spoke with head bowed in hushed, embarrassed tones.

"Your Highness, *please* forgive me for treating you like some common piece of driftwood last night. I had no idea you were the Prince of Kelnia. I mean, you hardly look princely, now, do you? And my husband failed to tell me anything about this scheme beforehand, so it's not like I was expecting princes to be waltzing willy-nilly through the door of the pub, announced or unannounced. You will forgive me, won't you?"

It was Telvyn Rakahr who lifted his wife from the floorboards in front of the speechless Starbane. "Telize, please! There's no call for court pleasantries or theatrics here. Let the lad be at his meal." He turned to the Prince as his wife rose on cracking knees. "You'll have to excuse her, Your Highness. She's a bit overwrought, now that we've had you for company. She's always been a very devout royalist, I might add. Until your sister Oblixta came to power, of course."

"It's quite alright, I'm sure," said Starbane, sitting down to a scrumptious plate of honeyed cakes and cream.

"There was no chance for introductions last night, given the situation. My name is Telize," said Rakahr's wife, pouring tea from a huge kettle for her visitor.

"Pleased to meet you, officially, Ma'am. And there are no hard feelings. Believe me, I'm in your debt for the hospitality. As a matter of fact, I would've turned *myself* away last night. A bath and some clean clothes would have been ideal before meeting either of you, but those things have been hard to come by in my 'new life,' I'm afraid."

"That's nothing to be ashamed about," said Rakahr. "We're simple folk, as you can see, and we'd dare not judge peasant or prince, and for Dryndym's sake, Telize, would you *stop* gawping and pass the boy some biscuits?"

Telize shot a withering look at her husband, who seemed to shrink just a bit. "Here, Your Highness, have a nice biscuit or two. Made them myself," she said with a bashful smile. "My father was a great supporter of your family. I'd like you to know that. Though we were all born in Corydia, we moved to Kelnia when I was just a wee thing and it's been home to us ever since. Everyone loved your dear parents. Real proper rulers, they were. As good as King Sye ever was, my dad used to say. You know, my dad fought hard when ... when *she* took over." A dark cloud seemed to move across Telize's pink, freckled face as the Prince shoveled bread and honeycomb into his famished maw.

"I know it must be awful. To be at odds with your own flesh and blood now," continued the woman. "But you're doing the right thing, Your Highness, and we know you'll find this wonderworker, Rowan Blaize, down in Corydia, and get him to help you restore this kingdom to its former glory. My poor old father lived and died with that hope. We'll do the same, if necessary."

Starbane paused over his breakfast, stomach growling, and stared at Telvyn Rakahr. "Pardon me, but how do you people actually fit into all of this? Why should you—a couple of innkeepers—be involved with the webs that I've been spun into?"

"Have you ever heard of the Corydian Order of the Kashizma?" asked Rakahr.

"The famous spies of King Sye? That's you? Or, you are *them?*"

"Well, two of them, at least," answered Telize. "Though he's not stepped in to do much, yet, King Sye has kept his eyes—many of them, to be exact—on what's been happening since Oblixta began her treacherous rule."

"I should have guessed that you'd be spies," said Starbane. "You Kashizma people are the only ones in this realm doing anything active to undermine my sister, if I hear correctly. It makes sense that you were the only ones to whom Celintha could send me."

Rakahr nodded, and not without pride. "We are honored to be part of the Kashizma, as are the other members living in the city. There are a great many of us, Your Highness, though we are quite elusive. You are not alone in this world."

"I'm sure I don't know much more about your order," said the Prince. "But it had become rather famous at the castle when I was still a boy, or at least more of a boy than I am now. The ongoing problems of Castle Cadrach are not the first cause you've taken up for your Corydian king. Even my father and mother didn't quite mind your spying on them, but that's because they were the good ones in the family."

"Have some of these nice bristleberry preserves, young prince." Telize passed him a bowlful. He spooned a dripping heap of the stuff atop a slice of bread and was tempted to carry on the conversation with his mouth full, but thought better of scandalizing his hosts.

"My father *did* come to realize something of your value, when Oblixta first imprisoned us all," he said. "Word got through of your deeds, of your efforts to stir up resistance. Yes, my father and mother heard about the way the spies of King Sye rallied the people to demand our release and the restoration of the throne. They were heartened by this news, though I don't suppose it did much good. No one rescued us. No one rose up. We'd hoped that King Sye's armies would come to our aid. Why didn't they, if Sye's been so bent all these years upon nosing around in our realm?"

Rakahr's brows knitted with dismay. "King Sye is old, and Corydia is very wealthy and well-protected, as you know. Plus, he believes his whole nation to be under the magical protection of this Rowan Blaize. He opted not to get involved because he felt Kelnia's problems didn't concern him, at least not enough to declare war or press an invasion."

"No offense to you, but I'd say that's rather cold," noted Starbane. "And what of Sye's wizard? Doesn't this magician know that my sister has been *collecting* wizards in her march toward domination? Isn't he the least bit worried about that? And if King Sye isn't going to help Kelnia overthrow Oblixta, then why is he bothering to have his special order of spies help *me* in my dilemma?"

"That's just the thing," said Telize. "We think King Sye wants to know more before he makes any ultimate decision to intervene. It's our understanding that he was quite intrigued once he heard that you'd been set free and were on the way to seek his aid, and that of the warlock. We know nothing more about that, ourselves. Particularly in terms of Rowan Blaize. No one's even seen him in hundreds of years, for Dryndym's sake."

"What?"

"Now, now, Majesty," urged Rakahr. "My dear wife is not entirely accurate about everything. Forget about Rowan Blaize for the moment. The key right now is knowledge about how this situation with Oblixta came to pass in the first place."

The Prince rolled his eyes, nibbling at a biscuit. "You may be spies for Corydia, but you *do* live in this kingdom. Look around you. Anyone can see how it all came about. Don't tell me you don't know the stories. How am I to help you? Someone should've helped my parents—they'd be able to tell much more than I ever could. We were separated, you know, my parents and I, at some point during our imprisonment. I think about a year into our captivity, though I can't be certain. I lost track of time, under those conditions."

Rakahr glowered at the Prince, pity in his eyes. "And we know that much of terrible import has transpired, Your Highness, in the time since. But the Kashizma network has grown, despite the efforts of your sister to destroy us."

"Yes, we've become more active than at any other time in our order's history," added Telize. "And all because of this cause."

Starbane chewed at his breakfast with less enthusiasm now, somewhat uncomfortable among these strangers, solicitous though they were. Talk of causes and orders confused him after all that had been going-on throughout his sequence of very immediate dangers and dilemmas. Rakahr sensed his creeping unease.

"Listen, Majesty. I know something of what you've endured. Of your escape, at least. I know that you were shot off into the wild like an arrow from a bow, and that you must be quite wary of everyone. Old Gragan burned you with his sigils because of some ancient bargain he struck with Rowan Blaize and then Celintha sent you to seek help from us and from a foreign king who may, or may not, be willing to assist. You are uncertain. That's to be expected."

The Prince put his food down and brandished the scar on his fore-arm once again. "You *do* see this, right? I was indeed told by that foul old mage in the dungeons that Rowan Blaize in Corydia would be obliged to help me, if I show him this sign. Celintha agreed, though she could give me no details as to why such a weird thing might be true, beyond a vague legend she herself had heard over the years, to say nothing of the bizarre ways and dealings of magicians in the first place. But she said that Gragan would not likely have lied to me, given his hatred for my sister and de-sire for revenge upon her. Seeing as how I've been thrown into this mix and Celintha's efforts were the ones that set my rescue in motion, I am inclined to trust her. Moreover, I aim to show Rowan Blaize this mark, this "bargain scar" or whatever it is, if someone shows me the way to find *him*—whether he's been seen in hundreds of years or not."

Rakahr and his wife exchanged swift, nervous glances before the old man peered with momentary concern at the bandage and bit of scar tissue on the boy's cheek. "There is much that you deserve to know be-fore anything else happens, Majesty. There's also much that you can tell us, things that may help the Kashizma in its own work, here, among the people of Kelnia."

"What can I tell you?" wondered the Prince aloud. He felt they were unquestionably keeping something from him, these kindly spies. "I don't remember much beyond our imprisonment, and even that seems like a distant dream, now. As I said, I lost all sense of time while Oblixta had us locked away. It … it was beyond horrible. That's all I know."

"But you do remember things that took place before your impris-onment, do you not?" prodded Rakahr. "You remember, perhaps more than anyone now alive and fighting on the side of goodness, the events that led to your sister's rise and the downfall of your father and mother?"

"I certainly do. But these are things I want very much to forget."

"And no one can blame you for that," assured Telize, patting the Prince maternally on his hand. "But much of what the Kashizma knows about such matters is the result of hearsay and guesswork. Not one of us has ever been able to get as close to the Demon-Queen as you have, and lived to tell of it. Not one of us really knows how her mind works, and that's something very crucial to our cause."

The Prince laughed, a bitter sound invading the safety of the cheerful space. "If you think *I* know how her mind works, you're mistaken. No one ever *will* know, I expect. That's why Oblixta is so dangerous."

"Even so, whatever you can tell us about her exact history may be useful," said Rakahr. "Perhaps we can uncover some weakness, some vulnerability—"

"She *has* no weakness and no vulnerability," interrupted Starbane, his cheeks beginning to burn. "Surely you must know this by now!"

Rakahr and his wife looked at each other with the same discomfort. The Prince also saw in their eyes something extraordinary, perhaps some strange kind of underlying passion he had never witnessed before, but one he felt he recognized in his deepest instincts, all the same. He wanted to know more about their efforts as Kashizma spies for the Southern king, and why *they* were thrust into the whirlwind of his escape. Celintha, the old castle witch who had single-handedly set him upon this wild path, had told him precious little. In turn, it appeared that she had told them very little about *him*. Answers were obviously due.

"Celintha told you she was sending me here, that much is apparent. What else did she tell you? Why don't we start with that? She would know far more than I."

"She told us nothing else," said Rakahr with more than a trace of sadness and exasperation. "We—the Kashizma—knew only that she was attempting to set you free at your sister's castle. How she was going to manage it and when it would take place, exactly, were things beyond our knowledge. We lost all contact with Celintha after her last message arrived."

"How did you know her in the first place?"

Rakahr sat wearily down in a chair beside the Prince. "Let's just say that old Celintha had become a friend, an ally of the Kashizma. As you know, she'd been posing as an old washer-woman at the castle. Last year, she helped two of our spies escape certain doom at the hands of Oblixta's warlord, Kerrion. We've been thankful ever since, even though her information has been sparing and often cryptic. But she had her own purposes, and we respect that."

Starbane's mind raced back to the days leading up to his escape, and even further back to the time of his initial imprisonment. The barrage of images and feelings rose like gnashing phantoms to engulf him. He took a deep breath.

"I'll tell you everything that has happened, everything I know," he said to his hosts. "For it must be told. Whatever I can do to avenge the deaths of my parents and restore the kingdom they once loved, I will do. Though, I don't know how I'll ever be of much use in that respect. I don't even know how to fight, or draw a sword. I was thrown in a cell before such training was to properly begin in my life. You won't believe how I managed to escape the fangs of Eskanthian werewolves just to get this far, but I'll try my best to give a proper account."

"We understand, Your Highness," said Rakahr, nodding encouragement. "Do continue."

"Oblixta has ruled this land utterly for four years now," said the boy. "She is full of hatred, as you know, wanting only to conquer and destroy. Everyone in Kelnia and its neighboring lands knows this much, I expect. But what many of them *don't* know is that her rise—or more to the point, her fall—started long ago, before I was even born. When she herself was a child. You may have heard stories and bits and pieces of her tale, but I know what truly happened, because it happened within my family and *to* my family. Worse still, it happened to the whole kingdom, which is mine, by rights, to rule."

The Prince looked absently at the remnants of his meal. His lips broke into a thin smile tinged with the heaviest of regrets or, at least, regrets far too heavy for one so young. He shook his head. Rakahr and

Telize said nothing; it was as if the very breath of the world had been drawn inward, waiting.

"My kingdom," the tousle-haired youth whispered. "That's the reason we're all here in the first place, the reason we have all met within the context of such calamity, isn't it?"

Then, Starbane Cadrach, the Prince of Kelnia, told them his tale.

❧

For seemingly innumerable years, the mighty realm of Kelnia, with its vast, bountiful plains and majestic coastlines, had been influenced, to one extent or another, by the Family of Cadrach. The history of this powerful clan was indeed convoluted, and as fraught with winding turns as the infamous Dalorum hill country from whence their forebears hailed. Over centuries that seemed to churn with intrigue, the Cadrach rulers witnessed devastating losses in periods of political and economic upheaval, and were beaten into submission by rival clans who sought to increase their own fortunes. This happened on more than a few occasions. Entire generations often passed while the glory of the Cadrach tribe faded into little more than the reflection of a memory, like an image seen shimmering for a mere instant on rippling water and then lost.

The greatest members of the Cadrach line, however, were noteworthy survivors. They were resilient. More than that, it was widely said among the inhabitants of Kelnia that Cadrach blood, were it spilled, could cause warrior legions to spring out of the very soil, like so much wheat in the thrall of a golden and nurturing summer. These legions, it was believed, would inevitably rise up to avenge their predecessors. Without question, many great warlords bearing the Cadrach coat-of-arms were able to reclaim castles long-stolen and lands that had fallen into decline, or into the grip of less durable families. Like the slowly surging tides and great curling waves that lash the beaches of Harsperu, Cadrachs *always* came back into power.

True, many Cadrachian lords and kings had been thieves and murderers. Most were wily businessmen. A few were reasonably upright ...

and fewer still were actual saints. Their range of influence had extended, at the outset, from possession of a few sturdy villages and farms in the Dalorum hills to a claim upon the greater part of the Kelnian realm itself, at their peak. The jewel that symbolized the height of their glory and achievement was the colossal Fortress Cadrach—an impenetrable rose-granite edifice in the city of Grohal that was built to loom like a chiseled mountain over the verdant Filean plains at the zenith of the clan's power. After it was constructed, the hallowed Throne of Cadrach was installed and the line produced a dynasty of unchallenged monarchs for over three centuries. During that particular period of success, the Cadrach Kings garnered a reputation for treating their subjects with kindness and wisdom, especially when it came to the poorest of the lot. Fortress Cadrach became Castle Cadrach, and its armies were potent, affording the people constant, crushing protection against those foolhardy competitors or marauders that dared trifle with outlying Kelnian provinces. The moral leadership of the Three Hundred Year Cadrach Kings inspired an allegiance that became the envy of sovereigns in neighboring realms, with their endless policy failures and domestic blunders.

No less revered than his forefathers was the stalwart ruler, Adraeus Cadrach, who had assumed the dominion of Kelnia directly upon the death of his aged sire, King Larcul. From the moment Adraeus was pulled from the sweat and struggle of a military training field one winter, all drenched hair and wind-burned cheeks, he seemed fated to govern particularly well. When the following harvest was marked by severe famine, the new King had dispensed wheat from the Cadrach family's personal granaries to nourish those provinces that were most imperiled. Then he sent battalions eastward to conquer the fruitful farming colonies of the more belligerent kingdom of Cyr, whose people he swiftly but beneficently assimilated. When the elemental spirits again bestowed favor upon Kelnia proper, King Adraeus enjoyed a national loyalty more pronounced than any in his lineage had ever experienced. Thus began what would be a long and mutual love-affair between a ruler and his subjects. Such popularity was only helped by the fact that Adraeus took as his queen one who would become as widely beloved as himself: the fabled beauty, Laredana. She was, in fact, his third cousin, herself a daughter of the ancient Dalorum hills and prized child of one of that region's most hallowed noblemen.

Laredana quickly became a guiding force in the administration of Adraeus. She proved herself his equal in every virtue and facet of wisdom, while their love became the stuff of song and legend. Queen Laredana devoted herself to the needs of Kelnia's widows and orphans, guarding their welfare through acts of imperial beneficence as if they were her own kin. In turn, such unfortunates would often rise to become her bravest knights. Laredana also managed the building of great homes and communities to which the aged could retreat to spend their dotage in comfort, if there were none to look after them. Such ventures endeared her to the Kelnian people on plain or near the rolling sea, consolidating the already formidable devotion secured by King Adraeus, and making it easy to downplay the host of smaller problems that inevitably plague even the greatest realms.

In the fourth year of Adraeus's reign, Laredana gave birth to their first child, a girl. The months leading up to the birth had been full of great anticipation for the entire kingdom, given the venerable status of its rulers. Celebrations were held across the land in the wake of the happy event and, when after five days the girl-child was given the ancient Cadrachian family-name of "Oblixta," more festivity ensued. All of this took place during a time of marked economic prosperity and, as the child grew up within the labyrinthine halls of Castle Cadrach, Adraeus and Laredana lavished her with the riches and attention befitting a princess of her stock.

For Oblixta were fashioned the finest robes and gowns, stitched with gleaming gold thread from Colstra and colored with the most exquisitely radiant dyes procured in the coveted marketplaces of Shensu. The finest craftsmen from Anasha were employed to design elaborate toys and other playthings for the Princess, while an entire stable of sleek horses was bequeathed to her care before she could even toddle. Moreover, the small city of Galarue, near to Castle Cadrach, Grohal, and its precincts, was consecrated to Oblixta—every man, woman, child, and institution within the walls. Such attention was lavish, even by the some-times ostentatious standards of Kelnian royalty. Yet, there had existed such anxiety during the first three "barren" years of the royal marriage, that Adraeus and Laredana spared no expense to make known their gratitude for the blessing of this daughter. As for the Princess, Oblixta basked in the splendor with which she was surrounded and grew quite accustomed to it. She wanted for nothing, and likewise had nothing to fear.

This truth, perhaps more than all else, made things more difficult when certain problems arose in the sixth year of the child's life. By that time, the era of peace and abundance was beginning to show peripheral signs of strain and possible decline. Simmering land-ownership tensions between the Kelnian border and a number of lords in Colstra had fi-nally erupted in scattered cases of armed conflict. The problem was seri-ous enough to warrant the military presence of King Adraeus himself. While he was away from the castle for extended periods of time, Queen Laredana handled matters of state in his stead. All seemed in hand until, during one of Adraeus's expeditions, the radiant Laredana fell gravely ill with a fever and died after a brave struggle of four agonizing days. This tragedy was to permanently alter the once-idyllic atmosphere of Castle Cadrach … and the nation. While King Adraeus mourned—hav-ing arrived too late from battle to Laredana's deathbed—the armies of Kelnia launched a full scale war upon Colstra and, in its zeal to honor the departed queen, won handily. It was at this juncture that disturbing phenomena began to affect the life of the equally grief-stricken Princess Oblixta.

The Princess Cadrach had been carefully shielded from the trials undergoing the kingdom, but the loss of her mother was another matter entirely. Her reactions were not said to be unusual, at first. Indeed, those appointed to attend the royal child noticed only that Oblixta began to spend her nights tossing and turning, complaining of dreams of loss and abandonment. During the day, when a haggard and distracted Adraeus sought to console his daughter in his exceedingly spare moments, Ob-lixta betrayed no memory of her night terrors and carried on about the castle as she normally did, charming one and all with her winsome ways as if nothing had ever happened to her mother. But this was only the beginning; her troubles soon became manifest in other, far more unsettling ways.

Seven months after Laredana's death, with the kingdom finally but reluctantly coming to grips with the loss, Oblixta took to running away from her governess, a generous but watchful soul. When this occurred, the entire castle was thrown into panic and uproar as they searched for the missing child, almost always in the thick of night. How could it be possible, so many wondered, for such a small and naturally communicative child to elude so many caretakers in the deadening silence? Eventually, Princess Oblixta would always be found, but it always seemed to be on *her* terms, rather than by the concerted efforts of palace personnel. For example, she might be discovered hiding and playing with her dolls in some ancient cupboard in the remotest part of the castle, oblivious to the fuss she had caused at midnight. Too, she could sometimes be found roaming and singing strange chants in the cool darkness, along the lush avenues of the small garden and exotic animal reserve that Adraeus had built long ago for her pleasure. This was all well and good, save for the fact that these areas had already been thoroughly searched by frantic servants and guards in advance of the child's "sudden" discovery.

After more than two months of this behavior, the kindly governess explained to the King that such problems were perhaps best solved by a heavier discipline, but the distraught Adraeus would hear nothing of it. In response, he simply doubled the already considerable staff of servants and other guardians responsible for his daughter's welfare, certain that, through sheer numbers, he could eliminate any further nonsense. Overwhelming numbers were, after all, one of the great king's favorite remedies for most any situation.

While this approach did seem to quell young Oblixta's string of disappearances and so-called "pranks," rumors of even more bizarre events began to make the rounds at Castle Cadrach in the ensuing months. One story, passed along in fretful whispers, told of how the Princess had been observed on several occasions calling out to flocks of birds as they passed outside her bower window. The dainty child in her court finery would stand on tiptoe, beckoning and coaxing the creatures to alight upon her balcony. In one harrowing instance, and to the amazement of those present, an entire flock of starlings blasted with full force into the royal bedchamber and wrought tremendous havoc. Hundreds of the shrieking birds swirled like a cyclone of confusion, scratching at the hair and faces of the helpless adults and destroying the beautiful tapestries and other furnishings that adorned the room. Then, the starlings darted out the window as one black cloud of whirring bodies, as quickly as they had entered. Pecked and bleeding nurses and attendants collected their addled wits just in time to see a laughing, bemused Princess Oblixta waving from her balcony at the departing flock, wholly unaffected by the phenomenon.

As if these episodes were not disconcerting enough, castle gossips were occupied night and day by tales of Oblixta's sudden fits of rage and her blood-curdling tantrums, typically thrown when goaded to obey her keepers, even in the most insignificant matters. Word spread that the child became so fierce and agitated, so full of fury, that objects would literally and without warning tumble from shelves, or fly across rooms like dangerous missiles aimed at those who were only trying to pacify the raging girl. At first, the child's devoted governess was too baffled and afraid to relate such weird incidents to the King. When they began to transpire with greater frequency and intensity, however, those in charge of Oblixta began to entertain the creeping fear that the Princess might be under the power of some malevolent charm or spell. Such afflictions were not unprecedented in royal histories. Worried that silence would implicate them, should this be the case, the Princess's overseers at last informed the withering Adraeus, and his response was one of angry disbelief.

In a minor fit of his own, the King dismissed the governess and all her underlings from both the castle and their service of the Princess, accusing them of insurrection meant to undermine his rule at a time of relentless grief. In his eyes, it was either that or they were all out of their minds. "No child of mine shall stand accused of sorcery or possession!"

he had railed. Even so, it was not long before Adraeus himself witnessed firsthand the oddities he had previously dismissed as nonsense. One day the child threw such a monstrous tantrum in his presence that the very pennants adorning the high arches of the throne room were ripped, one and all, from their lofty frames and sent hurtling to the marble floor. Aghast at this display, Adraeus summoned the kingdom's most renowned healer to examine his beloved daughter. When the arrogant but wise expert discovered nothing to be amiss with the child physically, one of the chief prophets in the temple of Dryndym was called upon to keep watch.

Angered by the daily prodding and interfering presence of strangers, it wasn't long before Oblixta lost her temper and the same wild manifestations were again revealed. The observing priest, ashen-faced from his experience, promptly told the King that his only child was the hapless victim of an evil spirit and that she needed an immediate and thorough exorcism. Horrified but convinced at last (for Adraeus harbored deep respect for the prophets of Dryndym), the King authorized the temple liturgists to do whatever was necessary to free the girl from her oppression and rid the castle, once and for all, of such awful intrusions. Thus it was that the prescribed and ancient rites were performed upon Oblixta with all the pomp and solemnity at the temple's disposal, though the child found all of the chanting and bell-ringing and bowing and fragrant censing to be little more than diverting entertainment. When the hoopla was finished and the chief prophet of Dryndym declared that the Princess was now free from her unnamed invisible "tormenter"—*was it the despondent ghost of dead Queen Laredana, as many had been speculating?*—all breathed a sigh of relief, expecting the castle to reclaim its hitherto normal existence.

But such relief was short-lived. The Princess's "affliction" came back with an even greater vengeance as soon as the child was sufficiently agitated again, which didn't take long at all. Now at a complete loss and poised on a cliff's edge of despair, Adraeus was consoled by Oblixta's new governess, a wise old woman who hailed from the king's own ancestral lands in the Dalorum hills. She spoke to him and recommended the counsel of another woman known in those parts—a reclusive soul said to be skilled in the arts of sorcery and possessive of great knowledge. As Adraeus pondered his options one desperate evening, he recalled that his own people had had occasion to consult this renowned witch in times past, long before he was king. Still, it was with a foreboding reluctance that Adraeus heeded the new caretaker's advice and dispatched a messenger to the region of Dalorum to find this enchantress, whose name was Celintha.

When, after a month, Celintha arrived at Castle Cadrach, King Adraeus was skeptical, to say the least. The fabled creature was ancient and bent, little taller than a child herself. She was riding an especially cantankerous mule, to make the scene even more unpalatable. The simple brown tunic Celintha wore was embroidered with a host of arcane signs and sigils, and from her long, stark white hair dangled feathers and charms intricately knotted with leather chords. Once within the castle, she looked suspiciously about the interior, great dark eyes moving side to side as she both scrutinized and turned her hooked nose upward at the grandeur. The servants snickered behind their hands at the sight of her, and despite the gravity of the situation, but when Adraeus questioned the weathered old crone in the company of his closest advisors, she amazed one and all with the scope of her wisdom and self-assurance.

Duly impressed by her charisma—and hoping they were not *all* under some sort of spell themselves—Adraeus gave Celintha immediate and complete access to Princess Oblixta. She spent several days with the child, behind the closed door of the royal chamber, coming out only to request food and drink, along with clean clothes for the girl. Though curiosity ran rampant from the throne room down to the most menial cook in the great subterranean kitchens, it was only after a week that Celintha emerged in a spirit of triumph and approached the worried king to deliver her diagnosis. To the amazement of those present, she informed Adraeus that, far from being under the influence of any curse or malevolent entity, his daughter was herself the source of all the bewildering phenomena.

With a mixture of horror and fascination, the monarch of Kelnia listened as the haggard Celintha told him in no uncertain terms that

Oblixta was one of those very rare individuals born with what the ancients of the Dalorum hills and elsewhere called *lathua*, or "The Peerless Gift." Oblixta, she said, had the innate ability to consort with and even compel certain facets of the elemental powers governing the world in its course. She reminded the King that no one knew exactly *why* some were born with such a gift, and that it would likely be a long time indeed before anyone would realize to what extent the Princess herself was actually "gifted." In Celintha's esteemed opinion, barring a clear history of other, similarly talented fruit from the Cadrach family tree, the release of Oblixta's powers had likely been instigated by the distress attending the death of her mother. Adraeus was beside himself at such a revelation. Like anyone in the realm, he greatly feared the mystery of sorcery and all of its attendant arts, but asked Celintha to stay on at the castle and, if possible, dissuade the child from any further pursuit of her "abilities." Such things might be acceptable for wizened old ladies hailing from the midnight crossroads of distant provinces, the King thought, but not for a royal daughter. Celintha, however, spoke gravely to the mighty ruler:

"If your daughter possesses but a small strain of the Peerless Gift, it may indeed be possible to suppress some of her instincts. However, if she has just a fragment of the power I feel she *may* have, such a route will be most impossible. Then, she must be educated properly in the ways of true sorcery, lest the kingdom itself should one day fall under the weight of her untamed strength and petulance."

Leaving herself proudly in the service of her master, Celintha did linger for some time at Castle Cadrach to carefully supervise and observe the young Oblixta. She became a trusted friend and counselor to one and all, completely winning the child over—not through any enchantment or through the sharing of magical secrets, but through simple teaching of the ways of Truth, the infectious love of nature, and the pastime of heartfelt laughter. Very soon, the unsettling disturbances no longer came to afflict Oblixta and her handlers at Castle Cadrach, even during the child's most difficult moments, and soon she began to live her life as any other happy, beautiful girl, albeit one full of the energies and opportunities afforded by a privileged life and a sorceress for a constant teacher and companion. As for King Adraeus, he thanked Celintha for not overtly encouraging his daughter's proclivities (as previously requested) and, in turn, Celintha confided that, perhaps, the Princess was not as gifted in extraordinary ways as she had once surmised. It was best for all, the old witch agreed, if the greatest "magic" in her existence turned-out to be simple and abiding happiness.

When all seemed calm once more in the tiny universe of the great castle, old Celintha went back to her own province, refusing all material gifts of gratitude, and the storm of Oblixta's crisis seemed, at long last, to have been weathered. Closure even in the death of the beloved Queen Laredana had been attained. Though the next few years were marked by continued tensions between Kelnia and rebellious Colstra, Oblixta was unaffected by her father's nagging worries and grew into a lovely young lady. Though spoiled as ever by her doting father and retinue of servants, she was happy; the tutelage of Celintha had been a powerful influence.

One summer, when the Princess was thirteen years of age, word began to spread like a rapid fire throughout Kelnia that Adraeus was finally ready to take another wife. This was news of immense importance, for though Adraeus was generally adored by his people, it had become a worrisome rumor that he would never again marry and thus would never produce a male heir to the throne. The happier rumor proved to be true and, in the following spring, Adraeus took as his second wife the Lady Mirysta, fair daughter of a Colstran nobleman. Not only was this marriage a diplomatic coup in the hitherto strained relations with Colstra, but it soon produced the male progeny so desired by the Kelnian populace. The realm rode a wave of festivity even more exuberant than it had following the birth of Princess Oblixta. At the appointed time, the new Prince was given the name "Starbane," for on the first night that he was placed in his elaborate cradle as a newborn, the midwives and nurses gasped to behold from a window that the sparkle of the entire firmament of stars was eclipsed across the heavens, as if in deference to the light of the royal newborn beneath their gaze. It was a glorious portent, they concurred, and shared the wondrous news with Queen Mirysta, who was bewildered but joyfully agreed.

Naturally, Adraeus bathed the infant Prince in all the love he had shown to his first child and hoped that Oblixta could share with them the exaltation of his arrival. To be certain, the Princess appeared to love the baby as much as her father and new stepmother, but it was said that—from the beginning—the new Queen Mirysta became jealous of any attachment Adraeus had for his first child and therefore treated the budding Oblixta with a cool disdain. As she was still quite young, the Princess could only be perplexed by the subtle cruelty of this sentiment.

As the years rolled onward, the upbringing of the Prince began to assume far more formal characteristics. After all, he needed to be groomed to one day rule in his father's stead. Thus, the attentions of the King and Queen were turned almost exclusively toward young Starbane's development. It was during this period that, many believed, a sliver of envy first began to pierce the heart of Oblixta. She had assumed that all of the fuss would fade away after her brother passed the stage of infancy and was no longer able to display the endearing qualities that only happy babies can employ to win hearts. She was disheartened to see that her step-brother's first steps and first words had come to be awaited with far more anticipation and excitement than her own notable achievements. In the preceding years, she had learned to ride the sleek thoroughbreds in her stable with an expertise that astounded her trainers. She had likewise learned to paint with deft strokes that drew high praise from far more experienced castle artisans. Still, the Princess came to feel quite secondary, and not without reason, if the rumors are true.

Of course, King Adraeus still adored his daughter, but a new child tends to be more consistently fascinating—if not more beloved—that the one that came before. Queen Mirysta, for her part, was calculating in her efforts to keep her husband's attention riveted upon their son. Old enough now to sense this disparity, Oblixta gradually began to withdraw and, in her furtive introspection, she delved deep into places and instincts long thought to be buried and forgotten. Now, however, no one in the castle seemed to give much notice to the changes in her personality, so caught-up were they in the latest developments concerning Prince Starbane. Slowly, back came the sleepless nights of Oblixta's early childhood and, with those nights, came the strange longing to wander alone in the darkest hallways of the castle or its most secluded groves and gardens. The Princess found her interests drawn away from the activities typical of a young lady of high estate and replaced with a wild desire to haunt the woodland expanse that bordered the castle grounds, particularly as dusk fell. That was Oblixta's favored hour—the murky passage from day into night, a transitional encounter between worlds, a time and place where even shadows met their defeat.

The Princess began to keep constantly to herself, venting her frustrations by avidly exploring the strange impulses that seemed to engulf her from every conceivable corner of existence. Trapped in this mindset, she sought to distance herself from regular people and cultivate friendships with the nocturnal creatures of the forest, forsaking the cheerful and exotic beasts sequestered within the animal reserve that had been built for her pleasure alone, and which was now the favorite domain of the tiny, curious Prince Starbane. At night, Oblixta would slip with ease past the omnipresent castle guards, willing herself to vanish down dark corridors and eventually into the thick forest beyond the enclosure walls, unafraid to roam amid sinister-looking trees, breathing the scents of the living woodland and hearkening to its lonely sounds. Before long, nothing in that untamed blackness alarmed her and with boldness she dared to spy upon the hidden and magical beings known to inhabit such places. These were creatures that normally shunned the sight of people, preferring instead to work mischief upon them while their backs were turned.

But Oblixta found a new home among such immortal denizens of the night. The wood nymph, the sprite, and even the reclusive dryads came to the girl, irresistibly drawn to her innate magical presence like moths to torchlight. They sensed her burgeoning powers, and the desires that such powers inspired deep within the Princess's soul. At first, Oblixta was wary of their inquisitive looks and baleful whispers, but as months passed, she found herself beckoned to their most secret hideaways and meeting-places, unrestrained. There, she was made privy to scenes that few in the mortal world ever saw, save those unlucky enough to stumble upon them by chance, or foolish enough to observe them uninvited. Such interlopers often paid harsh penalty for their intrusions, but Princess Oblixta of Cadrach was a welcome and regular guest at these revelries. Such mystical and clandestine forays gave Oblixta an overwhelming confidence, lifting her spirits out of their former state of brooding within the castle walls. The strange new companions began to encourage her in shrill admonitions to forsake the ways of mortals altogether and join them entirely and forever as a true Daughter of the Forest.

The Princess's parents would approach her, the toddling Starbane in tow, urging her to share their insatiable interest in the boy, but she would join them only for scant moments and then race swiftly away to her own ethereal affairs. From time to time, she still tried to win King Adraeus's attention by showing him some new painting, a bit of complex needlework, or by inviting him to watch her jump the gables and puddles on Warwing, her most prized steed. Alas, when the King and Queen were not burdened with affairs of state, they remained transfixed by the Prince. Oblixta finally stopped trying to impress them altogether. Even so, her existence was not completely void of human interest during these days.

One autumn she became enamored of a young groomsman at her stable, a strapping, handsome lad who was himself captivated by the ever-growing beauty of the Cadrach Princess. Although he was the son of a worthy local farmer seeking to gain some form of royal favor, Oblixta took great pleasure listening to his unpolished talk and found herself oddly mesmerized by tales of simple country life beyond the splendor of the castle. Having become adamant about her desire for unsupervised freedom—and capable of securing it by numerous acquired skills, if necessary—Oblixta was likewise assisted by her bevy of impish immortal friends. These cohorts would help her steal the groomsman deep into the woods, and they watched hungrily as the two shared laughter and secrets beneath the creeping cover of the mighty trees.

Thus it was that, at the time in her life when Oblixta felt most abandoned and ignored by her family, and most jaded with her life at court, she discovered the simple pleasures of youthful, romantic love.

But the eager assistance of those in the magical realm had a counter-productive effect, as far as their own unsavory goals were concerned: Oblixta's mystical leanings began to languish and the desire to consort with the Denizens of Shadow gave way to the need for intimacy with her suitor. For his own part, the Princess's would-be lover was frank about his fear of being discovered. He would often remind her that he could never take any proper place at her side, and this angered the willful Oblixta. Naively, she assured him that her father the King would never find out about their relationship. Her eerie companions of the woodlands and deep caverns, however, had by this juncture grown jealous and infuriated with her deepening neglect of their revelries. To them, enjoying proximity to her inner-power had been as intoxicating as the radiance of moonlight itself. Messengers from the fey world were duly sent to the King himself one evening, as he stood gazing in admiration near the bedside of Prince Starbane. In their sly and invisible manner, these regents of the Mischievous Realm whispered to the King's deepest intuition a disloyal tale of Oblixta's secret, girlish dalliance.

For the first time in a long time, the Princess recaptured her father's full and undivided attention, though not in a way she desired. The normally even-tempered Adraeus flew into a rage, castigating his daughter at the very thought that she, Princess of Kelnia, would consort romantically with a mere stable-hand. The unfortunate fellow was soon apprehended by castle guards and thrown into the dungeon until it could be proved that Oblixta's virtue had not been physically compromised. This latter diagnosis was obtained by the Healer-Prophets of the Temple of Dryndym, their cold examination a shameful experience for the weeping, protesting girl. Luckily for her companion, their encounters had not yet become physical and King Adraeus sentenced the boy to exile, rather than torture and death.

Strict orders were given to Oblixta lest she ever think of fraternizing with such undesirable types again. Moreover, at the behest of the hideously gleeful Queen Mirysta, the Princess's freedoms were curtailed altogether. The decisions were brutal and longstanding. Oblixta's reaction was one of swift, unparalleled depression. She remained in seclusion in her apartments—though not by choice—and there she wept for her lost love, vowing never to speak with her father again. As the days passed she allowed and even *willed* her heart to grow colder in its regard for him. Adraeus merely assumed his daughter would get over the entire incident and, goaded again by Mirysta, he unwisely left her well alone in her mounting despair and anger. Bereft of family and friend, cast aside to gnaw upon regret, the Princess began to entertain a seething bitterness in her heart, one that would engulf her entire being, in time.

This rancor became a chosen affliction, a new "romance" for her, of sorts. It was a disposition welcomed by both the passion of her resentful thoughts and by the reinvigorated support of those deceitful demons that, having once betrayed her, soon flocked to console her. Even as the initial sting of the incident began to fade and Oblixta's tears dried forever, she did not simply *find* herself to be rife with anger. Rather, she *devoted* herself to the emotion. Those few who knew her well and preserved such intuitions in their hearts were to look back in later years, pointing to this particular time as the most pivotal in her developing career. Indeed, all of the separate ingredients were in place at the right instant for the entire brew of her life to turn irrevocably sour.

At the height of Oblixta's misery, a particularly malicious sprite named Grimalgeron, who had lately been "possessing" the form of one of the stone gargoyles decorating the ramparts of the castle keep, encouraged the Princess to run away from her family to seek-out the old witch, Celintha, who had so impressed her childhood with tales of magic, and of the special powers available only to a chosen few. Grimalgeron, in his sly gargoyle trappings, and with his raspy gargoyle whisperings, told Oblixta that this woman could teach her how to work charms upon her father and perhaps regain the attention she had long ago lost to the prince. In her steady cultivation of dark thought, the Princess agreed, thinking that her spirit-companions had only her best interests at heart. In truth, however, the meddlesome lot wished chiefly to wreak havoc and interfere with the lives of unsuspecting mortals in any way they could. In choosing Oblixta as their potent medium, they had no way of knowing that they were sealing their own doom, as well.

So it came to pass that, under cover of night and with only scant possessions, the Princess escaped Castle Cadrach and made for the distant hill country of Dalorum, where she knew Celintha might be found. After a grueling month of travel with the help of her familiars and certain kind strangers who saw her wandering the roadways disguised in tattered rags, she reached the fabled province of her ancestors and was eventually directed to the tiny stone cottage of the sorceress. The place was sequestered deep among arid, rocky vales, well away from the teeming towns and villages. Celintha was genuinely amazed to see the Kelnian princess; Oblixta's immortal companions had hidden her approach well, though they themselves had withdrawn in fear before reaching the actual doorstep of the witch. The girl did not hesitate to inform Celintha that her father the King had experienced a change of heart and now wished his child to be educated in the ways of sorcery, after all. With kind, humble words and a seemingly genuine desire to develop her dormant gifts, the Princess charmed the elderly enchantress, who agreed to shelter and teach her, if such was the wish of the King.

Though Celintha was indeed skeptical about the very sudden manner of the Princess's arrival and the true nature of her intentions, she decided to honor Oblixta's word and not explore the matter immediately to her own satisfaction, as she could well have done. First, she warned the girl that the process would be long and arduous, but made an apprentice's place for her in the crumbling cottage all the same. Thereafter she began to instruct her unexpected pupil in the ancient and secret ways, revealing to Oblixta the forbidden disciplines, languages, and charms that only a person truly blessed with *lathua*—the Peerless Gift— might employ to any real effect. It was indeed a difficult and, at times, dangerous path for Oblixta. The old woman did not cater to her royal status. As a willing novice of the Mysterious Arts, the Princess renounced comforts and worked as something of a handmaiden to her mistress, sweeping floors even as she memorized bizarre chants and circuitous incantations. As time passed in their seclusion, Oblixta proved a swift pupil and more and more of the "experiments" Celintha contrived for her met with success.

The elder witch was careful to remind the Princess that she was learning a mere "beginner's sorcery," and that such lessons drew only upon one small dimension of her inexperienced talents ... not to mention the unique relationship that she shared with the hidden, elemental powers. Oblixta would often spend entire days, from dawn until dusk, struggling to channel her abilities simply to make a cup topple from the edge of a shelf onto the floor. Celintha, though miserly with praise, was in her heart quite impressed by the progress of her charge and, in due time, she discerned what she had suspected since meeting her long ago at Castle Cadrach: Oblixta's potential was great, indeed. As the girl honed her skills and practiced feverishly the often excruciating exercises required to draw the inner gifts to the visible realm, she begged Celintha to take her to the next level, even deeper into Magic. There she hoped to discover the wellspring that would empower more complicated forms of the Craft.

Celintha's refusal, however, was adamant; the desire to rush was natural, but any attempt to do so was foolhardy at best and potentially lethal, at worst. Even so, Oblixta began to envy the older woman's powers. Whereas the Princess needed to suffer and strain to ignite the tiny wick of a candle, Celintha could set an entire hearth full of logs aflame with the same spell and little effort. When Oblixta lifted her milk-white arms toward the heavens to beg rain from the clouds, only a few meager drops would batter her eyelids—if she was lucky. Celintha, on the other hand, could bring down a luxurious shower with a mere pass of one gnarled finger.

The girl's impatience grew unbearable. At night, when her trusted mentor was asleep, or during the day, when they were not off among the hills or in the scraggly woods searching for this or that ingredient for a potion, Oblixta secretly delved into Celintha's sacred books. What marvels were contained within! There, she discovered skills and secrets that she was certain the old sorceress had been deliberately hiding from her out of fear that she would learn too much, that the student would come to outshine the teacher. With stealth, Oblixta read the tomes and memorized as much as she could and, when free time was available, she ventured off alone to practice what she had learned in secluded places.

Of course, while all of this was going on deep in the Dalorum hill country, the rest of Kelnia was in an uproar over its missing Princess. Within days of her initial disappearance, a distraught Adraeus had orchestrated massive, kingdom-wide efforts to locate his eldest child. Having only the rarest contact with her neighbors in the Dalorum region and having promised not to magically scrutinize Oblixta's original intentions, Celintha had remained ignorant of the frantic search. One day, however, a small contingent of soldiers from Castle Cadrach found its way to her door. They had been sent to beg the sorceress's powers in the effort to find the King's daughter. Realizing at once that she had been misled from the beginning, the trusting Celintha turned Oblixta over to the men and, in her anger, chastised the girl for such a cruel and unworthy deception.

Oblixta was trapped, but resolved not to go back to the castle to face her father's wrath—much less the gloating punishment of Queen Mirysta—under any circumstance. Throughout the first day's journey home in the custody of Adraeus's henchmen, she plotted her escape. That very night, using certain spells she had been acquiring (openly and in secret) from Celintha, the Princess conjured an illusion that allowed her to slip away from the tent in which she was confined and beyond the sight of the sentry guards. Grimalgeron, her gargoyle servant from Cadrach Castle, was slavering, waiting in the midnight mists, to receive her. No one at Castle Cadrach was to see Oblixta again for many years.

∾∾

"So, the stories we have heard are true, for the most part," said Telvyn Rakahr, staring in solemnity at the floor. "She was touched by black sorcery even as a child."

"Not necessarily," countered Starbane. "You have to understand that my parents encouraged virtue, despite whatever faults they themselves may have had, particularly my mother. Oblixta was gifted, but not always evil, I believe. Besides, there's much more to the story. More that happened *after* she escaped from the guards that night on the road back to the castle."

"Ah, yes," said Rakahr with a grim nod. "The tales about Oblixta and Cabrus the Mage, and the more recent tale of Oblixta and Gragan. Just two of the great wizards she ensnared. We know how Gragan ended up, but in ancient times he was said to be good and merciful, before wandering onto darker pathways. How he fell into association with the Southern warlock, Rowan Blaize, is largely unknown to us, but legend holds that the two originally met here, in Kelnia."

"There's also that business with the Legion of the Viper," added Telize. "Let's not forget about them. Are those stories true as well?"

Starbane closed his eyes and sighed. "I'm afraid so. But I know only bits and pieces of these matters, things my parents managed to tell me that they, in turn, learned secondhand over the years from their spies and other sources."

Rakahr took a long drink of goat's milk from his cup and sat rigid, a new determination crossing his wrinkled and weary visage. "Those stories must be for another time, Your Highness. Above all, you must now be told why *we've* involved ourselves in your deliverance."

"Yes, I've been a bit curious, to say the least. Especially after all of this running about and blasted secrecy."

"You already know that you're going to be taken to Corydia and the court of King Sye," said Rakahr. "It is crucial that our Kashizma operatives get you there safely and, once there, that you seek asylum and remain under the protection of the powerful king until further notice."

"After what's happened to me, that sounds like a fine plan," agreed Starbane. "But I was likewise sent to seek the help of Rowan Blaize, this sorcerer everyone keeps going on about. The Gragan branded me for this purpose, and Celintha soon set me free from the castle to see that this same plan was fulfilled. They want me to get his magical help to take their revenge—*our* revenge—upon my sister. I can't linger forever as a refugee in the domain of King Sye, who won't even cross the mountains to fight her. Besides, I know that Oblixta's minions are after me. I'm lucky to have made it here without being caught and carted back to her dungeons already. How, exactly, are you going to get me out of the city, much less over those fearsome mountains? Surely my sister has posted watchmen at every conceivable escape route."

Rakahr raised a hand of reassurance.

"Not to worry. Not *too* much, at least. To begin, you'll have to speak with King Sye about the issue of Rowan Blaize, whoever he is. This is where our work and the particular goals of Celintha and the Gragan wizard intersect, but do not necessarily agree. We cannot instruct you in magical ambitions, for that is beyond our jurisdiction. In terms of your escape, we've thought of everything. Now, around the back of my tavern there is a covered buckboard loaded with empty beer kegs that need to be filled with water from the Charbex Springs, which flow just beyond Kurda Road, at Voyager's Pass, the first of many passes that lead up the side of the Great Pyr Mida Mountain. I go to the springs about twice a month to fill my kegs and return. I use the water to brew my ales and lagers and so forth."

"But if these springs are beyond the official borders of Kelnia, how do you manage it? Hasn't Oblixta forbidden everyone from crossing? I recall that much from my days in the dungeons beneath Castle Cadrach. And what, pray tell, does my escape over those mountains have to do with empty beer kegs?"

Rakahr stared mischievously at the curious youth. "You're right about the border restrictions. No one's allowed to cross. But I've gotten to know the lieutenant in charge of the sentry post at Voyager's Pass and, though I despise the trade-off, I give him one keg of my best stuff each month to look the other way and let me cross the short distance to the springs. Oblixta may have all of her legions in some sort of magical thrall, but even sorcery can't quell old-fashioned greed in the human heart, apparently. It's inside one of those empty kegs that *you* will be hidden when we approach the border patrol."

"You've got to be kidding!" said Starbane.

"Not at all," replied Rakahr, stroking his moustache thoughtfully. "It's really an excellent means to get you through. Like I said, my associates and I have spent the night planning it all out."

The Prince's mind began yet another whirl into some vortex. "But ... I don't understand. Aren't springs normally frozen in winter, or have the laws of nature changed with my sister's domination? Wait, don't answer that. The better question is whether the border patrol will somehow discover me if we even try such a thing. It sounds awfully risky."

"First of all, the Charbex Springs have never frozen," replied Rakahr. "Not even in the most ferocious winters. It's a hot spring that many believe was enchanted by some itinerant magician—some even say it was Rowan Blaize!—passing through our land long ago, as an act of benevolence, but that's hardly important now. Trust me, the freshwater springs are positively gushing, as usual. Once we have reached them, we'll meet-up with a special escort chosen by the Kashizma. He'll be waiting in the woods nearby. Our man will then take you over the mountain and all the way to Sye's castle, deep in the heart of South Corydia. It'll be quite a journey, but once you're over the peril of the mountain, everything should be rather straightforward ... no pun intended."

The Prince gnawed nervously at another hard crust of bread, still not satisfied. "You say it's just one man who'll get me to the other side of the mountains? Excuse me for seeming doubtful, but I might've expect a few more than that, especially if you knew I was coming. You know, for security. I realize I don't look the part, but I *am* a prince, in case you haven't forgotten."

Rakahr shook his head. "One escort only. The more bodies involved, the more complicated and slow the progress, as well as more potential for trouble. These mountains aren't exactly free of danger. Bandits and cutthroats call the Great Mountain home, out of hatred for Oblixta and pursuit of their own foul plans that have nothing to do with any kingdom, good or bad. But the one who'll accompany you is unquestionably the most fearless warrior and accomplished scout in our order of spies. You're lucky to get him—he's usually busy with other, more dangerous matters this time of year."

"Dyrndym forbid *my* plight take him away from his regular duties," said Starbane, peeved and restless now. "More dangerous matters, indeed. What's his name?"

"Talthagar," replied Rakahr.

"Never heard of him."

"You don't *need* to have heard of him. He's the best. That's all you need to know."

"Well, I certainly hope this works, Rakahr. I've got a sorcerer to find, no matter how much your order of spies may wish me to hide behind the robes of King Sye. I suppose I haven't got much of a choice, either way."

"Our plan must work, Your Highness and, no, you don't have any other choice. We wouldn't even let you go back to Castle Cadrach at this point, if you were insane enough to want it. Your destiny lies elsewhere. King Sye will be open to receiving you and learning more of the things you've told us. That's what he wants. And, when the Kashizma can boast that it has led you safely to the court of the Corydian king, we can perhaps make critical inroads toward mobilizing that portion of the Kelnian people who have yet been ever on the brink of joining the rebels' cause. Your living presence, even in Corydia, might give them the push they need, for we fully expect Oblixta to go to war with King Sye at some point, Rowan Blaize or no Rowan Blaize!"

"It seems you're forgetting something rather important here," said Starbane, leaning forward in his chair with a grim smile. "Namely, that my sister is a very powerful, very *dangerous* sorceress on her own. It's not men or swords that King Sye—or any of you—will be facing when her wrath is revealed. How do you think she got as far as she has over the years? Sure, that putrid General Kerrion and his legions do all her dirty work now, but I guarantee you, if she sees things going even slightly off-course, she'll step in and curse the lot of you. What'll you do then? That's why I've been set free and advised to seek out additional magical help. Not only by the good hag, Celintha, but by that festering old Gragan himself. The one who burned his ring into my skin while we were *both* prisoners of Oblixta! This Rowan Blaize would probably like to be warned that Oblixta is collecting magicians like trophies these days."

Rakahr frowned, raising one of his magnificent eyebrows.

"Yes, yes. We are well aware of the problem of your sister's magic. The Kashizma have been wrestling with this matter for some time. But as we've told you, King Sye must be consulted before you go trifling with an enchanter that he considers to be his own royal property, as it were. And we're not certain how much the King himself knows about Rowan Blaize, who supposedly lives practically under his nose, in the Forest of Shadnai!"

"Yes, your dear wife alluded to some very disheartening things in that regard, earlier," said Starbane with a glance at Telize. "What's all of this about Blaize not having been seen in centuries?"

"Again, that's business you must take-up with King Sye," said Rakahr.

"And again I say to you that Celintha—and obviously Gragan—felt that I should seek the aid of this rival sorcerer, someone disposed to lend his skills for the sake of bringing Oblixta down. I'm assuming that Celintha knew all along she wasn't strong enough to challenge my sister, but she seemed certain that this other creature might be, and once she saw the mark on my arm, she was even more enthusiastic. She did set me free, after all."

"Again, good Prince, I can only tell you that we know nothing with certainty about the magnitude of Rowan Blaize's powers," said Rakahr.

"I don't suppose you do. I'm probably mad to even attempt such a thing. By the gods, dealing with another sorcerer, *any* sorcerer, is foolhardy enough."

"Well, I don't blame you for being wary of magic. We members of the Kashizma have always had our reservations about it, or at least we did until Celintha became a friend and ally some time ago. The old girl's idea, and the Gragan wizard's insistence, may prove to be a dead-end. In her letters, though, she seemed quite determined. She spoke highly of Rowan Blaize, as we said, noting the past association he shared with the Gragan wizard, and the legend that Blaize himself did not even hail from this particular world, but from another. Now, however, he supposedly dwells in the farthest reaches of Corydia, past the boundaries of the Turbax Diadem Lords, in the Shadnai forest I mentioned, not far from King Sye's castle itself. In the old legends, he's feared by the distant peoples, but has a reputation for—how shall I put it?—occasional benevolence. Sye and the rest of the kingdom believe an old tale telling of their own ancient pact, one allegedly made between the sorcerer and Sye's forebears to protect Corydia from all usurpers. We know nothing more about it, and haven't a clue about how much more Sye may know, as I said."

"Ha! I'll believe in benevolent sorcerers when I see one, which may never happen, because all the ones *I've* ever heard about are vile, like Oblixta. Of course, Celintha is excluded from that despicable company. If this one's benevolent he must indeed be the last of his kind. But I plan to give it a go, no matter what. I've come too far to give up now." The Prince frowned over his breakfast, having little desire to inquire about any magician, good or otherwise. He had had enough of spells and enchantments to last him several lifetimes.

Rakahr rose from his place at the table and gazed upon the burgeoning day from a nearby window. The sun was shining across the snow-covered city, an almost blinding jewel in its ascent toward the vault of the morning sky. "Time runs away from us," he said after his eyes adjusted to the brilliance and he had taken a careful look around the parameters of the tavern. "To catch it we must leave at once. Please get the few things you have, Your Highness, dress warmly, and prepare yourself as best you can. Two of our men, the two who always ride to the Charbex spring to help me lift the kegs, will be here soon."

"How long will it take to reach this spring or collection of springs?"

"It'll be an hour's ride, if all goes according to plan." Rakahr paused, looking the lanky young prince up and down. "I'm afraid it won't be very comfortable for you. Like I said, our plan is to put you *inside* one of those kegs. They're large kegs, to be sure, but you're all arms and legs. It's going to be a bumpy trek to the Voyager's Pass."

"To get out of this nightmare I'd squeeze myself into a teacup, if I had to," sighed the youth.

He rose and thanked Telize for the hearty repast before returning to the little bedroom. There, he looked with dejection at his possessions—really just his boots, fur coat, and the satchel that Rufthar and Ona had given him upon leaving the encampment. Once more his nerves began to quiver at the prospect of danger and he wafted a quick prayer to Dyrndym that this latest, seemingly hasty, plan would actually work. He still didn't know much about these Kashizma spies—perhaps they *were* just a bunch of wayward trouble-makers, like Rufthar had said—but Celintha had been their friend and Telvyn Rakahr was the sanest person he had met in ages. He had no choice but to trust them now. He was "in the thick of it," as his beloved father was often fond of saying, and only a successful passage over the stern, snow-shrouded mountain could possibly get him out.

≈∽

"For once, Xerbex, I have to admit you've at least *finished* an important job. I won't discuss how long it took you to do it."

The festering rat-troll grinned and drooled, shifting back and forth on its haunches, pleased with the tempered satisfaction of Oblixta.

"You are certain that you saw the Prince Starbane?"

"Yes, my Queen," came the hissing reply. "The trail was hard to uncover, but once I did ... well ... time. It was only a matter of *that.*"

"I can't believe a sentinel-gnome led you to him," said Oblixta, staring out at the gleaming day from her tower. "I haven't been very nice to the woodland faery-types, lately. If ever. I'm sure the news about what I did to Bryn Tramayda has been spread about, too. And this spirit said that my brother was first attacked by Eskanthian werewolves and *survived?*"

"Yessss," hissed Xerbex. "I thought I'd have to interrogate one of the Ice Dryads to get anywhere, but the miserable sprite I caught had once been in the magical service of that old hag you killed, Celintha. The spell was broken when you executed her, but the sentinel-gnome kept following the boy, hoping to get hold of his things, if he were to meet with an ill fate."

"Ha! Those sorts of faeries can never be trusted unless you've got them positively *speared* with magic," snorted Oblixta. "So Starbane did indeed meet with trouble."

"Yessss, and once the boy had fallen, the gnome stole his things. It claimed to have had a satchel in its possession, one belonging to the boy. It said the Prince fended-off the Eskanthian beasts with some sort of fire spell."

"Nonsense," said Oblixta. "He has no magical skill. It must have been some potion or talisman of that viper-tongued besom, Celintha. Anyhow, where is this satchel?"

The troll drew a fetid breath. "The sentinel-gnome would only say that he'd taken it back to his own kind. He wouldn't reveal the place, of course. They never do, even when you've managed to sneak up behind them so perfectly, and when you've got them in your hands, and they are so stunned they can work no magic, and you are about to crush them like twigs. No, they never tell you where they live."

"I didn't ask for a lesson in sentinel-gnome courtesies," muttered Oblixta, casting an impatient eye on her servant. "Nor am I interested in your dietary fantasies, Xerbex. What else did the gnome tell you before you ate it?"

"Only what I already said," answered the troll. "The boy killed the beasts, somehow, and stumbled off into the forest. He was wounded. Bleeding an awful lot. The gnome followed for a distance, hoping to loot the whole body, once it fell, but the Prince managed to reach the edge of some mortal village or camp of some sort, where he was discovered by one of their women. The gnome was too frightened to go closer, or so it claimed—mortal women have charms against their kind, you see, and the gnome said it could feel the presence of iron in the vicinity while ..."

"Shut up already about the gnome!" snapped Oblixta. "Tell me again everything *you* saw."

"Well, Vuzbahg and I ate the wicked little thing up—Oh! Its thighs were most tasty!—but not before it at least pointed the way to this woodpile. It was near some sort of human hunting camp, I'd say, but I'm no expert in mortal things, of course. Many little houses. At night I kept myself well-hidden and glimpsed in windows when I could, where the fires were burning. In one of those little houses, I saw the Prince, sleeping in a bed, he was! Some women were looking after his wounds.

There's no doubt that it was him. I came back as soon as I could to tell you, but I can't help that it has taken me so long. I tracked him far, far away, Majesty. And it was far, far to come back. We trolls are not as swift as gnomes or dryads, to say nothing of your precious gargoyles!"

Oblixta drummed her talon-tipped fingers rapidly on the smooth obsidian stone of yet another ritual altar. "It's been a month since you left that place. I wonder if he's still there, if his wounds were severe enough to keep him there. You're certain he wasn't dead when you saw him?"

"No, no, Great One. I saw the breath rise and fall in his chest. I made sure to watch for that," added the troll, pointing at its skull in a grotesque attempt to indicate wisdom. "He is alive, your brother. Or, at least, he was when I saw him."

Oblixta paced back and forth between altar and tower window. "Whatever the case, I must act at once," she growled to herself. "He may be dead, but maybe not. If not, he may elude me again."

She turned to one of her blind, wraith-like handmaidens, standing near the door of the chamber with head bowed low; none of Oblixta's servants were allowed to look at her directly unless commanded to do so, and it was a boon that these specialized ladies could not do so even if they desired.

"You. Get word to General Kerrion that I wish to see him at once, and *you,*" she added, turning in the gloom to behold the filthy troll. "You may go with her to tell the General yourself where to find this camp of little houses."

Xerbex shuddered right down to the biting fleas beneath his matted fur. None of the trolls in Oblixta's ranks cared to cross paths with Kerrion, even with good news to relay.

"Get someone to dump a bucket of boiling water on you," said Oblixta as the foul creature bowed and began to slink away behind the silent maidservant. "You smell *worse* than a troll."

"As it pleases you, Mistress."

Alone, Oblixta allowed herself to gloat in the likelihood that Starbane would soon be within her grasp once again.

Eskanthian wolves, indeed! She laughed within the very midnight tar-pit of her soul. *How could that pampered little fool have survived the journey, much less an attack? Celintha must have done her very best.*

When Kerrion arrived she planned to dispatch a contingent to this place, wherever it was, from the Pyr Mida garrison and pluck the boy away, if he was there. The fools who had been hiding him would be tortured and killed, for good measure. Perhaps *that* would atone for some of the frustration she had endured in the past month. Meanwhile, she would accelerate and finalize her plans to get rid of Rowan Blaize and King Sye of Corydia. Her war-famished legions would finish everything else off, after that. Oblixta blessed the bloodcurdling spell-chamber with a scimitar smile. It was going to be a Spring to remember.

VI

Princes-by-the-Barrel … Demons-in-the-Downdraft

Not five minutes away from Telvyn Rakahr's tavern, the Prince was wracked with pain from head to foot. Bounced and jostled around in the empty beer-keg, barely able to breathe and struggling not to bite his tongue with every dip of the wagon wheels, he decided this plan was simply *not* going to work.

Rakahr and two burly accomplices had helped him into the back of the wagon, which had been parked in an alley and, once he was inside the first of four sour-smelling kegs, they had fit a round end back on to conceal his presence and popped it into place, leaving only two very small holes for ventilation. Whispering nervously all the while, the men tied the kegs firmly in place and then stretched an enormous patchwork leather canvas across the back of the wagon, leaving the Prince in total blackness. Now, the throbbing in his jiggled brain was making him angrier and more claustrophobic by the minute.

Trying to shift his body around in the receptacle offered no relief; it was all too cramped no matter how he maneuvered. Rakahr was right—he seemed to be nothing but interfering arms and legs, much to his dismay. In desperation, the boy kicked at one round end of his keg and the lid flew off against the inside of the wagon bed. He took in deep gulps of what meager stale air could be gulped underneath the canvas and worried about being able to get the lid back in place, should he need to do so in such a tight spot. Then he remembered that Rakahr said he knew the sentry at the border and passed unhindered all the time. No one was going to check the back of the wagon. Why Rakahr had put him to all of this inconvenience was an issue he determined to raise once they were safely onto the Voyager's Pass.

With an awkward and painful wiggling motion, Starbane crawled out of the keg, careful not to loosen it from the restraining ropes and bring it rolling against his back. He soon found that there was enough room to lie almost supine across the width of the wagon bed and stick a bit of Bog Bear glove out to lift the rawhide canvas in certain places, peeking outside. He could no longer see the city of Pyr Mida from his vantage point. There was only a glimpse of the road, a snake-like swath of slush and dirty snow with winding gray forest on either side.

Already, the fresh air coming in from the canvas peepholes made him feel at ease. If they stopped, or if he thought something was going wrong, he planned to crawl back into the barrel as fast as he could and pull the lid on behind. For what seemed like an eternity, he heard nothing except the creaking groan of the kegs and the slow whine of the wheels in rotation. If Rakahr and his henchmen were conversing up on the buckboard, he certainly couldn't hear them. Then, the vehicle came to an abrupt stop that made the Prince's heart pound with new anxiety, but his body was so jammed in its current spot that he didn't have enough time to crawl back into the empty barrel as planned. Instead he froze, holding his breath and straining to hear what he could. There were voices, muffled and yet sharp in tone. Rakahr was talking, but it didn't appear to be with his helpers. The fur of Starbane's hooded coat made it impossible to catch more than a few, scattered words and then, unmistakably, the sound of a young female voice.

What in the name of the gods is going on?

A moment later, he heard the crack of the whip and the jingling of the reins as the wagon resumed its course. Very discreetly, he opened another little viewing space in the oppressive canvas and was stunned to behold the face of a heavily bundled girl, trudging alone on the roadside as the wagon pulled away. *How bizarre,* Starbane thought, before his eyes nearly spun around and then out of his head. He recognized the forlorn figure—it was Ilyssa, the troubled girl from the previous night's drama at old Wyrnie's house! It was she who had come so desperately in search of refuge, and the Kelnian prince's heart fell to think that, in his own mad dash to secure the help of Telvyn Rakahr, he had forgotten all about her!

He yanked off a glove and quickly fumbling an entire hand through a canvas opening, he grappled for a few seconds, took firm hold of a crease and yanked with all his strength. Amazingly, the canvas flew back off the wagon-bed from the corner. Starbane stood up and nearly tumbled into the snow.

"Stop the wagon!" he yelled.

Rakahr and his men had already turned around, stunned, when the canvas had nearly flown over their heads. Now they saw their secret passenger, wobbling on the wagon bed, and their jaws dropped.

"What in the name of every god that lives are you *doing?*" hissed Rakahr. "Get down this instant! Have you gone mad?"

The Prince echoed his command to stop the rolling wagon and spun to face the girl, Ilyssa, who watched the whole strange scene, frozen and dumbfounded in a spot by the road.

"Stop this vehicle, Rakahr! That's a royal order!"

The thing came to a jolting halt that knocked the teetering prince from his already precarious stance and over the edge, head-first, in a full flip. He landed on his back in a snow-bank, unharmed, and called out to Ilyssa, fighting to extract himself from the awkward position. Ilyssa looked at him as if he were some wild and lanky beast—one that knew her name, no less!—and she turned to run for the forest. The discombobulated boy finally got to his feet and gave chase, which frightened the girl even more. By this time, Rakahr and his men had jumped from the buckboard, yelling and chasing after both the Prince and the girl in a chaotic procession.

Ilyssa didn't get far; she tripped over a snow-covered limb and this was all Starbane needed to overtake her, tumbling down beside her as she began to unleash a frightful howl. He clamped the furry Bog Bear glove he still wore to her mouth and stared into her eyes. They were a petrified blue.

"Ilyssa, it's alright! It's me, Starbane ... I mean, Gremm. I mean, *that's* how you would have known me last night. Don't you remember?"

She didn't. He took the glove away and the scream continued as if it had never been stifled. He put the glove back across her face.

"Now listen! I saw you last night at *Wyrnie's* house! I know all about your troubles. Don't you remember, even a little? I was one of the men that came from Rufthar's hunting encampment."

Ilyssa's eyes narrowed, but with clear skepticism. She obviously remembered the setting at Wyrnie's house, but still had no idea who this boy was. It had to be some sort of horrible trap. It was too bizarre *not* to be a trap.

"You must have escaped somehow," the Prince went on, half to himself, as Rakahr and his men approached out of breath through the mounds of snow. "I was going to help you last night, but so much has happened since then that I completely lost my head. You see, I'm on the run, as well. These angry men about to descend upon us are friends. They're helping me get out of the kingdom and into Corydia!"

Rakahr and his huffing, puffing brutes had stopped just short of the fallen twosome, begging Starbane to come to his senses.

"Your Highness, what's gotten into you?" begged Rakahr. "Do you want to get us all killed? Leave this girl and get back into the wagon immediately!"

"He's lost his mind," one of Rakahr's helpers marveled to the other. "He's crazy. We're all as good as dead."

Rakahr silenced his assistant with a cuff on the back of the head.

The Prince gathered a huge breath while maintaining his grip on the terrified Ilyssa.

"Rakahr, I know this girl," he said. "We've got to help her. She's trying to escape, too."

"What do you mean? When we stopped to ask her what she was doing way out here she told us she was out looking for a lost cat!"

The Prince looked at Ilyssa, but her eyes were still wide with bewildered fear.

"*I'm* telling you she's scared. She's running from Oblixta and her forces just as surely as I am. I insist we take her with us over the mountain into Corydia."

Rakahr moaned in exasperation, gazing this way and that along the lonesome stretch of road. "Please, Your Highness, there's no time to mess with this … this *girl,* whoever she is! If you don't get into the wagon we'll soon be caught and strung-up like pigs before the sun has set on this very day. Is that what you want?"

Starbane ignored him and faced Ilyssa, who by now was starting to get angry as well as terrified. "Listen to me, Ilyssa. I realize that you don't remember me from last night, but I was there, with Wyrnie and Rufthar and the rest, and I know your story. I know Ona and Wylla, back at the hunting camp. All of them! I'm a friend. These men are helping me get onto Voyager's Pass, past the Kelnian sentry, in the back of that wagon. If I insist, they'll let you come, too. Now tell me—do you want to get over this mountain alive and into Corydia, where you'll be safe from that Prefect? If so, you'll get up at once and walk with me. No screaming. Telvyn Rakahr, here, will hide us and we'll be off. If not, we're probably going to have to leave you here or risk getting killed ourselves. The choice is yours, but it's going to have to be a fast one. What do you say?"

The girl had stopped sniffling and looked the strangers over, one by one. She nodded her head and Starbane removed the glove from her lips.

"If you idiots really think you can get me out of this lousy country, I'll go along. I don't have a clue who any of you might be, and I'll thank you to get your miserable paws off my body, boy. But other than that, count me *in.*"

"Then it's settled. Come on." The Prince jumped up from the snowdrift and, pulling Ilyssa along in a stumbling flurry, faced Rakahr. The other men had already been sent back to the wagon.

"Rakahr, we're taking her with us. I don't care how we do it, but we're going to get it done. Find a way to get us both past the sentry. By the way, I am speaking to you as the son of Adraeus Cadrach and only *true* heir to the throne of this miserable kingdom."

Starbane tried to make this last bit sound as weighty as he could, but was nevertheless uncertain. Beyond the occasional dinner request or childhood indulgence, he had never given a serious royal order in his life. Rakahr, meanwhile, looked as if he had aged another ten years since the youngster had jumped from the wagon. He stood blinking at the two before him, caught between the instinct that this new twist was guaranteed to bring disaster and the realization that the Prince was not going to relent. Ilyssa was now staring agog at them both, after absorbing the "only true heir" declaration.

"What kind of weird, crazy world was I born into?" she muttered. "What kind of screwed-up dream am I having, out here, on a mountain road, where I'd just as soon lay down and die? Did you just say you're some kind of royalty? Am I already losing my mind from the cold? Who *are* you people? By the gods, I should just take off and throw myself over a cliff before my life gets any more insane."

"Okay. Alright," said Rakahr, trying not to hyperventilate. "The girl goes, if she can keep her mouth shut. We'll figure it out, but you've both got to get in the wagon without delay! We'll put the girl in the other empty beer barrel, but if she panics and loses her nerve in the dark and screams, we're all dead and this'll be *your* fault, Your Highness, no offense meant. Oh, gods … what am I doing?"

"Right now you're babbling," said Starbane, leading Ilyssa toward the wagon.

"And I'm not gonna scream because of a little darkness," snapped Ilyssa. "Do you have any idea what I've been through since last night alone, old man? I will *take you down* if I hear insults from you or anybody else in this crazy dream. Er … did you really mention a beer barrel?"

"Let's just get out of here," urged the Prince. "I'll explain everything to you as soon as we're safely onto the Voyager's Pass."

&∼&

An hour later, with only one grand curve left in the circuitous roadway before reaching the Charbex Springs, Tel Rakahr wiped nervous sweat from his brow and rejoiced silently with his men at their success. They had made it through the border sentry's checkpoint with the usual bribe of one splendid keg of Telize's best brew and not a peep from Starbane and Ilyssa, hiding as they were in two of the three empty barrels.

Love of beer saves the kingdom, mused Rakahr, feeling frightened and a little daft. He ordered his equally relieved men to keep an eye out for interlopers, but knew everything was accomplished; the guardhouse—with its satisfied sentry—was now a mile behind them. The team of white mares pulled the ramshackle wagon off the main road and onto a narrower path hidden behind a massive hedge of Moab bramble. They came to a halt some two hundred feet ahead in a circular clearing. The wintry meadow was surrounded by a thick army of white Thadnus trees and, rising in the middle, was a rugged array of gray, steaming boulders. From the cracked center of one such rock gushed a steady stream of hot water. This fountain bubbled merrily down and melted a winding channel in the snow before vanishing in the deeper woods. Above them soared the largest of the Pyr Midan mountain peaks, crowned with thin clouds that lingered like obsequious ghosts around the head of some disdainful god. Cyr Mida and Val Mida, the smaller but ruthlessly sheer sister-mountains, kept watch on either side with their coterie of perilous canyons and ridgelines.

In the clearing, Rakahr instructed his men to free the precious-but-secret cargo. The jostled youths emerged, dizzy and disheveled, from their barrels; the Prince was already full of questions.

"Yes, yes, everything went off without a hitch at the sentry post," assured Rakahr. "Oblixta would skin that sentry alive, or worse, for breaching security on account of ale, but he and his cohorts will be too drunk to care for the next few days, I expect."

"Then we've made it! You *are* a master spy and no mistake."

"That may be, but you're not out of the woods yet, and I do mean that literally," replied Rakahr, glancing around with concern at the menacing forest. "How about you, girl, are you alright?"

"Yes ... I'm ... I'm fine. I'm alright. Just a little banged-up. But I must say that I still am not quite certain that any of you really, truly exist. I'm beginning to wonder if I may be dead, after all." Ilyssa stood rigid against one side of the wagon as Rakahr's men rolled the kegs into the snow. "They say you see strange things when you're dead, and you people are about as strange as they come. But, I've pinched myself several times, and felt my head smacking into that beer barrel as we rode to wherever we are now, so if this *is* death, then it's better than death, which is what I was expecting, anyway."

"Well, that ... er ... answers *that* question," mumbled Rakahr with a wide-eyed glare at the shaken lass.

"I'm sorry to have put you on the spot back there, Rakahr, but I met this girl yesterday evening," Starbane explained. "She was about to be handed over to the Prefect of Pyr Mida and Rufthar from the encampment wasn't able to——"

"It's a long story, I get it," interrupted the old spy, pressing a palm to his aching forehead. "I'm also familiar with that miserable Prefect. I don't blame you for wanting to help her. There's much we didn't have time to learn about your adventures last night and I'm afraid we're in the same situation now, Your Highness. No time. I trust you about this girl, of course. One day, perhaps, you can tell me *all* about how you two managed to meet up, but my present concern is sending you off. Quickly."

"Right," said the Prince. "Out here in the middle of nowhere, too. What happens next?"

"*He* happens," said Rakahr, pointing behind them with an enormous sigh of relief.

Starbane and Ilyssa turned toward the sound of the powdery thud of snowshoes coming from a thicket.

"Glad you're finally here. I got a little scared, waiting alone in the trees," said the most impressive man Starbane had ever seen. A head taller than his famously tall father, Adraeus, with raven-black hair to the shoulders, the boxed-jaw of a lion, and a build that would have matched any of his father's best warriors, the Prince was momentarily stunned as the brutish figure swaggered into their midst. Chewing absently on what looked like a piece of bark, the buckskin and Bog Bear fur-clad man stared at the boy and the girl with eyes the color and intensity of thunderclouds.

"So. I take it *this* is the Prince Starbane everyone's been talking about, Rakahr?"

The behemoth held out a huge hand and, after initial hesitation, the Prince shook it, his fingers slightly crushed by the grip.

"Yes, I am the son of King Adraeus, the Prince Starbane Cadrach of Kelnia," said the boy, drawing himself up as regally as possible, though it seemed to be a wasted impression.

"Yeah, right. It's a regular honor to meet you," said the man, his voice tinged with mock reverence. With an almost imperceptible bow of his head he turned next to Ilyssa.

"And who's this? No, don't tell me. You're a prin*cess,* right?"

"Watch it, smart-mouth," warned Ilyssa. "I've just had the worst night and morning of my entire life and if you don't think I'm up to scratching the eyes right out of your square skull, you've got another thing coming. I hate sarcasm. Anyway, who *are* all you people?" Ilyssa turned with a maddening gaze to her new companions. "Starbanes? Barrels? Kings? Giant oafs coming out of the woods? Is this some kind of cruel joke?"

"Now calm down, young lady," said Rakahr. "Get a hold of her, Your Highness, I do think she's looking a bit faint, or hysterical, or both. In any case, there is nothing to worry about. This is Talthagar, the finest warrior-spy and scout in the Order of the Kashizma. He'll be leading you both over the mountain and into Corydia. Really, Talthagar, you're a sight for sore eyes."

"Hey, you asked me to be here," drawled the warrior. "But could you lay off the 'finest warrior-spy' thing for once, Rakahr? I get so sick of hearing that. Why does a warrior-spy always have to be the 'finest-ever' when one of these crucial end-of-the-world situations comes along? Answer me that. It puts a lot of pressure on a fella, and somebody still ends-up writing a song about it. Besides, I'm tired of this gig. And what's with the girl? You said I'd be traveling with the royal what's-his-name *alone.* The ride's gonna be rough enough without a chickadee to slow me down. No offense, Miss, before you decide to scratch the eyes out of my square skull. What gives, Rakahr?"

Starbane felt his cheeks flush as he helped the unsteady Ilyssa sit on the back of the wagon bed. "Her name is Ilyssa. She's not a 'chicka-dee,' and I might as well tell you right now that she's coming with us over the mountain! Now stop frightening her with your condescending talk, you brute." He turned to Rakahr. "Is this the kind of warrior you think can get us safely to King Sye in Corydia?"

"What did you say, you little twerp?" muttered Talthagar.

"Oh, of all the *impertinence!*" gasped Starbane. He had heard his father use this expression often to powerful effect; now seemed as good a time as any to try it out for himself.

"Stop it, both of you," snarled Rakahr, trying to think of a diplomatic solution to the dubious first-impressions being made. "Talthagar, there's been a change in plan, I'm afraid. You'll have to make due. The girl is going along. It's to do with some business concerning the wretched Prefect of Pyr Mida, as far as I can surmise. Who knows? And Prince Cadrach, I highly recommend that you watch your temper with Talthagar—your life is in *his* hands and crossing this mountain is not going to be an afternoon stroll in the palace garden!"

"That's sure as heck right," said Talthagar.

"A little respect for the Royal wouldn't hurt on your part, either," growled Rakahr.

"*That's* sure as heck right," said Starbane.

"Alright, alright," said Talthagar, rolling his storm-cloud eyes. "But listen close, Starbane Whoever-You-Are. You and your girlfriend here can start getting ready for the trip, because like Rakahr said, this ain't gonna be some court waltz. I know what's going on. I've been briefed." He twirled his hand at the sky in mockery. "Yeah, I know all about it. You're the one who bears the mark of some gabbling old wizard because you're supposedly seeking some *other* wizard to help you bump-off the witch that's your *sister.* Please keep in mind that, if the added burden of this girl slows us down and we run into trouble, you can blame yourselves, not me. Otherwise, I'll stand by you and defend you to the death. Fair enough?" Talthagar leaned in close and smiled, teeth shining white as the snow.

Starbane fought a rising tide of adolescent wrath. "I *suppose* it'll have to do."

"It will," said Talthagar, seriously.

"Please, you two," said Rakahr. "We've wasted enough time as it is. The pass patrol will start to wonder what's taking us so long and my men are still filling those kegs from the spring. Talthagar, get them out of here, and you two," he added, turning with feigned fatherly affection to Starbane and Ilyssa, "… put your trust in this man. *Please?* He's your only means of reaching King Sye's realm safely. He wasn't lying when he said he'd guard you with his life. Just disregard his manners, if it comes to it."

Ilyssa emerged from her shocked agitation and began to shiver. "The old codger is right," she said. "The patrol, or whatever he's talking about, may come looking. We need to get out of here. And I'm *freezing*. If you people are princes and warrior-spies and such, can't you figure out how to light a fire under your rear ends and hurry it up?"

"Testy, ain't she?" said Talthagar. "Alright, you kids follow me. My horse is just ahead in the thicket. I've got supplies and snowshoes enough for both of you. The girl's going to need more warm clothing than she's got on, but she can ride on my horse while we walk alongside, Prince Starbane." The warrior's smiled now flashed with sarcasm at the boy. "It won't ever be said that Talthagar is not a gentleman."

"I'm perfectly happy walking," spouted the Prince as Talthagar sauntered toward the forest. "Been doing a lot of that lately, I'll have you know."

Telvyn Rakahr turned to the boy a final time before they followed their new guardian. "It *has* been an honor to meet you, Prince Cadrach, I must say. This whole mission has been an adventure. The older I get, the more these sorts of thrills become a *real* bother, but we can't do much about that, can we? I know I haven't had time to explain more to you from my end of things, but Talthagar will do that. He knows what's been going on, as he indicated. For what it's worth, I'm not sure I could have done what you're doing, when I was your age. But, I suppose that's what comes of being a prince. Special breed and all. Must be in the blood."

Starbane placed a kind hand on the old man's shoulder. "I don't know that breeding has anything to do with it. Good people seem to make the difference, though. And luck. I can only thank you, Master Rakahr, as I've thanked everyone else who's somehow come to my assistance thus far. If I ever have any power to make it so, I'll see that your efforts are rewarded."

"We'll settle for you getting safely across the mountain. Forget about any reward. Please promise me that you'll tell King Sye *everything* when you see him. He's slow to interfere in Kelnia, as we've discussed, but he may be moved by your plight, as a fellow royal. So many have misinformed him, and your sister has had much to do with that. Part of her plan, I suspect. Perhaps you can persuade Sye to persuade Rowan Blaize to help. Perhaps you can do so yourself, if the legend about that signet-ring scar on your arm is true at all."

"I promise to do whatever I can. Though I don't know exactly what that might be, just yet. Goodbye."

With that, he and Ilyssa joined Talthagar and vanished into the encroaching natural corridors of the nearby wood. The sunlight waxed through the high tops of the bare-limbed trees, as if to acknowledge this new leg of their journey.

"How long will it take to reach the other side of this mountain?" Starbane asked Talthagar, breaking a dead but still-sturdy limb from a Thadnus tree for support in the drifts. "Here. Ilyssa, take this. It'll make you feel better to carry it in forests like this. I should know."

"If all goes well—no delays, obviously—then we should be off the mountain and into the first Corydian valley in two or three days." Talthagar stole another skeptical glance at the girl, who was whispering angrily to herself and struggling to plow through the deeper snow with her new staff. "That's with *no* delays," he reiterated.

"You said you've got a horse with you?"

"Yeah, up ahead. Behind those bushes."

"Not to seem ignorant," ventured the Prince, "but how is a horse going to go over a mountain of this size? I've never heard of such a thing. Won't *that* slow us down more than anything else?"

"Don't believe everything you've *never* heard about," advised Talthagar. "That's where my expertise comes into play."

"Oh really?"

"Of course. You see, we won't be scaling the side of the mountain all the way to the top, like creeping Caltressian spiders. We'll be going around it, by way of certain passes and trails that I know like the back of my hand."

They turned along the narrow pathway between the trees and passed a briar thicket to behold a horse as impressive as its owner. The beast's hide was the same dangerous gray of Talthagar's eyes; its sleek and bulging muscles exuded steam in the cold. They watched it paw the ground, restless at the sign of their approach.

"What a beautiful horse!" Ilyssa gasped, approaching to touch it, sheepishly, on the nose. She received a gentle nuzzle in response. "I like horses so much more than I like people."

"That's about right," noted Talthagar before reaching for a couple of satchels. "It's love at first sight, then, because he likes people so much more than he likes horses. This, good friends, is my steed, Skull."

"Bit of a pedestrian name for such a noble animal," said Ilyssa.

"Don't call my horse noble, you pedestrian," warned Talthagar. "He's got enough of an attitude already."

Within moments, they were on the move, Starbane properly fitted with snowshoes and walking astride while Ilyssa, warm in an added sheepskin jacket Talthagar gave her, rode atop Skull. Vast slopes loomed ahead through the upward grade of woodland, looking insurmountable and forbidding, but the forest floor was not yet difficult to travel. Over the next several hours, Talthgar cautioned them against speaking, for fear of enemy spies, but was true to his prior word as he revealed a keen knowledge of otherwise hidden trails that wound, one after the other, toward numerous small and opportune passes. Progress across the rising side of the Great Pyr Mida was steady and the deep silence afforded these sudden acquaintances a chance to assess the gravity and wonder of their situation. Ilyssa was still reeling from her headlong rush into the strange affair and spent much of her time shifting her gaze nervously from warrior to prince.

"Are you sure you two aren't part of some spell cast by that witch who's made life so rotten for everyone in Kelnia?" she burst out suddenly as they rounded a small canyon ridge. Talthagar and Starbane stopped in their tracks.

"What did I say about talking too loudly before we reach tonight's campsite?" muttered Talthagar.

"Why don't you leave her alone?" said the boy. "She's likely scared to death."

"I am not!" protested Ilyssa. "I'm not afraid of anything, after what I've been through. I just wanted to know if this is some freakish spell, is all."

"Well, *I'm* a bit spooked by all this silence and a little hungry, too, if you must know," said the Prince to both of his new companions. "Besides, no one has explained much of anything to Ilyssa. That's probably why she's so miserable."

"Hey!" snapped Ilyssa.

"Oh, this is just great," said Talthagar, closing his eyes as he trudged onward.

"I don't mean to delay things," whispered the girl, her bell-like voice absorbed by endless carpets of snow. "I'd simply like some idea of what I've gotten myself into, or what I've been pulled into. And with whom, exactly. Nothing seems to be what it is. You tell me," she continued, pointing at Starbane, "that you were one of those in the group of hunters at Wyrnie's house, when you say you first saw *me*. Then, today, when I'm escaping to let *myself* die in the cold, rather than lift my skirts for the lousy Prefect, I see *you* and learn that you're the prince of this whole nutty kingdom. It's a bit ridiculous, if you don't mind me saying so."

"I know it seems bizarre," said the lanky royal, walking up to grasp Skull's reins. "But we're living in a time of insanity. I think some of the gods must be on our side, or something, by the way things have worked out for us. Quite uncanny, I admit. None of us should be on our way to freedom, by rights. But it's true, Ilyssa. I *am* Prince Starbane."

"I'll vouch for that," added Talthagar, "but only because Rakahr insists, and he's supposedly got the Gragan's scar on his arm."

"I do have the scar!" boasted Starbane, struggling to display it with little success due to his heavy garb.

"What scar? And what's a Gragan?" bleated Ilyssa.

"Enough," said Talthagar, exasperated. "Can we move along, children? We're not even close to our campsite and it looks like it might snow any minute."

Ilyssa was not satisfied. "How can you be the Prince of Kelnia?" she questioned. "Everyone says the royal family was killed by Queen Oblixta. Everyone knows she killed her stepmother, her father, *and* her step-brother."

Talthagar looked with a piercing, sideways interest at the boy, whose face became a mask of instant and unmistakable anguish. He spoke quickly and compassionately on behalf of the heartbroken youth.

"Only King Adraeus and Queen Mirysta were executed," he said. "By Oblixta's warlord, Kerrion. You can believe me on that count, girl, and say nothing more about it."

"How did you know that?" asked Starbane. "How did you know it was specifically that monster, Kerrion, who murdered my parents?" He stared away from them into the sweep of forest below, one tear stinging the cold, dry surface of a cheek, then falling to melt, forever lost, a tiny crater of sadness in the infinity of snow.

"The Kashizma spies of King Sye know much. We have our ways. And General Kerrion is every bit the monster that Oblixta is, too," said Talthagar with an ominous shake of his head. "He's been that way ever since he was with the Legion of the Viper."

"Legion of the ... *what?*" said Ilyssa, drawing her shawls tightly around her shoulders.

"The viper," replied Starbane in the midst of his reflective sadness. "Long ago, my sister ran away from castle guards sent to fetch her from an old sorceress named Celintha. She escaped those guards in a fit of anger at my parents."

"Where did she go?"

"To the Galpern Valley, or so it is said. There, she fell-in with the Legion of the Viper. A bunch of rogues and bandits and murderers that haunted the region and pillaged many cities and towns. Butchered anyone who stood in their way, really. Oblixta's kind of people. It was from their ranks that my *half*-sister first began to raise an army that would eventually conquer Castle Cadrach and take over the realm."

"But not before they brought her to the sorcerer, Cabrus, way up in his fortress on Galpern Mountain," interjected Talthagar, suddenly eager to participate in a bit of Kelnian history.

"You know about that as well!" marveled Starbane.

"Some of us have kept our eyes and ears open for a long time, Prince. The Legion of the Viper had been Cabrus's henchmen for ages, kidnapping people and bringing them to the skinny old conjurer so he could enslave them. He met his match with your sister, though. They say he fell madly in love with her."

"There's no accounting for taste," said the boy, miserably. "But it's true."

"Can we stop talking about wizards and Queen Oblixta," pleaded Ilyssa, looking about the dense mountain woodland with a shudder. "The whole kingdom has heard enough of such evil. That's why all of our lives are in ruin."

"It's alright, chickadee," said Talthagar. "She can't get you here. But I think the Prince knows I'm right about Cabrus. The story goes that Oblixta was kidnapped by the Legion of the Viper and that she tricked the magician, somehow. Made him gradually powerless while *she* grew stronger in sorcery. No one knows how she did it, but pretty soon she was running the whole show in the Galpern Valley. She whipped that scabby Legion into shape and had them take over every town, village, and city in the neighboring provinces—called herself 'Queen' and forbid any allegiance whatsoever to her father, Adraeus. At first it was a bit of a laugh, because the Galpern and its neighbors weren't much in terms of territory, in terms of prestige. Pretty desolate and populated with wealthy criminal families. Most decent folk had always been scared-off from settling there by that fact, and the fact that mighty Cabrus was atop his mountain."

"Then Oblixta started going after the Dalorum hill country of our ancestors," said the Prince, remembering all that his parents had told him during their years of confinement. "That's when my father first got wind of what was happening. He refused to believe that it was her, at the beginning. She took the walled city of Nargos, her first really big prize. The warlord she has now, Kerrion, was also a general at Nargos, under Lord Cabrisius. Oblixta either bribed him or put some spell on him, and they assassinated Cabrisius. That's when she started sending messages to my father, demanding he cede her half the entire realm of Kelnia! He thought she'd gone mad, of course, until he saw her power firsthand."

"The war," said Talthagar with a sigh. "She used dark magic to build her army and finally came back to Castle Cadrach, but *not* for a family reunion party."

The Prince felt his face grow hot with the painful flood of memories.

"Why'd she keep *you* alive?" asked Talthagar. "Many of us have wondered about that. If you'll pardon me for saying so, it made no sense to let you live, after what she did to your parents, and Cabrus, and others, and eventually to the Gragan wizard himself."

"Thanks a lot!" snarled Starbane. "Do you always fly-off at the mouth like this? I'd really like to know, seeing as we're going to be traveling together for heaven knows how many days."

"Hey, I begged your pardon," shrugged Talthagar. "If I'm out of line, you gotta tell a guy like me."

"Whatever," said the irritated lad, kicking at the snow. "I suppose you have a right to be as curious as anyone else. The fact is that I don't know why Oblixta left me alive. I didn't even know about my parents' fate until Celintha told me, though I'd had my suspicions. We'd been kept in separate cells in the dungeons of the castle since the second year of our imprisonment. At least I'm pretty sure it was the second year. One loses track of time in places like that. From what I managed to hear, and from what I discovered for myself as I was being transferred to another cell one day, she kept the Gragan wizard there, forced him to reveal the secrets of his sorcery. Later on, her guards confined me to a chamber high in the west tower of the castle and that's where I remained for a short time. Celintha was my only friend. She was posing as a maidservant in the castle. She was a spy, too, as it turns out, and saw to it that I was fed properly and had someone to talk to, if only for a few moments every now and then."

Starbane peered over the treetops at the dreary tufts of low-lying clouds hanging in the sky. The sun that had been so bright that morning was now hidden. A few snowflakes drifted down in the stillness and the three travelers heard nothing but the steady footfalls of the horse and the sound of their own snowshoes dusting the terrain.

"How did you finally get away?" asked Ilyssa, breaking the solemn spell.

"Celintha," replied the Prince. "The old sorceress of Dalorum set me free, at the 'appointed time,' or so she called it. I woke one morning to find the door of my tower cell wide open and the old woman standing there. She beckoned me to follow her quickly, for the sake of our very survival. I didn't know what to do, at first. Was it some sort of trap of Oblixta's doing? By that point, I hadn't much room to care, one way or the other. I had to take a chance. When I joined Celintha outside my cell, I found all the guards fast asleep. By torchlight she led me down the winding stair and then into some strange underground passage I had never known to exist in the castle. It wasn't the dungeons, though. Nothing to do with them. It seemed to wind forever into the darkness and I was nearly in a panic. I thought for certain that one of us was going to slip and fall to our deaths. That's when Celintha revealed exactly who she was, that she'd been the famous friend of my parents and even my sister, at one time. She said she'd been living in the castle, magically disguised as a serving-woman, hoping for an opportunity to set all of us free and send us into hiding. She told me of my parents' deaths at the hands of General Kerrion, but she didn't give me any time for tears, and I was far too wild with fear to shed them, anyhow. At least at that moment. She told me I must head southward through the wilderness to the city of Pyr Mida, where I'd meet Telvyn Rakahr."

"You must've been mad with questions!" gasped Ilyssa.

"I was. But Celintha knew about the Gragan burning his signet-ring into my flesh during my transfer from the dungeon, and she explained the wizard's words to mean that I must indeed find Rowan Blaize in Corydia, the sorcerer who is said to owe the Gragan something. A magician who is still, presumably, good in spirit. I was not to worry, Celintha said, because there would be a protective spell around me, guiding me until I reached my destination, or at least until she could no longer maintain the enchantment—whichever came first. When we ascended from the earth and into the light of day, she gave me a satchel, a map, some supplies, and a rather strange fire-potion. Even a set of fur clothing was waiting. I was astonished to look back and see the castle so far away in the distance behind us. I had no idea we'd traveled so far and so long."

"She'd found an old subterranean escape-tunnel," said Talthagar with an approving nod. "Well done, on her part. All castles have at least one, if they're any kind of castle at all."

"I wasn't about to argue with her devices," said Starbane. "There, at the edge of the forest, I was told to flee for my life and the life of the very kingdom itself. 'Find Pyr Mida and Telvyn Rakahr,' she said. Thereafter, I must reach King Sye and find Rowan Blaize. When I protested that I had no idea which way to go, she literally pushed me and said I didn't need to *know* anything. I was merely to go, and walk wherever my feet felt like walking, and look for the hidden shelters I would find at the end of each day. She sent some sort of really sarcastic faery to guide me, at times. But it ditched me because her spell supposedly was broken. It was all so strange. I could feel the spell coming over me when she first cast it, though."

"Old Celintha was something special," Talthagar said. "Rakahr had told me that she offered her magical services to the Kashizma operatives, hoping to rescue you and your family. It's a shame that she might be dead—or worse, knowing Oblixta—now. As strong as she was, I don't think her powers were any match for those of your sister."

"I know. I was afraid of the same thing. Especially considering what happened to me before I even got to Pyr Mida."

The Prince told them the rest of his story and they listened in grave silence to his account of the Eskanthian wolf-attack and how he had come upon Rufthar's camp by sheer good fortune. Talthagar was visibly impressed when the boy showed him the necklace of werebeasts' teeth that Ona and Wylla had made for him. Ilyssa, meanwhile, had calmed down considerably and, in her turn, told them of her own woes and near escape from the clutches of the Prefect. She also voiced her opinion that the gods must have personally arranged everything, so improbable yet perfectly timed was their luck in meeting.

"Still, when *everyone* is suffering, it's not so improbable that suffering people might meet each other, is it?" was all Starbane would say.

As they pressed deeper into the mountain passes, the jolting change in the course of Ilyssa's own fate had finally begun to sink-in. Her existence, like that of the Prince, had been entirely uprooted in a matter of hours. She tried not to think about what might be happening to her parents at that very moment.

"Well, neither of you has anything to be afraid about now," said Talthagar, a confident grin curving across his jaw. "Not with me leading this little expedition. By the way, after this mission, I am seriously going to consider an early retirement. Hero-gigs are getting rather old."

They kept to their path among hordes of trees, preparing to ascend a new slope toward one of Talthagar's "short cuts." Starbane looked down behind them from time to time, knowing that they were indeed climbing a mountain, though not realizing it in their sidewinding mode of escalation. He could see it, however, when able to behold the mountainside's steep downward slope, with the endless rows of Falthurns and bristle-topped Thadnus growing smaller and smaller in an eerie visual descent. He looked up at Ilyssa, safe and warm on the back of the stalwart Skull.

"Are you hungry, Ilyssa? I gather we have lots of provisions so we won't—"

"We eat later," snapped Talthagar, keeping his eyes on a particularly treacherous bit of hairline ridge straight ahead.

"But she probably hasn't eaten since yesterday," countered Starbane. The girl's wan expression seemed to confirm this. Talthagar turned around and poked the boy once on the arm, hard enough to hurt.

"Ow! What did you go and do that for?"

"Let's get one thing straight, Prince of Kelnia," said the warrior, lifting the same offending finger for emphasis. "Until I get you to King Sye's very door, I am in charge. Do you understand? This is *my* element, this woodland. Not yours, werewolf-slayer though you may be. You'll do exactly as I say, and I say we wait to eat because I want to get to this special cave I know about before the trolls, the ice-fey, *and* the Eskanthian wolves come looking for dinner of their own. Got it?"

"It's fine with me, Mister," said Ilyssa, peering through the deepening murk of the forest. "I'm not hungry a bit. No way."

"Glad to hear it," said Talthagar. "Cooperation with my methods is what'll get us safely to the other side of this mess."

Starbane frowned, his ego as bruised as the spot on his arm. "I was just trying to look after her," he explained. "By the gods, you must've had despicably mean parents to have turned out as pushy as you are."

Talthagar cocked a disdainful eye at his charge. "I have no desire to discuss *my* childhood," he said, tartly. "I've heard enough tales of woe today. Besides, if you judge someone's parents strictly by the kind of children they've produced, then your parents don't measure-up very well, considering our dear Oblixta."

"Oh, gods," huffed the Prince. "That's a vicious thing to say, but point taken. At least you didn't insult *me* outright, this time."

"I was going to," Talthagar shot back, "but your sister is more accomplished than you are, so I picked her."

As the prickly royal stewed and muttered, they continued to make their loping way along what passed for a "trail." With little daylight remaining, Talthagar insisted they pick up the pace. Though still fearfully aware of the mountain's hidden dangers, the two youths looked at the enormous man, and at the sword dangling from his hip. Feeling somehow fully protected for the first time in a long while, they journeyed onward in silence, safe in the company of their surly and mysterious guide.

あ〜

Oblixta paced relentlessly before the gathering of officers in her reception hall, her face a veil of stagnant fury. The men said nothing as she moved back and forth; they all knew that some sort of thunderbolt was about to strike, but to what extent—and upon whom— was anyone's guess. None of them dared breathe but for the very necessity of oxygen. When at last the Queen turned to speak, her tones were calm.

"When my brother escaped, I was patient and willing to accept the fact that not everything always goes according to plan," she said. "Even *my* plan."

Something was coming. They braced themselves.

"I left the matter in your capable gloves, General Kerrion. You were to delegate this task to these men, who, in turn, set their own underlings to the mission. Days and days go by and invariably I hear, 'But Your Majesty, the search has yielded nothing, yet. We *do* remain hopeful.' Idiots!" spat Oblixta. "The best trackers and scouts in the history of this kingdom and you can't find one half-witted boy wandering about in the forest?"

Her voice had risen in volume. Kerrion and the others knew it would rise even more.

"Now, I ask you, who is it that finally locates the little wretch, over a month later?"

Oblixta glared at the ceiling of the morbid hall, as if she expected its assembly of leering stone gargoyles and carved demons to answer before her own men. "A *troll* locates him! A stinking rat-troll that probably can't find its way out of the castle grave-pits where it's currently feasting on the remains of our dearly departed prisoners. General Kerrion,

I commanded you to send word to our forces in Pyr Mida to have them capture the Prince at this … this *hunting* lodge I've learned about, and now you tell me that he is no longer there."

Oblixta moved closer to the General, her dragon-skull crown casting horrific shadows in the torchlight.

"The interrogation and subsequent obliteration of everyone in this encampment reveals that the boy had already ventured into Pyr Mida, and a few days of torture *there* brought us the happy news that he has apparently escaped across the border in a beer keg. A *beer* keg."

"We did the best we could, based upon what we knew," rumbled Kerrion, hanging his head low. Hardened murderer though he was, he could not face the piercing steel of Oblixta's gaze. "The boy slipped away from us and had help, obviously, in doing so."

"He had help, indeed," retorted Oblixta. "For he was given passage across the border by your men, Kerrion, and they *are* your men—I don't care how far out in the wild they're posted." Her eyes rolled toward the ceiling. "Finally, we learn by the further torture of those who aided him that Starbane has now affiliated himself with the Kashizma spies. He's hooked-up with those whom I despise more than anyone in the world, save King Sye himself, and it's to *that* old goat and presumably to Rowan Blaize that the Prince is now running!"

Oblixta stalked back to her immense slate throne and practically threw herself into it, pounding a fist hard on the armrest.

"I want punishment," she growled. "All possible accomplices and their families are to be put to death."

"We've *already* destroyed them all," assured Kerrion. "The hunting village and the family that nursed the boy after his attack. The Kashizma operative, Rakahr, and his wife. She's the one who told us the most under torture. But she died before giving us details about other members of the movement in Pyr Mida. We executed our own sentry at the border patrol after that, along with *his* wife and children. Then we burned half of the entire city itself as a warning. Would you have us burn the rest of it, Your Majesty? I would advise against it. Pyr Mida is too valuable, even at half-capacity. We must face the unpleasant fact that your brother simply got away."

Oblixta had ceased paying attention to Kerrion and seemed to be calculating, her eyes darting about and dagger-like fingers drumming on the cold slate. "It's been four days since he left Pyr Mida, so he should be in Corydia by now," she reasoned aloud. "He *did* have an escort, you're certain of it?"

"One of their finest warrior-scouts," answered the General, "as far as we can surmise. The spies we have in Corydia have already been alerted. Do you wish us to send a contingent after the boy, Great One? Our assassins, perhaps? They have a great lead on us, but if there was any difficulty in crossing the mountain, then perhaps—"

"Kerrion, please," scoffed Oblixta. "Do I look like a fool? You, whose men have failed me in every aspect of this task so far, would ask for yet another chance to blunder?" Her rage was now beginning to simmer perfectly below the point of eruption. Her fists clenched and unclenched, revealing small drops of blood across her ivory palms. "No. I've grown tired of your services in this regard. It shall be a drain on my own resources at a crucial time, but I have no other choice than to handle this personally."

She rose from the throne and, gathering robes spun from the silk of countless venomous arachnids, descended the dais, elbowing some of the officers violently out of her way as she stepped onto the flagstones. A group of servants worked in distant quadrants of the vast hall, busy replacing torches, deliberately hearing nothing. Oblixta dismissed the lot of them.

"All of you out. Now!" she howled.

The slaves gathered their wits and their tools and made swiftly for the main doorway. Kerrion and his men, assuming the Queen referred also to them, began a slow march toward the exit as well, but Oblixta whirled around in her billowing cape to stop them.

"No, General," she said, pointing a ghastly finger in his direction. "You and your fearless associates will stay. All of you will witness how *I* am forced to deal with things you cannot seem to manage." She turned once again to the line of departing servants. "Everyone else out," she blasted once more. "Everyone but ... *you.*"

This last was spoken to a young maid who had not yet managed to join the line of those filing out of the cavernous place. Earlier she had been scrubbing flagstones, but turned as if impelled by some unseen physical force, melting under the stonier glare of Oblixta.

"Me, Your Majesty?" she whispered, bowing and clutching at her threadbare bodice. No more than twenty years of age, the mousy-haired wench began to glance fitfully back and forth from the Queen to the cluster of soldiers that had stopped in their tracks nearby.

"Yes, you, woman," answered Oblixta in soothing tones. "You shall stay, in order that you might serve your kingdom in a far more important fashion than floor-scrubbing."

Sensing that something was quite amiss, the girl rose and began to back away. The queen advanced upon her. "Wh—what do you want with me?" bleated the object of all attention, dropping her water-bucket and brush and grabbing at her filthy skirts. "What have I done?"

"Nothing," replied Oblixta. *"Yet."*

She gestured to the officers with a mere toss of her chin and two came running to flank her on either side. "Seize the girl," she commanded.

They obeyed, snatching the cowed, whimpering form up from the floor.

"Bring her," commanded the Queen, and she motioned for the entire group of officers to follow as she led them across the hall and through an archway. With the girl wailing now in terror, they gathered in a small antechamber dominated by a massive rectangular block of obsidian. "Put her on the altar," instructed Oblixta. The maid's entire body now shuddered with every sob that escaped her lips, void of coherent words.

"No, not like that," snarled the witch-queen. "Like this."

She approached and showed the men how to take the girl's arms and pin them behind her at cross-points, while placing her flat on her stomach atop the smooth stone.

"Hold her down and grab her by the back of her hair."

One of the men ripped off the girl's dirty kerchief and grabbed a handful of greasy locks.

"Now slowly lift her head up from the table until it's pointing toward the ceiling," said Oblixta. The second of the two assistants did as he was told and, while his cohort held fast to the girl's struggling torso, he pulled her head backward by the hair until she was curved slightly upward from the glittering black table in an arc. The maidservant had by now seemed to go into shock, her body still and her tear-streaked face strangely impassive.

"Hold her just like that and don't allow her to move, do you understand?" hissed the Queen. "Kerrion, come here," she added out of the corner of her mouth. "I have a new job for you."

The General moved like a shadow of dread to the side of his queen, anxious as to the purpose of this strange scene.

"Cut her throat."

Kerrion looked at Oblixta, hesitant for a moment, as the girl twitched back to life and screamed at the top of her lungs. But she was held fast.

"Do as I say, General. Cut her throat now or it will be your own."

Kerrion whipped a vicious, curved dagger from its sheath at his hip and pounced toward the girl on the altar, drawing the blade swiftly and cleanly across her exposed neck. The wretched victim began to choke and hack as blood gushed from severed veins and arteries in torrents, straight out and onto the nearby wall, onto the ghost-white faces of the officers holding her, and onto the obsidian surface itself. Oblixta came forward, pushing the General and his dagger out of the way. She stuck an open palm beneath a pulsing fountain of black arterial blood, letting it fill her hand and then spatter down upon the cruel altar.

"By the power of this still-warm life," she chanted to begin the spell, eyes narrowing. *"Tyrinox, lathua. Pyr ferestus harsperu!"*

With a vile finger, Oblixta began to draw a series of signs and sigils in the spreading blood-pool, chanting and muttering under her breath as she did so. Finally, she raised a scarlet fist above the table and extended her other arm across its width. Her body began to sway gently even as that of the girl trembled with the onset of death.

"*Tjayef!*" spoke Oblixta, in a word that seem to billow and grow and echo like a peal of thunder in the antechamber and out across the reception hall beyond. Her eyes closed and she stepped back from the grisly scene, taking deep breaths that made her nostrils flare in great black circles.

"Drop her where she is and move away, if you value your lives," said the Queen in her strange sing-song voice. The pitiful corpse was dumped face-first with a sickening thud into the blood. One of the girl's arms flailed, lifeless, over the side of the stone. The officers, panting in fear and with anticipation, stared at Oblixta as she continued backing away slowly.

An eternity of moments seemed to pass. Then ...

"It's working," whispered the sorceress, as if in answer to their collective thoughts.

"Can't you *smell* it?"

Kerrion looked at the others, grimacing. Yes, they *could* smell it.

The odor was subtle, at first, but not for long. Soon it grew pungent as it seemed to well-up all about them in the chamber from no apparent source. To the men, it was a scent like the putrefaction they knew too well from years of slaughter on the battlefield, only much more intense. They glowered around the room, choking as their lungs struggled to process the now-fetid atmosphere. Kerrion thought he heard Oblixta speak, short and sharp, to someone or some*thing* unseen near the west corner of the place. Looking, he was stunned to see—even in the gloom—a deep black shadow blossoming and slithering across the stone tiles of the floor. Having no form or cohesion, it simply kept growing in length and began to writhe and twist inward, upon itself, over and over like a cyclone. The air was now saturated with corruption; the eyes and lungs of the men started to burn.

"Don't even think about leaving," Oblixta called out to them in the same peculiar tone. "It is dangerous for any of you to move right now."

The slippery thing, naught but a shadow, congealed suddenly and changed color from pitch black to smoky gray, and then from gray to a mottled brown. It changed shape, too, becoming an oblong form that rested upon the floor in a far corner, hardening before all eyes like hot wax suddenly exposed to cool air. Within moments, any further change became imperceptible as a hideous entity began to unfold itself with terrifying deliberation.

First, two massive wings emerged from the fleshy body. With a wet, sucking noise, these wings unfurled to expose a scaled backside dotted with hundreds of spines and bristles. Two spindly legs ending in clawed feet next stretched forward across the floor, followed by dark, sinewy arms that reached upward to the ceiling, as if heralding a massive awakening. Finally, and to the utter horror of all but Oblixta, a shiny, bulbous head turned to the onlookers and rolled malevolent black eyes in their direction. Caustically spying the altar, the now fully constituted creature—a living version of the stone gargoyles above them, come-to-life!—began to slide weakly across the flagstones, fluttering its wings like a newly emerged moth. Oblixta watched it crawl with great interest, smiling and nodding at its progress until it came to the foot of the altar and began to laboriously pull itself upward. When its head peeked over the edge of the stone, the beast eyed the corpse of the girl and its maw, riddled with gleaming ebony fangs, opened wide to set loose a slime-covered tongue that fluttered and licked its way hungrily toward the fare.

"Not yet!" commanded the Queen with bracing authority. "First, we speak, you and I."

The demon merely eyed her with disinterest and resumed its slow crawl toward the dead girl.

"*Tjayef ferestus!*" cried Oblixta, making a series of complicated signs in the air with her spidery fingers. At this, the thing drew itself into a fetal position and rolled off the altar, cringing as if in pain. When it had fallen in a heap, Kerrion saw the Queen extract a small blue box from the inner folds of her cloak. He had no way of knowing it, but the lid of this box was marked with the same sigils first drawn in the blood atop the stone. From the box Oblixta took an unseen substance and, stooping down to the great monstrosity, she placed this substance close to its rank lips. Immediately the creature came to attention, slurping and licking her fingers clean like an eager pup. Oblixta stood, proud and potent.

"There, now. That should satisfy you … for the time being."

Animated by the mysterious offering, the gargoyle-devil stood on legs increasingly muscular and strong. It flexed the enormous chest muscles that caused great wings to beat and plow through the toxic air of its own presence. With a voice that the officers thought could only have echoed from the Abyss, the thing spoke.

"Thou art Mistress, O Woman."

"That's as it should be," said Oblixta, nodding. "Do not forget that I am the one who has summoned you, and you remain in my power. Your task is this: find the one whom I see in my mind's eye but cannot touch with my hands. Find the one who carries in his veins the blood from which I have drawn my own life. Bring that one to me *alive and unharmed*. Destroy all those in his company. Obliterate any who dare to stop you. Leave at once and fail me not in this task, or it shall go ill with you, indeed."

Oblixta pointed, herself a specter of unspeakable death, toward the one window of the chamber. General Kerrion wondered how the beast would possibly manage to get out, for it was indeed the size of two or three grown warriors, not counting its enormous, veiny wings. The demon bowed low but, before it turned to leave, eyed once again the corpse of the sacrificed girl on the altar. Sheepishly, it glanced at the Queen for approval. Oblixta nodded once and pointed again to the window.

Swift as a leopard, the conjured atrocity reached out and snatched the body of the maidservant by one arm and flung it off the table with an awful cracking of bones. Clutching the girl to its scaled breasts like a rag toy, it unleashed a piercing scream that made the General and all of his men shiver beneath their armor. Then it dashed for the window. Once there, the thing squeezed through easily, like a flattening snake, and took off on pounding, membranous wings into the night. Oblixta turned to face her officers in triumph. Never had they feared her powers more than in this moment; as one, they fell to their knees in submission. She said nothing. Instead, she stared at each of them for an instant before walking slowly out of the chamber. She glided like a towering, robed phantom into the reception hall and toward the deeper confines of her castle, leaving Kerrion and his men alone and astonished—ignored bystanders in the silence of the bloody, blasphemous room.

అఈ

General Kerrion rapped at the door of Oblixta's personal apartments in the East tower of the castle. There was no response. It was the second time since dawn that his efforts had gone unanswered and well past the time when they had agreed to meet in conference. It was unlike the Queen to keep him waiting, especially when matters of grave importance were scheduled for discussion. Still, the General had no desire to disturb her, given the previous night's harrowing experience and the possibility that she might be sleeping. Worse, she could be in the middle of another foul conjuration. All of the Queen's closest aides knew she often chose the first hours before dawn to perform her sorcerous tasks. Kerrion turned to walk away after one final knock, eager to depart this most unsettling portion of the palace.

The instant he turned away, however, there was a sharp creaking of the great door. Glancing over his shoulder, he could barely see one of the Queen's eyes, peering at him in almost reptilian fashion from the crack.

"What is it, Kerrion?" she croaked. "Why have you disturbed me?"

Clearing his throat, the General walked a step closer and hesitated. "Majesty ... I ... I awaited your arrival at dawn in the Great Hall. For our meeting?" He felt the air between them grow thick with tingling energy. "But surely I was mistaken about the hour. Forgive my error. I'll leave you at once."

He heard her mutter something from behind the door and slowly she opened it the rest of the way. She receded into her room, her back to his face.

"You're right, of course," she said. "Come in, General. Come and sit. We'll conduct our meeting here, but it must be brief."

Kerrion stepped into the stark chamber he had never before entered. There, he spied only a large canopy-bed of rich, dark wood, its frame and various panels carved with every manner of grotesque devil and sculpted forms that seemed in the throes of agony or wicked elation; it was difficult to discern. He forced his eyes to look away. A small writing desk, decorated with the same sinister ornamentation, was nearby. Oblixta walked to this desk and sat, visibly pained, in its chair.

"I do want to discuss the problem with the cavalry," she said at last, gesturing. The General sat dutifully on a seat near the immense, empty hearth. The room, all of its window shutters flung open, was stabbed by icy gusts from without. When Oblixta finally turned to confront Kerrion, he could not help but gasp in shock at her appearance. The Queen's once-smooth brow was now wrinkled and bruised, her eyes sunken and languid in their sockets, their surfaces glazed and lifeless. The noble cheeks, though always on the pallid side, were quite emaciated. Her usually stern but moist lips were cracked and encrusted with dry streaks of blood.

"Majesty ... you are ill," stammered Kerrion, trying to compose himself. His gawping had been an impertinence she would not appreciate. "Perhaps we should meet at another time."

Oblixta merely scowled, creating a new, oozing fissure in her desiccated mouth, and she brushed his concern away with a pass of one gnarled and chapped hand.

"It's just the spell, General," she said between rattling coughs. "Don't get anxious to sit on the throne so soon." Reaching for a silver cup amid the rolls of parchment on her desk, she sipped with an almost dainty poise at its contents. "Ah. Yes, that's much better," she breathed, and cocked a suddenly keener set of eyes toward her warlord.

"As I implied, dear General, my current appearance is simply one of the more inconvenient side effects of the spell I cast last night. If I must tell you, it takes an inordinate amount of power and will to keep a gargoyle-demon of that particular kind under control. It's most rebellious, that brand of fiend, but very effective nonetheless. We shall see this presently for ourselves. Until then, every hour it spends in this world drains *me* physically." Her gaze trailed out the nearest window to the snow-capped mountains so distant in the South. "The completion of the beast's work is near. I can feel it."

Kerrion nodded, far from able to comprehend such matters and thoroughly unwilling to extend any conversation about the creature he and his men had seen the night before. His head was still rank with the remnants of a dream about it. "I trust fully in your wisdom, as always, Majesty."

"As well you should. Now then, let us discuss that one aspect of our legions I'm willing to consider, in my present condition. The cavalry."

"What are your thoughts, Majesty?"

"My thoughts? There are simply far too many of them," said Oblixta, hacking slightly into a shiny square of black fabric cupped in her alabaster palm. "Bringing that many horses through the sorts of passes we'll eventually be taking in the Pyr Mida Mountains is foolish. It will only slow us down. King Sye's initial retaliation will be huge, of course. I'm expecting that. His men will rush up the side of the mountain from that infernal valley to meet us as we descend. For this reason, I want greater numbers on our front lines. Cut the cavalry by a third and transfer those men up to the front, once they have been trained. And make the training swift, do you understand? I want a guaranteed response to whatever Sye may throw our way off the mark. Once we've pushed them back a comfortable distance with swords and bows and axes, we can bring the rest of the horsemen over the Pyr Mida."

"A wise move," admitted the General, nodding slowly. "I shall see to it this very day."

The Queen sneezed into her handkerchief and then drew a deep, unsteady breath. She leaned back in her chair, a debilitated crone. "This is all I care to discuss with you now, Kerrion. When the demon returns with the boy, which should be sometime after nightfall, I'll send it back to its own world. I will require rest until then. We'll lay more plans on the table tomorrow morning and you can help me deal with the miserable little Prince. I shall then turn my attention to the ultimate issue—

that of King Sye and his patron wizard, this Rowan Blaize we've heard so much about. Leave me until I summon you again."

The General rose and bowed low, departing the room in stunned silence. He had never seen the Queen in such vulnerable shape and it both unnerved and tantalized him. Alone again, Oblixta closed her eyes and forced her brain to concentrate. *Yes.* She sensed the progress of her conjured servant, felt it deep down beyond the painful pulsations that wracked her body and being. The demon was getting closer to the boy, wherever he was. Perhaps it was even now watching and waiting for the perfect moment to strike, to snatch him from those who sought to aid his effrontery. Yes, Starbane would be in her grasp soon. Eyes still shut and her black hair whipping in a new blast of air that accosted the tower, the sorceress of Cadrach Castle began to cackle.

తిఅళ

"Well, which one do you like, Starbane? Choose among these six. And make it fast, will you? It smells in here."

"It's a horse barn," said Ilyssa. "What do you expect? Some warrior *you* are!"

Starbane, Talthagar, and Ilyssa stood crowded by the great rumps and swaying heads of horses in a small stable of King Sye's Fourth Valley Regiment, a battle-camp at the foot of the Pyr Mida—*his* foot—on the outskirts of the town of Trindyll. In three days' time they had crossed the great mountain without incident and, with an almost explosive sense of relief, had entered the realm of the Southern kingdom near sunset the previous evening. Seemingly unnoticed by the taciturn Corydians milling in the streets, the three weary stragglers were rejuvenated after a night of comforting food, shelter, and dreamless sleep at one of the sprawling town's more discreet inns. Eager to resume the journey, Talthagar had taken his charges to the busy war camp to retrieve the happily lodged Skull and choose some horses of their own for the rest of the journey.

"They're all fine looking animals," concluded the Prince, wrinkling his nose against the odor and dodging the whip of various tails. "You seem to get along best with horses, Ilyssa. Why don't you choose for me?"

The previous night's rest and a hot bath had served Ilyssa particularly well. Her freshly braided hair was a radiant auburn even in the dinge of the stable; her blue eyes—previously so sad and evasive—had regained a measure of their former sparkle. She was beginning to believe that an actual future might somehow exist for her. The world had changed in an instant, on the back of a wagon, across a mountain. Nothing would be the same, but *possibility* was better than nothing. She looked each of the horses over carefully and decided on a brown stallion for Starbane and, for herself, a white mare marked by one black splotch between its gentle eyes.

Talthagar turned to the stable-hand, a crouched old fellow with the build of a scarecrow. "Saddle these two up and throw at least one extra bag over each." The keeper approached to begin his preparations and Ilyssa asked whether her horse happened to have a name.

"A name?" repeated the stable-hand, giving the girl a strange look. "No, can't say that she does. I suppose you can call her what you will, though. The mare is yours, now."

"You should call her 'Wyrnie,' I think," said Starbane with a snicker. "After Rufthar's old sister. There's a resemblance."

Ilyssa laughed as well, the ringing sound of her amusement a pleasure to all who heard it. She herself could not recall the last time she had laughed.

"Yes, 'Wyrnie' it is," she agreed, stroking the mare's flank.

Starbane turned to Talthagar, a look of suspicion upon his face. "You said this is a stable belonging to King Sye's army, right?"

"Yeah," replied the warrior. "So what?"

"I'm curious as to how you, a fairly grubby spy, can simply walk into one of the Corydian king's stables, on the edge of one of his battle-camps, and pick up horses. It's a bit strange. Even the stable-hand knows you and takes orders from you. Spies aren't known among their own. I learned that much as a child in my father's court."

"I'm really *really* close to the King's inner circle," said Talthagar.

Starbane raised a brow. "Just as I thought—*more* than a spy. You've been keeping things from us."

"Yeah. Lots of secrets. I'll explain later, if I feel up to it. For now we've got to get those horses over to the regiment captain's tent, when they're ready." He instructed the old stable-hand to bring the animals along as soon as he was finished saddling them. "Tie them up next to Skull. You know my horse well enough."

The Prince and Ilyssa then followed Talthagar out of the stables and across the bustling encampment to a line of soldiers situated against an even longer row of massive blue tents. The Kelnian royal guessed that there were at least one hundred men in the formation and all stood at attention as a burly, heavily decorated officer in chain mail walked along their ranks, inspecting them one by one. Starbane watched as the man commended some and chastised others for whatever quality he found bountiful or lacking on that particular day.

"Who is that officer, Talthagar?" whispered the boy in awe.

"Only one of the most renowned generals in King Sye's army. His name is Coragus. They've stuck him with this mountainside unit in Trindyll because they know war is on the way, one of these days. Whenever your sister decides she's arrogant enough to finally start one, Rowan Blaize or no Rowan Blaize. These valley regiments have to be made as tough as possible, given their numbers. More legions will be on the way from the provinces, if I know anything about war games. But Coragus will whip these mountainside men into shape pretty quick. He's a military genius, to put it mildly."

The General continued his inspection but it wasn't long before he noticed his rapt observers. He lumbered over, following a sharp command for the line of soldiers to remain at attention. Starbane and Ilyssa marveled as he approached; the man possessed that rare ability to utterly intimidate by physical bearing alone. His size, carriage, and stoic expression all served to overwhelm the two youths as he neared. Talthagar tipped his own head and extended a hand; the General shook it readily.

"Good to see you again, General Coragus. The ranks are looking rather fit," said the warrior, though with none of the usual sarcasm underlying his tone.

"They need some work, but they'll soon be ready," replied Coragus in a voice that seemed to roll and boom like distant thunder. Still, there was a curious twinkle in his beady eyes. "I'd heard that you might be coming down the mountain, Talthagar. But I *hadn't* heard all that much about your latest mission. I'm glad you stopped by." Starbane and Ilyssa appeared to swallow hard under the giant man's scrutinizing gaze.

"General, I'm pleased to present Prince Starbane Cadrach of Kelnia and his companion, Ilyssa. I am escorting them both to the castle of King Sye."

Coragus was only partially surprised by this introduction, at least as far as anyone could see. One of his great hairy nostrils twitched and then the eyes were twinkling once more.

"Well, well," he rumbled. "It is indeed a pleasure to meet you, Prince Cadrach. We have, of course, heard *rumors* of your survival and escape." The General glanced fleetingly at Talthagar. "I am glad to know that these rumors are true. It's difficult to discern the truth when so many tales abound in these unsavory times, wouldn't you agree? Yes, I am honored to see you—though, under such impending adversity, I am dismayed as well."

"The honor is mine, General Coragus," said Starbane evenly, shaking a cold mail glove. "You are as formidable a man as I have been told by our new friend, Talthagar."

"Is that so?" smiled Coragus. He stared at the Prince a bit longer, bowed politely to Ilyssa, and turned again to Talthagar. "I'm taking this as a great portent for our side, having the true heir to the Kelnian throne on Corydian soil. Certainly the King has a masterful plan in mind for him. If I had more time, Talthagar, you could perhaps update me on your new adventure, and even the status of your Kashizma associates back in Pyr Mida. But I see that you have as many pressing matters as I, at the moment. Our own reconnaissance feels certain that Oblixta will launch an attack within a few months, the way she's been jangling her legions about, this way and that. We aim to be ready for them."

"And you will be," nodded Talthagar. "I was drawn into this mission somewhat at the last minute … and somewhat not. It's a bit complex. Suffice it to say that the King is hoping to use the Prince, here, to rally a much more widespread resistance back in Kelnia, as soon as word gets out that he's safe in the stronghold of the castle. Hundreds of our operatives are training in Kelnia, in all the provinces. King Sye, of course, has more of his own ideas, I'm sure. I'm guessing he'll eventually put the boy at the head of a great legion, simply as a figurehead, of course. Anyone can see he's no soldier. The propaganda potential is obvious."

"Indeed it is," said Coragus as the "figurehead" marveled, a bit angrily, at how bits and pieces of the picture *not* given by Telvyn Rakahr were beginning to make sense. "I trust you'll have the full attention of the King, once you reach the castle. Whatever he may decide to do, I wish you all great luck. Tell me, are you in need of supplies? Horses?"

"Everything's been arranged, General," replied Talthagar. "We had a good night's rest after coming off the mountain and we're ready to hit the road any minute."

"Good. Then, if you'll excuse me, I must return to my men. You know, in some ways it's a shame you're the King's personal spy and High Assassin, now, Talthagar. I could use a swordsman of your caliber here at the front of the battle, *when* the battle arrives."

Coragus bowed his head before Starbane and Ilyssa a final time and then strode away to accost his waiting troops.

Within minutes, the new horses were ready and the three were mounted and trotting along the wide road that swung southwest away from Trindyll. The weather was still frigid, but a vast, dazzling sunshine heralded warmer temperatures to come, along with Spring in all of its emancipating glory. Starbane gazed around the desolate, snowy valley as they rode and grew melancholy at the thought of the region's potentially imminent transformation into a battlefield. He was also agitated by thoughts of King Sye's "plans," mentioned in his regard by Talthagar, and he was also bothered by General Coragus's reference to the warrior as Sye's personal spy and assassin. The Prince hadn't dared to question Talthagar about this matter in front of the General. Neither of them said much of anything to Ilyssa. Both were worried about engaging the moody and volatile girl too much. They knew she was still emerging from the shock of running away from home, the shock of being rescued, the shock of learning who was rescuing her ... *and* the shock of learning where she was about to be taken.

"Oh!" gasped Ilyssa, suddenly.

"What is it?" asked the Prince, snapping out of his little trance. He turned slightly in the saddle. Ilyssa was trailing last in their trio of riders.

"I'm sorry. It's nothing. Nothing at all, really," she answered, looking up at the sky with a half-eaten apple in hand to shield her eyes from the noonday sun. "An eagle. That's what I saw. Flying way up near that bank of clouds in the East. It was huge!"

Starbane followed her pointing finger, scanned the clouds, and saw nothing. He decided it was time to bother Talthagar up ahead.

"I think it's safe to say that you're not *just* some sort of spy in the Corydian pool, Talthagar. Am I right or not? There's no sense hiding things at this point. I'm not stupid, you know. I heard what that general said."

"Nothing's being hidden from you, Prince Starbane," said Talthagar as Skull made a quick jump over a Thadnus tree that had fallen across the road. "In case you haven't noticed, I've been a little too busy saving your butt to explain everything."

"Three days of silence up, down, around, and over that mountain? You could've told me then."

"Nope. I needed every minute of every one of those days to concentrate on our surroundings. Danger lurks around every corner for you, kid. At least until you get to King Sye's court. I know my orders."

"And I'd like to know what those orders really involve. Me as some sort of military figurehead? I'm here to see the King and supposedly find a wizard, in case you and your gang haven't forgotten. Besides, we're safe on Corydian soil, now. You said so yourself."

"I never said any such thing. What you've got to do now is wait—"

"By the gods!" screamed Ilyssa from behind.

"TALTHAGAR!" screamed Starbane ... from *above.*

A rush of wind whipped Talthagar's hair as he spun Skull around in a flash. He beheld a mind-numbing series of visions that seemed all-too-frantic, yet frozen in segments of time, each isolated but moving as a gruesome whole. He saw the apple in Ilyssa's hand drop, as if in slow motion, to bounce upon a rugged portion of exposed road. The girl was in danger of slipping from her horse, in a swoon, while Skull screamed a mixture of warning and terror. Most horribly—most impossibly of all—Talthagar heard another desperate cry from the Prince and he saw, with the blood seeming to rush from his brain to his sword-arm, the boy trapped in the clutches of a winged-beast from Hell.

The sword was drawn with a stinging slice from its scabbard even before Talthagar had landed from Skull's back into the snow. Ilyssa screamed. Starbane struggled to fight a thing eager to bear him aloft, eager to gain altitude. The frigid wind was edged with strange heat and the smell of rot. The warrior rushed forward with a wail that soared across the valley expanse.

By now, the Prince was mad with terror, gripping with both arms at the limb of a Falthurn tree as the gargoyle-demon snarled and yanked in frustration at his legs, which could have easily been snapped into pieces, had its orders been less explicit. Talthagar leaped up into the air toward a beast he had never imagined capable of inhabiting the world of men—a thing twice the size of General Coragus and armored from ghastly head to cloven feet with thick scales and spines. Its huge leathery wings twitched and battered the air, scraping against the branches of the surrounding trees. Ilyssa's horse reared in wild-eyed fear, dumping the girl soundly into the snow on her back. With sword flashing and a warrior rising behind it, the beast immediately let go of the boy's legs and whirled in flight to face the charge. Its noxious glare, coupled with the exposed mouthful of gleaming black fangs, was enough to nearly send Talthagar hurtling back to the ground in gut-wrenching retreat.

But not quite.

The thing bellowed a sound that dwarfed any cry ever heard by man or beast in the land of Corydia and it lunged for its mortal attacker with a stealthy adjustment of flailing wings. Talthagar had no time to cry out or bring down his sun-blazed sword before he was swiped aside by a brutal thrust of the creature's arm and sent tumbling through the air. His body slammed hard into another tree nearby and he crumpled in a heap at the base of its trunk. In that instant, the demon returned its voracious attention back to Starbane, who had crawled like a small, shrieking animal beneath a blessedly dense patch of vines and briars. Instinct had found for him an opening!

Wailing at the attempt of its quarry to escape, the great devil plunged a hand unharmed through the jumble of thorns, snatching for the Prince as he cringed and dodged, scrambling along the musty earth. With the other set of talons the enemy began ripping and tossing mounds of debris. Starbane rolled out of its grasp just in time, but was now jammed against the base of a much larger Falthurn tree, with no place left to retreat or scurry as the roadside thicket was being decimated. With a soundless scream he peered up through the remaining vines and into the fiery red eyes of his pursuer. The huge, slimy orbs were filled with an unmistakable malevolence and the boy knew he was as good as finished.

Unleashing a triumphant howl, the beast raised its claws for another clutching strike, but no sooner had the limb been raised than it was sent spinning into the edge of the forest beyond, severed at an elbow by a sword that now slashed in gleaming arcs and whistling songs of razor-sharp metal piercing the air.

Talthagar!

The monstrous hulk bellowed in pain or surprise—none could be certain which—and stared at the stump from which spattered a stinking and viscous yellow blood. It flapped its sulfurous wings against the thicket and whirled around to hiss at the attacker. From his hidden place, and between the mighty legs of the demon, the Prince could see Talthagar raising his sword again in defiance, his chest heaving in frenzied bursts to recover the wind that had earlier been knocked out of his lungs.

The great filthy gargoyle rose a little off the ground and swooped at Talthagar with renewed ferocity, but the warrior was ready. Swinging and sliding across the slush and ice like the superb swordsman he was, he rolled into a ball underneath the nightmare just as it came upon him. Then he somersaulted out the other side between its kicking legs and sprang to his feet in time to deliver a wicked hack to the demon's ankle as it turned to face him, three feet off the ground. This time Oblixta's minion howled so balefully that Starbane had to cover his ears for fear they would burst at the resonating sound waves.

Seizing yet another chance, Talthagar dove again for his foe, this time aiming straight for its neck. Talons swiped, fully exposed and ripping buckskin and trails of flesh from the warrior's chest. Another claw hooked the sleeve of the swordsman's coat and sent him flying even more wildly than before. Again he landed against a tree and fell upon his back, devoid of breath. Worse, the sword had been flung from his grip, landing not far from where the real target remained crouched amid the briars. Talthagar raised his head, fighting unconsciousness as blood trickled from his nose and busted lower lip, just in time to see the creature retract its wings and lurch toward him, limping on its mauled ankle. It spread its gargantuan legs and, with the only remaining arm, reached down to lift the dazed victim into the air, bringing him even with its hideous face. The demon hissed with pleasure as it brought the warrior's head toward its open maw.

Starbane watched in spellbound horror, noting perversely that his friend's head was going to fit without a problem. Ilyssa saw it as well, from where she lay, paralyzed with fright, in the snow. Now she vanished into a spiraling faint, her face plopping into the soupy drift. Talthagar struggled as best he could, but his eyes were beginning to flutter and darkness beckoned at the edges of vision. Alas, even his best efforts would have been in vain against the otherworldly strength of his captor. The Prince could bear to see no more and buried his face in a furry sleeve, praying to die. As the demon tensed its jaw muscles and prepared to snap the warrior's head from his torso in one bite, however, it was struck square in the mouth by a series of missiles that appeared to come from everywhere, and yet seemingly from nowhere. Though Starbane in the copse, Ilyssa in her swoon, and Talthagar nearly in the creature's mouth could not tell, these lethal arrows had come from eight of General Coragus's marksmen, who were standing less than one hundred feet to the north, in the road. Their bows were raised in unison and war cries soared to the vault of the sky.

Every shot had been true.

Down came Talthagar's battered body as the beast yanked frantically upon the feathered arrows buried in its choking, hacking throat. Unsteadily, it lunged for the men who had now closed-in to surround it on all sides. Breaking from their circle with an unbalanced beat of its wings, the struggling beast reeled, swinging talons and trying to snap its bleeding maw. The horses scattered as it landed blindly, teetering in a haphazard dance over Ilyssa's supine form, threatening to crush her if it landed the right footfall. One of the archers raised his crossbow and shot again at the demon's head, but it ducked in the nick of time and plunged madly until it had snatched the man who fired, gripping him by a leg. Erupting in pain and rage, the monster shook the man so violently that the leg snapped off entirely while the rest of him smashed into four others, who had no time to get out of the gory missile's way without serious damage to their own bodies. Another soldier snuck in and managed to drag Ilyssa's body aside as the rest drew daggers and took turns swatting at the increasingly confused behemoth.

Starbane heard the fighting, hollering men and had by now poked his head from beneath the thicket. His eyes met those of the recovering Talthagar, who labored to his feet and began to look desperately about for his sword.

"There!" yelled the Prince, though his voice seemed little more than a croak over the din. He jabbed with a finger and pointed toward the place where he had seen the blade land and sink into the snow. "It's right over there!"

Talthagar ran to retrieve the sword and, within moments, had rejoined the incredible fray. The rescuers were down to three in number, now, as more of their companions had been mauled beyond hope by the crazed-but-fading creature. Sensing its disorientation, Talthagar waited until it turned its pierced head to one quailing dagger-wielder. Then, with a final, aching cry and a headlong rush, he dashed behind and straight up its back of bristling spines to stand between the great wings. The demon reached up with its one arm and brayed an infernal squeal, beating the wings furiously in an attempt to dislodge the intruder. It rose a few feet off the ground as it fought, but Talthagar maintained his balance and, with all possible strength, drove his sword deep into the scaled back. The foul brute went limp, wings collapsing and its body slamming with a terrific thud into the utterly ruined portion of roadway. Talthagar, bruised and battered, succumbed to exhaustion as the demise of his enemy sent him tumbling, head-over-heel, to the side. The three archers that remained alive crowded cautiously closer to the fallen devil, daggers drawn and crossbows pointed. The sudden and total silence was almost deafening after such a storm of fury.

"I think … I think it's dead," gasped Talthagar, rising to his feet. His face was contorted with pain.

One of the men in the circle crept up and jabbed it hard with a dagger, deep in what *looked*, in any case, like an ear.

"I'll say the damned thing is dead," he spat. Placing a boot on the stinking back, the solider withdrew Talthagar's sword with a mighty grunt and wiped the foul blood from the blade against a thick patch of winter lichen. He handed the weapon back to its owner.

"It's dead because you killed it," said the man. "I'm not sure our arrows would've made a difference. Good stab."

Talthagar sheathed his blade and nodded, still struggling to catch his breath and somehow recover. He looked toward Ilyssa and dashed to her side in the snow. The solider that had dragged her to relative safety was dead and nearly gutted fifteen feet away. Kneeling, Talthagar eased the girl over onto her back and cradled her head in his lap. He patted her cheeks softly, calling her name. She started to moan and whisper, her mind fighting the desire of her body to regain consciousness, afraid of what it might behold in a return to the light of day. Another of the other stunned soldiers grabbed a saddlebag that had fallen from one of the horses and brought it to

Talthagar. He placed it under Ilyssa's head and left her, stalking toward the briar patch where he knelt to summon the shaken Prince.

"Starbane, are you alright?"

"If you mean physically uninjured, I ... I *think* so."

"You can come out now. We're pretty sure it's dead."

The boy crawled slowly through the rustling debris as Talthagar began pulling aside huge mounds of briar, thorns and all, to free him.

"Ilyssa," said the dazed Prince. "Is she ... is she ...?"

"No, she's not dead. She fainted, but she's going to be okay, I think. Probably the best thing that could've happened to her. She's coming-to right now, in fact. You'd better get over there, if you're able. Believe me, you don't want her to wake up and see the mess we've got on our hands."

"What in the name of the gods *was* that thing?"

"No time for that now. Get over to Ilyssa. I've got to see about these men who just saved our lives and lost many of their own."

Starbane emerged from the thicket and staggered to Ilyssa. The grisly scene along the road made him heave with disgust. It was the ghastliest carnage he had ever witnessed. The huge beast lay oozing its foul blood in the snow, stinking up the vicinity with the smell of sulfur. Men and parts of men were scattered all around, their bright lifeblood splashed against the immaculate backdrop of white. Wiping his mouth and choking back tears, the Prince reached Ilyssa, who was still not quite out of her stupor. He buried his face in her wet hair.

"Starbane?" Her voice was a chilling whisper.

"Yes, it's me. Are you hurt?"

"Where are the horses?" Ilyssa said. Her eyes were struggling to focus. The Prince, nose dripping, looked around the landscape but could not see the animals anywhere.

"They must've bolted. Can you move?"

She clutched at the boy, fighting to sit up. "Yes. I'm not hurt. We've *got* to find the horses."

Prince Starbane rocked her gently in the snow while Talthagar joined the stricken trio of surviving archers that huddled, ashen-faced, around the carcass of the demon.

"What is it?" one of the men muttered, bleak as midnight on the last day of the world. "I've never seen anything like it."

"A surprise from the Kelnian Queen," hissed Talthagar, putting a hand over the bleeding wound across his chest and praying that the creature's talons were not venomous.

"What do you mean 'from the Kelnian Queen,' warrior?" This question had come from one of the other survivors, a giant of a man who now looked boyish and lost.

"I mean that this is … was … some *thing* concocted by that witch and sent to murder us."

The others look at him, incredulous in their shock and exhaustion. Talthagar pointed at Starbane and Ilyssa.

"I have the Prince Starbane Cadrach, Queen Oblixta's half-brother, with me. She's been searching for him ever since he escaped the Kelnian castle and I think this thing was dispatched here to capture him, or destroy him. Or both. I saw it try to fly off with him, at the very least." He gave the gross cadaver a vicious kick. "Trust me, this is her handiwork."

Another of the surviving archers stared at the ground, babbling. "We all knew she was some kind of enchantress, but … well, it's difficult to believe such things until you actually see them. Such things as *this.*"

"Yeah. I know," muttered Talthagar. "But you don't exactly see these things flying about the countryside every day now, do you?" With surging pity he surveyed the bodies of the dead archers. "By the Gods. Your men were brave. All of you saved us, I have no doubt of that. How in the name of Dryndym did you get here so quickly? We were at least two miles away from the encampment at Trindyll."

"Me and the others were out on hunting detail since this morning by orders of General Coragus, in those woods, right over there," said one of the archers, pointing to a rather thick range of trees near the roadway. "That's why we had the crossbows. When we heard that awful wailing the hair stood up on the back of our necks and we rushed over here as soon as we could. We're no cowards, but … but this is a bit much." His voice trailed off and his mind seemed to wander along with it, nearer to one of the mangled corpses. "I sent Digger, one of the men in our group, back to the encampment on one of your horses. We managed to catch the white mare while you were fighting that thing and we were trying to take aim at it. All three of your mounts were getting ready to bolt on you when we got to the scene, and I can't say as I blame them. They'll send some men out here. Probably the General will come, too. He'll definitely want to see this."

Talthagar turned and looked for any sign of Skull. Soon he saw a set of distinct tracks leading off the road, away from the chaos. The warrior marched over to his charges.

"Prince Starbane, I'm going to find Skull. He's probably just up around the bend somewhere. Will you two be okay here for a bit? The men that survived will stay with you and some more men will be coming from the camp at Trindyll very soon. These guys were hunting nearby when all of this went down. One of them caught Ilyssa's horse and rode back for help on her."

"Then Wyrnie's alright?" said the girl, stirring. "At least horses have some sense."

"The horse is alive, which is more than can be said for the men lying yonder," said Talthagar. "But I don't want her to see any of this, Prince. Take her over near the trees and try to keep her warm."

"Oh, the two of you can stop fussing over my delicate constitution," Ilyssa snapped. "I'll live."

Starbane nodded. "It came from Oblixta, didn't it," he said evenly, his eyes searching the harsh landscape, seeing everything and seeing nothing at all.

"If I had to bet on it, I'd say so," replied Talthagar. "I've certainly never seen anything like that before, and I've seen a lot in my time. Even the dragons of Colstra."

Prince Starbane looked ready to weep. "Then it's my fault that those men are dead."

Talthagar lifted the youth's chin in his hand. "Listen to me and listen well. It's not your fault. We're here—all of us, in a sense—to protect you. Doing that, getting you to King Sye's castle, or to Rowan Blaize, is part of winning this war that seems to be so close at hand and yet so far away. The lives of these men are all on your sister's soul, if she has one. Not yours. Do you understand me?"

Starbane nodded reluctantly and Talthagar released him. "Now, look after Ilyssa while I look for Skull. When more men from the camp come and we get our horses back, we're heading faster than ever to King Sye. Time appears to be running out on us."

The warrior turned and glanced once more at the three surviving archers, who were now trying to cover the bodies of their comrades with their capes. He walked past them, his sharp whistle for Skull echoing across the macabre valley and into the distant reaches of the indifferent woodland beyond.

❧ ❦

"Unnecessary!"

This was the only word King Sye spoke as he turned his attention back to the circle of grim-faced advisors crowding his throne. He stretched forth a gnarly hand mottled with age-spots, but for all its discoloration it was still the sturdiest hand in the kingdom. The Princess Malinna, his four year-old daughter, looked up at him adoringly from her place on his lap. Sye's chief advisor paused and then scowled. In his mounting anxiety, he had bitten the inside of his lip and now tasted blood.

"Majesty, now that you've sent the third legion toward the Gleer-an Plains and alerted the Lords of the Turbax, we thought it might be a good idea to draft a few thousand more men from the Southern Tier. Have them ready to go, just to reinforce the castle."

"Again I say 'unnecessary,' Galtra."

"But surely you must know that we're thinking only of the security of the entire royal family, Sire. We simply have no idea when the Kelnian Queen may attempt to move over the Northern mountains and launch her strike. It could be a matter of mere *days*."

King Sye gestured to his child's governess, who was hovering dutifully behind the white marble throne. "Take the Princess to her mother, please. I believe the Queen is in the banquet hall seeing to a torn bit of tapestry or some such pressing matter."

The child was removed after a parting pat atop the head from her doting father and, once she had been whisked from the dire business at hand, Sye cleared his throat and faced his advisors with all the impetuousness for which he was legendary.

"If you think the miserable Kelnians will even get *over* the Pyr Mida Mountains, much less to the Gleeran Plains, then none of you have lived long enough in this kingdom!" snapped the monarch, feathers clearly starting to ruffle. "As I've said, we will move onto the mountain ourselves before they do and strike them hard the moment they try to cross, *if* they try. We'll cripple them in their tracks. If any of them make it past that hurdle there'll be so few with any fight left in them that the River Barons' *children* could do them in! It amazes me, the number of doomprophets with which I've apparently surrounded myself. Naysayers who fear I'm going to just *give* Corydia to that … to that … *madwoman.*"

"We've warned against underestimating her, Sire," said another of the robed counselors, but the King waved him away, equally annoyed.

"By the Gods, I haven't underestimated anything," he grumbled. "I know what she's done, and I know her capabilities. I'm also aware of the weaknesses present in those Kelnian provinces which allowed themselves to be so easily overthrown by her brigands in the first place. *Our* world, gentlemen, is not theirs. The Kelnian usurpers will scurry like rats back over the Pyr Mida and I just might have a mind to follow them," Sye added, wagging a crooked finger. "We'll have no trouble beating them back. I know my resources. I know my people."

A servant approached from a side-chamber with a tray of steaming fare and a goblet of wine. Sye lost interest in the briefing. "I suppose you daft birds will have to see for yourselves," he snapped. "Now get out of here, the lot of you. Go on! And don't come back until the day when battle reports confirm everything I've just told you. That is, as I said, if Oblixta even dares to cross at all."

"There *is* one more crucial matter, Sire," said Galtra, the chief advisor.

"Oh, for heaven's sake," croaked the King.

"We've received word that Talthagar is bound for the castle as we speak, only two days away."

"Ah!" said Sye with a slight clap of his hands. "That is fine news, actually. I look forward to hearing someone make some sense around here again. It's been so long since he and I have had a chance to sit and chat. I don't know why I allow him to be away so long on these little missions."

"That may be, Sire, but Talthagar's 'guest,' if you will, is of more immediate interest, in our humble opinion."

"A guest? Who is it? Not who I *think* it is, eh?"

"None other than the Prince Starbane Cadrach, half-brother of the Kelnian Queen and rightful heir to that kingdom's throne."

"Really now?" replied the King, raising a bristled brow. "Then the rumors that have reached my ears via you squawking murder of crows are true. The Prince is alive and no doubt seeking asylum—or seeking my sorcerer, Rowan Blaize! And what of his parents?"

"They, Sire," said Galtra, "are presumably still dead."

King Sye began to pick with long yellow fingernails and considerable discrimination at the rich assortment of food upon his tray. He said nothing at all for a deadening moment.

"Whatever the case may be, Your Majesty, we are certain that you and the Kelnian royal will have much of import to discuss."

Sye dipped a piece of bread into a bowl of fatty broth and snorted. "Possibly, but if the Prince indeed comes seeking my ancient wizard to help him reclaim his throne, then he'll be sadly disappointed. I won't risk any possible distraction on the part of our shy and reclusive Rowan Blaize while that hag to the north is stewing-up a battle. I aim to keep the old agreements and see that he's left well alone. Ah, well. I'm sure we'll discover all we need to know in due course. For now, I bid you all to leave me to my lunch. I'll receive this pathetic little Starbane exile—and

Talthagar—when they arrive. See that they are made quite comfortable until I send for them."

The tall counselors turned as one and departed the throne room in a susurrus of their elaborate, flowing robes. King Sye turned back to his hot meal with enthusiasm, not yet ready to ponder the bitter cup of conflict from which his beloved Corydia would soon begin to drink its fill.

❧❦

Oblixta frowned, leaning into the air outside the window of her Ritual Chamber. Night had fallen and a radiant half-moon glowed cold in the heavens as she gazed in all directions, as if half-expecting to suddenly see the silhouette of the demon, fluttering across the nightscape, the boy in its grip.

She knew, however, that this was *not* going to happen.

Since mid-day, the excruciating side effects of her sorcery had all but disappeared. Gone were the wheezing and the rattling coughs. The dehydration that had begun to crack the soft skin of her lips and mouth had also vanished. By twilight, the color and tone had returned to her face and, while these things made her much more comfortable, they also revealed a severe malfunction in the spell she had cast. The demon would not return to her. Not ever.

In the Queen's mind, there were only two things that could have interrupted the spell, one of them being the reacquisition, by the gargoyle-demon, of its own will and power. This idea she dismissed outright. The incantation she had used, and the amount of power she had exerted, had been supreme. Such potency would have been impossible, even for a beast of its formidable caliber, to resist. The other possibility was that her fiendish envoy had been destroyed by another party. This scenario, while also difficult for her to fathom, seemed most likely.

But how and by who? she wondered, rigid with vexation. Her brother could not have gotten to the wizard Rowan Blaize so quickly, and she would have sensed if the sorcery of another magician had crossed her purposes. Warriors, perhaps? It would take a small army to kill the demon, unless the beast itself had made some egregious tactical miscalculation. Unless it had struck too soon and too unwarily. Indeed, Oblixta was forced to ponder the likelihood that her brother was now in the protective company of King Sye's forces across the mountain in Corydia, if not quite yet in the very shadow of the King himself—or that of his fabled warlock. Some battalion had thwarted her devil; that was the only answer.

She stormed out of the chamber, sweeping away from its pulsating firelight. In the adjacent reception hall, she ascended the dais as if she were nothing more than a hint of shadow and sat on the slate throne. No one else was moving about the place; her blinded wraith-servants had been dismissed for the day and the lowly mortal slaves were trying their best to avoid her entirely after rumors had spread about the disappearance of the handmaid, the sacrifice.

A few slaves, she learned, had actually managed to run away from the castle into the doom of winter. Oblixta did not care. She drummed her eternally restless talons on the stone and contemplated her next move. General Kerrion had warned her that the legions would not be ready to enter Corydia for at least another month, and here she was, barking orders and demands for greater efficiency while her own methods were failing! What a dismaying turn of events—one she would not be swift to mention, by any means, to her Supreme Warlord. She had other work to do, now. It was imperative that she get the boy before he managed to get the Gragan wizard's little scarified "message" to the Corydian King and his Blaize conjurer.

The Southern King and his allies would have no power over her, she vowed, especially at the behest of her miserable half-sibling. Some sort of preemptive strike was now necessary, something far more personal than the summoning of a supernatural envoy to do all the work that even the most horrific of demons would not do, now. Taking a deep breath Oblixta closed her eyes in the throne room, murmuring again the unholy words that had allowed her to maintain power over the infernal creature and a certain level of sympathetic contact with it. Then she frowned, sensing once more that her groping and probing had found no point of contact. *It's dead,* she concluded, indignant. Somehow, some way, her brother had foiled her powers and plans again, almost certainly with the assistance of others.

And it was time for those "others" to pay dearly—kings, warriors, wizards, and all.

෨ං⇔

The remaining ride through the land of Corydia to the castle of King Sye was not nearly as uncomfortable or depressing as Starbane had anticipated. Although memories of the demonic attack kept moods dismal, at best, the trio had recovered their horses and their desperation to speed toward safety. Even more encouraging was the growing cheer of their surroundings; the farther south they ventured, the warmer it became and, as horses galloped at steady speed, they were able to shed some of the oppressive garments of winter and let their faces bask in the swelling glow of sunshine. Even the now-quiet and worried Talthagar commented happily on the huge portions of land from which the snow drifts were melting away. As the three riders bypassed the region known as the Gleeran Plains, keeping abreast of the rugged woodlands that encircled on either side, they smiled to see the faint glimmer of green grass in so many places. Spring was near.

The route Talthagar had chosen would take them across only a small corner of country marked by the Gleeran Plains. Despite the progressively muddy turf, the three began to sense that their traumatized minds were under repair at the sight of the majestic countryside, sweeping before them along the mighty Turbax River. Against this river were a series of six immense fortresses, rising like watchful sentinels from one corner of the horizon to the other; the scope was breathtaking—lands and villages surrounding these fortresses extended as far as the eye could see.

"Those are the fiefdoms of the five River Masters, the Diadem Lords," Talthagar had explained. "All of them are very powerful and loyal to King Sye, of course. These Lords are the ones who own most of the rich farmland that makes Corydia prosperous."

"And it is the farmland my sister covets," added Starbane. "But she won't get it. The closer we get to your king and to Rowan Blaize, the more confident I feel that I'm going to get my revenge. That scar is fairly burning on the inside of my arm."

"Don't get ahead of yourself," cautioned Talthagar atop the faithful Skull, who seemed to glide along the trail, so majestic was his gait. "I've told you that Sye can have very strange opinions of his own wizard, and we have no idea what opinion he may have of you, yet."

"He's bound to like me," said the Prince, allowing himself the luxury of confidence for the first time in what seemed an eternity. "Royals understand each other, Talthagar."

"Pardon me for forgetting," said the warrior with a roll of his eyes.

Even Ilyssa had to sigh.

"You two magpies seem to bicker an awful lot," she noted. "Between keg-rides, mountain crossings, gargoyle assaults, and the terror of meeting someone who'll actually *look* like a king, I'm beginning to wonder if it was a good idea to join this expedition. It might have been better to deal with the Prefect back in Pyr Mida. I could've stuck a knife in him when he wasn't looking, easy enough. Oh, yes, right between his ribs!"

Starbane and Talthagar looked at each other in surprise. Their heretofore overwhelmed Ilyssa had remained a trifle grouchy and more than a little bold in her sparse commentary since Oblixta's hell-spawn had nearly finished them off. She seemed to care for nothing except her horse, Wyrnie, ever since.

"I hope you're not seriously repenting of your decision to come along," the Prince called to her from his saddle.

Ilyssa shot him a quick, coy stare. "No, I'm not repenting it," she said over her shoulder as she galloped into the lead alongside Talthagar. "And I didn't have much of a choice in the matter, as you might recall. But for better or worse, we're here now, and I have a feeling things *will* take a turn for the better. I'm sorry if I seem a bit snappy. I'm hardly an ingrate, and don't want to be taken for one."

"It's alright," said Talthagar, with a sly smile. "I'm just glad to see you bounce back from all of this madness. Not easy to do, for a girl."

"I think you'll find that *women* can easily do the things that men sometimes find most difficult," was Ilyssa's tart reply, and then she decided to change the subject. "The fiefdoms of your River Masters look quite huge," she said with a nod toward the shimmering Turbax. "But why are their castles so close together?"

"The Turbax Lords are all members of the same family," answered the warrior. "An unbroken line for centuries. The Five, led by Lord Epernalus, are as sure a protection for this realm against invaders as any obscure sorcerer, or even King Sye for that matter. The five families have always been able to divvy-up those immense agricultural plots you see across the plains and somehow manage to get along famously with each other."

"Imagine that, a family getting along," said Starbane. "That certainly doesn't seem to be the prevailing tradition back in Kelnia. Will we be visiting these Lords and their cities?"

Talthagar shook his head. "No. Our journey takes us away from the Diadem Lords. Sye's castle is beyond and, to get there, we must travel toward the East, at first, Prince."

"Well done, then. And, by the way, after all we've been through in so short a time, I think you can start calling me 'Starbane.' Both of you. Let's face it, I'm no royal in this land and we're all friends by now, I should think."

"As you like. Rein your horses toward the East, friends, and ride with me these last wretched miles to see the great Corydian King," said Talthagar with a slight bow and mischievous grin. Ilyssa said nothing, but sneered as their animals turned as one into the southeasterly wind.

Onward they flew and, after several hours of arduous travel and the bypassing of all five Turbax River fiefdoms, they were struck again by new natural wonders that graced the region as if gilded by the gods themselves. Flatlands gave way to pendulous, rolling hill country while the road writhed and swirled through caverns, chasms with robust waterfalls, and barely hidden pools that shone like mirrored glass. At last they came upon a stony corridor banked on either side by steep cliffs of jagged limestone. In one sense, Starbane felt that they were no longer riding *upon* the world as much as they were sinking deeper *into* it. Engulfed by the sloping terrain, they paused only to rest and eat a little bit of lunch in the hushed and awesome atmosphere. When they resumed their trek, the snows were almost completely gone from the landscape and up from the ice-dripping crags they rose to behold a heavily wooded expanse once again.

Near dusk, they managed to enter the lush cover of a sylvan territory Talthagar proudly introduced as the Forest of Yur. The place instantly lulled the youthful riders with its towering trees and the beguiling fragrance of pitch that only thousands of budding Falthurns could give-off in the first throes of a warming springtime. They felt hypnotized. As evening shades fell with greater depth and the stillness of the region took on an even more striking quality, Talthagar informed his friends that Yur Forest had been maintained by King Sye for years as his own, private hunting reserve. More than once as they followed the well-beaten but manicured trail, the horses and riders were startled by the sudden rustling of hedgerows or the quick flash of white as deer turned tail and scampered into hiding.

The castle of Sye was just beyond the far edge of the wide wood, Talthagar warned, and all were filled with different sensations of anxiety as the last rays of the fading sun finally illuminated their first sight of the stunning edifice. Starbane and Ilyssa were unprepared for the grandeur spread before them, even as it was cast in the subdued, glimmering shadows of a dying day. Indeed, the castle of Sye rose as a complex, spiked mountain of red-tinted sandstone from the middle of a lake whose waters were a placid, breathtaking reflection of rose upon gray. Along the crescent of the shoreline, the forest's far reaches were curtained with a swift-rising mist, the colors of the distant trees blending almost imperceptibly with the slate hues of the lake-water. Despite the immensity and magnificence of the scenery, the youths were overwhelmed with an almost irresistible sense of being secluded and, somehow, *embraced.*

"It's unreal," whispered Ilyssa in open-mouthed reverence. Starbane found himself nodding agreement without even realizing that his head was moving and that his own jaw had dropped open.

"Far more wonderful than even my father's castle," he said. "I'd heard stories of its beauty since I was very small, but they didn't prepare me for *this*." He turned to Talthagar, who had seen it many times and was still careful to slow Skull to a near crawl so that he, too, could soak in this vision. The three horses clopped idly out of the forest and downward upon the stony road that curved toward the shore of the entrancing lake.

"Sye's forebears chose this island as the seat of their power ages ago," said Talthagar. "It was here that my mother served as a lady-in-waiting for Sye's first wife, Scilde, who died very young. It's also where my father, who was one of Sye's greatest knights, met my mother and they married. I think I was actually conceived in those woodlands behind us. The lake is named 'Scilde,' in fact, after Sye's first wife. The new queen, though, is Adurra, and she is just as beautiful, everyone says. And just as young. I agree. But you'll see for yourselves soon enough."

The Prince fixed his gaze upon the majestic bridge that flew gracefully from the great boulders along the shore of the lake all the way to the castle's stately entrance gate. There, several wagons and horsemen could be seen milling-about in the distance, preparing to cross. Talthagar pulled ahead to lead them down the final stretch and noted that everyone had to stop at the sentry posts to receive clearance from the multitude of guards.

"Once we're over the bridge, and then over the *drawbridge* part of the bridge," he emphasized, "we'll head into the castle courtyard and then up to the keep itself."

"Will we actually get a chance to see King Sye tonight?" inquired Starbane as they took their places in the long line of those seeking admission. The warrior shook his head.

"I highly doubt it. Sye usually retires, with the rest of his family, to the private apartments, right around sunset. He's very old, but don't let his age fool you into thinking he's a dotard."

"I'm not sure what a dotard is," said Starbane, "even though I've read that word a lot in books about places just like this."

"What?"

"Never mind. Does it mean 'crazy old man'?"

"I guess. But King Sye is far from *that*. Moreover, he won't meet anyone as stinky as we are. We'll need a good night's rest, hot baths, and some excellent food, for a change. Trust me, I'm ready for it."

"So am I," muttered Ilyssa, gazing in wonder at the impossible surroundings. She felt like pinching herself. "I can't believe we finally made it here, seeing as we were almost eaten by a devil, or a gargoyle, or whatever it was."

"Was there ever any doubt, with the good men of General Coragus to intervene and *me* along to protect you?" said Talthagar. "And forget about that thing. It's dead and nothing Oblixta hexes-up will be able to touch you here." He breathed his own discreet sigh of relief when he saw the drawn and pale faces of both protégés. As they finally reached the sentry post, a bevy of soldiers crowded around and scrutinized the three in lantern light. The travelers recognized the famed insignia of King Sye across the many breastplates and shields and helmets. Its chief symbol was a full moon pierced with a sword, and had been known—with respect among the common people, at least—even in distant Kelnia. Talthagar hailed the curious, questioning guards, many of whom recognized him at once, and he wasted no time in explaining the identity of his companions. Brows were raised beneath all shining helmets at mention of the Prince Starbane Cadrach. Looking at the stern faces of the royal sentries caused Ilyssa's heart to beat with mounting distress. It was still difficult to trust a soldier, she thought, no matter the place or circumstance.

One of the sentries informed Talthagar that word of his impending arrival had already come down from the King's inner circle and that they were to be admitted to the castle without delay. Thus it was that the last portion of their long escape from despair offered only the splendid bridge before them; they crossed its expanse with a sense of accomplishment that seemed to flood every limb, every vein. Once beyond the drawbridge and massive entry-gates, with their carved scenes of King Sye's numerous military excursions and victories, the three entered the courtyard, which was really more like a labyrinthine hamlet, bustling with people who paid them no notice. The little "town" within the castle seemed to hum with activity despite the onset of darkness.

"Everyone here works, in some capacity or another, for the upkeep of the castle and the welfare of the royal family," said Talthagar as the tiring horses hung their heads a bit and plodded past tailors' shops and smithies, bakers, and carpenters. "There are hundreds living within the walls of this great place."

"I can see that," said Starbane. "I do know how castles tend to function. And these people are obviously prosperous. Look at their storefronts. Their clothing. Even the streets in here are paved to perfection."

"We didn't have that much, even in a city as big as Pyr Mida," said Ilyssa. "What a dump it was, compared to this. I'm extra glad I left."

"You'll find that things are much different in the Southern kingdom," said Talthagar. "Particularly in these times. I'll show you as much as I can tomorrow, assuming we're not summoned to meet the King at the crack of dawn. Right now, I want to get these horses stabled and get all of us settled inside and fed."

"You'll get no disagreement from me," said the Prince, putting a hand across his grumbling stomach.

The massive and ornate iron doors of the keep were still wide open after they entrusted Skull and the other two mounts to a solicitous bevy of stable-hands. Ilyssa's vision soared along the sides of looming obelisk towers piercing the night sky like needles and, once within the keep, she marveled at the opulence of the courtyard gardens. A stunning carved fountain of nymphs, dryads, and smiling fauns veritably roared in greeting amid the spray. Soldiers and servants of all ranks were gathered everywhere. The monolithic central tower made both Starbane and Ilyssa feel dizzy just to gaze upward. This heart of King Sye's castle was itself surrounded by a second wide moat of clear, clean lake water, its ramparts boasting pennants of varied colors that snapped and fluttered in wind currents high above. The round tower rose in a sweeping layer of tiers dotted with seemingly innumerable windows and arched doorways. People could be seen scurrying in and out of these openings like ants on a conical hill of dark sand. In many places, winding stone stairwells abounded, their flights guarded by grotesque but exquisitely crafted gargoyle statues that reminded the youths not a little of the malefactor they had encountered on the road from Trindyll.

In the distant windows above, shrouded by the settling night, there flickered the lights of myriad hearth-fires, while smoke plumes wafted heavenward from unseen vents. Ilyssa, for all the adrenalin pumping through her body at such a sight, felt a strange weariness, and the need to perhaps pinch herself again for possibly dreaming such a scene into existence. It was almost impossible to believe that she would actually be sleeping in such a place. Starbane smiled at her awed countenance as Talthagar led them through the crowd.

"I don't imagine you've ever been in a castle before," he said, even though he was nearly as amazed as was she. Kelnia's Cadrach Castle was great, but nothing like this. *Little wonder Oblixta covets the wealth of Sye*, he thought.

"No, I haven't been hanging about in many castles," said Ilyssa with a sigh. "Which goes along rather well with the fact that I've never happened to meet princes jumping out of wagons and beer barrels before, either. These aren't typical city-girl experiences, even in bizarre days like these. When I left Pyr Mida that day to let myself freeze to death in the mountainside forest, I had no idea that royalty would, quite literally, be on tap. Do you think the gods are playing tricks on us, Starbane?"

"I think they've always been playing tricks. On everyone, everywhere."

Ilyssa could only stare at her new friend with a mixture of suspicion and bewilderment.

Talthagar, meanwhile, had caught the attention of a lieutenant who soon led them to the edge of the moat. It glistened below, reflecting rippled shards of moonlight above, and the officer called to a sentry tower. The signal was received, for a great cranking noise was heard and the gargantuan inner drawbridge was lowered. The thing groaned and whined as it descended on chains of linked iron as thick as a man's torso. When it reached their side of the expanse, the Corydian soldier held up a hand and asked them to be patient as he awaited clearance from within the tower's torch-lit halls. Starbane and Ilyssa leaned to peer within, astonished again by the long hallway visible with its rows of polished granite and limestone pillars. Soon another guard, this one armed with a devastating spear twice as tall as he was, stalked across the drawbridge and greeted the arrivals.

"If you'll follow me, we shall see that you are sheltered for the night. King Sye and Queen Adurra have retired for the evening, but wish me to express welcome to all of you, particularly the Prince Starbane Cadrach of Kelnia. King Sye gives assurance that the Prince and his companion are honored guests and he bids you peace. You, too, are welcomed, Talthagar," added the dignified soldier. "The King looks forward to meeting with all of you tomorrow morning, after breakfast. You will be informed of the exact time, of course. Come, follow me."

Starbane stifled a gulp as they were led away. The air had suddenly become cold in the wake of the rising yellow moon's appearance and Ilyssa shivered as, at last, the three of them were escorted across the drawbridge and soon lost in the vast, engulfing womb of the incredible palace.

ৡৣ

PART TWO
Oblixta's Revenge

I

All Fessed-Up and No Place to Go

"Ilyssa, you're the most beautiful thing I've ever seen!"

For a moment, Starbane felt like reaching up and clapping his jaw shut, for he was certain it had to be hanging open in foolish wonder. At the top of the stairway, Ilyssa beamed down at him and then burst into laughter, pointing in gentle mockery at his brazen admiration. She was beautiful, and she knew it, twirling around a bit for his pleasure on the stairs in the luxurious white-lace dress her new "handmaidens" had given to her for the upcoming audience with King Sye. Her auburn hair was washed and arranged in plaits that seemed to mimic golden fields at the hour of sunset; it was spread, shiny and thick, across the delicate ivory of her shoulders. When she lifted the hem of her gown slightly to descend the marble steps, the Prince could see two embroidered shoes upon her feet. He also thought he could hear the rustle of some lacy undergarment. By the time she reached the bottom of the stairs, he was so agog that Ilyssa felt the self-conscious need to blush and cuff him, quite hard, on his shoulder.

"Oh, stop staring, Your Gloriousness," she muttered. "It's only *me* underneath all of this finery and scrubbed skin."

"I can't help it. You look like a princess yourself."

"No, just a poor girl on the run from a sorceress-queen and dirty, slobbering old men," she said, and then drew Starbane confidentially aside into the shadows of the plush and columned corridor. "I've got to tell you ... I spent the most unbelievable night *ever* in my life. In the most incredible bed I've ever seen!" Her eyes were afire with delight. "I could never have imagined the like of it. I had three maids, and all of them tended only to *me*. First, there was this magnificent meal of duck and wine and candied oranges and then, after supper, they poured this huge marble pool in my room full of hot water and all sorts of sweet-smelling potions and perfumes, for my bath, you know? Then they gave me a night-robe with feathers on it and turned back the furs of that bed. And to think that, only a matter of days ago, I would either have been frozen dead with my eyes pecked-out by birds and my body eaten by beasts in the wood *or* I'd be doing who-knows-what for that abominable prefect in Pyr Mida. Actually, I'd be dead in either case, because I would have found a way to knife the filthy monster by now. But this? *This* is incredible!"

Starbane frowned and laughed, a bit nervously, at the sudden vision of Ilyssa's eyeballs being pecked away, and of her slaving for (and then murdering) a drunken prefect. She certainly had turned out to be a cavalier sort of girl.

"Well, heh ... you mustn't ever, ever think about that fate again," cautioned the Prince with a bright smile of his own. He took Ilyssa by her arms and, for the first time, she had a chance to notice his own transformation.

"Please forgive my vanity, Starbane," she gasped. "I was so caught up in my own new trappings I hadn't had time to notice yours. You look ... you look—"

"Like an actual member of royalty for the first time since you met me?"

"Something like that, yes."

"Then I duly thank you, as well," he said, with more than a hint of pride, inspecting himself and tugging at the fine outfit, which was dark blue and featured a cape of exquisite silk. *"My* bevy of servants said these clothes belonged to King Sye himself, when he was a young man like me. Said they required a frightful amount of dusting, but they look quite good now, in my opinion. Wow. It's been awhile since I've dressed like this."

The Prince then recounted for Ilyssa his own night of comfort, appreciating it every bit as much as she, though from a different standpoint. It had indeed been so long since he had experienced the actual pleasures of royalty that he often feared he would forget how to act like royalty altogether … if the need was ever to arise again. Now, the time had come, however improbably. His first exposure to King Sye's excellent hospitality was a reminder of much happier circumstances. They had already eaten delectable breakfasts brought to them in their bedchambers. There was no sign of Talthagar, however, and they wondered if his first night had been as luxurious. No one deserved it more, they concurred, given all he had done to get them this far along.

"I'm still hungry, would you believe it?" said Starbane. "I don't imagine that Talthagar's going to meet us here in the halls. Besides, it's drafty in this spot. Let's find the great dining hall. There's always one of *those* in a proper castle, and I should know. Talthagar can find us there, if he wishes. He'll need to, if we're to meet with the King as planned."

Thus the two began to make their way through the gleaming corridors, inquiring of the first servant they encountered as to the dining hall's location. It wasn't far. When at last they descended another flight of spiraling stone stairs, they entered the tapestry-festooned chamber and were stunned to find Talthagar himself, finishing a plate of quails' eggs and dark bread.

"Ha! I thought you might be here," said the Prince, striding proudly up to the tremendous long-table. "We had our morning meals served to us in bed, I'm pleased to report. But we're still hungry. I hope you haven't gobbled everything up. You're quite stingy."

"Very funny, little Prince," said the warrior. "You're a perpetual fountain of laughs. As a matter of fact, the servants will be bringing some more trays presently. You two piglets have nothing to worry about."

"Did you hear that, Ilyssa? 'Piglets,' he calls us. I hope you're not this charming when we meet King Sye. I daresay he doesn't put up with your nonsense."

"The King knows that I am a perfect gentleman," insisted Talt-hagar through a mouthful of food. Ilyssa rolled her sapphire eyes as she reclined rather awkwardly in a massive gilded chair.

"Men. Always jousting, even over eggs. I pity the women that'll ever have to put up with either of you."

"You look perfectly Starbanely this morning," said Talthagar, ignoring Ilyssa's remark and pointing a skewer-fork at the Prince's blue ensemble.

"Well, I'm used to being dressed this way. Or at least I was, once. Are you jealous, Talthagar? I notice that your wardrobe hasn't changed much since last night."

The warrior had also received a fresh set of clothes, but his were almost identical to those he had been wearing: a simple woolen shirt and buckskin trousers, with a scabbard and sword at his waist. The only difference was that his hair was washed and braided, his face was clean-shaven, and the shirt bore the distinctive insignia of King Sye.

"All of these pleasantries aside," said Talthagar, laying down his fork, "we've got to figure out what we're going to say to the king. They'll be announcing us in about an hour, you know."

"What do you mean about what I've got to *say?"* asked Starbane.

"I mean that, after I've introduced you, you've got to formally request political asylum in his court, for one thing. Didn't you know that?"

"No," replied the boy. "How am I supposed to know? Do you think I run from realm to realm every day, asking kings for political asylum? Besides, my whole purpose in coming here was to ask for the help of his sorcerer, Rowan Blaize, so I can get my *own* father's throne back. It's my throne now, by rights."

Talthagar suppressed a growl and forced himself to be patient.

"I told you before that just waltzing in and bothering King Sye about Rowan Blaize isn't a good idea, right away. He doesn't *own* Rowan Blaize, if Rowan Blaize even still exists. Rowan Blaize isn't really *his* wizard. Their only association, like I said, is some arrangement between Blaize and Sye's ancestors, made centuries ago, some deal wherein the wizard will magically protect the castle and its descendants, so long as he's given the Forest of Shadnai to live in, so long as he's left *alone*. Sye won't be willing to mess with that agreement, if I know anything about him. His father didn't. Nor his father's father. None of them ever bothered Rowan Blaize, according to legend, mainly because nothing rotten has ever befallen this kingdom."

"Well that's just great," snapped Starbane. "The smelly old Gragan warlock burns his own 'strike-a-bargain' sign into my arm in Oblixta's dungeons, then he and Celintha tell me to escape to find Rowan Blaize, and then you keep telling me the magician might not even be around here, after I've come so far? After nearly being abducted by a gargoyle? After years of imprisonment? After being attacked by tusked werewolves? Look, here are their teeth. Did I ever show you these beauties?" added the Prince, pulling the necklace of fangs from his elaborate collar. "I'm practically a prophecy-boy, for crying out loud!"

"I haven't said anything to intentionally discourage you," replied Talthagar, lifting his palms defensively. "And you've already shown us the teeth."

"Then where is Rowan Blaize? I can't waste any more time."

"In Shadnai Forest, supposedly."

"And where is that place, *supposedly?*"

"A few miles south of the castle and the lake," said Talthagar, now a bit more testily. "Look, if you're planning to talk to the King like this, I can tell you right away that you'll be asking for trouble. And the fact remains, kid—King Sye agreed to use Kashizma spies to help rescue you, but what he's willing to do beyond that is anyone's guess. You need to start by thanking him and asking, formally, for asylum. Let the rest happen when, and *if*, it's destined to happen. There were a lot of forces at work in your initial escape and he wasn't involved with each and every one of them. He'll want to mull matters over for a while, I guarantee."

"And let the murders of my parents go unpunished?" said the Prince, coldly. "Let Oblixta get away with trying to kill us all? Let her get away with ruining the lives of the Kelnian people? Is that what you propose?"

"You know I'm not saying that," said Talthagar, feeling genuine compassion for the youth. "But these matters are not so simple, and kings are not so easily goaded to action, by anyone. Much less by fallen royals from foreign realms. They take their own counsel."

"He's probably right," said Ilyssa, digging into some of Talthagar's eggs. "I'd play it a little more subtly, if I were you."

"And what would *you* know of it?" snapped the boy.

"In case you didn't notice, life hasn't been all white lace and down pillows for me, up until this moment," retorted Ilyssa. "I'm no royal, Master Fancy Pants, but I've suffered with the rest of the Kelnian people because of *your* sister, or half-sister, or whatever she is."

"I didn't mean to imply anything else," said Starbane. "I'm sorry. This is all a bit overwhelming. But no matter what you say, Talthagar, I'm going to ask the King what I mean to ask him about the wizard. I have the right."

Talthagar nodded slowly. "Yeah, you do. I can't stop you. And my advice is probably worthless. But don't blame me if you offend old Sye at your very first meeting. Remember, Princeling, you need *him* far more than he needs you. Ask him for asylum, and ask the same for Ilyssa, too, while you're at it. Never hurts to be thorough ... and official."

One of the King's lesser counselors entered the dining hall and, after clearing his throat conspicuously, signaled that the monarch was now ready to receive them in the Throne Room. Ilyssa, for all of her forced confidence, was trying not to shake in her fabulous slippers and the Prince affected the most regal posture he could recall from his father's long-lost example as they departed. Morning was at its peak and sunlight flooded the hallways, rendering everything dreamlike as rays coursed through windows of exotically colored stained-glass high above. A man in pompous scarlet clothing stopped them at an appropriately imperious marble archway. Boasting a black moustache that flowed from lip to ruffled shirt collar, he scrutinized the three visitors.

"I am Calix, and I shall announce you to the royal family," he sniffed. "Names and official titles, if you please."

"Well, you know *me*, Calix," said Talthagar, wiping away a few breakfast crumbs from his chin. "And you know that I've brought the Kelnian Prince, Starbane Cadrach."

Calix wrinkled his nose and stared expectantly at Ilyssa.

"Oh, this is the ... uh ... the Lady Ilyssa, handmaiden of Pyr Mida in Kelnia," explained Talthagar. "Guest of the Prince."

"Alright," said Calix, after a second or two of hesitation. "I suppose you're all ready to meet the royal family. You appear clean and properly groomed."

"Of course we're clean!" said Starbane, incredulous.

"Then wait for my signal and enter, slowly, your Young Majesty. And ... handmaiden. And you, too, Talthagar."

Calix disappeared behind a rippling waterfall of velvet curtains and the trio was soon struck rigid by the piercing sound of many trumpets blaring in unison. The booming voice of Calix followed.

"May I present Talthagar, Champion of King Sye and his Queen Adurra ... Talthagar, Scourge of the Foes of Corydia," he brayed in a great, nasal call that was almost as unsettling as the horns.

"That's me," said the warrior. "Just do as I do when he says your names."

"I may be young, but I haven't forgotten how it's generally *done,*" said the impetuous prince. Talthagar swept into the throne room. The voice of Calix boomed a moment later.

"May I present to the Glorious Court His Royal Highness, Starbane Cadrach, Son of Adraeus, Esteemed Prince of Kelnia, along with his ... er ... companion, the Lady Ilyssa of the principality of Pyr Mida."

Trumpets blared anew. "Follow along a step or two behind me, Ilyssa, and don't be afraid."

Starbane held his head high and with dignity, though he wished he had his old diadem for the occasion. *It likely wouldn't fit now,* he realized. *It was starting to get too small for my head four years ago, before ... before.*

Before.

Still, beneath his silken shirt, he felt the slight pressure of Eskanthian werewolf-teeth against his skin. Somehow, the necklace on its simple rawhide cord was better than a crown, he thought. It would have to do. Ilyssa marched with surprising grace at his side, though she felt as if her legs had been suddenly cast in stone and was certain she would trip and fall flat upon her face at any moment.

Even before they reached the gleaming dais, the Prince found himself enthralled by the mere sight of a royal family that even he, as child of another great ruler, had so often heard about. This was the redoubtable Sye, resplendent in a robe so richly indigo that it appeared luminescent against the sparkling white of the marble walls. He sat, as ancient, stern of face, and wise-looking as anyone could ever have imagined. His famous white beard really *did* travel all the way to his knees, like a cascade of snow spilling down a mountainside.

Beside the King sat his celebrated Queen—and second wife—Adurra. She seemed as young and warm as her spouse was gnarled and distant. Lovely as a nymph, she watched the approaching guests with shimmering hazel eyes that moved ever so slightly with an air of mystery and fascination. Standing at the arm of her throne they saw the child Princess, Malinna, who was every bit the miniature image of her mother, but with all the playfulness to be expected in the face of a four year-old. Starbane and Ilyssa joined Talthagar in bowing gracefully before the dais as trumpets blasted a final crescendo.

"Their Majesties King Sye, Queen Adurra, and the Princess Malinna," said Calix, who had accompanied them. Talthagar rose first and smiled broadly at the bemused King, who managed to crack a slight grin of his own.

"Talthagar, what a welcome sight you are in these times that try the soul," said King Sye in a voice far more resonant and powerful than Starbane had expected in such an old man. But he, of all people, knew that kings were not like ordinary men, young or old.

"I've missed your presence at court. Please," he continued, gesturing toward the Kelnian Prince with an arthritic claw that grasped a long silver scepter. "I have waited with much anticipation to meet the son of Adraeus."

Talthagar gently pushed Starbane forward as the King and Queen watched with a stolid scrutiny. The Prince lifted his eyes to address them.

"Your Majesties, it is a pleasure to meet you both at last. With your gracious help, I have come to you through much peril and danger. I rejoice to find your kingdom such a beautiful land, blessed by the gods. With all humility and recourse to your kindness, I seek refuge from my enemies—and yours—beneath your banner."

The youth could think of nothing more to say, but was inwardly quite pleased with himself as he bowed his head a bit, keeping eyes and ears open to discern the King's reaction. Sye looked at him for a moment and then smiled. Lifting his staff, he tapped its end loudly, three times, upon the granite platform, calling out as he did so.

"Let it be known that, from this moment, the Kelnian Prince Starbane Cadrach is granted full asylum under the hallowed wings of the Corydian Realm and my own dwelling!"

Silence reigned after this proclamation, though Starbane was waiting for another wild scream of the trumpets, or perhaps applause from the long line of observers in the galleries on either side of the immense rectangular hall. Instead, the King bid the boy to come closer, along with his companions. Though his expression appeared stony to one and all, he couldn't have been more genial as he proceeded to speak.

"It is a shame," said Sye in his gravelly rasp, "that your first visit to my realm could not have occurred under happier circumstances. It does fill my heart with gladness, however, to know that you survived and escaped the dire conditions that have befallen your native land. I assure you, Prince Cadrach, that you have my complete protection and hospitality. For as long as you wish, even unto the end of your days."

"I am more than grateful and in your service, Majesty," replied Starbane. "But it is my fervent hope that I shall not require this inestimable grace of your hospitality *forever*. I want very much to reclaim the throne of my father in Kelnia. And I have come here to seek your aid in this matter." Next to him, Talthagar grew tense.

"Come for my aid, you say?" said Sye, slightly befuddled, as if hearing the unexpected birthday wish of an eager child. "And what, pray, would you have me do to help you, hmmm?"

Talthagar murmured a strange sound, but the Prince was not about to be diverted.

"Well, it would be wonderful if we could sit together and discourse," he began. "There's much to talk about. I suppose you've been told *something* about the more explicit purpose of my pilgrimage to your land, since your own Kashizma spies are involved. I would like it very much if Rowan Blaize, your fabled wizard, could assist me in avenging the deaths of my parents and reclaiming what is rightfully mine from my half-sister, Oblixta."

"*My* fabled wizard, eh?" chuckled Sye, as if savoring the punch-line of a little joke.

Starbane was perplexed by the reaction, but not entirely thwarted.

"Your legions might do, if the wizard is indisposed," added the Prince.

Sye's brows knotted and his chin trembled. "I find that a most bold and audacious form of speech, Prince Cadrach. In practically one breath, you would request the use of a wizard I do not command, and of an army that I do command, but which is indeed *not* available for such a task as you have so specifically in mind."

"Told you," muttered Talthagar from the corner of his mouth.

Starbane ignored him. "I don't understand, Your Majesty. Begging your pardon, of course. You're telling me that you do not have an alliance with the wizard, Rowan Blaize? How can this be?"

Sye glanced around the silent throne room, as if expecting an eruption of guffaws.

"How can this be?" he repeated. "How can this *be?* Young man, no one in this kingdom, to my knowledge, has ever even *seen* the wizard, Rowan Blaize, to say nothing of any alliance."

"But is he not bound to your dynasty?" pressed Starbane. "Does he not protect Corydia from all harm with his magic, according to ancient agreement?"

"Oh, my! That is what some old wives' tales purport," conceded King Sye, his voice tinged with frost. "But I tell you again, this mythical Rowan Blaize is not under my jurisdiction, and may not even be alive, for all anyone knows. Any alleged alliance with him is the rag-tag end of some apocryphal story, if you must know. We do not disbelieve it, but we do not place too much stock in it, either. It is my powerful army, built over centuries by my forebears, that protects these lands. What any wizard does or does not do is unknown here. Unlike in your own, *former* kingdom—which has been tragic for you, I admit—practitioners of the magical arts do not interfere with Corydian policies and politics."

"Then you have never so much as *seen* him?" said the Prince, crest-fallen.

"Indeed, I have not. As I said, I've never even heard of anyone *else* seeing him."

"But he is said to dwell in the Forest of Shadnai, to the south of your very castle."

King Sye frowned. He hadn't expected such a pesky intrusion. And it wasn't even close to lunchtime.

"We do not go to Shadnai," he said. "No one goes there."

"Why? Are you afraid of Rowan Blaize?"

"Certainly not!" thundered the King. "Shadnai forest is simply … why, it's … simply off limits. Traditionally speaking. No one ventures there, not only out of longstanding respect to the legend, whether or not the wizard still dwells in Shadnai—which is so far from certain as to be improbable. But old myths must be respected, young man. Do not forget it. Tales, of course, are told of those who venture into Shadnai, those who go there out of foolhardiness, but such fools are said to never return."

"I don't understand," said the Prince. "If this wizard's forest is so near to your castle and this place—"

"I daresay you don't *need* to understand, whippersnapper!" blustered the King. At this, Ilyssa and Talthagar drew in their breath and Queen Adurra, who had been content to watch the odd exchange, cleared her throat and decided to change the Royal Subject.

"Prince Cadrach," she said in tones like honey dripping from the comb, "we have so been looking forward to dining with you this evening. Perhaps we can discuss lighter matters at *that* time. You are weary and overwrought. Understandably so. Tell me, what is your favorite dish?"

"Stewed jerboas in red wine," said the flattened youth.

"Excellent," said Queen Adurra, smiling radiantly. "It shall be prepared and you shall enjoy a repast with us tonight, on the condition that you give your thoughts a rest from the disasters that have preyed upon them for so long. Let this night be one of recuperation and the forging of new, productive friendships."

Starbane bowed low as Sye's jaw worked in consternation. At this point he preferred not to share a table so soon with one so impertinent, but he was far more reluctant to contradict his Queen, whose skills of diplomacy he respected more than anything.

"I'm afraid I have offended you in my earnestness," lamented the boy. "Do forgive me."

"Think nothing of it," said King Sye, with little apparent sincerity. "As the Queen has indicated, you shall join us for much more pleasant discussion this evening. Talthagar, you and I will talk privately much *sooner,*" added the ruler. "I want to discuss your departure from Trindyll and the atrocity that seems to have occurred along the highway."

"Yes, Sire."

"Pretty girl," giggled the cherubic Princess Malinna, who had moved onto her mother's lap by this time. The child pointed at Ilyssa, who grew red-faced.

"Prince Cadrach," said the Queen, smiling and parrying further, "I am certain we should like to meet this lovely lady who comes to us as your companion." Her hand on the throne's armrest lifted one fluttering finger, a weary butterfly's wing, to point at Ilyssa. The nervous girl bowed fully once again, now thoroughly bewildered by the proceedings.

"Yes ... of course," stammered Starbane, turning slightly to give his hand to Ilyssa. "This is the Lady Ilyssa of Pur Mida. I would humbly ask on her behalf for your royal protection, as well. Sorry I forgot to ask earlier."

"Consider it done," mumbled King Sye, although with no enthusiasm now and only one, rather weak, tap of his scepter on the dais.

"Welcome to Corydia, and to the castle, Lady," said the Queen. "So you are from Pyr Mida. I assume that your family members are nobles of that Kelnian city?"

Ilyssa froze and felt like fainting at the same instant. She tried to speak, but the voice that emerged was barely a whisper.

"Yes," the Prince interrupted. "Yes, her people are nobles of the Pyr Midan countryside."

Talthagar and Ilyssa turned to look at him as normally as they could manage, but wondered if he had lost his mind.

"You see, her family and friends were really quite helpful to me in my escape, at one point. They asked me to see to Ilyssa's safety before any further ... um ... *trouble* came about. That sort of thing."

"What a good princeling you are," nodded the Queen, "and what a brave and loyal family you must possess, Lady Ilyssa. You, too, must come to dinner this evening as well. Talthagar, when you have time, see to it that our honored guests are given a full and proper tour of the castle and its grounds, as you know this place so well."

"It would be my pleasure, Your Majesty."

"Would you like that, young Starbane?"

"Sure. We love tours where I come from."

"Avoiding the edges of Shadnai Forest," added King Sye. "And don't forget our own meeting, later." The King ogled the warrior. "We'll have some lunch, though from what I've heard the topic at hand will not be conducive to proper digestion." After this the King beckoned and a bevy of servants emerged from the flanking galleries and approached the dais.

"Until our dinner later, Prince Cadrach, I bid you enjoy the comforts of the castle," said Queen Adurra. "As the King has decreed in his goodness and wisdom, it is your refuge for as long as you wish. Explore it freely and know that you are welcomed here by one and all."

With that, the audience came to an abrupt end. Starbane and the rest had time only to bow once more before being officially escorted from the place. Following the lead of the Royal Guard and the stoic servants, the hushed group surged down the corridor and, at Talthagar's request near a columned terrace that opened onto an inner garden, he, the Prince, and Ilyssa were left to their own devices. Once in privacy, Starbane was ambushed.

"I can't *believe* you told the Queen that my parents are nobles! You idiot," Ilyssa gasped.

"Sorry," said the Prince. "It sort of just came out."

"But my father is an apothecary's assistant!" continued Ilyssa. "He and my mother were going to give me up to the Pyr Midan Prefect as a plaything. 'What a brave and noble family you must have' the Queen said. By the gods, Prince, I felt like I was going to melt into the stones!"

"Yeah," added Talthagar. "I mean, we all like Ilyssa, but do you really think it was such a good idea to lie to the Queen of Corydia?"

"Oh, give it a rest, you two. No one will ever know the difference, seeing as *all* of Kelnia is nothing but a dank pit right now. Besides, if I wanted to, I could pronounce Ilyssa a noble on the spot. I *am* the rightful ruler of my native land, if you'd kindly remember."

"Can he really do that?" asked Ilyssa, suddenly bright-eyed with interest. "Can he just pronounce me a duchess or baroness or some such?"

"Yes I can," said the irritated royal. "Consider yourself a big fat contessa from this moment onward, if it suits you! Anyhow, Talthagar, *you've* got to help me get to this Shadnai Forest, where Rowan Blaize lives. The King is playing games with me, I can tell. But I've got to find this sorcerer and show him the scar left by the Gragan. I've got ask him to help me fight Oblixta!"

"Hold on, there. You heard what Sye said about Shadnai."

"I know. I suppose I don't really think he meant it."

"He did, believe me."

The Prince chewed at his inner lip. "He's lying to me about never having seen Blaize. I know he is. Like any other king, he's greedy and wants to keep his possessions to himself. I'll just have to go on my own, then. Where is this Shadnai Forest, again? It must be pretty close, or the King wouldn't have told you to avoid showing it to me on a tour of the grounds."

Talthagar shook his head in wonder and walked out into the sunny garden. It eventually ended near a ledge on the third tier of the castle's central tower, exposing a panoramic view of Corydian forest and farmland to the north, and, on the other side, a stretch of pale woodlands to the south. In the distance, the white peaks of the Pyr Mida Mountains could be seen. Prince Starbane and Ilyssa followed the warrior's gaze and soon all three became momentarily lost in the horrors and adventures that had already befallen them in such a short time. The boy shook such thoughts from his mind and looked to the south, beyond the lake.

"That's Shadnai Forest over there, isn't it?" he said.

"Yes, that's it," said Talthagar. "But you didn't hear it from me. Got it?"

"Yes, I've got it. Though, I'm sure I could've asked around."

"You know, as good as I am at what I do, it's hard to believe I made it this far with you two tender-horns," said Talthagar.

The Prince took swift offense. "Please. We more than held our own on the trip. You thought it was going to be worse than it actually was."

Talthagar shot him a doubtful look. "Actually, that demon bit was a little over the edge, if you catch my drift."

"I won't disagree with you there. But I do disagree with your King Sye. If Rowan Blaize the sorcerer still dwells in Shadnai Forest, yonder, then I'm going to find him, with or without permission."

"Do that and you lose Sye's protection," warned Talthagar. "And reap nothing for your troubles, more than likely."

"Maybe he's right," agreed Ilyssa. "Isn't it good enough that we've gotten to safety after all of this? Why wreck it? Not that I'm ungrateful, mind you. But maybe now that you're safe, your sister will not trouble you again."

"Neither of you seem to grasp the magnitude of my predicament!" growled Starbane, running a hand madly through his wavy mane of hair, ruining the coif prepared just for his glorious—and disastrous—morning audience with the Corydian royals. "This journey has been much more than some sort of self-imposed exile, or runaway scheme, right from the beginning. And you, Talthagar, know this more than anyone. I was commissioned with a task, and part of that task involves seeking the sorcerer. This whole expedition did not simply start once we met you on the Voyager's Pass outside Pyr Mida. It started with my parents' murders, and my long imprisonment, and with Celintha, who also lost her own life, apparently. It started with this scar burned into my arm by some foul creature in the belly of the world's most despicable prison." He tore back his sleeve to display for them the red and intricate scar made by the Gragan's signet-ring.

"This little adventure involves good people like Rufthar and Ona and Wylla, and the gods only know how I may have jeopardized their lives with my pilgrimage to this land. Don't look away from me, Talthagar, as if I am a fool that doesn't know his own mind! You and Telvyn Rakahr and your King and his Kashizma henchmen are all involved in this, politically, thick as thieves—even if it's only for purposes of espionage. Damnation to politics, I say! But it's *my* life that hovers in the center of this cyclone! I am the one who has the most profound responsibility, here, not only to my ruined kingdom in Kelnia, to the memory of my parents, and to those who have so bravely assisted me, but to myself. You know the King was lying to me back there, Talthagar, at least about his relationship with this Rowan Blaize character. Oh, he and his forebears may propagate the notion that no one has seen the wizard in ages, but I know better. I sense it. Tell me the truth, Talthagar, if you are anything close to the honorable warrior you pretend to be!"

"I don't pretend to be anything, Prince," said Talthagar, drawing near with a harsh whisper. His eyes were frantic, searching the face of the young refugee. "Of course King Sye was lying to you. At least, partly. I know he has seen the sorcerer of Shadnai with his own eyes. He has told me so, on evenings when I have been 'privileged' enough to share his drinking table next to a proper fire, when the poor old creature has lost even *his* legendary good sense and has run off at the mouth due to too much wine and the pleasant feeling that comes with trusting someone else when the whole world is not to be trusted! Curse the day of my birth for even telling you such things, but, yes, King Sye has seen Rowan

Blaize. Once a year he traipses out at midnight, follows that blasted little river, and makes a secret journey into the Forest of Shadnai to confer with him. But of the things that transpire during those conferences, the King has never, ever spoken, even in the most inebriated state of loose-lipped camaraderie. All he has ever told me, otherwise, about the matter—sober or not—is that the sorcerer's forest is perilous, and one does not go there uninvited. Not ever! I thought that you might, one day, have a chance to get through to the King after a period of time concerning this wizardly affair. I told you not to rush in your petitions. But you disregarded me, and you have angered the King, and likely the Queen, as well. Of course the King was not going to simply draw you a map to this magician's door upon first-sight of you, begging as you were for asylum, with an entire gallery of his subjects watching on all sides! Have you no sense of royal protocol whatsoever, despite your youth? Now, I do not know if he shall ever arrange for you to meet the conjurer of the Dreaded Woodland, but I do know one thing, Prince—you cannot and you *must* not try to seek out Rowan Blaize alone. That would be the negation of all that has taken place to preserve your life and future, and it would lead to your likely ruination. You will not risk it."

Starbane gritted his teeth and whirled away, his borrowed blue cape billowing as he stalked some unseen vision down the majestic hall. He stopped to look at his companions only once, and he smiled. "You told me all I need to know, and I thank you for that," he called back, but not too loudly. A king spies best in his own house, after all. "I won't betray your confidence to King Sye. But I *can* take any risk I wish, Talthagar. Gragan and Celintha sent me this way for a specific purpose. Rufthar, Ona, Wylla, Telvyn Rakahr and others have risked their lives to help me. You two have risked most of all, perhaps. Innocent men have died. Each has his or her own reason, his or her own agenda. But again I remind you that *I* am positioned as some sort of interesting little political toy in the midst of all these reasons. Does any of this have meaning or does it not? Has the preservation of the world become some game, wherein lives lost or lives ruined are considered mere peripheral nuisances? Enough! I am not the same person I was when I fled the castle in Kelnia. Of that you can both be assured. I'm going back to my room to rest. You two can try to dissuade me all you wish, but until one of you ever gets thrown into the bitter wild with orders to find a sorcerer tough enough to destroy your own sister, I'm going to follow my own heart and listen to my *own* advice, thank you very much."

The Kashizma warrior and the newly noble "Contessa" Ilyssa stood, dumbfounded, and could only watch him go.

❧

Majesty,
Our spy in the court of the Corydian King
reports that Starbane has arrived in the company
of a warrior and a girl from Pyr Mida. Sye has granted
the boy asylum. Starbane has inquired about the wizard, Rowan Blaize.
I await your instructions.
—Kerrion

Oblixta could barely see the words of the note in the darkness, but then again, she did not need to see them. She had already read the message five times and there would not be a sixth. Angrily, she crumpled the paper in her fist and tossed it onto the red coals of the brazier. It burned up in a crackling whistle. Putting her hands calmly behind her back, she began to pace slowly across the length of her library, black robes merging seamlessly with the engulfing shadows. To an onlooker, it might have appeared that she and the shadows were of one and the same substance. The only window in the book and scroll-filled room was now shuttered against a howling wind that kept pace with the acceleration of her rage. All around, numerous tables were cluttered with bottles, phials, and strange vessels filled with all manner of grotesque or exotic substances. As the coals in the brazier glowed and pulsed with sinister radiance, the witch kept to the deepest shadows of the chamber, waiting as patiently as she could. The return letter to Kerrion was already rolled in a silver cylinder and on its way to the castle barracks:

*I'll be taking matters into
my own hands, General. Bring six of our best
men with you into Corydia, in secrecy, and wait
in hiding on the Gleeran Plains
until I contact you.
Find a way in, evade the enemy patrols,
and do not fail me—your lives
hang in the balance. Leave at once.
—O*

Moments later came the knock at the door, its sound penetrating the atmosphere of the unhallowed room. The Gragan wizard's Tome sat on a pedestal, its pages open, waiting, watching.

"Enter," said Oblixta, her icy voice seeming to emerge from far more distant corners of existence. Torchlight from the outside corridor flooded the library, but she remained in her place, a malignant specter, half-illuminated. The two expected servants entered only a few paces, their hearts beating with dread as the first of them held out a small velvet bag tied at one end with a long tress of recently cut human hair.

"We've brought the things you required, Majesty," stammered the first servant while the second began to grovel. "The roots and the … *pieces,* just as you said. From the boneyard."

"Yes," squawked his companion. "It took some time, too, for the ground is still frozen hard. We managed to get seven, though. Isn't that right, Jarra?"

"Yes, seven. Some very fresh. Oh, very fresh, indeed."

Oblixta could smell the fear oozing from the very pores of these seasoned henchmen as she swept from her secluded corner, billowing against the faint glimmer of the brazier. Her presence extinguished the torchlight like an arid, deadening wind. Only her eyes remained afire.

Jarra squinted in the murk. "Are you sure you don't want us to fetch Rundl, that goat what you like to ride of an evening? For your flyin' purposes I mean, Highness."

"Shut up, you filth," said Oblixta. "If I'd wanted the goat I'd have asked for it. Butcher it and eat it, for all I care now. Just keep in mind that Rundl is apt to make a meal out of you sooner than you could make one out of him. Devil-goats *do* have fangs, you know."

"Odd, I never saw any fangs on him. He always looked like such a nice little goat, if you arsked me."

"No one 'arsked' you, Jarra! Just give the bag to me and leave this place. Close the door behind you."

The order was obeyed with haste and, once alone, Oblixta untied the parcel and extracted just one piece of its foul contents. It was a whitish root that she placed immediately in her mouth, chewing furiously as she stood leaning over the coals of the tiny ritual brazier. Its particular bitterness made her salivate profusely as particles of dirt scratched and gritted against her teeth and caked on the roof of her mouth. She dipped into the bag once more and withdrew something else. This thing was moist and stinking and round. It was slimy, and it stared at her as she turned it in the faint light. Into her mouth it also went and she bit down, careful not swallow any of the gushing, putrid liquid that popped and squirted as she chewed. One by one, the remaining six were placed in her mouth and chewed to a hideous pulp. When finished, and when her cheeks were ready to burst with the fullness of their contents, she lifted both palms, cupped together, and spit into them the entire mouthful. She held her fist over the brazier and closed her eyes.

"*Turanthox, Caubus, Thothibexus!*" she whispered.

Her cadence was soft and deliberate. With a squeeze of her fists she allowed the masticated juices and chunks in her hands to drip and plop onto the coals, which began to hiss and bubble with much more violence than they should have displayed. A putrescent plume of smoke rose from the brazier and Oblixta leaned forward even more to inhale it, murmuring under her breath the words she had learned from the Gragan's Tome.

"*Ahnkeet, Caubus, Naufrett!*"

Sweeping a hand quickly over the surface, the brazier erupted in a huge, incandescent flame of green. Its luminosity turned the dark library into a ghost-world of writhing figures, sharp and agonizing as they offered glimpses of otherwise hidden entities. Even the shadows, hitherto unchallenged, retreated in dread. The Tome on the pedestal seemed to radiate approval. The Queen stepped back and regarded the fire and its strange light. Her vision penetrated into the raging white heart of the flame, searching. She raised both hands, and removed from her abysmal cloak the stone statue of a small gargoyle she had yanked from one of the palace archways. She placed it amid the fire on the brazier. Now, with clenching gestures that beckoned and coaxed, she manipulated the desired results from her spell. Slowly, the flickering tongues of fire parted in the middle atop the brazier, giving life to the stone form that began to undulate and grow upon the exposed madness of the flaring coals.

Pleased, Oblixta bent closer, her face fixed upon her craft with even greater intensity. Within a moment, the figure she had conjured from the flame leaped with a small screech from the brazier and onto one of her tables, knocking a myriad of objects to the flagstones. It twirled with some exuberance, savoring a fit of fiendish glee, and then sat in the trembling green light of the fire that still waxed nearby. It cast a doleful glare at Oblixta and began to peel from its chicken-sized body a membranous film that had completely covered its limbs and torso. Had Kerrion and his men been present, they would have recognized this thing immediately as a much smaller version of the great beast their Queen had first conjured to capture the Prince. For her current purposes, however, this demon was not only much smaller, but more singularly gifted and easier to manipulate.

She approached the thing and it eagerly accepted the morsel she placed in its mouth, a bit of the same substance she had once fed the much greater beast. This depraved food had been contained in the tiny box hidden in a belt-pouch she now wore. Alongside the box were four phials of amber liquid—four *very* important phials. The beast, animated and strengthened by the mysterious offering, began to stretch vigorously, unfurling and then batting its own ample set of wings in the gloom. It spoke to the Queen, being much more coherent and personable than its larger cousin.

"I am here at your bidding," droned the hell-spawn. "It is under your power that I move about this world, whither you desire. Speak, and your commands shall be obeyed."

Oblixta nodded. "Do you behold the place I see in my mind's eye?"

The gargoyle demon bowed. "Indeed I do."

"Excellent. Then it is to this place that you must take me with the utmost speed. Allow nothing to interrupt our journey. I may have lost my patience and ruined a chance to use the wings of a Fey Empress for my flying spell, but I figured the Gragan's Tome might have an alternative. You'll do for the time being, slave."

Double-checking the crucial contents of her belt-pouch, Oblixta gathered her robes and moved to the library window, throwing wide the shutter. A blast of cold wind entered, causing sparks to fly from the smoldering brazier. Stabbing a finger toward the night sky, she watched as her demonic assistant bowed a final time before taking to the air. As it rose in flight, it grew by half and, with the powerful claws of its hands and feet, gripped the Queen by the edges of her outer garment and, holding her fast, carried her through the window into darkness beyond.

ॐ

"This place doesn't look so intimidating," said Starbane, reining his horse at the edge of the Forest of Shadnai. His voice was shaking, nevertheless.

At long last, he found himself at the destination to which he had first been sent with such urgency, the place that—if he were to be truthful—most gripped his heart with fear, aside from being in the very clutches of Oblixta herself. He forced himself to regard this mythical forest with a façade of bravery, though no one was there to watch and appreciate it. He had run away from the castle of King Sye to reach the lonely frontier at dawn and no one had apparently followed him. Not even Talthagar.

It was not yet mid-day, and though the sun was shining, the woodland itself seemed shrouded in tendrils of mist that weaved in and out of the legion of trees. Shadnai Forest, with its gently budding cover of leaves and gloomy interior, had looked far more menacing when he had first seen it from the window of Sye's palace and earlier from a nearby canyon's edge. Then, it had appeared to be an imposing wall, jutting abruptly from the otherwise flat terrain.

The steady rush of a little river flowed through the middle of the forest—this was the one he had been able to follow so easily in order to find the place, at the conveniently unwitting advice of Talthagar. He wondered now how his friends would react upon their discovery that he had left the castle. Surely they would guess his plan and, though this unapproved side-trip would not do a thing for his reputation at King Sye's court, he was less concerned about that than he was about any search party that might be galloping after him even now.

Drawing a deep, resolute breath, the Prince considered the gentle roar of the nearby water, which flowed out of Lake Scilde, and he spotted a haphazard sequence of boulders and smaller rocks at a bend in its course. Tying his "borrowed" horse to a Thadnus sapling, he moved closer to the water and discovered that the sequence of rocks was ideal. They were practically steps, close enough together that he could stride from one to the next, or leap without much danger of falling into the swirling, steady current. In a few moments, he had hopped successfully onto the opposite bank, which was steep and not quite as pebble-strewn as its counterpart. Scaling this bank with a couple of steps and gulping nervously, he entered what he presumed to be the boundary of Shadnai. There he stopped, at an edge between worlds, it seemed, waiting. Nothing strange or malignant occurred. No enchantment befell him. Scrupulously, he looked down at himself and his surroundings and found everything to be quite as it should.

One thing however was different.

The scar on his forearm—the insignia of the Gragan wizard— began to tingle.

"There's *something* magical about this place," he whispered in the stillness as he headed deeper into the wood. There, Starbane noticed several things along the crunchy, debris-laden earth. All signs of snow had gone, but there were none of the shoots and sprouting plants of springtime he had seen earlier in the southern portion of Sye's realm. Too, there were apparently none of the annual varieties of tree that so flourished in Corydia and Kelnia, littering forest floors with mounds of decaying needles. No Falthurn trees, with their smooth white trunks could be seen, either, and the youth had never failed to see a forest grow Falthurn trees in abundance. This alone struck him as rather odd. As he moved between the branches of columnar white poplars, not at all certain about which direction might be best, he noticed that there were also no briar thickets or bushes that were normally common to a woodland expanse.

In fact, there was no sign of life *anywhere,* save for the rigid, budding trees of white. He did not even hear the calling of birds, or the buzzing of insects recently hatched from winter hideaways. No squirrels scampered about, rattling branches and skittering across bark. Close to him, the poplars were evenly spaced and provided more than enough room to walk comfortably. Further on, however, where he saw the blanket of forest floor begin to dip and rise in places, the trees seemed to merge into an almost hazy gray cloud. After several minutes of aimless walking, he glanced back only to discover that he could no longer even see the little ridge near the winding river where he had first entered. Nor could he hear the river itself, which had snaked away in an opposite direction.

"Just keep walking," he muttered, absently hoping that the horse would be safe, left behind near the water. Talthagar hadn't said anything about any dangerous beasts lingering in or near this alleged magician's forest. Now, however, as he walked alone, searching for any sign of life or activity, Starbane was tempted to holler out the sorcerer's name, but thought that this might be perceived as incredibly rude. Moreover, if Sye had sent anyone to apprehend him, he didn't want to attract *that* sort of attention, either.

After an hour of wandering, the Prince stopped at the base of yet another white poplar, identical to all of the others, and sat down in frustration. He opened his satchel and removed a bladder of water. The Gragan's scar had stopped tingling.

"This place may be enchanted, but it's certainly lifeless," he complained to the ceiling of intertwining limbs between himself and the sky. "There's no one here. There's *nothing* here! Not even a lowly insect."

He sat like this for a few minutes and then rose on aching joints to resume his walkabout. After another hour of travel marked by the same, infuriatingly uniform terrain, he did finally stop and scream "ROWAN BLAIZE!" at the top of his lungs. Unsettlingly, however, the sound of his voice didn't seem to carry much past the spot upon which he stood. It was a disturbing, suffocating effect. Again he called and this time the immediate sensation was shocking, as if he had merely whispered a word to someone standing nearby. There was no echo, nor the slightest reverberation among the trees. Now that he was thinking about it, he could no longer hear the wind. In fact, there *was* no wind, no breeze moving a single branch in the entire forest, that he could detect, and there had not been any wind since he had entered. Realizing this for the first time, the silence soon became frighteningly oppressive.

"By the gods, what's going on in here?" Starbane said ... or *thought* he said. For even though his lungs had pushed air past his vocal cords, his tongue had formed the tone, and his lips the shape of the words, no sound came forth from his mouth. Going rigid in surprised horror, the Prince tried at once to yell again and kept on screaming until his throbbing, aching throat gave up. Panic clutched his heart.

He had become deaf!

What would soon begin to drive him to the very brink of paralyzing madness, however, was the fact that the only sound he *could* still hear—the voice of his inner mind—was beginning to fade into nothingness as well. Deaf inside his own mind!

Frantic, he whirled and dashed off in the direction from which he had come, gulping and gasping for air. His eyes felt ready to fly from their sockets as he ran at top speed. In the thickening sense of death that pressed against his very soul, he raised his hands and began to slap madly at his head and face, as if it were being swarmed by a cloud of angry but invisible bees stinging the sanity from his being. On and on he raced, slamming into trees and falling, scrambling to his feet and starting again. His mind whirled and spun and then finally froze in a state of complete disorientation and, with what seemed to be the last threads of some dying knowledge, he realized he was losing ... *himself.* He fell to his knees, and finally onto his back, the beat of his heart slowing to the point of termination. Just as he was on the edge of irrevocable insanity, the entire, excruciating sensation came to an abrupt, wrenching halt.

There was a blissful moment of pressure upon his entire body, a comforting squeeze.

Then, the roaring return of sound and all things sensible was akin to the instantaneous bursting of a damn—powerful and charged with elemental energy. The onset of actual noise, even the noise of his own thoughts, boomed like an exploding volcano in his eardrums and surged as a bolt of lightning throughout his entire being. He began to shake and shudder. Flopping backward onto the moist dark soil of the forest floor, he gave in to an overwhelming exhaustion, filled with a dull pain he had never felt before that grievous moment. His teeth clenched and his eyes squeezed to narrow slits. A small rivulet of saliva ran from one side of his mouth and down his cheek onto the earth.

Only with the passing of what seemed like countless moments did he begin to regain some measure of equilibrium and rationality. He sat up, everything ahead of him in the forest now appearing calm and normal, though this did nothing to subdue his thundering heart. His father long ago had once warned him that men were known to have gone mad in cursed or enchanted forests—why had he not heeded such advice on this day? What had possessed him to make a run for this forbidden spot after the clear discouragement of Talthagar and King Sye himself? The Gragan's sigil-scar, however, burned anew and more painfully than ever on his forearm. Gingerly, the Prince rose and decided then and there to abandon his search for Rowan Blaize. If such a creature truly existed in this particular woodland, then it was doubtless he who had wrought the kind of maddening doom-spell that seemed to hang over it like a pall. Like his peers, Gragan and Cabrus, Rowan Blaize must have also fallen into the pathways of Darkness.

Starbane felt then, for the sake of his sanity, that facing Oblixta in all her wrath might be preferable to meeting this latest wonderworker, if it came down to it. Looking around with a head that seemed to wobble, he tried to get his bearings. If he were somehow able to retrace his tracks, he might find a way out of the despicable Forest of Nothing and No One! The river still could not be seen or heard; he had apparently run much too far away from it in the grip of his distress. From every direction he saw only the same formations of trees and realized that there had never really been a single landmark he could have kept in mind for purposes of retreat.

"Stay calm, you idiot," he breathed, thrilled to hear his own whisper and hoping his heart would cease its relentless pounding. "There's got to be a way out of here. Just *find* the river."

He looked above, hoping to gauge something by virtue of the sun's position in the sky, but beyond the interlaced canopy of thick tree limbs the heavens were an unrevealing haze of creamy light that seemed to tremble in his vision. Suddenly, he *felt* the ground tremble beneath him before he actually heard the Awful Sound. The sensation came in short, shuddering jolts that he could feel quivering up through his boots, and rattling the bones in the tips of his fingers, and the teeth at the very back of his mouth. One tremor came after another, each only a few seconds apart. The boy spun in every conceivable direction to ascertain the source, but it was the slow, distant snapping of a tree off to his right that heralded the first glimpse of an answer.

Starbane's eyes grew enormous, his heart tried to leap into his throat, and he dropped like a stone onto the moist earth. He wished with all of his being that he hadn't looked in the direction of the snapping tree, for what he saw, not even two hundred feet away, was enough to make the forest's earlier "Insanity Spell" seem like some harmless game. Coming closer with every footfall and standing as tall as any of the poplars in the forest was the unmistakable form of a bull ogre. The Prince covered his head with the hood of his new blue Corydian cloak. He dared not look, but sheer self-preservation and chilling curiosity, of course, demanded that he do so. There it was! Its awful snout and curved tusks—*why was he always running into fell creatures with tusks?*—were held high as the monster snorted and sniffed the musty forest air.

The Prince held his breath and prayed that the thing could not smell him, especially when it began to glance around and paused, facing his direction. The tortured youth began to pray, begging every god he could name, great and small, for the power of invisibility. He was so desperate that he tried to will his body into the earth, where it might melt into the concealment of the sod. This, of course, did not work.

Go away! his mind screamed at the gigantic thing, though he hoped not too loudly. Ogres were not telepathic, at least that he knew of, but they were awfully sensitive to smells and hunted in that fashion, he remembered. People were never excluded from their menu, either. *How could King Sye allow a bull ogre to exist in a forest so near to his own castle?* he wondered. Then he recalled that this area did not really belong to Sye.

It was supposed to be the domain of a warlock named Rowan Blaize, yet here was an ogre, grunting and smashing another tree like it was a twig. *Boom! Boom!* drummed its boulder-sized feet, each clad in badly tanned animal skins sewn together with dark, dried gut. *You can't see me,* Starbane repeated over and over in his brain, pressing himself so flat to the ground that his back felt ready to snap like one of the ogre's trees. *Go the other way!*

The behemoth leaned against another tree, which likewise split and crashed to the ground. Then it raised its hideous maw to the breeze and snorted again. Even from a distance, the sound made the interloper's stomach begin to churn with fear. Darkness was still quite some time away, so he could see the beast far more clearly than he wanted. Only once before in his life had he seen an ogre; fortunately for him, it had been a dead one. That particular specimen had crawled out the hills near Cadrach Castle in Kelnia one night many years ago, during a violent storm, and had died propped against the very walls of the outer fortress. As a boy, Starbane had been on hand to watch with his father as soldiers and townspeople were forced to hack the gnarly thing apart just to haul it away. They said it had been struck by lightning, and that it was a female.

Mostly, he could remember its hair, as thick as grass all over its body, and tusks that curved like meat-hooks beneath the gruesome maw. That memory alone would have made him shiver, were he not able to look upon a living specimen just a stone's throw away, now, in the Forest of Shadnai. This beast—unquestionably a male because of its rancid codpiece—was much larger than the dead thing he had seen as a child.

The Prince stared; the ogre was still ambling idly, it seemed, among the trees and perhaps if he was careful he could rise from his crouch and move quietly away. Even if he managed that, he could not remember exactly what his father had once told him about ogres, though his mind wracked itself trying to do so. Did they have keen eyesight and poor hearing? Or was it the reverse? Did their sense of smell guide them solely to their prey? He couldn't recall! The fiend started to move with purpose once again as Starbane swiveled his eyes around almost painfully in arcs to follow its progress. The impact of its steps, the sickeningly dull but powerful booming, continued to send chills down his spine. The titan swung away from the boy and, for a moment, it appeared to be heading back into the more dismal recesses of the forest.

Please! Keep going that way!

Almost as if it heard his silent plea, the ogre loped toward the blurry, gray depths. The Prince soon sensed, however, that it was not going directly away from him as much as it was swinging around, making a kind of arcing path through the trees, several more of which came falling in its wake. Where once the ogre had been a few hundred feet away and in direct line of vision, it was moments later *behind*, at roughly the same distance. From that angle, the Prince could see the beast only by moving his head, which was a frightening proposition, but he dared not lose sight of the thing. He had to know exactly where it was at all times, despite the chilling signals given-off by its lumbering.

Slowly, to avoid scraping the slightest bit of soil, Starbane lifted his head to take a look. There it was, of course! Right behind, only a few hundred feet away and sniffing the air again. His neck muscles straining, he watched the creature make a half-circle, stare into the deeper forest, and then turn to look in his direction. He could actually see the ogre's flaring nostrils, and the flicking of its veiny, purple tongue as it "tasted" the rather slight breeze that had cropped-up only at this fateful moment.

Then, to the Prince's horror, it began to make a steady path straight for him.

His instincts now played a tortuous tug-of-war. He could remain where he was, still and undetected, and hope the enemy switched position in the interim distance and wandered elsewhere. Or, he could get up now with as much stealth as possible and make a run for it while there was still time to maintain a lead. But where would he go? This forest seemed an endless, formless maze! Besides, he had no idea how fast ogres could move when they *felt* like moving fast, and his dark blue court clothing was hardly good camouflage amid the pale surroundings. His brain throbbed as the beast maintained its lugubrious pace. If he stayed where he was and it didn't veer from its path soon, the thing would step right on top of him! *He had to run.* Seized with terror, he knew that doing this would certainly draw the ogre's instant attention and bring it after him in a fury. But it had come down to a choice between certain doom by staying-put and mere "likely doom" by making a dash. These beasts were well-known to crave the flesh of men, when hapless men could be found in the wild.

He took one more look. It was closing-in, thumping and plodding, swinging a gigantic spiked club this way and that, crunching trees on every side. Starbane had to flee now, or being eaten alive was an imminent reality! Steeling his heart and summoning every fiber of his courage, he clasped one of the werewolves' teeth on his necklace for luck and patted the portion of his arm bearing the Gragan wizard's signature scar. If it possessed any benevolent magic at all, he would have need of it.

He scrambled to his feet like a frightened, clumsy pheasant whirling off into the air. The moment he got a grip on the terrain, however, he knew he had been discovered. How? He peered back and saw the ogre bent double in surprise as it gave a quaking, baleful cry that froze the blood in his royal veins! With a wrenching jerk of its entire body, the beast fixed its lidless gaze upon the youth and exploded into a gallop that sounded like the onset of a particularly vengeful thunderstorm.

"No!" Starbane screamed, but it was far too late for protest. The ogre barreled toward him, blasting trees out of its way and kicking up turf in furious clouds, bellowing all the while. The youth tossed his satchel of lunch—he was about to *become* lunch—and forced his legs into motion, digging so hard upon the forest floor in his first few leaps that he almost sprained an ankle. He ran like he had never run before. Past tree after tree he sped, arms pumping madly and a low wail escaping his heaving torso all the while. Behind him he heard the pounding of the ogre's feet become louder. Its screeches and screams rattled the inside of his skull. Instinctively, he wanted to look back over his shoulder and gauge the distance, but was afraid of what he might find out, afraid that there would be no lead at all, and that he would turn to see the filthy claws reaching, the purple tongue lolling and lapping for him.

As he raced onward, the energy of his initial sprint began to exact a toll. In helpless horror, he sensed his legs beginning to weaken, his arms unable to pump as high or as quickly. The air in his lungs felt like it was going to split his chest open and spill everything inside-out. Quite suddenly he came to some sort of break in the dreary forest, a spot where the maddeningly uniform trees parted and the sun—By all gods, the sun!—shone down in such glittering shafts that one might imagine nothing horrible *ever* happening in such cheery surroundings. Leaping over a fallen log, he noticed the conspicuous green of moss that was just beginning to grow in the Spring air. Beyond this was a small clearing surrounded by another cluster of the smoky, white-colored poplars, but when he entered this alcove he likewise came upon a rather abrupt ledge, one which hovered over a little waterfall and a roiling expanse of rapids that seemed to tumble and roar away for miles.

The river. My, how it had grown!

BOOM! BOOM! thundered the feet of the ogre, closing in behind.

Starbane pulled insanely at his sweat-soaked hair, not willing to dash once more into the woods. That plan would never work. He tiptoed to the brink of the waterfall's ledge and peered down. The drop was numbing and the blood drained from his flushed face, but the sight was not nearly as petrifying as the thought of being gored upon the tusks of the oncoming devil. He closed his eyes. All it would take for him to jump from the ledge—even if it be to his death—was another tree crashing, another jolt of giant footfalls, or another ear-shattering bellow from his pursuer.

He heard all three at once an instant later.

Without a thought, he jumped off the ledge and hurtled down, past the lip of the falls. Plunging, he turned once in the air, head-over-heel, before he struck the frigid water flat on his belly. In some ways, he was fortunate to have landed as he did, for the basin was relatively shallow and, had he entered head-first, the results would have been disastrous. As it happened, however, the air was knocked from his lungs before he pushed himself wildly out of the froth, struggling to fill his chest with breath lest it be inundated by churning water. Flipping and soaring like a confused fish in the current, he finally took a few hacking breaths and attempted to scramble with at least the tips of his feet to get some traction on the gravelly bottom.

There was no stability to be obtained—with the water now up to his neck and the current pushing relentlessly, he was swept further down the frothing channel and into an even more perilous section of the rapids. First, the Prince was shoved completely under by the force of the flow, but this time he held his breath and managed to right himself, trying to swim as best as he could and navigate the treacherous strait. This, too, was impossible, for he merely continued skating through the foam, his rear and torso bumping against every rock that was hidden beneath the white-capped swell. When the rapids threw him next upon his back and he was facing the sky, swallowing water, he imagined through the gurgle and sloshing that he could hear the call of the awful beast and just glimpse its head poking-out past the same ledge from which he had jumped.

Starbane's arms flailed. He was ingesting too much of the wild river. The turbulence sped him onward and every time he felt as if he managed to get some sort of grip on the slippery bottom, it was ripped way. Moments later, when he felt ready to succumb to the raging force of the torrent, he seemed to be jettisoned like an arrow into a somewhat less aggressive pool, though one that was clearly deeper. Try as he might, he could not touch bottom and, with waning strength and soaked garments weighing him down, his mind began to flash visions of his entire past life. To say that he tried to save himself by floating was inaccurate; the boy lost all strength and tilted, beyond will, onto his back.

When the world began to spin and all sense of hope seemed to be fading, he felt a sudden, almost miraculous surge of relief. His feet slid onto a piece of slippery rock as he drifted, face just above water, in the pool. The rock beneath soon inclined to packed mud and the drowning victim discovered that he could take weak steps, edging little by little toward the bank. It took what felt like an eternity to reach the haven of shore and, when he finally dragged his body painfully onto dry land, he sighed as if entering paradise itself.

Starbane lay for some time, as still as a corpse, spent, before wobbling into a squat and then wobbling even more frightfully to his feet. He was dazed but alive, and that was more than he thought Fate would offer on *this* day. Standing upon the pebble-strewn bank made him dizzy enough to fall right back down, so he spun like a wounded bird and vomited a stomach-full of clear river-water that had been swallowed on the harrowing ride downstream. Groaning for mercy from the gods, he forced himself to make for a flat bend of trees up ahead, nearer to a place where the river pooled once again and made an almost perpendicular turn.

The sound of the rapids was still loud in his ears, but behind him now. Hesitantly, he looked back for any possible sign of the beast that might still be on his trail. Peering and squinting in the welcome sunshine, he judged himself to be at least a mile from where he had leapt from the ledge. He was so exhausted that he half felt the ogre deserved a good munch on his bones ... if it cared to catch-up with him now. Then again, he only *half* felt it, and decided to put even more distance between himself and possible disaster, utterly exhausted or not.

Staggering toward the sharp bend in the river, he stayed close to the bank that wound much more lazily around an outcropping of diverse foliage. Gone were the odd gray poplars that he was now convinced must have been deliberately trying to drive him mad. Falthurns, Moabs, Cirstea, and Thadnus trees were growing in smaller clusters around this portion of the woodland. The sound of birds, a blessed relief after the tomb-like silence of the prior forest, rang with a decency and brightness almost foreign to his ears. He forced himself to move, though his legs felt as if they had been filled with all of the water of the reckless river. His stomach unleashed a fierce growl that could be heard beneath his soaked shirt and he began to feel rather ill again.

Ogre or no ogre, he had to find a place to hit the ground and recover, or he was going to have no choice in the matter of hitting the ground permanently. He looked back again, listening for any sound of thunderous feet or snapping trees, and then scanned the banks ahead for possible shelter. What he saw in this direction made him stop in his wavering tracks, though not in the same manner as had the fell beast of the upper woodland. Ahead, near another, slighter bend in the slowing waterway, stood a person. Starbane had to rub his eyes and shake his head to rule out the possibility that he was dreaming.

Yes, there was someone there. Not a hundred paces away, a young man, perhaps no more than four or five years older than him, stood garbed in a pair of brown buckskin trousers and a rawhide shirt. The young man stooped down toward the river with a long pole across his shoulders and two buckets dangling at each end of that. He noticed that the fellow's hair was inky black and shoulder length, but spiked, instead of wavy like his own. He even heard the stranger curse mildly as he tried to steady himself on some slippery rocks along the bank with little success. He nearly fell into the water as he dipped one crude bucket down toward the languishing current.

"Thank the gods," breathed the Prince, more dazed in his sudden exaltation at seeing another person than ever. He half walked, half stumbled toward the fellow, who didn't even notice Starbane until he was only a few feet away, kicking up gravel and sputtering water from his mouth. He paused in the midst of filling his buckets and looked slowly upward at the visitor.

"Hey," panted the Prince, grinding to a halt. "Hey, Mister … you gotta help me … we gotta … we gotta get outta here. Do you know some place safe?" He teetered up the bank a little, stopping to clutch the trunk of a tree for support. The world was spinning away from him yet again.

"Excuse me?" said the young man in buckskin. He stood erect, balancing his pole and water-buckets, gazing with no small measure of skepticism at the soaked Prince, who leaned against the Moab and instantly slid onto his rear in the dirt. He pointed with a shaking finger in the direction of the rapids.

"There's an ogre after me, Mister. Big one! He'll get us both if we don't get out of here. Oh ... Oh, Dryndym help me, I think I'm going to be sick."

The Prince slumped to his left and heaved more water into the bushes, trying to hide his face as best he could. The stranger, meanwhile, set his buckets aside and stalked slowly toward the retching youth, stopping a few feet away to inspect the pitiful scene.

"Did you fall into the river?" he asked calmly, with a curious tilt of his head.

Starbane finished throwing up and looked up with a violent cough rattling around his throat. He could only nod that, yes, he had *indeed* fallen into the river.

At this, the young man lifted a sinewy, tanned forearm and casually rubbed the tip of his nose with the back of his hand. He glanced upstream for a moment with what could only have been described as nonchalance.

"Well, I've got a little place just over the hill, there," he drawled, with a toss of his brow. "I don't know who you are, or how you got here, but you're welcome to come up to the cabin and dry off by a fire. Maybe you should have something to eat, as well. If your insides can handle food right now." He looked Starbane up and down once again and abruptly spun on his heels, gathered up his pole and unfilled buckets, and pinched his thumb in the joint of the awkward contraption.

"Ow!" he said, and started sucking the wounded digit. "Are you coming or not?" he asked, shaking the pain out of his thumb. Without waiting for a reply from the collapsed Prince, he sauntered up the riverbank and onto a small hillock that rose toward the forest. His nausea subsiding, Starbane sat up as best he could, grappling with the tree for support. He was on his feet a moment later.

"Mister, wait for me!" he called. "I'm a little shaken up, if you don't mind. And what about the ogre that's after me? Didn't you hear what I said before?"

The spiky-haired youth kept walking up the hillock, buckets swaying. He turned once more to look upstream with the same blank expression and said nothing about the ogre.

"It might be a moment or two before my place warms-up enough to satisfy," he warned. "I don't normally stoke the fire up good until dark, now that Spring has sprung."

He disappeared from view around a thick patch of budding Grizzleberry bushes. The Prince staggered after him, afraid of being left alone, now that he knew he wasn't alone after all. The path taken by the fellow was winding and rocky, but he felt slightly better for throwing up and managed to follow with little delay. He came close behind the stranger as they ascended a pile of gray granite slabs near the crest of the hill—rocks that had been formed by the elements over centuries into a beguiling natural stairwell. The fellow turned to look at him.

"I hope you won't feel insulted," he said, "but would you mind hanging back a little until we get to my cabin? You smell like puke. I don't like the smell of puke, though I daresay there are few who do."

Starbane was taken aback, at first, but after looking down at his sopping, filthy clothing and realizing that he had vomited on most of himself as well as upon various portions of the ground, he felt more embarrassed than insulted.

"I ... I'm sorry," he groped. "I guess I didn't realize I was—"

"Never mind," interrupted his host, turning to resume the climb. "I've got some clothes you'll be more than welcome to borrow, once you've washed up."

The Prince waited a moment and continued upward, though hanging back as requested, like a timid pup. The walk came to a sudden end in a secluded but tidy clearing. The view of the sky here was somewhat obscured by the ceiling created from budding, outstretched limbs of several encircling Moab trees. These gave the entire spot a deliciously woody fragrance and cast playing shadows where the afternoon sunlight managed to shine through. At the center of this haven was a small, unremarkable house built from oblong stones layered roughly, one atop the next, the cracks filled in numerous places with daub. The roof of the dwelling was thatched and seemed as idly assembled as the walls, which were drooping in a precarious slide toward the left.

It looked to Starbane like the entire roof would fly off in a strong wind, or even with a hearty shove. A chimney straddled the right side of the humble abode and this was the only feature of the architecture that appeared to be sturdy. Around its base lay a host of buckets, domestic tools, and nearby, a long plank formed a table between two craggy old tree stumps. Some sort of derelict plowing device was upturned in the grass beside the table. The woodsman set his current buckets down in a spot by the chimney stack and motioned for Starbane to come closer. The Prince, however, lingered hesitantly near the entrance to the clearing, not wanting to head straight for the house, smelly as he had been told he was.

"You can come closer than that," said his unexpected guide, who grabbed a small stool from behind a barrel filled with rainwater and placed it in the middle of the path. "Sit on this and wait a little bit. I'll go inside and get a fire blazing and get you something to put on your stomach until you're ready to wash up and change clothes."

Shivering as a breeze wrapped itself about his garments, Starbane nodded and sat down upon the stool. The woodsman loaded-up with wood split and stacked near the open door of the stone house and, while the Prince noticed that the fellow was not much taller or heavier or even older than he, he was much more fit. His muscles were toned and his skin a soft brown from what was clearly a life lived almost entirely out of doors.

"My place isn't much to look at," he said to the soggy boy, one foot poised to go within the dwelling. "But that's because I built it with my own hands and I'm afraid I've never been much of a carpenter, or a stonemason. It's home, though, for now. As soon as you're cleaned up you can come inside and we'll figure out what's troubling you."

Starbane watched the almost elfin face, which was stoic and smudged from work, but handsomely set with striking gray eyes that belied a confident sincerity, or perhaps even arrogance. Through the one open window of the cottage, he could hear logs being tossed upon the hearth and moments later heard the slight crackle of flames kindled.

"You live way out here all by yourself?" the Prince called, glaring fearfully in all directions, feeling awkward and exposed.

"Yeah. Woodsman to the core," was the answer. The man had stuck his head and shoulders out of the window, rough-worn hands grasping the stone sill. "I've got a decent garden in the glade beyond those Moabs," he added, pointing. "I'll be planting within the next couple of days, now that the ground has completely thawed. The river's full of fish, too. In winter I store berries, nuts, dried apples, and all sorts of things in the cellar. There's a small barn I built, just down the path behind the house, on the other side of the garden plot. I've got goats, you know. Plenty of milk and cheese throughout the year."

He popped back inside again and, when he next came out, he offered Starbane a wineskin along with a plate loaded down with some cheese and a hunk of fluffy, fragrant bread. In a little clump in the middle of the bread were some thick red preserves that looked heavenly to the famished youth. "By every god, I thank you, sir," mumbled the Prince, stuffing his mouth to capacity. "It's been a whole day since I've eaten anything and I lost my supplies back there in that freakish forest. This is like a feast!"

"Take your time eating, if you please," said the youthful woodsman. "My dooryard may not be much, but I don't want you to retch all over it. Believe me, if you took in a lot of water, your stomach will handle the food much better if you gobble slowly."

Starbane looked up, feeling quite the pig and truly having the look of one; a mishmash of food was practically oozing from his packed mouth.

"Obviously, it's not going to take you long to finish," said his host with a raised brow. "I'll get some linen and soap from the house. You'll want to wash-up. I have clean clothes on hand, too."

Back into the house he went and, by the time he reemerged with the appointed articles, his guest had licked the little plate clean of every crumb and was draining the wineskin. "I feel better already," puffed Starbane. "This wine is delicious. It makes me feel unbelievably warm and I need *that* right now more than anything."

"I'm glad you like it. I make that wine every summer with the juice of crushed Chrebus berries, and a few Grizzleberries thrown in, too, just to top-off the barrel." The Prince accepted the neatly folded but simple garments, a small set of linen cloths, and a hunk of lard soap.

"Over the knoll behind us, through the Moabs, you'll see another rocky step, just like the one we climbed at the edge of the hillock. At the bottom of this step is a small alcove where a channel of the river pools into an oval basin. I'd like you to wash yourself thoroughly down there." Though politely offered, the words had an insistent drive behind them. "When you're finished and changed, come back up to the house and you can sit by the fire. I'll have some more wine ready."

He took Starbane's plate and turned to go back inside the hovel, but the Prince was not about to budge, not yet. He peered at the narrow pathway just visible through the trees, a path which snaked up a stubby knoll beyond. "I'm not so sure about going down there, or over there, or wherever it is," he said weakly.

"Did you say something?" asked the woodsman, pausing on the front step of his hovel.

Starbane was not the least bit embarrassed now. "Um, I don't know if you remember me telling you, but there's a *bull ogre* running around these parts. It nearly caught me half an hour ago! You've been really kind, Mister, but please don't be too surprised if I'm not keen on heading back into the trees. I have no intention of running into that monster again."

His host was as coolly unimpressed as ever.

"Don't worry. That thing won't bother you here. By the way, when you're finished washing, please give your soiled clothes a good rinse and leave them on the rocks downhill. They can dry a bit in what's left of the day's sunshine and we'll collect them later."

Then he went inside the house.

Starbane was decidedly perturbed by the strange attitude of the fellow, and thought it quite a foolhardy stance to take for someone who lived in such a dilapidated dwelling, with ogres in the neighborhood. How did he know the beast wouldn't come calling? Did he even know what an ogre *was?* Grumbling to himself, the Prince arose and walked, dripping with every step, up and over the knoll and onto the path that led down to the run-off pool.

No matter what the odd stranger had promised, he was going to be very swift about washing up, that much was certain. Descending the rocky stair, he stripped down almost frantically in the cool air, finding his nakedness to be excruciating for many reasons. Self-consciously, he squatted at the edge of the freshwater pond and splashed about, rubbing the soap all over his numb body and scrubbing with the cloth as diligently as could be managed. Once relatively clean, he could tell from the smell of his discarded clothes just how offensive he must have been to the forest-dweller.

"I'm never going to know what it's like to be royal again," he griped as he dried himself with one other linen towel that had been provided. Fearful of catching a chill, he scampered quickly into the simple tunic and trousers loaned to him and trotted on tip-toes up the stone steps in his bare feet. Sticking his head bashfully into the open door of the house, he saw the woodsman kneeling by the hearth, stoking flames with a rusty poker amid the logs.

"Finished already?"

"I was in sort of a hurry, if you know what I mean," said Starbane. "But I'm clean enough."

"Of course. You may come inside, at any rate. Sit by the fire, just here, and warm up." He gestured to a chair made from logs, with bark-slabs for slanting arms. There was a down cushion atop the rough-hewn seat. The Prince sat, feeling strange in the change of clothes, though they were almost a perfect fit. By now the fire in the hearth was roaring and snapping. He leaned forward and held his fingers and toes outward, turning them slowly before the radiating heat. Then he looked bashfully around the small abode. There was a bed, a table with one chair, a little cupboard, and the hearth with its iron kettle and various other utensils. That was it.

"Are you feeling better?"

Starbane stopped his temporary snooping and raised his brows in agreement. "Yes, much better. Thank you."

The woodsman handed him one of two cups filled with wine from a smaller kettle dangling across the hearth flames. Swirls of steam rose from the drink and the boy felt his senses quicken at the peculiar, spicy aroma. One sip left a fine, lingering trail from his tongue all the way to his gurgling belly. His host had taken the seat nearby at table.

"This wine is different from the one I gave you in the front yard. Not as sweet, but more powerful than the other, so drink slowly. It'll get rid of any chill you might be feeling."

The Prince cleared his throat politely and chided his forgetfulness, even as his head seemed to be in the grip of a slight swoon. "Please excuse me, sir. I'm sure you must think I'm completely out of my mind. Here I am, invading your dooryard, eating your food, wearing your clothes, enjoying your fire, and I haven't so much as introduced myself the entire time. I don't know what's become of my manners. My name is Starbane."

The handsome young fellow smiled and the radiant warmth of his gaze seemed as consoling as the warm wine in the cozy shelter. "Don't worry about manners, Starbane, because I don't recall introducing myself, either. It's good to meet you. My name is Rowan Blaize."

The Prince's hand contracted so hard upon his earthenware cup that the vessel popped from his grip, flipped, spilled, and then smashed all over the hearth stones. He was too stunned in that instant to do anything except stare in bewilderment as his host bent swiftly to pick up the pieces, a look of mild annoyance on his face.

"You really are a bit jittery, aren't you?"

"I … I'm sorry," said the Prince. "But I was startled by something I'm sure I misunderstood. Or misheard. Did you just say that your name is *Rowan Blaize?*"

"That's right," replied the fellow as he tossed the broken shards of the cup into yet another bucket and proceeded to pour another cup of warm wine for his clumsy guest.

"I don't believe you," said Starbane, though not with rudeness. He was genuinely stupefied.

"What—you don't believe I know my own name?"

"No, no, it's not that," replied the Prince, slinking back as far as he could into the chair, eyeing the one before him with frightful scrutiny. "It's only that I came to this place, this forest in the domain of King Sye, to *find* a person named Rowan Blaize. You can't possibly be the one I'm looking for. It's ... there's been some sort of mistake here. A big one."

The fellow's interest was piqued. "You're coming from King Sye, eh?" he said. "How interesting ... and rather unexpected. In any event, I'm the only person named Rowan Blaize living in this forest. You can trust me on that. And you say that you were looking for me? What in the world for, young man?"

Starbane shook his head in protest. "No. No ... you see ... I'm looking for a great and renowned wizard. A sorcerer of incredible power and prestige. You're obviously not him, so someone has gotten the myth all wrong and I've been led down a most wasteful pathway!"

The woodsman paused, mulling over the boy's words with an air of faint amusement. He tossed a cloth soaked with spilled wine into the nearby bucket where it landed with a plop.

"Now I'm truly curious," he said, settling back into his own chair and staring into the dance of flames across the hearth. "You must tell me why you've been seeking me. I know the Corydian King would never *send* you here. It's against all the arrangements that I have ever made with that line of silly old men. Forgive me, but all this time I thought you were merely some poor lad foolish enough to get himself lost in my forest. There have been others, in the past, after all."

"*Your* forest?" Starbane's mouth fell open. "Wait a minute. Again I say that there is no way that you could be the person I'm looking for."

Rowan Blaize feigned indignation at this assertion. "Am I being insulted in my own hovel?" he said with a sly grin. "What makes you think I'm not the one you claim to be looking for?"

"Well, I mean ... er ... *look* at you!" Starbane said, impatient and thoroughly discombobulated now. He gestured at the humble surroundings. "Don't get me wrong. You seem to be a nice person, what with the wine and the clean clothes, and the pleasant fire to sit around. But ... but you're a lowly woodsman. In a *very* small house, I might add. And you've got—what? Cows? Goats, did you say?" He stared for a quaking moment at his new friend. "Great wizards don't have goats."

Rowan Blaize laughed so hard that his own cup of wine sloshed and spilled a bit onto the rush-covered flagstones. "Why in the worlds and worlds-within *don't* they have goats?"

The Prince was duly offended. "Because a wizard would have no need for such trivial things," he explained. "And I'd appreciate it if you wouldn't make sport of me, sir. This joke has gone far enough as it is."

Blaize struggled to hide his amusement. "Oh, my stars! You've got it all wrong, don't you? Goats are *most* necessary, to the wise and witless alike. Milk and cheese are never free, and I need to eat like everyone else, if I may say so. Especially here." He frowned after these last two words, looking around his cabin as if not quite convinced of his own avowed comfort, after all. "Why, if I used sorcery for every little whim and need in this particular corner of the worlds-within, I'd be so drained that I'd never have a chance to get to the next worry."

The Prince was horrified.

"This has become a most dreadful business," he said. "You're no sorcerer. You can't be! By the gods, I'd say you're not five years older than I am! The wizard Rowan Blaize is ancient and mysterious, with crabbed claws and pockets that contain magic amulets and a voice like thunder at the crown of a mountain. That's what my father once told me about proper sorcerers, anyhow. And stop chuckling at me! I've been through near destruction for the last several years of my miserable life and this past month alone has been the pinnacle of horrors. Just a bit ago I was chased by a ferocious ogre in my attempt to find the *real* Rowan Blaize, if such a person exists. I've got very serious reasons for finding him, too."

The owner of the humble hovel continued to laugh his soft laugh, eyes aglow in the firelight. Starbane narrowed his own steely gaze.

"If you know where to find Rowan Blaize, please just tell me and I'll be on my way, to trouble you no further." He placed his cup of wine dismissively upon the mantelpiece above. "Ah ... I know!" he added in a sudden burst of inspiration. "You're likely the wizard's gardener, aren't you? His manservant. Wizards always have roughshod and capricious young fellows in their service, or so I've heard. Now you're enjoying a good laugh at my expense, but I assure you that I'm here on the most pressing of matters, so you had best take me to your master at once. Where is he?"

Rowan Blaize forced himself to stop smiling, but it wasn't easy. He took careful note of the Prince's frustration—indeed, his disorientation—and didn't wish to completely unsettle his guest. Leaning forward in his chair, he stared deeply into the eyes of the boy.

"I'm sorry to disappoint your expectation of what I should look like or *be,* young Starbane, but as you can well see, I live very simply. Admittedly, this is not always the way I prefer to live my life, but it *is* the manner in which I must conduct myself while occupying *this* specific world. There are worse ways to get by, believe me. I am not trying to fool you, or to make fun of you, either. By the by, I am no one's 'manservant,' and I require no servant—at least not usually, and certainly not the kind of servant that can be seen, in any event. Besides, wouldn't you be petrified, like most people, to confront a wizard that looks like the one your father described?"

The Prince glowered in silence, unconvinced of anything except the fact that he was in the company of a cruel jokester at best ... or a lunatic at worst.

"By the Gods, indeed," muttered Rowan Blaize as he began to glance with some measure of irritation about the parameters of his meager surroundings. "People and their need for signs, wonders, and *demonstrations,*" he spat. His eyes fixed at last upon the hearth itself. "That will likely do, for the moment."

Without a word, he extended a hand toward the flames and Starbane saw him stare at it for an instant while muttering a series of strange words under his breath. Then, with a sucking inrush of air that seemed to come from origins unknown, the entire whipping, crackling fire was extinguished in the blink of an eye, leaving not a single spark or pulsating ember in the bare basin. There were only untouched logs. The cheery little inferno had vanished entirely.

After a jump and a great gasp, the Prince stared at Rowan Blaize, who was again leaning comfortably back in his chair with folded hands. The wizard's distasteful expression indicated that he was far from proud of the display.

"Y—you … *are* a sorcerer," whispered Starbane.

Rowan rolled his stormy gray eyes. "Ta *da.*"

"I'm so sorry," insisted the awestruck youth. "I didn't know. That is, as I said, you simply don't *look* like a magical person, at least not any of the magical people *I've* known."

"You really ought to believe people when they tell you something, unless you have compelling reasons not to trust them," sniffed Blaize. "This world—like most others inhabited by the sentient—isn't entirely full of liars, you know. And you claim to have met magical people before, is that correct?"

"I know that everyone is not a liar," replied Starbane. "And yes, I most certainly have met magical folk, though I wish I hadn't … present company excepted, of course. I think. I suppose. Even so, in your regard, all the legends that I've heard so far—"

"Legends? Ha! I'll tell you, feisty young lad, that legends are very good things, indeed. In all the thinking universes. But you must keep in mind that their primary purpose is to instruct, to teach, and to inspire. Not to furnish accurate and irrelevant details. Legends seek—at least the better ones do—to provide people with a glimpse of the abyss between right and wrong, light and dark, heaven and hell, and so on and so forth. It's all called different things in different dimensions. The point is that beings should pay far more attention to what worthy legends are trying to say, rather than *how* they are saying it. You can trust a sorcerer on that."

The sorcerer flashed a toothy smile and, in the very instant he did so, the fire in the hearth roared back to enthusiastic life. Starbane jumped once more from his chair.

"Believe me," said Rowan Blaize, "In this difficult, dreary world, I could have expended far less energy going out to the woodpile, grabbing a few logs, and kindling a fire like I always do. The magical way is certainly quicker and it's a totally *different* sort of energy, I admit, but don't doubt for an instant that it requires effort. Don't doubt that there is a cost. *Always* a cost. Especially on this somewhat backward enigma of a planet. Alas, it's impossible to explain such things to someone who doesn't have The Gift."

The Prince nodded gravely. "You don't have to explain anything."

"Let me see. I'm sure you expected me to live in a gloomy castle," continued Blaize. "Surrounded by riches and faery servants and all sorts of trimmings gained through the use, or misuse, of my powers. Is that the story currently being circulated in the age of King Sye? I haven't bothered to keep up with all the adventures of this ongoing line of monarchs. Dreary. Every one of them. I meet him once a year to listen to him gripe about his job and he's usually drunk as he does so. But that's the pact we made when I asked for sole dominion over this little parcel of forest some two hundred years ago."

"You've been around these woods for *that* long?" gasped Starbane. "Like I said, you don't look much older than I do, and I'm only a teenager."

"I'm afraid I have been here for a little over two hundred years, but this is not my original home, mind you, and this is my second—and far more unfortunate—visit to your world. As for the way I look, please keep in mind that I am not cut from *quite* the same cloth as your kind."

"Then you'll have to forgive me, but, yes … I would expect to find you in a castle filled with faery servants. That's frankly what I picture in a wizard, or whatever you are. At least in a powerful one."

"Mind you, I have enough skill to manage the kind of environment you mention, as do a few of my peers on this exceptionally dismal rock. In other realms, my energies tend to find themselves channeled in more efficacious ways. There's something lugubrious about the occult continuum, here. I still haven't quite figured it out. That being said, do not doubt that I can accomplish considerable things in this existence, if I so choose. But while in this dimension I have discovered that it is much wiser and easier not to overuse the abilities I possess. Where I originally come from, your sort of person would refer to that dynamic as 'saving up for a rainy day.' Have you ever heard that expression, boy?"

"No, I haven't."

"I didn't think so. At all events, I live here in solitude and simplicity, for the time being, trying to respect and explore the forces at work in this domain, even if it *is* within my power to control them. True, I don't bother with the mortals here, very much. As is the case in other worlds I have toured, I often find *them* more abusive of the world in their relative weaknesses than I've known certain wayward wizards to be in their strengths! But that is my prerogative. This forest—Shadnai, I believe it's called—was given to me in my days as a neophyte, here, by the ancestors of this Corydian dynasty. They bequeathed it to me in return for a modicum of magical protection, and I found the arrangement convenient. Ha! Not that I could have offered them unbeatable protection, way back then, at least, but it is not as if these kings have ever seemed to need it, either. This lot has always been about military supremacy. But they've always fancied themselves more intimidating with a sorcerer on the premises, too. And I like this forest well enough. These kings have believed that our bargain keeps me close to them, when in fact it keeps me quite apart. I haven't enchanted the woods as much as the so-called legends would lead anyone to believe, but it *is* enchanted, as I am certain you discovered, and the exaggerations of mortals have served my purposes well."

"That bull ogre," said Starbane. "Is he part of your enchantment?"

"No, I found him here when I first decided to settle down. He was injured and I came to his assistance. We arrived at a mutually beneficial understanding, me and him. Something of a lost soul, himself, to be honest. Trust me, youngster, when one finds one's self banished, there are far worse places and worse predicaments. I have seen such places and I have been in such predicaments. At least I have power to wield amid my current state of banishment, when I wish to wield it. Things could have been much worse."

"What do you mean about being banished?" said the Prince, accepting another pour of the beguiling spiced wine from the wearying host. "I don't understand. If you're a sorcerer, and so famous and feared throughout these lands, how can you speak of banishment?"

"You express a great many opinions and ask a lot of questions for one who is a guest in *my* home, and for one who has yet to explain anything substantial about himself and his present purposes," said Rowan Blaize, more than a trifle petulant. "I get to ask the questions, now, dear boy, and if you know what's best for you, you shall answer them truthfully and with expedience. Oh yes, you've got some explaining to do. Normally, no one in their proper mind in Corydia would even think of venturing into my forest, at least not intentionally. But you have done so, on a recommendation, no less. You have entered my territory to the point of risking your life in order to find me. I want to know exactly who you are and what is the nature of your business. Let me begin by asking why you are called 'Starbane.' I have never heard that moniker in all my considerable travels through these kingdoms."

The Prince took a deep breath and tried to speak without trembling. "My parents gave me that name because it is said that, on the night I was born, all of the lights went out in the heavens. They took it as a good omen."

Rowan Blaize shrugged, unimpressed. "It could have been an omen. It could have been a big cloud. Next question: Who are your parents?"

"I ... I am actually the Prince Starbane Cadrach, son of King Adraeus and Queen Mirysta of Kelnia. The *former* King and Queen, that is." He paused and waited for this to sink-in, but Blaize remained unmoved.

"So you are of royal Kelnian blood. What of it? That only makes your presence in my forest, this far away from your homeland, all the more preposterous."

"You don't understand. I have come to you after a period of unjust imprisonment and now self-imposed exile. I come to you because I am seeking to free my native realm from oppression and restore *my* rightful place on the throne."

"I fail to see how this has anything at all to do with me," said Blaize, sipping indifferently at his own cup of wine.

"Oh, it's got a great deal to do with you! You're involved, whether you want to be or not."

"I call that a most amusing claim!" laughed the sorcerer. "Look, young Starbane, I have no trouble believing that you are who you say you are, but you're going to have be more specific than that, if you want to really get my attention, especially on mortal political matters, which are things that do not usually concern me in any fashion whatsoever."

"You might change your mind when you hear me out," said the Prince, gloomily. "I was sort of sent to you through the political machinations of King Sye and a few other interested parties, but as I have discovered, that entire enterprise has been fraught with … well, *politics,* and I agree with you completely, insofar as your distaste for such things may be concerned. The real problem is my half-sister, Oblixta. She's set herself up as Queen of Kelnia and of all the lands north of the Pyr Mida Mountains. She killed my parents a couple of years ago and kept me prisoner until I escaped with the help of an old witch named Celintha and a group of spies under the auspices of King Sye. It was Celintha who agreed that I should find you, as did the King's network of spies, but Oblixta's awfully displeased and has been after me ever since my escape. And it's not just my problem, because she's after you, too, apparently! That's part of this whole disaster. She's planning to wage a war to take over the kingdom of Corydia, just as soon as she gets rid of *you*. You've got to help me fight her, if you can."

Rowan Blaize had listened intently, chin in the palm of his hand, and looked at Starbane now with gentle perplexity. "That's quite a story, young Prince, and my heart does indeed go out to you. I have no interest in how such things may have come about in your kingdom, especially at the hands of a sister, but apparently the world of mortal-types has not changed much since last I was interested in their company. Ever have kings and queens in all the worlds and worlds-within been the victims of their own sinister bloodlines. Tragic, but I can at least understand it. War is a scourge of your own making and must be resolved through your own solutions. I don't even protect the Corydian king with magic, as I indicated—he and his ancestors have liked to think so, but in truth, it's the legend of my presence here that enhances his reputation. He's on his own. They have all been on their own."

"But I need your help!" implored Starbane.

"Sorry, but as I may have indicated, I make it a policy never to interfere with the machinations of mortal potentates and despots. Not here. Not anywhere, if I can avoid it, and I can."

"But you don't understand …"

"I understand that sorcery is not meant to be used to influence the outcome of politics, Prince Starbane. Not even in a case as obviously unfortunate as your own. I'm afraid you've come all this way to see me for nothing. The only thing that remotely piques my curiosity is why this naughty sibling of yours feels it is imperative to do away with *me* in order to wage her campaign with King Sye of Corydia. That part is a bit intriguing. Also, you mentioned an old witch, one named Celintha. Is this witch a hag that hails from the far Northern hills of the Dalorum province, by any chance?"

"Yes!" said Starbane. "You have heard of Celintha?"

"At whiles, at whiles. Let us just say that her reputation preceded her when I had occasion to spend time in Kelnia myself, long ago. More to the point, you said that she helped rescue you from this alleged imprisonment of which you speak. You said specifically that she 'agreed' that you ought to seek my aid. I find that a curious word, in this context. With what—or with whom—did Celintha 'agree,' O Prince?"

"Gods, with all due respect, where do I begin?" lamented Starbane. "She agreed with that other blasted wizard. Don't you see? It's not just the growing armies of Kelnia that we will be up against. King Sye lied and told me that you were just a myth, even though I knew better. I pushed him too quickly on that count, and it's my mistake, but I came here of my own volition today, all the same. No matter what happens, now, the whole world will be contending with my sister herself. She's a sorceress! She's used her black magic to crush the decent peoples of the North and, if she has her way, this realm will be hers, too. All she needs to do is get you out of the way like she did the other magician. It was despicable, even as much as he probably deserved to be gotten out of the way."

Rowan Blaize raised a brow, the only perceptible change in his placid expression. "What do mean by 'sorceress' and, most of all, what 'other blasted wizard' are you speaking of, Starbane Cadrach of Kelnia?"

The Prince's shoulders sagged with relief. "Oblixta, my half-sister, is a witch. The most powerful in the world, I should think. She's been … I don't know how to describe it … *collecting* and killing-off great wizards and warlocks for quite a few years. Her goal has been to crush the best ones, and she's managed a number of those already. You, I am told, are next. The Gragan seemed certain of it. That's why he did what he did to me."

"Preposterous!" thundered Rowan Blaize, rising from his chair. The fire in the hearth exploded outward in pace with his anger.

"What? That you are next on her list?" blubbered Starbane, shrinking in his chair, thoroughly frightened.

"No! That you speak of the Gragan wizard! How dare you mention that name? I should smite you to cinder where you cower, boy. Speak while you have a tongue to form the words. Are you one of that wretched old goat's spies sent to torment me?"

The boy was too mortified to speak, for Rowan Blaize was now towering before him, seemingly taller than the vault of the unseen sky itself, enshrouded with crackling, sizzling, snapping bolts of blue lightning that coursed all around his furiously trembling form, and especially throughout his windblown mane of spiked obsidian hair. With a trembling hand, the Prince reached up and rolled back the sleeve of the tunic he had been given, revealing the scar burned onto his forearm by the Gragan, deep in the dolorous dungeons of Cadrach Castle. It radiated an eerie orange glow in the dim interior of the hovel. Upon sight of the signet-ring scar, Rowan Blaize's eyes grew wide and from their depths flew clouds of screaming, searing sparks.

"Impossible," he hissed, unable to look away. "That *cannot* be the Gragan's monogram!"

"But it's true," said Starbane at last. "The nasty old conjurer was just about powerless when I encountered him in that awful cell beneath my father's castle. Oblixta had brought him to ruin. He had only enough magic left to burn this sign into my flesh and tell me that I must seek you out and warn you. There was a poem he recited, but I forget it now. He said that there was some connection between the two of you, because of this sign, though I didn't know what he meant, and still do not know. He said he had been taunting my sister about you for some time during his own imprisonment. Celintha and the others were not able to explain much to me after my escape, I'm afraid. She did mention, as I recall, that the Gragan told my sister about our encounter. I wish I could tell you more, but that is all I know. I swear it. All I can do is show you this scar, which is what I was told to do, and now it is done. May the Gods help me!"

Rowan Blaize's fury faded and his face became pale and drawn. The sudden anger that had overtaken the small dwelling like a storm was now just a flicker of shadows cast by the ebbing fire. Through a window, the afternoon waned and a blood-red sun was rolling away over the distant treetops.

"Oh, there is a connection, alright," whispered Rowan Blaize to himself, falling into his chair as if pushed by some unseen force that had drained the very spirit from his being. "That *is* the monogram of the Gragan wizard, and if what you say is true, then we have reached a most extraordinary crossroads, indeed, Prince Starbane. Coming to me as you have done, though it would seem an act of despair and folly in the minds of many, is quite clearly a gateway to freedom for both of us."

The boy shook his head in consternation. "I can't take any more confusing hints or riddles or allusions to mysterious circumstances!" he insisted. "My mind cannot endure much more double-talk and if I go stark, raving mad the entire battle I've fought just to survive this long, just to get to you, will have all been for nothing."

"Your tribulations will not be counted as vain experiences," said Rowan Blaize. "I can assure you of that. And believe me when I tell you that you will not go mad."

"Then explain matters to me as plainly as you can, sorcerer! I may be just a child in your eyes, but I am an educated one, even if I can't wield a sword or charge into battle the way some royal offspring are able. My progress as a prince has been interrupted, heinously so."

"An explanation shall be yours, good soul, for you now deserve one as much as I have deserved a truthful delineation of matters. Listen well and bend your mind to the understanding of what I am about to reveal to you. To begin, you must realize that I am not from this world."

"What? Do you mean you're not from Corydia? I already surmised that much. You said you traveled all over the kingdoms."

Rowan Blaize shook his head slowly, and with an ancient, solemn patience. His eyes closed in deep contemplation. "You misunderstand, Prince. When I say that I am not from this world, I mean exactly what I say. I am not from Corydia. Or Kelnia. Or any other kingdom or province that may exist in or upon this particular planet. I come from another place, from another time."

Starbane struggled to braid the disparate threads of his reasoning skills together. "You ... you mean you are from the stars? The expanse above us? I have heard legends and tales of those who came down from the heavens to dwell among us."

"No, not even that. There are doubtless many worlds and wonders in this universe—places millions and trillions of light-years away, and some of those places habitable. But I do not come from this universe, Prince. I come from another."

"By the Gods, then how did you ever get here, and why?"

"That, my friend," said Rowan Blaize, raising an instructive forefinger, "is where magic comes into the proverbial picture, if you catch my meaning."

"I don't," moaned Starbane.

"Look at it this way. What you see in front of you, what you can feel, touch, smell, sense—this is one particular dimension. But there are hundreds, thousands, even millions more, layered and hidden beneath all typical vision and awareness. These worlds are veiled from all but the most penetrating Powers and Watchers, who, if they are wise enough and careful enough and foolhardy enough, often seek to slip in-between the barriers that separate these worlds and explore the mysteries that are concealed beyond. This is accomplished through magic. Potent magic. Only a few have the skill to manage such adventures, and I am one of them. Yet, even as I sit before you, an example of one who is crafty enough to undertake such expeditions, I also sit before you as an example of how things can go very, very wrong. My current situation is an example of the dangers inherent in such practices, even for wizards and warlocks and witches and their ilk."

"You mean there are roads that lead from one universe to another?"

"Hmm. Not roads. That's not what I would call them. More like corridors, or gaps, if you will. Gaps that can slipped through the way a bit of thread slips through the eye of a needle, but even that is not a wholly telling analogy. It is more like a passage from light into shadow, and the other way around. My kind calls such places the 'worlds-within,' at least where I originally come from."

"And where is that?"

"Last time I was there, it was still being called 'Europe,' but that is not important for you to know. What is crucial is that you realize that my kind of people are very curious beings. Most inquisitive. We poke and prod at the edges of existence, of multiple existences, if we can. My father was the same way. He disappeared into another world, and I was sent to look for him."

"Where did he go? Did you find him?"

"No, I did not. Oh, we had a few ideas about where he might have gone, but some of those places I did not have the power to enter. Others I did not dare to enter. The passageways into *this* world, however, were navigable enough, so I came here to have a little look around, just over two hundred years ago, as time is reckoned in this world. As it turns out, the entry-point to this particular existence had a specific location—in Kelnia, your own homeland, to be exact. I worked the necessary spells and slithered in like a snake, albeit a harmless one. Oh, I must have spent at least six or seven months here, asking around and searching under every rock for signs of my father's presence, but after a while I found the place so cold and underwhelming—please, do not take my assessment as a personal insult; it was winter—that I could not imagine my father having secreted himself into such a relatively dismal dimension. There are, after all, so many more intoxicating worlds to peruse. So I went back to my own country."

"Just like that?" whispered the awestruck Prince.

"Well, it took a modicum of effort, but yes … just like that. When I returned to my true home I discovered that, even though I had spent over six months in your world, as mentioned, only a day or two had passed in London, while I was away."

"You must have been shocked out of your mind!"

"Hardly. Discrepancies in time are to be expected," said Blaize, as if it were something the Kelnian royal should have known as well as he knew how to add a simple column of figures. "The only mystery rests in what may be the extent, or parallel, of the discrepancy. In some worlds, there is no discrepancy at all. But that, my most welcome guest, is also of little import to your role in this unfolding drama. The key to understanding this predicament is to be found in the fact that, when I first found my way to Kelnia and when I departed Kelnia, my passage did not go unnoticed. I was being spied-upon."

"Not by your father?" said Starbane. "I thought you said he never came here."

"No, not by Father! I was spied-upon by the Gragan himself."

"What?"

"Oh, yes indeed, my boy. You see, the Gragan wizard had his own little curiosities about how one might go about peering into other worlds and dimensions—we cannot fault him for that; he is a sorcerer. Worse than cats, we are—and he had discovered on his own the particular location of the little gateway, the occult corridor that I employed to make my journey to this world. He had been monitoring this junction in the cosmos for some time, seeking to solve its riddles, and that was when he saw me enter and, months later, when he watched as I left. The Gragan himself, however, was not powerful enough, not skillful enough, to undertake a similar trek of his own, although he wanted nothing more than to do just that. As I later learned, he had made inquiries about my person and purpose during my first visit and, after I returned to my own lands, he seethed with envy regarding my ability to cross back and forth as I pleased. Knowing I had been on a search for my father, however, he did manage to concoct just enough magical wit to stage a ruse, and believe me when I tell you that it was a clever one."

"What did he do?"

"He managed, through dark sorcery, to send a message through the otherworldly passage—a message for me, purporting to be from my father, asking me to join him. This little piece of wizard-bait arrived only six days after I had returned from Kelnia and, overcome with renewed curiosity, back I plunged by magic through the Wasteland On the Edge of the Void, through the Unknowable Corridor into Kelnia, where an entire year had passed since my prior departure ... and where the Gragan, vile and sly as a spider, had set a trap for me!"

"How could he have trapped you? If he was not powerful or skillful enough to go between worlds, as you said, and you were indeed powerful enough to do so, then how could he have bested the likes of you?"

"Poor dear Prince, you know little to nothing of the ways of wizards and warlocks. Please keep in mind that I was reentering *his* territory, and moreover I was unaware of any machinations that had been taking place behind my back and beyond my awareness. A great many unfortunate things can befall a sorcerer—even the most formidable one—when he is caught by surprise. The moment I emerged from the Secret Emptiness to breathe the air of Kelnia, I found myself betrayed by a cruel wizard's webbing of spells, right at the door!"

"By the gods, what did you do?"

"Well, what *could* I do?" said Rowan Blaize, shrugging his buckskin-clad shoulders in the thickening darkness of the interior. "The moment I entered the land of Kelnia, the Gragan used a most potent enchantment—one he had clearly been working on for months—to shut the Mystical Passageway completely. Again, it was his world, his land, his domain. He had certain powers over its hidden exits and entrances that

I, being but a visitor, did *not* possess. Thinking he had me at his mercy, the fool laughed and ranted and raved and danced about, certain that I would reveal to him the exact rubric of the spell I used to shift between worlds. I, however, was properly offended and, in my own petulance, was not about to share that information in light of such a deplorable ambush. The Gragan was sly enough to block the passage back home in such a way that I could not circumvent his spell, but he was not potent enough to compel me to tell him a thing about my own methods; nor was he was certain about his chances of defeating me in a duel. 'Go ahead and hide the damned doorway,' I told him. 'I am resourceful enough to find another route of return on my own.' Oh, he was livid, I can tell you, when he saw that I was not about to budge, not by any means. 'Go on, then!' he squawked at me. 'I'm not convinced I can out-trick you, spell for spell, where we now stand, but I can keep you from this doorway, at the very least. Until you make amends to my offended sensibilities by revealing your secrets or by performing some other service that I require of you, the secret gateway in this place shall remain closed forever, even if I should perish, so don't even think about trying anything sneaky.' Really, Prince Starbane, he was a bitter, intractable old bunch of baggage if ever there was one."

"I know. I met him in the dungeons and felt the sting of his ring, if you'll recall. But tell me the rest! What happened after that outrageous encounter, Rowan Blaize?"

"Magicians, my vagabond friend, are stubborn creatures, whether they are Good, Evil, or In-Between. I knew something that the Gragan did not know—namely, that in Kelnia six months were but a few days in my native world. Plus, I really did think I was intrepid enough to find some other magical corridor, somewhere, if I looked hard enough, and eventually head back on my own. I determined that I would be more than content to wait the miserable little devil out. Besides, at that moment, I thought it might behoove me to spend a bit more quality time in your world, exploring its magic, its people, its nooks and crannies. Basically, I fooled myself into thinking I would treat the whole episode as a vacation. A *two hundred-year* vacation was not, however, in my plans."

"Oh!" gasped the Prince. "So, I take it you did not find another doorway back to your own realm?"

Rowan Blaize grinned, but it was not a contented expression. "Obviously."

"So, you've just been here ever since?"

"Here and there. I made-do with what I had to work with, and got some sightseeing accomplished on top of all that. I still had my magic powers, though they don't work quite as effectively in this sphere as they did back home, as I mentioned. Occult forces tend to be relatively constant throughout the multi-dimensional continuum, in my personal experience, but magic works a little differently, here. Took me a few days to tap into the proper wavelengths and what-not. Even then, it has been important for me to conserve magic over the years, which is why I live like a pauper. But what a likeable experiment it has been. Furthermore, I established this little forest-rental with the Corydian royalty after performing just a few showy tricks for the court, if you can believe that. What a gullible lot they were. I also learned extraordinary amounts of lore, in Kelnia and in Corydia and elsewhere. Knowledge is always a marvelous thing, young Starbane, for I shall be the envy of my peers when I return and am able to record all of this data in the proper manner. My book will be a fabulous addition to the Worlds-Within section of any magical library worth its salt."

"But you can't go back!" countered the Prince. "You said yourself that the Gragan has blocked the passageway with magic and you have not been able to find another escape route, thus far."

Rowan Blaize threw his head back and laughed; it was actually the most comforting and encouraging sound that Starbane could recall hearing in years. Then the sorcerer grasped his forearm in a flash and stared him ferociously in the eyes.

"Oh, but I *can* return to my own world, Prince of Kelnia," said the warlock. "Behold this scar you have shown me, which is none other than the insignia of Gragan, as I concurred when first I saw it. Behold the favor that he himself, apparently quite down-at-heel, sent you to beg of me, here in my solitude, here in my lonesome Forest of Shadnai. This insignia, once shown to me, confirms—as do your own words—that I have been asked to perform a favor and make 'amends' to that irritating wizard. Once this is accomplished, then the gateway will open and I can be on my way, whether the wretch who walled it up is alive or dead. That was and remains the rather reluctant 'agreement' between Gragan and I, my boy, and that is how magic works in most worlds, for better or for worse."

"Then I hope you know how grievous is your peril," whispered Starbane in the blossoming shadows of twilight, as birds sang soft songs to welcome the evening outside the stone cottage.

"On the contrary," said Rowan Blaize, settling back in his chair, taciturn once more. "I have no idea, it would seem. I have never heard of your half-sister, Oblixta, and though you tell me she was born with great gifts, even *I* find it impossible to believe that she has evidently conquered the Gragan and Celintha and these nameless others to whom you allude. Perhaps you should tell me her particular tale, so that I am more fully apprised of my 'grievous peril,' as you describe it."

Starbane proceeded, then, to outline for the increasingly surprised Rowan Blaize the entire tale of Oblixta's fall into dark pools of deceit and malignant magic, placing particular emphasis upon her victories against the wizards Cabrus and Gragan and the overwhelming strength of her warrior legions. The fire had died to embers by the time he was finished.

"She'll be coming for you. Everything she's done since I escaped has been to prevent me from warning you. But as you now know, that was all part of the Gragan's foul plan, as well. He wanted to pit you against her, even if he did not survive to see who might defeat the other. Politics. It's unavoidable for any of us," said the Prince.

Rowan Blaize remained silent for several moments and then rose solemnly from his chair and slipped from the house. Starbane made to follow him but, upon entering the dooryard, the magician was nowhere to be seen. The area was moon-flooded and empty and quite still, save for the slight rush of an evening wind and a rustling of the nearby bramble. He called out once, but discerning no reply, felt frightened and far too aware that he had set something quite serious in motion. Something from which he could not back down. Not now. Not ever. He returned to the listing house and took his place by the buzzing coals in the fireplace. Tucking his knees up under his chin he prayed that, wherever the curious and otherworldly Rowan Blaize might have gone, he was even now plotting his strategy to destroy Oblixta and restore balance to the desolate and woe-begotten world that cared little for either of them, once and for all.

II

The Wizard that Toasts is Toast

Night had descended upon the castle of King Sye. A heavy wind surged through the air, its current first high and straight as it bullied northern clouds toward the southern tier of Corydia, and then dashing abruptly downward upon Lake Scilde to swirl around the island fortress. On a thin stone ledge outside the main window of Queen Adurra's bedchamber, Oblixta stood motionless.

Had anyone passed far below with a mind to look upward in the dark, she would have easily been mistaken for just another of the gray, sinister sculptures that adorned the castles of magnificent realms. Her conjured demon had brought her to this place, coursing through the air without obstacle, at great speed blazing above the peaks of the Pyr Mida Mountains. General Kerrion and a handful of his men had been on their way by rather more arduous means far below. The flight-demon had been relieved of its duties and now occupied a place among the other gargoyles of stone that decorated the exterior of Sye's impregnable domain.

Slightly hunched and grotesque, wary to keep her footing and balance in the rising gusts of wind, Oblixta paused. Magic had indeed brought her here—it was something she should have done from the start, she now realized—but there was little more strength to waste by steadying her body against the soaring stone wall. There was work to do on this night, and all the physical and mystical power she had left would be required to fulfill the task. She glanced up into the sky, her palms pressed flat and gripping the cracks between the massive slabs of stone. The remaining height of the central tower was just as dizzying in its flight upward as it was in perilous descent to the courtyard below. While perched as she was, a snaking finger of the breeze found its way underneath her cloak and caused it to flutter and billow. Startled, she very nearly lost her balance. Knowing it would be very difficult to conjure a spell against impact in the few seconds it would take to plunge to the terrace, Oblixta clutched with renewed fury at the castle wall. The long talons on her fingers began to split and every muscle in her lithe frame went rigid. One last look around revealed that no guard would see her enter the bedchamber window in moonless dark like this. That, too, had been the result of her handiwork—though, in summoning the massive cloud, she had not counted on the gusts that accompanied it.

A quick Spell of Foresight had revealed all she would need to know about the chamber beyond and what she should expect at this time of the evening. The room was darkened, save for the pithy embers of a hearth-fire, and the youthful Queen Adurra was fast asleep. It was time to learn *exactly* what her enemies were planning and plotting in this fortress, and long past the time to see her own schemes brought to fruition. Slowly she scuttled, crab-like, a few paces along the ledge to reach the open, arched window of Queen Adurra's bower. Her fingers curled and edged around the sill. It was time to go in. She whispered a foul incantation that rendered her form temporarily unseen. Even without benefit of the moon's blossoming glow, it would do no good for the Queen to catch sight of her silhouette, if perhaps she was tossing and turning in the bed. Visible form faded and became one with the very air as Oblixta hopped down onto the flagstones of the chamber.

Cancelling the spell, for every minute of magic drained her now, Oblixta scurried like a spider into the utter blackness of a nearby corner. Once there, she drew a deep breath, as if preparing for a long and treacherous dive, and listened in the stillness for the sound of her prey. It was a matter of moments, alone in the shadows, before the witch's heartbeat ceased pounding in her ears. The passing ghost of impatience brushed her soul and only when she heard the sound of Queen Adurra's light snoring did she relax, knowing the moment had arrived at last.

From where she stood, there would be only the monarch's huge, canopied bed in the middle of the large room and, directly across from that, a table resplendent with toiletries and mirrors against the wall. On the other side was the softly humming and popping hearth, its glow a dull, pulsating red amid the gloom. Near the hearth and the various furnishings on the exquisite rug before it was the imposing door to the Queen's private suite of apartments. Oblixta knew, from her earlier, perceptive spell, that it would be tightly closed, but *not* locked. On the other side, two sentries stood guard through the night. Oblixta realized that these men—or perhaps a servant—might creep in at any given time to tend the waning fire for Her Majesty's comfort. Indeed, there were two other doors in the room, both smaller portals in the east and west walls leading to auxiliary chambers and other passageways. One, Oblixta had discerned, led to the very apartment of King Sye himself. The other led, eventually, to the small bedroom of the Princess Malinna.

The Kelnian witch was concerned only with this room, for the moment. With the stealth of a cat she slinked across the floor, pulling her black cloak around her body like a shroud, fixing her heightened senses upon the Queen's bed. Halfway across, she bumped into an object that rocked a bit noisily on the flagstones. Cursing herself in her mind, the witch bent to steady the thing—it was a miserable footstool—and cocked an ear to discern whether the sound had awakened Adurra. Devilish luck was with her; the distinctly feminine snoring continued to filter through translucent curtains draping the bed canopy. Oblixta squinted and caught the vague outline of the Queen's head, poking from beneath the coverlets, resting amid a cluster of white pillows. Relieved, she maneuvered around the room, sneaking close to the vanity table, and approached the hearth. Its dwindling light began to reveal the borders of her cloak and form, but this did not matter now. She was almost upon the door and, once it was locked, she would make haste to secure the other two portals. Then, no one would disturb her planned activities.

Oblixta reached the main door of the chamber and caressed its surface with her fingertips, pressing an ear close at the same time. The thickness afforded no hint of what might be happening in the corridor on the other side. Certainly the guards were keeping their silent watch. With nerveless hands she felt for the huge slide-bolt below. Finding it and looking down, she also noticed the tiny pinpoint of light visible through a keyhole. Once the bolt was secure, however, no one could possibly gain entry. Even though she planned to have her work accomplished before any interloper had a chance to intrude, she muttered a potent Shutting Spell over the entire door as she slid the bolt in place. The thing slid easily and made no sound, despite its age and heaviness.

Finished!

Next she turned to the other, smaller doors and threw Shutting Spells against both as if she were tossing coins. This would do for her purposes. Creeping forward, with every fiber of her being focused upon the sleeping form in the middle of the great room, Oblixta came to the bed. One of the few remaining pieces of wood on the fire began to hiss a warning just as she passed and it waxed bright for a few seconds, causing her shadow to loom large and dragon-like for an instant upon the vaulted ceiling. Then the light faded and she found a partition in the draperies. She brushed them aside and placed one foot upon the dais surrounding the base of the elaborate bed. Placing a knee upon the down mattress and its thick covers, she sensed Adurra shift slightly in her deep sleep, head now lazily facing the one that hovered, wide-eyed, mere inches from her own.

Oblixta brought her other leg full upon the bed and the canopy curtains closed around her as she straddled the form of Queen Adurra. Ever so slightly, the young Corydian ruler began to rise from the protective embrace of slumber, her puffy eyes opening and seeing the ethereal face of the sorceress. At first she saw her enemy's visage indifferently, as if it were part of some dream to which she still clung. Adurra would indeed be pulled entirely from this waking trance, but only for a few horrible moments.

Oblixta lashed out and placed her chilling fingers around the Queen's neck, snatching one of the pillows with the other hand. She squeezed Adurra's throat so harshly that the poor woman could only emit a faint, rasping gurgle as her windpipe was bruised and then crushed. Up from beneath the coverlets flew one of Adurra's arms in desperate reaction, clutching at her attacker. But the witch threw the full force of her weight upon Adurra's body, pinning her beneath the blankets even as the victim began to thrash and spasm. The hand with the pillow went instantly across her face and Oblixta smashed it hard against Adurra's nose and mouth while maintaining a vise-grip on her throat. The midnight sorceress scowled in pain when her arm was briefly raked by Adurra's fingernails, so she pressed her shoulder hard against the smothering pillow, feeling Adurra's jaw gape beneath it, trying to draw breath or perhaps desperately bite a way free of the suffocating cover.

"Die, you wretch," Oblixta murmured dangerously above a whisper. Then, as if the words had been one of her dark incantations, Queen Adurra's futile movements ceased abruptly beneath. The body heaved one last time, nearly knocking Oblixta from the bed and onto the floor. But this was life's last, desperate grasp at survival. After a moment of twitching, the free arm of Adurra flopped away from her murderer and it was over.

Oblixta sat up quickly, listening in the glorious silence for any rattling or pounding at the three doors, but all remained undisturbed. Success! She flung the pillow aside through the drapery and lowered her ear to the open but lifeless mouth. There was no warm breath to be detected, so she slapped the Queen's cheek twice. Nothing. Lastly, and for good measure, she reached down and took Adurra's head between her forearms. With a slight grunt and one deft heave, she twisted the slender neck until it snapped.

"That's the end of you," muttered Oblixta as she lifted the body from the bed and dragged it with some difficulty to the rug in front of the hearth and dropped it there. Nearing exhaustion, she propped Adurra's torso against the base of the fireplace and stood back. The next portion of her work would require light, so she concentrated briefly upon the nearly extinct fire in the grate.

"*Rua, chnokobex, saboth!*"

The embers began to glow and then billow in bright flame that fed upon some unseen, supernatural fuel. The chamber was at once illuminated and great shadows began to swirl about the cavernous ceiling, catching features of Oblixta's profile and rendering them in wholly grotesque form. The sorceress next whirled around to the dead Queen's vanity table and, not finding what she sought, moved instead to a small bedside chest of drawers. On its surface she saw an earthenware pitcher and basin. She grabbed the little basin and emptied into it a small amount of water from the pitcher, muttering all the while in her secret tongue. The amount had to be small. *For purposes of dilution only,* she reminded herself. Otherwise, the spell's effect would be distorted.

Moving back to the body, she set the basin beside it on the rug and passed both hands over the Queen's ruined figure once, and then again, chanting softly. When the beginning of her cold rite was finished, she reached into the folds of her vast cloak and produced the thin blade she had sequestered before flying off from the castle in Kelnia. The knife was razor-sharp, but no longer than her middle finger and no wider. Its surface shimmered in the brilliance of the now eerie firelight. The small handle was carved from bone—fashioned by the Gragan wizard himself centuries ago. It had been the sorcerer's Third Ritual Blade, the smallest but by far the most powerful of the many Oblixta had acquired in her plunder of the dead magician's lair. As a High Sorceress in her own right, now, her use of this blade was crucial to the spell she was about to complete.

With steely concentration, Oblixta lifted the Corydian Queen's right arm and positioned it so that the wrist was arched downward and over the basin. She strained to see in the flickering light of conjured flame, searching for a spot she knew well from past exploration of various "practice" victims. But it would be difficult. If she cut the wrong vein or even spilled so much as a drop of blood outside the basin, the entire charm would have to be aborted. Only the proper incision would produce the correct flow and amount of blood she required. Finally, lifting the slight blade to Adurra's pale wrist, she cut a straight incision lengthwise, no more than an inch across, and smiled as the first trickle of blood emerged and ran slowly down the forearm to drip into the receptacle. Oblixta took great care to cut the languid stream off with the rim of the basin and, when the slightly elevated limb had yielded all that could be drained, she raised the Queen's elbow and massaged another supply downward.

"It's a good thing your heart's no longer beating, my lady," whispered Oblixta with a sneer. "Else we'd have a right good mess on our hands, wouldn't we?"

The witch-queen chanted the final few lines of her Introductory Plea, beckoning the dark powers to assist in her heinous work. With a gruesome stare, she caused the fire in the hearth to wax higher and brighter. After folding Adurra's desecrated arm over the torso, Oblixta greedily brought the basin to her lips with her long fingers. She swallowed once, twice, and then a third time, draining the vessel of the blood and water and the sinister magic with which it had been mixed. As if she were the prim guest at some macabre tea, Oblixta placed the empty vessel beside her and stood, gathering the cloak and hem of her gown. She went back to the bed where, moments before, her victim had lay in such innocent and peaceful slumber. She parted the curtains and spread her own body across the pillows and finely embroidered coverlets, going rigid as a scepter. Her moist eyes searched the pulse of shadows cast by the magical fire on the canopy above her.

Suddenly, Oblixta felt a rumbling in her chest and a trembling in her belly. The sensation was at first laborious in its effort to nauseate her. Her ivory-skinned face contorted at once into a half-smiling, half-grimacing mask. In another moment, the churning of her insides passed, as she knew it would. She knew as well that other, far more severe pains were yet to come and against this she braced herself with every portion of will at her command. A sharp tingling invaded her body after this, and moved across the surface of her flesh, as if the circulation of blood had been abruptly obstructed from head to feet. This numbness segued into a prickling so unbearably painful that she nearly cried aloud, though she had long ago trained her mind and body to withstand such agonies. A small moan did manage to escape her twisted mouth, but it was lost in a gust of wind that blew in from outside the tower at the perfect moment. Oblixta's arms flexed and bowed, and her hands began to clutch and claw desperately at the fabric beneath her.

Spasms wracked her legs, causing them to buck and twist uncontrollably and then her entire body seemed to crack upward in a brutal arc. It was only after this that she began to change. The transformation was slow at first, just as the onset of agony had been slow, but once it took hold, the completion was swift. Guided by the power of her spell, Oblixta's once harsh and striking features began to throb and her cheekbones undulated beneath pallid skin. Her mouth and lips stretched and pressed hard against teeth that were themselves being molded into an alternative shape. Her fingers and hands went limp, quivering with each jolt that reduced their length to a shorter form. She endured the tumult, drenched in sweat until her face glistened with an almost snake-like sheen. She drifted into a brief state of unconsciousness but quickly summoned her reserves to pull herself back from the brink.

Eyes fluttered open and with a gasp the witch sprung from the bed. She stared for a moment at the fire, which was beginning to dwindle again to little more than a handful of embers. Only a new, dusty panel of moonlight kissed the wall in its radiant race through the great window. The chamber door was still undisturbed, so Oblixta limped over to the hearth, stepping across Adurra's corpse, and bent low to repeat the Fire Spell she had used before. Nothing happened and her memory emerged from a temporary stupor caused by the spell. Nothing *would* happen. There would be no more magical powers, at least for the duration of her stay in this castle. But she had come prepared for all of that.

She grabbed a few logs from a nearby bin and quietly put them on the ebbing heat of the coals. Next she moved through the murk to the dead Queen's dressing table. There, in the well-polished mirror, she gazed at the results of her arduous conjuring. The reflection staring back was not her own. The black cloak and gown were still hers, along with the large pouch at her belt, but the face was that of the murdered Queen Adurra. Oblixta raised a now curvaceous brow and smiled as flashes of waxing firelight revealed the new, beneficent gaze of stolen eyes. She raised a hand to pinch the cheeks, much rounder and far less handsome than her own, but with a quick glance back at the fallen Adurra, she saw that the magic had been astonishingly accurate. Her new shock of blonde hair was shoulder length and tousled, while further investigation revealed that the entire body had followed suit in the successful shifting of shape. Still, there was the voice. The voice was often a problem in a spell of this kind. Oblixta cleared her throat and spoke a few soft words. The sound was undeniably *not* her own, but that of a much younger and less husky-voiced lady.

"Excellent," whispered Oblixta-Adurra.

Through the window she saw that dawn was perhaps only an hour away. The ordeal had taken much longer than she now remembered or had anticipated. Any lingering in the chamber beyond daybreak would certainly rouse suspicions she wished to avoid, so she put her new body to immediate use. In the hour that followed, she managed to find another set of clothes in one of the Corydian Queen's linen troves. In these she garbed herself, fixed her cosmetics using the toiletries at hand, and at last rekindled the fire from scratch. Pre-dawn birds could be heard chirping across the lake outside when she was finally ready to tackle the problem of the body. The corpse, now marred by rigor, was regarded as little more than an unwanted piece of furniture. Disposal was perhaps the second most important task she must complete in the darkness, while evil spirits still held sway.

Grabbing the belt-pouch she had placed on the foot of the great bed after changing clothes, Oblixta removed the four crystal phials she had prepared for this malicious adventure before leaving Kelnia with the aid of her gargoyle-demon. Each phial was filled with an amber-colored liquid and each had a stopper with a different sigil-marking. Each was crucial to her plan. She chose now one of the four and placed the others safely in the bodice of her new ensemble. Bustling over to the cadaver of Adurra, Oblixta proceeded to drag away every nearby chair and other item of furniture until a safe radius had been created on the flagstones. She lifted the dead Queen up and shoved the body roughly against the hearth so as to take the tapestry rug from beneath. This she rolled up and carted away for the time being. Once the floor was entirely bare, she grunted as she pulled Adurra into the middle of the cleared space. The effort was not negligible; Oblixta quickly discovered that "Adurra's" physique was not nearly as strong as her own.

Standing over the body, she removed the stopper from her phial and winced at the pungent odor released. She poured the syrupy contents onto her pathetic victim and stepped back quickly as the potion did its work. The fallen queen's form began to smoke and sizzle in a most agitated fashion and, although the replenished hearth had reached a healthy blaze by now, its crackling could not compete with the rising din caused by Oblixta's concoction. Under her watchful new eyes, the entire corpse was suddenly consumed in a hissing cyclone of destruction—flesh, fabric, and bone seemed to liquefy and blend into an unrecognizable sludge that soon bubbled and steamed as if the flagstones beneath were really the surface of some great furnace. In moments, the pitiful remains were nothing but ash and the turbulence was finished. Oblixta stepped closer, cool and triumphant, kicking the toe of her slipper against the little mess. It crumbled into dust upon contact.

So much for you, mused the witch.

Working quietly, she covered the dust with the tapestry rug and replaced the furnishings around the hearth. Any apprehension she had felt before was now nonexistent. At this moment, she *alone* was Adurra, Queen of Corydia and Wife of King Sye. She placed a hand to her bosom and clutched with malevolent glee the three remaining crystal phials sequestered there—potions that would be instrumental in her final victory as the days passed. With a wretched smile painted upon her borrowed face, she moved to the bedchamber window and stuck her head out in full view of the billowing dawn. She stared at the guards now visible in their patrol of the ramparts directly across from the central tower. At least one of them looked up at her and bowed his head in deference. Oblixta leaned against the sill, the soft fingers of her new hands drumming against the stone. She nodded back. The guard who had first saluted her stared wistfully at the high tower, at the cherished figure framed like a portrait in the window.

"The Queen is up a bit early this morning," he said.

He and his immediate companion took pains to appear more sturdily at attention.

"Let's move on to the East lookout," muttered the second sentry, "before she thinks we're loafing and reports us to the Commander."

"She's kind of heart," said his comrade, moving all the same toward the suggested destination. "There's not a mean-spirited or spiteful bone in her body, you know. I've always been able to tell."

The guards marched from the spot and, in their absence, drifting across the breeze, came the bitter laughter of Oblixta. It rose up over the North wall of the castle and then plunged down across the surface of the brilliant lake. There, it shattered into a million pieces of stinging glass and rode gentle waves to the distant shoreline beyond.

ॐॐ

Five days later, the castle of King Sye was in an uproar of confusion and awe. If Prince Starbane's sudden disappearance just one day after arriving had caused a tremor in the monarch's court, his return *ten* days later with a wizard in tow caused a veritable earthquake. No one could believe it, at first.

Not Talthagar, who had initially wanted, in his annoyance, to pursue his young charge all the way to the Forest of Shadnai (for that was where he had gone—*everyone* knew it).

Not Ilyssa, who, despite her new "Contessa" status, had been quickly relegated to the role of playmate for Princess Malinna, who she discovered to be an utterly impossible brat.

Not King Sye, who had forbidden Talthagar or anyone else from following the Kelnian upstart to the edges of the mystical forest.

"His fate is in his own hands," the decrepit ruler had first grumbled privately to Talthagar. "If he is punished for his impertinence by the temperamental Rowan Blaize, then it is not our fault, indeed."

Nor could "Queen Adurra" believe her eyes.

Certainly not Queen Adurra, who had been acting a little funny lately, anyhow, and who was the most astonished of anyone when the Prince returned to the palace reception hall riding on the back of a gigantic raven. When that raven swiftly transformed into the wizard of legend, for all to see, the Queen had erupted in a brief fit of mad laughter while the others at court remained frozen in disbelief. But the Queen's odd reaction went unnoticed amid the greater hubbub, which suited *her* just fine. The fact that the blue-cloaked Rowan Blaize was young and handsome, instead of withered, snaggle-toothed, and one-eyed, only made jaws drop even lower. Tongues between those jaws began to wag throughout the castle and its fiefdom, and soon they wagged throughout the entirety of the kingdom itself.

The news spread relentlessly: Rowan Blaize, Dweller Within Shadnai, had agreed to journey with the Prince Starbane Cadrach back to Kelnia and do battle with the vile half-sister and usurper, Oblixta, thus helping restore the throne to its proper heir. The brave young royal's dangerous mission had not been in vain, after all. There was also much talk about the significance of some sort of scar in the various negotiations associated with the plan, though no one could quite figure *that* part out.

The announcement of this campaign, though it set King Sye, Talt-hagar, Ilyssa, and everyone else on their ears with wonder and anxiety, had thrilled Queen Adurra, who was conspicuously alone in her proposal that the upcoming endeavor called for the most extraordinary celebration ever seen in the history of the realm. She did, in fact, *insist* upon planning the feast entirely on her own.

"When shall I—I mean *we*—ever again possess the good fortune of entertaining the fabled Rowan Blaize before he sets off on such a pivotal adventure, with such a brave little boy as the Prince Starbane of Kelnia at his side?" she queried with an odd, perhaps even a *hungry,* look in her eye. No one thought to question Her Majesty, and that included the discomfitted King Sye.

So it was that Starbane made apologies to his friends Talthagar and Ilyssa, sought and received King Sye's forgiveness for running away to the enchanted wood without permission, and generally distracted all of them by showing off the incomparable new ally he had attained in the suddenly quite available Rowan Blaize. For his part, the reclusive sorcerer found the wave of reverence and attention to be surprisingly flattering, especially after so many years of solitude in his stone cottage.

He warmed to the idea of a feast before battle with a most rude and impertinent sorceress, and was the first to applaud the Queen's almost hysterically enthusiastic idea to invite *all* of the nobles and military leaders throughout Corydia to the glorious event, which would be held in the gigantic castle ballroom. No expense, of course, would be spared.

Before anyone knew it, the feast came to pass, with all of the powers and potentates of Corydia in attendance and all excited to behold the famous magician and co-rulers of their realm on the very evening before Rowan Blaize was to take off—via powers unquestionably supernatural and mysterious—to help the lanky Kelnian teen defeat his sister, avenge his poor murdered parents, and gain the dominion that was rightfully his own. How well and good it all was! Stories and songs were certain to be composed about the hullaballoo forthwith; everyone was certain about that. Barons, ladies, mayors, generals, dukes, duchesses—they came in droves. Most of those gathered in the gloriously decorated Festival Hall were in complete agreement that it was wise of the moody Blaize warlock to come out of retirement and make a pre-emptive strike against a witch-queen that had already cut down some of his famous confreres. All concurred that it was *the* sensible thing to do, if one was gifted with such powerful magic: hex or *be* hexed, they agreed. Any details other than that were beyond their comprehension and would be of interest only after the battle (or whatever it turned out to become) had taken place and new myths could be created apace.

Lining the ornate and well-appointed long-tables of the ballroom, these elite guests sat and laughed and drank and feasted. On the dais above them was an even greater table for the most select guests, with King Sye doddering in the middle, flanked on either side by his Queen, Rowan Blaize the sorcerer, Prince-and-future-King Starbane, Talthagar, and even Ilyssa, who had been allowed to sit in such choice company solely because of her association with the Kelnian Prince ... and because she'd been putting up so well with the irritating little Corydian princess, who was rather fond of pulling her hair for laughs at regular intervals. The cavernous room was alive with music and the typical sounds of overwrought celebration and spectacle when Starbane was startled out of a little trance.

"Have you been enjoying the celebration, Prince Starbane?"

It was Queen Adurra.

Rowan Blaize nudged the youth discreetly with his foot beneath the shining white tablecloth.

"Wake up," he whispered. "It's the second time she's asked you."

Starbane collected himself and turned to face the Queen. She was leaning slightly forward in her gilded chair, smiling and full of sweetness. One of the last speakers had concluded his toast (there had been an endless string of toasts all evening, which naturally helped everyone enjoyed their drinks even more) and servants were scurrying everywhere, trying to keep an eye on the slightest finger-movements of the demanding King Sye and other Very Important Persons.

"Aren't you feeling well, young Starbane?" asked the Queen, suddenly quite maternal in her concern.

"Yes, Your Majesty, I'm quite alright," he replied. "Perhaps a bit lightheaded from all the excitement and from all of this toasting. That's all."

"Mind that you take only small sips after each raising of the cup," counseled the Queen amiably. The Prince noted that she hadn't seemed more at ease since the shocking day he and Rowan Blaize had arrived in such grandiose style from the enchanted forest.

"It's part of the ritual," she explained. "If we emptied the cup after *each* honor given, the place would look very much like a common drinking hall, now wouldn't it?"

She laughed, then, and the weird coldness that seemed to lurk beneath the sound made Starbane feel decidedly uncomfortable, though he was not about to show it. Nodding politely, he turned his attention away and glanced about the main table. Talthagar, Ilyssa, and the rest of the guests, except for himself and Blaize, were showing signs of rather dubious sobriety, despite the Queen's talk of etiquette. For example, Starbane and Blaize both happened to catch sight of a Corydian Lord named Khadmar as his hand crept through the folds of an equally inebriated servant-girl's robes ... even as the Lord's wife sat at his side. She, however, was too preoccupied with her hiccoughs to correct her husband's lack of couth.

"Typical mortals. They're exceedingly drunk," whispered Rowan Blaize as the Prince fought the urge to snicker at the bizarre spectacle. He had been eager to leave for Kelnia with his new friend immediately. Only the Queen's ferocious insistence on a great "pre-victory party" and Talthagar's injunction to wait a few days had halted their plans. Indeed, Talthagar had made it known from the start that he wasn't about to trust Rowan Blaize completely, but he was coming around on *this* night. As tipsy as anyone in the hall, he was slurring his words as he regaled the ambivalent sorcerer with stories about his exploits as a swordsman, assassin, and spy for the King. Starbane shook his head and leaned back as lazily as he could in his grandiose chair. The magician tried to ignore Talthagar as he shot the leisurely youth a disdainful glare.

"Please don't tell me to sit up straight, Rowan Blaize. I'm exhausted. You can't begin to know what a long life I've had."

"Don't talk to me about long lives, Princeling. And I've been hearing all about your adventures, thank you kindly. At least I'll know exactly what I'm up against when I face your dear sister. I'm starting to wish we had left to fight her immediately, rather than lingering for this overblown revel."

"Gods, don't even mention my sister's name, not tonight," said Starbane, wishing he could fall asleep where he was. "It's going to take me three days to recover from all this celebrating and you and I are supposed to leave for Kelnia in the morning as it is."

"We may have to think about that idea a bit," said Blaize, raising a goblet to his lips. He was clad in his best conjurer's clothing—a cloak as blue-black as the darkest galaxy, bedecked with embroidered runes, and shirt and trousers to match. His hair was no longer in woodsman's disarray, but shining like spun strands of dark crystal across his mighty shoulders. He always felt it paid to advertise when one was out amongst mortals.

A Springtime humidity had congealed in the hall, its thickness churned by the crowd and held in by walls that boasted windows too small for adequate ventilation. The season's first bottle-flies had long dismissed themselves, for the most part, but they were succeeded by an annoying barrage of gnats eager to escape the cooling night outside. These insects flitted and spiraled, taunting faces and descending upon plates, always just beyond the swiping fists and napkins that snapped out to crush them.

"Try to stay awake for a little longer," muttered Blaize. "Queen Adurra is the only one left who hasn't given a toast and she's the last of the night, according to her own words. She says it's going to be a salute to remember."

Starbane's head began to swoon. He looked over at Ilyssa, who seemed completely out of place at the event. He had discovered upon his return that she, of course, was not best suited to being a governess for the reprehensible little Malinna. Between anxiety for her treacherous parents and fear of offending her esteemed hosts under such beneficent circumstances, the Pyr Midan runaway who had just happened to cross their paths seemed suddenly more miserable than before, if such a thing were possible. Their eyes met for an instant amid the merriment and, in their depths, he could sense that no rescue, no matter how royal, would erase the brutal ache of a life betrayed.

But Starbane Cadrach had little time to ponder Ilyssa's sadness; Queen Adurra had now risen with a pert flourish from her throne beside King Sye. Two servants behind her clapped their hands high into the air, signaling to every august personage in the ballroom that the mistress of this triumphant event was at last ready to pay her own long-awaited respects. The murmur and gaiety of the assembly dwindled like a vanishing tide and all eyes fixed upon the beautiful Adurra, down to the most minor servants that had paused in their duties for the evening's crowning moment. King Sye, Starbane, Rowan Blaize, Talthgar, Ilyssa, and even General Coragus (who had come to the party all the way from his battle-camp at the foot of the Pyr Mida Mountains) gave the Queen their undivided attention. She stood and paused, basking in the sheer magnitude of the venerable silence.

"Honored citizens of Corydia and guests of the royal family," she began, lifting her voice so that it could be easily heard throughout the place. "It is with profound gratitude that I thank all of you, loyal adherents of my husband the King, for joining me in this special tribute to the alliance formed between our remarkable enchanter, Rowan Blaize, Lord of the Sacred Forest of Shadnai, and the Kelnian Prince Starbane Cadrach, seeker of vengeance against the injustices done to him, his family, and his throne. Indeed, like the rest of you, I stand amazed that this mere boy, one so young and one who has endured so much hardship, has come far enough to not only bring *our* legendary sorcerer out of hibernation, but convince him to aid in the destruction of a particularly hideous witch that has laid waste to all the Northern realms!"

The raucous crowd erupted in cheers at this pronouncement. The Queen's words caused hearts to swell with pride for King, country, and conjurer, even as her beauty was unveiled as a beacon. None could remove their eyes from her.

"Yet," continued the Queen, smiling, "there is one ultimate honor I need to bestow upon this exceptional night of feasting and, dare I say, this forecasted triumph." She raised a delicate hand and summoned a servant nearby. The man brought a large bottle of wine to the queen, along with a tray upon which two gilded golden goblets of inestimable quality had been placed. Begging the pardon of the bemused Rowan Blaize, the Queen placed one of these goblets down in front of him at table.

"The entire realm rejoices in the appearance of the great magician of Shadnai Forest," she said. "Moreover, I lead all of our people in wishing you, Rowan Blaize, great magical success in your upcoming battle against the wicked and false Empress of Kelnia." She glanced briefly at Starbane as she spoke and the Prince saw the same, simmering look of hunger that had been piquing his curiosity all evening. A boisterous round of applause welled-up from the far end of the hall and surged like a great wave across the gathering, but the Queen stemmed its tidal sweep with another display of her upturned palm. Rowan Blaize's vision now seemed lost in the gleam of his golden cup, though he listened carefully to every word.

"I have reserved for the sorcerer's honor the finest vintage found in the glorious cellars of my husband's vast private reserve," boasted the

Queen as King Sye nodded approvingly to the noble sycophants around him. "This is a wine we had been saving for some very momentous occasion and we agreed that there can be no greater moment than *this* one, in which our renowned spell-caster embarks upon a journey of honor and deliverance!"

Another joyous cheer soared through the hall and Rowan Blaize was clearly charmed by the gesture. Everyone stood, then, the steady and the unsteady, cups and goblets in hand, to pay homage to the fabled sorcerer. Starbane smiled, happy for himself and, of course, for his new magical champion. The Queen instructed that the two goblets be filled from the open bottle, first her own and then that of Blaize. The steward—*did Starbane find him somehow disturbingly recognizable?*—tipped the vessel slightly and poured the rich red liquid into the vessel. Instantly, all at the main table were enchanted by the exotic spiciness of the aroma. This was indeed a magnificent vintage. Silence reigned, for this was the special moment of the Queen as well: she, after all, had been the mistress and architect of such a memorable repast. As chief recipient of the night's final honor, Rowan Blaize would be the first to taste of the gift, in accord with Corydian tradition. Eyes afire, the Queen raised her goblet with open-mouthed awe, gripping its basin with both palms. With a simple nod, she instructed the sorcerer to do the same and he lifted his cup to meet her own above the festive crowd.

"Rowan Blaize, who came to us in ages past from lands unknown, in my name and in the name of my great husband, Sye, I salute you. You bring joy and honor to all who dwell in the realm of Corydia. Drink with pleasure this vintage I offer. May its sweet taste symbolize the flavor of the success you shall experience in all your endeavors against an enemy you shall surely crush beneath your feet!"

With a quick wink of her left eye, the grinning Queen waited with the rest of the multitude for Rowan Blaize to taste and he did so without delay, looking first upon the gathering and raising the cup jovially in their honor as well. Then he took a long draught from the goblet and savored the wine with visible appreciation.

"Excellent vintage, Your Highness!" he remarked, placing the bejeweled goblet very gently back upon the table. "Certainly the finest I have had the pleasure of sampling in ages, though I do confess it has a rather beguiling aftertaste that I do *not* recognize from all my vast years of experience as a drinker of exceptional beverages. Indeed, the honor you have done for me this evening is incomparable."

"It is also your last honor," hissed the Queen in a low but vicious whisper. Only Starbane and Rowan Blaize, facing her, were able to hear these words. The Prince tilted his head, as if not quite certain he had heard correctly. Rowan Blaize shifted uncomfortably in his chair and stared, unblinking, into the eyes of the Queen. She had not deviated from her standing position and had conspicuously failed to take the traditional sip from her *own* goblet. After a moment of odd silence, the wizard's eyes grew wide and a look of bitter recognition flashed across his visage. There was little time for anger, however; a frightening pallor soon wiped away every trace of color from his ruddy flesh. His gaze seemed to burn into that of the Queen, who stepped back a few paces to watch his every move with raptor-like interest.

"It's *you!*" gasped the sorcerer, pointing an accusing finger. "I should have known."

These, unfortunately, were the only words he managed to utter at that moment. Starbane leaned toward him, now quite bewildered at the strange turn of events. Talthagar dropped his own goblet, spilling its contents upon the table as he pushed forward to get a look.

Soon everyone was watching as Blaize's hands clutched awkwardly at the tablecloth, squeezing it until his knuckles were white and trembling.

"Rowan, what's wrong?" said Starbane, placing a hand upon his friend's caped back. But Rowan Blaize was oblivious to everything and everyone. The hall erupted in a storm of curious whispers.

The Prince stepped away from his chair and looked at the Queen, whose own face was now a mask of pure contempt. Her cup had been placed back on the table, its sinister contents untouched. Nearby, the King began to mutter and smack his lips at the spectacle while one of his generals stood and, across a platter of roasted capon, asked quite foolishly whether something might be amiss.

"Rowan Blaize, speak to me!" begged Starbane, taking the sorcerer's hand into his own when he saw that the mage was beginning to breathe in spasms that kept time with his increasingly flipping, flopping, trembling body. Guests throughout the place were now whispering and pointing.

"It's a fit!" cried some.

"No, it's poison!" screamed others.

"He's working some spell!" hollered a few.

"He's just drunk," slurred at least one. "Like the rest of us!"

Starbane looked over his shoulder, frantic, at the watchful Queen and at King Sye, who was peering from behind her skirts. "Summon a healer, Majesties!" he pleaded. But no one moved to help except Talthagar, who held the wildly shuddering Blaize from behind as best he could. Rowan seemed to be fighting whatever had come upon him. He managed to grab the Prince by the sleeve as the heavy chair went flying from beneath him. Then he fell, shivering and quaking upon the floor of the dais behind the table. Confusion and more catcalls engulfed the hall as people rose from their seats to gawk. Starbane knelt to the floor to try and get hold of the twitching arms, but his efforts were in vain.

"What in the name of the trickiest god in Dryndym's Drinking Hall is going on?" snapped Talthagar.

"I knew it! This place is as crazy as Kelnia," wailed Ilyssa. "I should have died in the snow like I planned. You're all *so* not worth being here!"

"You'd think a wizard of such repute could handle himself with a bit more dignity," complained old King Sye.

"Someone help us!" bellowed Starbane.

Then, the Prince saw a strange look in the sorcerer's rolling eyes and he was gripped with the terrible realization that it was far, far too late for help.

"Prince Cadrach ... g-get ... *away,*" rasped Rowan Blaize in a final burst of choking lung-power. His words had been garbled by a weird pink froth that had begun to fleck his lips and exposed teeth.

"Can't you tell me what's wrong?" begged the terrified youth.

Suddenly, it all became apparent, *what was wrong,* there on the floor behind the banquet table. Most of what happened next was hidden from the troubled guests at the lower, front tables, guests who were clamoring for explanations, but the "happening" part of it all was quite evident to King Sye, Talthagar, Starbane, Ilyssa, everyone else nearby, and most particularly the Queen.

Rowan Blaize was changing.

In every place where it was visible, the sorcerer's skin began to move and undulate, as if being stretched by unseen hands and remolded to the point of rupture. Poor Rowan let out a painful yowl that struck terror in the hearts of the assembly and it was after this that his limbs began to twist and crack with the most hideous sounds imaginable. First his arms appeared to tie themselves together in some sort of bizarre knot while his fingers writhed and curved inward, one upon the other. His head was yanked back with such a force that Starbane, who had fallen in shock and astonishment against the skirts of the supervising Queen, thought he heard the warlock's neck snap altogether. In fact, Rowan's facial skin had been pulled so tightly in profile that only dimpled slits remained where his eyes had once been and the hairy brows above them suddenly burst forth like wild black grass to grow down the sides of both cheeks and then the very front of his previously handsome features.

After this horrific display, bristling hairs pierced through the remnants of pallid skin-like spines and Starbane's eyes nearly flew from his head as he watched these whiskers meld with the sorcerer's formerly luxurious hair. The color of this hair was becoming much different now—black as tar in some spots and gray as slate in others. More terrifying (if possible), legs and arms started to shrink and wither and retreat backward into the openings of Rowan's shirt and breeches. Next, everyone could hear sounds like the ghastly sucking of flesh and the dreadful snapping of bone. Soon, the gnarled and unrecognizable head of the mage had receded altogether into his collar. An instant later, there was a little puff of green steam and nothing could be seen except for Rowan Blaize's clothing, which was twitching and shaking as if some horrible thing struggled within, trying to break free. Even his "special occasion" troll-skin boots were left empty and askew in the tangle beneath the chair.

"I say, what's he *done* with himself?" muttered King Sye.

"Is it something we said?" grumbled Talthagar.

"I'm sorry I ever laid eyes on *any* of you freaks!" shrieked Ilyssa.

"Wizards!" sniffed one of the Corydian River Masters, munching on a duck's leg. "What show-offs they tend to be."

Starbane pulled on the tablecloth in a desperate attempt to scramble to his feet. He would have preferred to scream, had he possessed the breath to fuel such a sound. Only a thin whimper managed to part his lips, though. Plates, goblets, candlesticks, and all sorts of food began to roll and clatter onto the flagstones around him as he tugged and bucked against the table, the sound forming a frightful harmony with the random shrieks of various noblewomen throughout the hall.

"ROWAN BLAIZE!" cried the woeful Prince of Kelnia.

Eyes were wide and jaws were agape when, a moment later, a large, angry raccoon darted from the pile of Rowan's clothing and leaped onto the banquet table, snarling, spitting, yelping ... with his ringed tail at full-bristle status. In the bedlam and fearful rushing-about that ensued, Starbane imagined for a horrified instant that the aggravated beast was actually trying to *say* something in its shrill squeak-of-a-voice. To his wild distraction, however, he found himself being suddenly lifted from the floor by the two servants who had procured and poured the wine for the Queen's final toast. These men were rough with the boy and, when one of them twisted his arm with a terrible jerk upward behind his back, the Prince knew—with grim certainty—that everyone was very, *very* much in trouble.

Amid the blur of screaming people, the pompous, besotted cries of King Sye for "order," and the vain attempts of Talthagar and Ilyssa to reach the Prince through the thick, maddened crowd on the dais, the larger mob below was beginning to rise up in a mounting panic. With the two powerful servants beginning to drag him, kicking and yelling, away from the scene, Starbane could not believe the horror before his eyes.

The raccoon—or whatever it was—that had emerged from Rowan Blaize's robes and garments was poised on its hind legs atop the table and Queen Adurra herself was gesturing wildly for a bevy of castle guards poised nearby with spears to cut the creature down.

"No!" screamed the Prince, but amid the tempest of so many voices no one could begin to discern his own. He struggled in vain as the grip around his arms tightened and he saw a guard with a curved sword begin to swing away at the furry thing that had been Rowan Blaize. Deftly, the chattering animal ducked the blow and scurried away, jumping down from the table and then beneath it. Talthagar was beside himself, looking around for his own sword and trying to keep Ilyssa close to his side in the press of frenzied guests.

"What is this gruesome business?" yelled the Prince at his new captors. "Where are you two fools taking me? I demand to know at once!"

Neither of the men dressed as servants gave an answer. In another moment they had made their way out of the tumult and were suddenly face to face with the Queen herself, who was still bellowing for the guards to find and kill the jabbering Blaize-beast that had dashed beneath the table.

"Queen Adurra, what's going *on?*" screeched Starbane. "Tell your servants to release me! I've got to find Talthagar and Ilyssa in this chaos."

The Queen whirled to look at him as if his words had completely revolted her. With a scowl smeared from one side of her face to the other, she lifted a hand and slapped the boy, with all her strength, upon the face. Her palm was hooked as it struck, the long nails scratching his cheek with a vicious sting. The Prince could only gape at her in horror as she peered nervously about and nodded to her henchmen. The outer columns of confused castle guards, meanwhile, were attempting to calm the hundreds of guests in the hall with little success. King Sye appeared to be slumped in his chair, grasping his heart in pain or pathos—it was now impossible for anyone to tell.

"Get this little wretch out of here now," barked Queen Adurra. "Do everything as we planned! Are Kerrion and the others waiting outside, beyond the lake as we expected?"

The hair on Starbane's neck stood up after hearing this name. *What was going on?*

"Let's move!" cried the Queen, gathering her robes, pushing befuddled servants out of the way, and dashing ahead of her cohorts away from the hall and into the narrow corridor that connected kitchen to banquet-room. Through the portal—and Starbane could see all of this because he was being dragged backwards—a flurry of castle guards caught sight of the Queen's flight and began to hurry after her through the maze of frantic people, eager to protect her, though they themselves didn't quite know from what. In that instant, she scrambled back in front of Starbane to face the guards as they came forward in a barreling unit. Reaching into the folds of her flowing blue gown she retrieved something that flickered and sparkled in the sizzling torchlight of the hall, something that looked like a crystal phial to the apprehended Prince. This the Queen threw with a terrible screech onto the flagstones before the onrushing soldiers.

There was a deafening roar, a rush of blistering hot air, and a flash of light that nearly seared the sight from Starbane's eyes. He coughed and choked and struggled with all his strength against the force of the explosion. There were now chilling screams and cries of terror throughout the great hall and, opening his eyes a crack, the helpless Prince vaguely saw Talthagar in the distance, beyond a sea of burned and burning people, rushing away in the opposite direction with Ilyssa flung over one of his shoulders. The Queen had somehow shielded herself from the awful blast, lifting the hem of her cloak and urging her entourage into the safety of the corridor. Once within, one of the men released his grip on Starbane and stumbled to shut the connecting door firmly behind them. He locked it with a triumphant snarl.

Though now in the grip of only one rattled captor, the youth was still too dazed to do much to help himself. The Queen howled another order and he was swept up again as the four sped through the rest of the passage and into the massive kitchen, past rows of petrified cooks and alarmed serving-men and serving-women. All of these began to cough in a rising storm of glittering, dusty smoke that seemed to be coming from everywhere and nowhere at the same time. They saw their Queen race by and called to her with pleas for some explanation, but none were forthcoming. As the foul cloud thickened and another great explosion— followed by a terrible crash—was heard from the vicinity of the festival hall behind them, the voice of the Queen roared above all other sounds.

"To the boats!" she cried. "Quickly! We must leave this island at once. It is doomed!"

In one hideous moment of recognition, the furious force of a conclusion rose with stabbing certainty into the Prince's brain. As the four rounded a tight corner and the Queen herself flung open the doors of a musty cellar and began to descend, Starbane knew that what he had *really* heard was none other than the voice of Oblixta.

❧◈◈

Even as the barge drifted across Lake Scilde toward the northern shore, Starbane could smell the smoke and hear the ferocity of the blaze. He was bound and shackled by chains to a chair, unable to look back, but at the edges of vision he could perceive on the water a shimmering reflection of the inferno they had left behind. The wine-stewards who had first grabbed him in the hall stood around him in a semi-circle with several more accomplices he did not recognize. Whether they had come from within the castle or some other place, he did not know. He was able to surmise that they were watching the castle of King Sye go up in flames due to their foul comments. Beyond his sight, he knew that Oblixta—couched so wickedly, somehow, in the form of Queen Adurra— was watching as well.

For her part, the disguised Queen smiled wretchedly at her handiwork.

The Corydian palace and its surrounding island fiefdom were now fully engulfed. Those who had been swift enough to escape were still doing so, she could see, rushing from every visible portal and even jumping from windows high in the towers. Many were even afire as they fled in desperate attempts to throw themselves into the lake. All in all, they ran about like insects dispersed from some great, crushed nest. This, Oblixta thought, was rather a fitting sight.

"Let them get away, if they can," she muttered. "Let them live while they can to spread word of my victory over King Sye and the ridiculous Rowan Blaize, idiot warlock of Corydia."

The servants—soldiers of Kerrion who had been secreted into the castle after their recent arrival in the realm—signaled that the pushing oars had finally struck the shallows of the lake bed. They were only a moment away from reaching shore near a scattering of high boulders that had been their prearranged destination. A number of tethered horses were sequestered close by. In their company was General Kerrion himself, who had been most swift and stealthy in his own, long journey across the mountains and plains, arriving by difficult pathways, elusively stealing into the environs of the Corydian castle, as commanded, to await his Queen's next orders. Everything was ready for the return-trip to Kelnia with the captured Prince Starbane. Still in the magical guise of Adurra, though disheveled and undignified because of the fray, Oblixta finally moved to face her captured half-brother, circling him on the barge like a satisfied panther. It was dark, but the moon and the great flashes of fire from the now distant castle provided enough light for their eyes to meet in dreadful recognition.

Oblixta-Adurra reached forward and, with the same fingernails that had raked Starbane's flesh at the banquet table, she loosened and then lowered the gag that had been placed about his mouth.

"I'm sure, by now, that you've guessed who I really am," she said softly. Some large water-bird squawked mournfully and soared out of the way of the drifting barge.

"Yes. I know that it's *you,* somewhere under that skin," said the Prince evenly. "How enterprising you are, sister. So gifted and yet so subtle. No one has ever been able to say you aren't a determined creature." The Prince's every word was delivered in a monotone of hatred and fear. "What have you done, may I ask, with that nice Corydian queen?"

"What do you think?"

"I think you killed her, as you tend to kill anyone who stands in your way, innocent though they may be."

"No one is innocent, you little idiot," murmured Oblixta. "And I haven't killed you, in any case, have I?" She leaned back as the barge gently struck shore, her arms crossed. "Not yet."

Starbane wanted desperately to spit in her face, but his mouth was bone-dry. He did, however, manage a brief but cutting laugh.

"Life associated with you is not one I have any wish to lead, so you might as well kill me," he said.

"Oh, don't worry," said Oblixta. "I intend to. But, as great practitioners of my craft have known for centuries, these matters have to be handled delicately. Otherwise, one could damage the magic."

The Prince cocked his head toward the swirling pools and little waves that lapped the shoreline. "There's the lake, Oblixta. I'm bound and helpless, thanks to you. Why don't you push me over and be done with it?"

The brutish henchmen scampered to shore, securing the barge with a set of ropes before disappearing behind the monolithic boulders. Oblixta sneered.

"If it were that easy I would've done it ages ago, instead of needing to follow the same procedures I used on our—on *your*—parents, back at Castle Cadrach. It's such a shame that killing blood relations is crucial to the acquisition of dark power, but we can't go changing the universe, can we? It's also a shame you didn't like the accommodations back home, a shame you felt the need to play runaway like you did. A minor crimp in my plans. But childish games are over, now, and I've got a far more complex end in mind for you. As you can likely guess from the destruction behind us on the lake, your Kashizma warrior friend, Talthagar, is not going to rescue you this time."

"Don't be so sure. He's dodged your arrows for longer than you or I realize. More artfully than you've shot them, I might add."

"That's as may be," laughed Oblixta, though she was hardly amused at such a reminder. "But I doubt he survived the Inferno Spell I tossed in there. He was right up close and in the middle of the action, after all. Otherwise, I have to admit you've been lucky during your little escapade—surrounding yourself with helpful friends, boy. Haggard old

Celintha, the woodsman Rufthar, his moron wife and child, that beer-brewer Telvyn Rakahr and *his* insufferable woman. I've since killed them all, you know."

"You didn't!" cried the Prince. "You couldn't. Not all of them!"

"Of course I killed all of them, fool. What did you expect me to do, after your juvenile little escape? I have wonderful ways of rooting-out insurrectionists and traitors and making them pay dearly. Why, once I truly got a fix on your trail, you led me right to them. You might as well have been the one to kill the useless numbskulls, yourself."

"Vile beast from hell!" spat Starbane, struggling against his pinions. "Why didn't you just leave them alone? They were all kind and loving to me."

"Yes, well, that was a foolish risk they chose to take, wasn't it? But I've no use for 'kind and loving' in my worldview, and much less respect for either. The people who aided you are dead and that's that. Their luck ran out and yours did, too, when you were foolish enough to seek the help of an obviously out-of-practice magician. But what a lark—you led him right to me and placed him in my grasp like a jewel! I thought things were going to be much more difficult when I first got rid of the Corydian Queen and assumed her flesh. I figured it might take me weeks to plot and plan once I, too, was settled in Sye's castle. But in a matter of days, there you were, flying in with Rowan Blaize himself, who proved to be quite the dimwit. If he even *was* the real Rowan Blaize, he didn't even have the sense to recognize that he was in danger. That you were *all* in danger. It seems I'd been worried about him for no reason, all these years, after all of the Gragan's threats and antagonism. Indeed, the Gragan seems to have greatly exaggerated his power. But that doesn't matter now. We'll put it behind us, shall we? Back to Kelnia we'll go, where there's a particularly foul place waiting for you, beside the remains of your father and that filthy wench he married. When you are dead—properly killed, mind you—then I shall bring my armies over the Northern mountains at last and take this realm without the slightest trouble. It's all become so deliciously perfect!"

"Do as you will, Oblixta," said Starbane, so calmly that the Queen blinked in mild surprise. "I won't resist you. I couldn't. We all know that. And I'll endanger no more lives because of their happenstance association with me. I know you probably even took personal pleasure in having old Celintha killed, and the same sick pleasure with Telvyn Rakahr, his wife, and those good people who saved my life at the hunting encampment near Pyr Mida."

"Correct on all counts," bragged the witch. "But let's not forget the fun I had smiting your wizard, your warrior, and your wonder-lit waif, Ilyssa, just a few moments ago."

"Fine," said the boy, his eyes filling with tears. "Then off we go indeed. But I want you to know something, and know it well—you *don't* frighten me anymore. Nothing you can do, whether by fell power of this earth or any other world, can frighten me. Never again."

General Kerrion, his men, and the horses were now gathered along the shore, waiting, but Oblixta wasn't finished gloating.

"Oh, you'll fear me," she promised, leaning forward upon the bound youth. She reached within her tattered, singed gown and produced the last of the four crystal phials she had brought for the working of her magic. "You see this, boy?" she hissed. "This is the result of *my* craft and *my* diligence. You've never accomplished anything in your miserable little existence, and you never shall. I, however, shall do so much more, and for so much longer, because of my skill. You shall indeed fear me, before the end."

Though Starbane's legs were bound together by chains, they were free to move in other ways. In a flash of anger and furious strength he brought his feet, heavy shackles and all, upward in a swift kick that grazed the hand of his tormentor and sent the phial spinning toward the granite boulders on the shoreline. The tiny vessel sparkled as it caught the reflection of the blazing castle across the water. Oblixta screamed and fumbled too late to snatch it out of the air. The thing smashed against the rocks, its dark liquid contents emitting a faint blue pulse of magical power on the granite and then vanishing altogether.

"Your Majesty, what has happened?" called General Kerrion, drawing his sword. Oblixta had watched the phial's destruction with desperate disbelief and now she turned eyes of wrath upon the fateful grin of her half-brother. "You worthless insect! You wretched pig!" she rasped. With a balled fist she backhanded Starbane so hard across the face that the chains on the boy made a rattling sound and Oblixta herself thought she had broken her borrowed wrist. It was annoying that the body did not truly belong to her—and in that regard her troubles were now doubly magnified.

"Do you realize what you've done?" seethed the sorceress, nursing her wounded palm as the Prince swooned in and out of consciousness from the blow.

"What?" he managed. "Has your magic deserted you?" He laughed and choked simultaneously, then passed out against the chair.

Oblixta was horrified, but hardly because of her brother's brief collapse. She leaned toward him once again and roughly grabbed his head, lifting both eyelids for an appraisal of his senses. "You'll live, imbecile," she muttered. "But only for now."

Her mind was racing. She had made a grave error in her fit of pride. The phial Starbane kicked away had indeed been the last of those she had prepared before the sinister journey to Corydia, and it had been the most crucial, particularly *now*. The elixir it contained—and which was now lost forever—had been a potion designed to transmogrify her body from that of Queen Adurra back into her genuine form. While in the body of the foreign queen she was still unable to work any magic from within her being, relying solely upon the disguise itself, guile, and her already prepared potions to carry out the remainder of the mission. Now, she had no means of turning herself back into the real Queen of Kelnia, and this in a hostile land upon which she had just dealt a grievous wound! The journey back to Kelnia would now be most perilous, potentially even fatal, without the powers she had been counting-on due to a necessary transformation!

Kerrion stomped onto the barge with a few of the other men and Oblixta felt faint. Kerrion was mighty, but he had brought only a handful of soldiers with him. What if they were to encounter members of an enraged Corydian army as they tried to sneak out of the country? What if they ran into a crowd of bandits, or a bevy of hungry ogres? Moreover, Oblixta dared not let Kerrion know that she was vulnerable in any fashion. Her warlord did *not* realize that she was without her magic powers while embodied as the Corydian Queen and this was a lucky thing. Her treatment of the General had always been severe, and she knew that he despised her—deep down—as much as he hated everyone else in the world. But any feelings of insurrection he may have harbored were always kept well in check by his fear of her sorcery. If he were to find out that she was presently without her magic …

"Majesty, what has this ingrate done? We saw him kick at you and then we saw something hit the rocks."

"It was nothing, General," said Oblixta, raising herself to Queen Adurra's full height (which wasn't nearly as full as she needed it to be, at this juncture) and affecting the most confident air possible. "The whelp was simply throwing a tantrum because I've killed all of his friends and his pet warlock, too. Behold, Kerrion!" she added, gesturing broadly at the destruction still raging over Lake Scilde. "See what my powers have accomplished for our purposes. Soon this castle, or what's left of it, shall belong to me, along with the rest of Corydia. Our army will have no trouble with King Sye in the future."

"Truly, your strength knows no limit," marveled Kerrion, his eyes glittering in the colorful night of fire upon the water.

"Correct," Oblixta said with almost visible relief before a sudden, amazing idea plunged into her mind.

Of course! *There was an answer to everything, after all.*

"We are ready to take the boy back to Kelnia," growled the General. "The horses are here, as you can see. It has been a difficult sojourn. Say the word and we shall fly."

"Let's get out of here," said Oblixta, gathering her skirts and stepping gingerly from the barge to the shore. "Take the boy in hand. But we'll not be heading back to Kelnia by the same secret roads you used to get here, General."

"No?"

"No. We're going to make a little detour first. I have one more piece of business to attend to. Come! I'll ride in front and the rest shall follow."

"Why this shift in plan?" asked Kerrion. He sensed something slightly amiss, some flicker of change that was not at all according to Oblixta's taste. "It will be dangerous to take any detours, with so few of us."

Oblixta glanced back at him with as much wrath as she could summon, given Queen Adurra's gentle features. "What danger do you fear when *I* am leading you, General? Obey me at once. I must deal with a small matter before I depart this fine nation. You and your men shall do as you're told. It won't take long."

"Where are we going?" asked Kerrion as his underlings fussed with chains and then lifted the bleary-eyed Prince toward the horses.

"You shall see in good time, General. By dawn, which isn't very far away. Now follow my lead or stay behind to burn with the rest!"

ॐ◈

III

Ashes and Umbrage

Talthagar and Ilyssa emerged from the Yur Forest on the back of Skull, weary and stained with soot and ash. They had escaped the previous night's evil inferno, along with a few hundred other residents of the castle and its island precinct. Most had not. Bodies of the burned and partially burned were scattered everywhere along the bridge and near the sentry gates. Weeping sounds mixed with cries of agony, and these awful noises echoed in every corner of the charred and smoking area, but few people could actually be seen. Most who had escaped unscathed had run as far as their feet could take them.

Talthagar had been one of the wiser members of the banquet party—he had guessed at some magical treachery as soon as he saw what had happened to Rowan Blaize, as soon as he saw the wine-stewards apprehend Starbane. Grabbing the frightened Ilyssa, he had powered his way in the opposite direction, through the drunken throng, knowing in his soul that something worse was about to happen ... even as the great explosion rocked the hall. Together they had run from the castle, breathless, all the way to the stables to find Skull.

Now, as dawn began to toy with the horizon, they were heartbroken by the scene before them. It was as if the entire lake was boiling and steaming with toxic fumes, and Talthagar knew that the great palace was no more. As Skull moved, his own head hanging low through columns of smoke swirling over the bridge, the hearts of the two riders fell in astonishment at the sight they beheld. The lake and foundations of the island, once the walls of ash parted in the shifting winds of the cruel morning, were as they had always been. The castle, however, was oozing like a small volcano, with smoke bubbling from every window and opening that could be seen. Even the great rock slabs that formed the exterior were scorched black in many places. The once majestic pennants of King Sye were singed, leaving not the slightest shred to whip and billow in the gusts. Talthagar slid from Skull's saddle, coming almost to his knees upon the bridge in his anguish.

"It's not possible," he murmured. "What sort of foul magic could have done this much damage? It's gone. Just *gone!*"

Ilyssa seemed as calm as the surface of the lake in her rigid pose atop Skull. But she, too, was in shock. "Do you think Prince Starbane and the royal family survived?" she managed to croak, feeling suddenly quite sorry that she had so resented the wheedling little Princess Malinna.

Talthagar glanced back at her in a daze. The world around the bridge seemed to spin, the sounds of harrowing cries still all around them in the murk.

"Survivors?" he whispered, thinking back upon the banquet of doom. "I don't know what's truly happened to any of them, Ilyssa, but you saw how relatively few managed to get out. Whatever the case, I've got to get over there and find out, if it's possible to know anything at all." He leapt back atop the horse. "You had better get off and stay here. It'll be dangerous further in and you won't be able to handle what you're going to see."

"You're not going to leave me alone in these charred ruins," snapped Ilyssa. "Anyone could be prowling about in this smoke. Besides, what I've already seen since hooking up with the likes of you and the Prince has prepared me for anything. Move on, but if you do, I'm coming as well. We owe it to poor Starbane, at the very least."

Talthagar nodded and spurred a noticeably reluctant Skull across the rest of the span. The great bridge-gate was wide open, though no person, alive or dead, could be seen in its environs. Racing through the arch and into the deserted, ruined hamlet, their hearts pounded and lungs were accosted by acrid fumes as they approached the inner drawbridge-gate of the palace proper. A stiff down-rush of wind relieved their vision and breath for a moment, dispelling the filthy vapors. It was only then that they saw more victims, soldiers, and others burned beyond recognition and sprawled all around the drawbridge. They were posed as if still crawling, on the verge of escape, as though the hellish inferno had pursued them to the bitter edge of oblivion. The riders halted; the castle interior was so hot and thick with destruction that it would be impossible to probe further. As the winds grew with the rising sun, the rest of the courtyard hamlet was discovered to be a wasteland of more crisp remains, heaps of scaffolding, and the skeletal remnants of various outbuildings.

"Somehow, some way, this has got to be the work of Oblixta," growled Talthagar, surveying the result of such atrocity. "Even if it was only for an instant, we saw Queen Adurra and those servants last night. How strange they acted!"

"It's like they were after Starbane," agreed Ilyssa, feeling sick to her stomach despite her previous claim of courage. "And after what happened to the sorcerer ..."

"Yeah, that was enough to get me running, and I'm glad we did," said the warrior, grimacing at yet another pile of human and animal carnage near the stables. Skull had stopped in his tracks, neighing and wheezing and refusing to go on. Talthagar jumped to the flagstones and Ilyssa followed, one hand clutching his cloak lest he should even think of leaving her behind. Another gale blew across the lake, fanning the crackle of flames still lingering in the mountainous ruin. He started to walk slowly onto the drawbridge, testing it in places, Ilyssa only a step behind. Smoke poured from the entrance beyond, belching as if from the maw of some fire-breathing beast. The two tripped over a portion of the great lifting-chain at the end of the bridge, but Talthagar managed to grab hold of it before they tumbled into the debris-strewn channel of cold water below.

"You'll find nothing in that castle but the dead! Even their ghosts would not remain here!"

Talthagar whirled around toward the courtyard. "Whah? What was that? Who said that? Show yourself!"

The shrill voice had come from behind a half-burnt platform near a smoldering sentry tower. The warrior and Ilyssa stumbled back into the courtyard, rubbing their eyes and squinting, certain that the smoke had made them delirious to the point of hallucination. There, atop the remnants of the lookout, sat a frazzled raccoon, clinging desperately to a beam and staring straight at them.

"What in the name of the daybreak gods?" gasped Talthagar, his chest heaving to take in as much oxygen as he could manage. The tiny beast spun around twice and chattered as if irritated, and then scrambled up the length of the remaining beam, hissing wildly.

Talthagar prepared to draw the sword at his belt.

"Don't you dare draw your sword on me, warrior," rasped the creature. "I won't survive another catastrophe!"

Talthagar and Ilyssa's mouths dropped open in astonishment. *It's not possible,* their minds first assured them, and then, *Anything is possible, these days,* spoke their inner "reminders." The beast on the beam sat boldly on its furry haunches, tiny hands spread wide as a black nose sniffed the air and ringed eyes dripped ooze from the swirl of irritants all about.

"Don't stand there looking so shocked!" chattered the raccoon. "Mouths agape, indeed. You've seen stranger things in your lives, I'd reckon."

Talthagar blinked, bewildered. "Wh-who the hell are you? I mean, you can't be—"

"It's *me,* Rowan Blaize!" answered the bothered beast. "I wouldn't blame you for not recognizing me in this condition, but didn't you both see what happened last night in the banquet hall?"

Talthagar stared and shrugged. "Uh … yeah. I saw something wild happen, but I had no idea what it meant, and … I can't believe I'm having a conversation with a ditch-rat!"

"Oh, just shut-up with your commentary and believe it," chattered Rowan Blaize. "We all found out too late what was meant by last night's little party. Gods, how blind could I have been? I really should've gotten out more among people the past hundred years or so. To be fooled so easily! To have let my guard down with such carelessness! Ah, she is most skillful indeed. Young Prince Starbane was right about her."

"Hold everything," blurted Ilyssa, taking a few steps forward, her hands held up before her filthy dress, as if trying to grasp the absurdity of the situation, of her life, in general.

"You are *really* Rowan Blaize? By Dryndym, this place is cursed as well as burned!"

"That's putting it mildly," puffed the raccoon. "Oblixta caught us all with our heads in our ... never mind."

"Oblixta?" roared Talthagar.

"Of course! Who else do you think it was? I wouldn't do this to myself, you pea-brain. I knew it from the moment I drank that blasted potion she must've put in the wine, and I knew it especially when I looked at her."

"What do you mean?" said Ilyssa.

"She disguised herself as *Queen Adurra,* my child. Must have killed the poor woman to craft the spell, too, I'm afraid. She foiled us all."

"Then Oblixta *did* have something to do with this!" growled Talthagar. "I felt it in my bones."

"Ha! You're not feeling it nearly as 'in the bones' as I am," snapped Blaize. "She must have planned this treachery well in advance." He curled into a pitiful ball, his ringed eyes buried in his hands.

"The others. The whole castle," said Talthagar. "Are there no survivors?"

"No! Those that were wise and able—like you—escaped before Oblixta's final, destructive blast. She had thrown another potion or something similar into the equation. I saw her do it as her minions tried to catch me. Everyone else is dead, including the King himself, I am grieved to report. The place is now nothing but a foul tomb, a sepulcher of savagery!"

"But you managed to survive," said Ilyssa. "How?"

"Only barely. And only by climbing straight to the top of one of the chimneys, through the only empty fireplace in the banquet hall. When the flames really began to sweep through this place, I held on for dear life, clinging to the outside of the rock at the rim. Imagine the irony—surviving a magical inferno by hiding in a chimney, of all things! But thank the gods for it, or else I'd be finished like the rest."

Talthagar moved closer to the debris, his eyes almost as fiery as the previous night's conflagration. "How could Oblixta have masqueraded as Queen Adurra?" he demanded. "How could everyone, including you, have been so easily deceived?"

"I told you already!" howled Blaize. "Her foolery was superb. That sort of witchcraft is among the most foul, among the vilest, almost impossible for mere mortals to see through, and not so easy for banished, out-of-practice warlocks, either."

"Starbane!" shrieked Ilyssa. "What's happened to the Prince?"

"She has abducted him," replied Rowan Blaize. "No doubt storming back to Kelnia, even as we speak, to have her way with him and prepare her army for a plunge into Corydia at last."

"Then we've got to stop her," insisted Talthagar. "I don't care what it takes. I haven't got a thing to lose now, with the King dead, the Queen dead ..." he gestured helplessly toward the ruins.

"Even the little Princess Malinna is dead, I suppose?" ventured Ilyssa.

"All of them are cooked, you can believe me," said the sneering raccoon.

"Such a ... *sweet* child," gulped the maiden, fingering a little bite-mark the 'sweet child' had left on her thigh during one play-session when a favorite doll hadn't been dressed quickly enough for the Princess's satisfaction.

"That does it. I'm heading for Kelnia now," snarled Talthagar. "We've still got a great army stationed at the borders of this realm and I'll be damned if I let that hag take us all down without a fight!"

"Perhaps," said Rowan Blaize, "but if you think you are a match for her by yourself or with *anyone's* army, at this point, then you are in for worse nightmares to come."

"I'm going after her all the same," scowled Talthagar. "For one thing, Prince Starbane has come too far to end up back in her talons and, like I said, there's nothing left to lose in *this* neighborhood."

He shook his head in disbelief. "Poor King Sye and Queen Adurra. Poor Corydia!"

"To Kelnia, eh?" piped Blaize. "Yes, you may get that far. But against Oblixta's sorcery your blades are useless. Take me with you and, as you work to rescue the Prince from his fate, I shall exact my own revenge upon that witch and finish her once and for all."

"You can fight her like that?" scoffed Talthagar. "You couldn't even help *yourself* last night!"

"Of course I can't fight her like this," spat Rowan, clearly rattled. He was running in circles, chasing after his own tail. "In this form I am fit only to fish for minnows or pilfer rubbish heaps. The spell that now binds me must be broken!"

"Who's going to do that?" said Ilyssa. "We're not magicians, and I doubt that Oblixta will make things right again, if we take you to her doorstep. You obviously can't change yourself back or you would have done it by now."

"What a clever girl. *Obviously* I can't do it myself, child. But let the Corydian warrior lead the way to Kelnia and bring me along. I know a brief detour we can make to find someone quite capable of breaking this spell!"

"Who?" said Talthagar.

"Never you mind, right now. Just get me down from here and let's get ready to go. There isn't much time. You'll know everything you need to know when we get to where we're going."

"I totally do not like the sound of this detour," lamented the warrior.

"Me neither," said Ilyssa.

"That's too bad for you both." Rowan Blaize tottered to the edge of the beam and motioned for Talthagar to extend his arm upward.

"Ow! Watch those claws," the swordsman muttered, wincing as the wriggling raccoon clung first to his bicep and then grappled its way onto his shoulder.

They withdrew from the drawbridge and walked back to Skull, who was waiting dutifully in the courtyard.

"I hope this side-trip of yours doesn't take too long, Blaize. Starbane may not have a lot of time."

"True, Talthagar. But without my help he'll have no hope, and *that* is the far greater tragedy, if it comes to it!"

☙❧

IV

A Bone for a Crone

Oblixta's "Adurra face" was drawn and haggard from thought and repressed worry. The loss of her transformation elixir was grave, to be certain, but she was glad she had thought of an alternative—unpalatable as the alternative truly was. Dawn had come and they had been riding non-stop since leaving the doomed lake. She would not travel without her powers much longer. She *could* not.

"We'll be heading toward those canyons, just beyond the trees," said Oblixta, who was riding in the lead, with Kerrion, his crew, and the bound-and-gagged Prince Starbane straggling a bit behind. Within moments they had crossed a small forest dell and entered a narrow expanse of winding canyon passes.

"This terrain won't allow us to go much farther with horses," complained Kerrion. His own mount had nearly twisted a leg in a deep gully and they had barely arrived. Oblixta kept her eyes focused ahead, her patience wearing as thin as the strange air of the claustrophobic pass.

"The place I'm seeking is not far ahead, General. We'll continue on the horses as long as we can and then walk the rest of the way."

She turned to look at the others. The rest of Kerrion's men looked as spent as their rides. Starbane was especially pallid, sitting limp in the grip of Vaedrus, one of her lieutenants.

"We ought to drag the little filth behind us on a rope," mumbled Oblixta under her breath.

The heinous party was now positioned about halfway up the sloping canyon's center. The area itself was almost like a hollowed-out bowl, with soaring ridges of sedimentary rock jutting around them in encircling fashion and then rambling on far away in more jagged formations. There were still a few trees and bits of scrub about, but these seemed to grow from the very rocks themselves in haphazard clusters. The place appeared scrabbled, as if some giant had tossed random piles from the flat tops of the cliffs above. Another half-hour's journey brought them to the most vaulting cliff they had yet encountered and it was here that Oblixta ordered the sagging horses and the uneasy men to stop.

"Yes, this is the place!" she exulted, jumping from her own lathered horse. The sun was beginning to heat the desiccated landscape. She looked around and then beckoned Kerrion and the others closer. What they saw when they had gathered to peer through a line of spiny Moab trees at the base of the cliff sent an ominous chill through every one of the men.

There was an archway before them, ancient and half-hidden among the Moabs—hewn, it appeared, from one very dark and gargantuan boulder. Carved into its apex was an image that none had ever seen, save perhaps in some forgotten nightmare. In the gray, red-flecked stone slithered a figure, half-dragon, half-person, and carved so perfectly that its form seemed to undulate like so much flowing liquid. The head on the image was hideous, springing up from the rest of the carving and lolling at the peak of the door, gazing down at all who might have the questionable nerve to enter such a place. Oblixta stared into the sculpted eyes of the bas-relief and, to the others, she seemed for a moment hypnotized in thought, calculating some unknown option. Starbane's battered body craned for a look and his eyes grew wide at the sheer malevolence of the carving.

"What is this place, Majesty?" whispered Kerrion, moving forward with his hand on the hilt of his sword. He was completely out of sorts. The strange acoustics in this geographical depression made even his whisper echo among the seemingly watchful rocks.

"Not a place you would know, General Kerrion, even in *your* extensive travels," answered the Queen, still gazing up at the sculpture. "Being Kelnian, I doubt you've even heard about it. Only a citizen of this wretched land would know the legend behind it, or a practitioner of the Darker Arts, like me."

Oblixta tip-toed carefully across strange piles of scree and other stones, moving closer to the eerie portal.

"What legend are you speaking about?" said Kerrion.

Oblixta smiled. "This, General, is the lair of the Galwyn Crone!" she answered, scanning the place as if it were an old, familiar haunt. "Or at least it was, last I knew."

"The Galwyn *what?* I've never heard of such a thing."

"I told you so. But what you've never heard about is of no importance to me. We are here now and, if you are very lucky, you'll have a chance to meet the crone yourself, quite soon."

"I don't understand. *Why* are we here?" pressed Kerrion, apprehensive. His warrior's instinct told him that the place was inordinately dangerous. He felt his alarm merited more of an explanation from the Queen. As for Oblixta, she spoke with none of her usual impatience. On the contrary, she seemed perfectly at ease.

"Oh, don't worry, my sturdy General," she said, lifting the hem of her tattered skirts a bit to cross the rocks. "The Galwyn Crone is an associate of mine, if you must know. A fellow sorceress. A right fine lady! We have taken this detour so that I may confer with her upon certain matters of imperative wicked witchery before moving onward to Kelnia. Besides," she added, throwing an icy glance at the others over her shoulder, "these men need rest and refreshment, things the Crone will certainly provide in honor of *my* visit."

"She will recognize you in such a disguised form?" questioned the General, still sensing some hidden doom.

"Of course she will!" shrieked Oblixta, perturbed by Kerrion's clever question. "Now leave these matters to me. You need only accompany me into her cavern and then come back to fetch the others once she has prepared a fine dinner for us all. All except the Prince, that is. He can subsist on scraps, outside, like the dog he shall eventually become."

General Kerrion nodded doubtfully and looked at his men. "They are to remain, then?"

"Yes," answered Oblixta, turning to face her team. "Tie up the horses and rest for a bit!" she ordered. "The General and I are going within to meet with an old friend. We'll send for you shortly."

Oblixta turned abruptly and motioned for Kerrion to follow her through the grotesque archway. As they passed beneath, the hardened warrior gulped and began to sweat. Things were certainly never right where Oblixta was concerned, he realized, but this felt like the *wrong* kind of wrong.

လ•ရ

"The *Galwyn Crone?*"

"Oh, don't say it so gruesomely, so … so *morbidly*. And put me down at once!"

They had halted Skull's trusty gallop near a glade of Falthurn trees. Talthagar, standing on the ground beside his loyal-but-wearied horse, held the wiggling, squirming Rowan Blaize up by the scruff of his furry neck. The transmogrified sorcerer tried his best to scrape and possibly nip a bite out of the warrior's arm, but his captor's grip was superb.

"What does that mean, Talthagar?" asked Ilyssa, standing at his side, arms akimbo and one brow raised with menace. "What's this 'Galwyn Crone' business?"

Talthagar was too livid to answer immediately and had been so ever since the purpose of their strange journey had dawned upon him. This had occurred upon catching sight of the horrid Galwyn Cliffs and Rowan Blaize's frantic exhortations to "Keep on moving! We're just about there! Not much further!"

"Perhaps you'd like to enlighten Ilyssa concerning the Galwyn Crone, my hairy little ditch-rat wizard." Talthagar shook the chittering, chattering bundle for good measure.

"Now what would be the point in alarming the child needlessly?" squeaked Rowan, extending a black paw in supplication. "After all, you and I will be the ones dealing with the Crone, Talthagar. Not this little girl."

"No way. Absolutely not!" bellowed the warrior. "There's not enough honor in the world to make me face the cursed thing that dwells in those canyons. Did you really think you'd get away with a trick like this?"

"Just what *is* the Galwyn Crone?" demanded Ilyssa, stamping her foot in frustration. Talthagar tossed Rowan to the ground with disgust; the diminished warlock landed with a series of humiliating somersaults.

"Seeing as we are not going anywhere near her, Ilyssa, I'll tell you," said Talthagar.

"No! We must go onward," shrieked Rowan. "There's no time for explaining."

Talthagar ignored him. "The Galwyn Crone is a hideous witch," he said to the girl.

"Oh, by the gods, not *another* one," replied Ilyssa. "I swear, I should've stayed in Pyr Mida and became the Prefect's wench! You princes and warriors and witches and sorcerers are all much worse, as far as one's chances for survival. This is insane."

"Hey, I'm not the insane one," protested Talthagar. "Just listen to this: the crone is half woman and half ... I don't know *what* the other half is. She is feared by every man, woman, and child in Corydia." He jerked his chin toward the roadside trees, to the ridge of cliffs beyond. "She lives within that canyon, yonder. That's where the ditch-rat was taking us. Nobody with a brain in this land dares to venture that way, not even the foulest brigands and thieves. But this half-burnt raccoon was going to just lead us to the picnic."

"Some brave souls have been known to enter her sanctum!" snapped Rowan Blaize, standing on his hind legs and shaking a little black fist.

"I bet they never came out again!" yelled Talthagar. Rowan jumped out of the way of Skull's restless prancing.

"You're not telling the full tale, warrior. The Crone is more than willing to grant favors to those in need. You didn't tell the girl about that."

"Oh, gee, I'm sorry I didn't tell her about *that,*" said Talthagar with an exaggerated bow. "By the way, Ilyssa, the Galwyn Crone grants favors to those in need," he sneered. "For a price."

"What's the price?" asked Ilyssa, agog.

"Sacrifice. As in *people*."

"And *you* were leading *us* to this Crone to seek a favor for *yourself?*" shrieked Ilyssa, kicking a spray of dirt and stones at Rowan. Her eyes burned with accusation. "Which one of us was to be the payment?"

"You morons! You've got it all wrong," squealed the sorcerer, picking a pebble out of his ear. "You've got to give me the chance to explain."

"I don't think so," snarled Talthagar. "You said yourself there's no time for explanations and, you know, ditch-rat, it's really starting to look as if you're far from the benevolent soul Starbane made you out to be. Answer me honestly or I'll have my horse stomp you to bits. Was it really your plan to have the Galwyn Crone transform you back into yourself in return for snacking upon me and Ilyssa?"

"Oh, how vile!" spat the girl. "Have Skull stomp him dead. Right now!"

"Don't listen to this nonsense, child," bleated Rowan in his constricted raccoon-voice. "The big, foolish sword-wielder, jumping to such horrible conclusions."

"Then I suppose you've got the nerve to deny that the Galwyn Crone has a particular fondness for mortal flesh?" challenged Talthagar.

"No, I don't deny that. But I assure you that I have a plan to restore myself by her formidable powers *without* the loss of anyone's life or limb. The Crone is very old, and nearly blind. I've met her a couple of times—strictly for purposes of observation, of course—and have done a lot of research on her during my years in this kingdom. I would wager that she could be tricked into helping us."

"Ha! That's rich coming from you, who was so easily tricked into taking a sip from Oblixta's little cup of Instant-Raccoon."

"Please, don't remind me. Rest assured that, when I am restored, she won't be able to enchant me again."

"Yeah, right. In the meantime, you've still not explained your little plan, or how it might fit into the fact that all the legends say the Crone demands a flesh-offering for her favors."

"As I said, the legends are correct. That *is* where you come into the equation."

"And that *is* where you can take a flying leap onto the tip of my sword," said Talthagar.

"No, fool! You will act only as a form of *bait*. Once I have been transformed—and she must do it, for that is her Ancient Law—I can rescue you from her clutches with my own sorcery. Then we can all make our journey into Kelnia to save Prince Starbane and confront Oblixta!"

"Forgive me, Rowan Blaize," scoffed Talthagar, "but I don't have much confidence in your powers of sorcery to rescue *anyone,* at the moment. Aside from flying into the castle in the form of a giant raven a few days ago, which was actually pretty thrilling, you don't inspire much awe. And I *am* a fool—a fool for letting you lead us this far off the beaten path already."

"You're wrong, Talthagar. When I'm transformed things will be much different, I can promise you. And speaking of confidence, I'd like to know where, exactly, you've hidden this bravery *you're* so renowned to possess?"

"Are you questioning my spirit of adventure?"

"Precisely!" snapped Rowan. "If you are the warrior you claim to be, this opportunity should be your meat and drink. It should make your mouth water with excitement or … perhaps … perhaps you're not at all the hero you think you are. Don't give me one of your looks! If you question my motives and character, then I shall question yours. Make a decision. We have no time to throw away and you're going to be beaten by Oblixta if you *don't* take the chance."

Talthagar looked cautiously at Ilyssa, who was clearly expecting him to reject such a foolhardy adventure. Yet, he knew deep down that the alternative—facing Oblixta on her own ground, without benefit of Blaize's powers (whatever they were)—would be suicide. Even more, his own inner penchant for the pursuit of serious risk had been well-triggered by the wizard's sly challenge. Once piqued, Talthagar knew he couldn't refuse such a summons.

"What about Ilyssa?" he asked.

"Talthagar, you cannot tell me you are seriously thinking about doing this!" blasted Ilyssa.

"Just hang on a minute. What about the girl?"

"She'll be quite safe," said Rowan Blaize. "She doesn't have to enter the Crone's lair with us. You can leave her outside with that ugly horse of yours. She'll be fine no matter what happens to us."

Talthagar was still skeptical. "You really think you can use me *just* as bait, to persuade that awful thing to change you back?"

"I'm certain of it! She owns an enchanted staff of immense power. It is the source of all her greatness, stolen over four centuries ago from the Dwarf King, Mandulis, during a territorial conflict. The Crone has been holed-up in those cliffs ever since, granting her notorious favors for those brave or desperate enough to seek them out. I'd say we fall into both categories at the moment."

"Please don't do this, Talthagar," Ilyssa begged. "I don't trust him. Nothing good has ever come from dealing with these magical folk. Haven't we seen proof of that in the last month alone? Let's just leave this animal here in the woods and get away. We'll think of something else."

Talthagar, however, grew ominously silent and Ilyssa knew that dissuading him was now impossible. Rowan Blaize sensed it as well and, with a feisty chatter, sprung up onto the trunk of a tree and then onto Skull's saddle.

"Now that this is settled, let's move, you two. We should be within the Crone's grotto in less than an hour and I'll explain my plan as we ride!

கூஒ

There was a slight, rough opening between two seams of red rock in the cliff-side. It was almost laughably small to serve as an entry. Kerrion looked at his Queen with grave doubt. Oblixta grinned.

"Would you care to go in first, or shall I?" she asked.

Kerrion did not reply.

"It doesn't matter, General. I'll go in first. See that you follow, and stay close."

Falling to her hands and knees, Oblixta proceeded to slide the lithe form of Queen Adurra through the strange, cracked opening and disappeared as if she had been swallowed by the canyon wall. It was far more difficult for Kerrion, with his bulk, but he somehow managed to slip through the impossibly tight space, as if by magic. This possibility, of course, did not surprise him. Once inside, he found Oblixta waiting for him in a most strange and cavernous space.

He was amazed, but not in a good way.

Torches blazed brightly in sconces everywhere, some jutting singly from holes in the damp walls while others were burning in clusters of two or more from various crags. The effect was ghostly, casting immense shadows and distorting the dozens of stalactites and stalagmites that rose like claws from the floor or ebbed in pale daggers from the ceiling far above. Apparently arranged to converge, the torches invited the visitors' attention toward another opening several paces away, which was much larger than the one through which they had just crawled.

"The Crone's chamber is just through that portal, if I recall correctly," said Oblixta. "When we enter, General Kerrion, you must do everything I say, otherwise she may react to your presence with suspicion, and we would not want that to happen. She's quite ancient and tends to be a bit nervous, but only at first."

Kerrion swallowed hard yet followed, hand on the hilt of his vicious sword, as Oblixta swept across the uneven floor. The General found it difficult to maintain his footing on the slippery surface, which was afflicted here, there, and everywhere with puddles of water that drizzled and dripped constantly from the ceiling. The so-called "chamber" they entered was as well-illuminated as its vestibule, but there the similarities came to an end. The place was half the span of the previous cave, but where the first had been rugged and natural, save for the torches, this room was clearly not crafted by the elements alone.

Oblixta stepped forward, but her footfalls were cautious. Kerrion drew an astonished breath and immediately wished he had not done so;

the air in the chamber was so oppressive with rot and dissolution that he could taste death upon his very tongue. Death normally rendered far different pleasures for him, but this place was an abomination. Filth of seemingly all descriptions lay strewn about the room. More fiery torches revealed animal carcasses, piles of moldy parchment scrolls, broken glass vessels, skulls, and crust-covered objects of indeterminate origin. So abundant was the stinking trash that the floor of the chamber was really not visible at all. The creeping, darting forms of rats and the slithering of other, less recognizable things could be detected in almost every quarter.

The sounds were those of oozing slime and a constant skittering, along with millions of rapid, sinister breaths. If there was a resident of such vile apartments, it was unseen and, while Kerrion looked about with clear trepidation, Oblixta waded without qualm through the debris until she reached a smooth, square block of gray stone directly in the middle of the place. She kicked and cursed a few rats out of her way, her voice booming and hollow as it bounced off the encroaching walls. Kerrion had seen much that was putrid in his day, but this was the first time his stomach had ever begun to turn at any single sight. It was more than the place itself, however; something beyond imagining layered the very atmosphere of this hole, an undercurrent of intelligent destruction.

"General, come over here," called Oblixta and he dutifully trudged the same path she had taken through the muck. Upon reaching the surprisingly clean, simple altar—or whatever it was—the Queen began to point at something he could not yet see. Only upon joining her was he able to glimpse a simple ram's horn, placed perfectly in the middle of the monument's polished surface.

"It is with this that you must summon the Crone," instructed Oblixta. "She is asleep in an adjacent parlor. Blow upon the horn three times and then step directly around to the front of this altar and blow it again."

"You wish *me* to summon her, Majesty?"

"Yes, Kerrion. It has everything to do with the Crone's ancient protocol. Believe me. Take the ram's horn, blow it as I instructed, then step around to the front of the stone and blow it *again,*" she repeated.

Kerrion could not imagine the concept of any "protocol" in such a fetid place, but he was in no mood to argue with Oblixta, even though she was in the far less intimidating form of the Corydian Queen, Adurra. He feared her powers too much to question her now. He picked up the horn and inspected it with disdain as Oblixta watched, her eyes sparkling in the torchlight, most interested. Judging the simple horn to be neither foul nor fair, he brought it to his lips and blew three times in succession. The sound made by the crude instrument was enough to chill the blood in his veins. Somewhat unsteadily, he meandered through the bones and rats and tentacle-ridden monstrosities, around to the front of the stone as instructed. There he stared in shock at the opening of a great, black pit, the circumference of which was at least four times as large as his battle-shield, and twice as deep as he was tall. Having nearly fallen in, his heart began to pound in his chest; he could even feel it thudding against his armor. He paused, aghast, before blowing the horn a fourth time, staring into the suddenness of the hole.

"Majesty, there is some sort of pit, here, some kind of—"

In his confusion, General Kerrion did not hear Oblixta tiptoe up to him from behind, but he felt it when she slammed him with all her strength, grabbing the horn from his hands with a vicious snap even as his hulking body went flailing into the pit. Without time to cry out, the General hit the bottom of the hole with a terrible crash, one of his knees shattering instantly against rock and one wrist broken as it was crushed by his own hurtling weight against a slimy wall. It was only then that he realized, in the midst of his panic, that he had been betrayed, that what he suspected in a faint way from the beginning had now come to pass in colors of white-hot agony. Enraged, he let out a gruesome howl that first found its power in sheer pain and finished with the fuel of unrelenting hatred.

"You miserable hag!" he screamed upward while struggling, in vain, to stand on his one intact leg. He slipped at once to the floor, covered as it was in centuries of rot and mildew. He felt parts of himself sinking, as if in quicksand. There was no way out. The pit was far too deep and he was far too injured to even dream of climbing. Even had he been uninjured, the walls of the hole were too covered in grease and fungi to allow for any escape.

"How could you have dealt with me so?" he seethed to the flickering darkness above. "I have served you long and faithfully! What are you planning, in your wickedness?"

Over the edge of the pit's rim, above, Kerrion saw Oblixta-Adurra poke a bemused, curious face, which was all the more maddening to the fallen warlord. She said nothing to him, at first, as she peered down uncertainly, as if not quite convinced that he couldn't get out. The General ripped free a dagger from behind his iron breastplate and hurled it expertly at her face with the speed of a striking serpent. Oblixta was too wary, however, and swerved just as the weapon hissed by her right ear and landed far behind in the garbage of the cave's floor.

"Do you think you can get out, General Kerrion?" she asked with such a voice of concern that the warlord thought for an instant that this had all been some queer accident indeed.

"What? Get out? No, I can't get out! My leg is broken. So is my arm. Will you help me?"

He fell back as a jolt of pain shot from his smashed kneecap to the very base of his brain. He screamed again in agony.

"Excellent," said Oblixta after this appraisal. "I wanted to be certain you were trapped, well and good, before I summoned the Crone."

She stood erect and turned, blowing the horn for its fourth call.

"What have you done to me, witch!" bellowed Kerrion from below. "I swear by all the foulest gods known in the Black Regions—if I were free this very minute I would cut your throat for such treachery!"

Oblixta was unimpressed. "If that's been on your mind, General, perhaps you should've tried it sooner."

"What's going to happen to me?" gasped Kerrion, now truly afraid.

"Relax, General. You'll likely have a bit of time left to ponder how the Crone is going to butcher you. She's quite old and clumsy, you see, and it'll take her a moment or two to get here. Then, of course, she and I need to strike our bargain."

Hopping up onto the stone altar, Oblixta tucked her legs demurely beneath the embrace of her arms and stared at a gaping orifice directly ahead in the chamber wall. Cragged torches burned ferociously on either side. Kerrion lowed like a distressed cow from the pit. A moment later, from within the blackness of the crevice ahead, came the sounds Oblixta had been waiting for. Kerrion heard them as well and shifted his broken body to listen in the grip of absolute terror. There was a shuffling, laborious sequence of noises, as if something huge was struggling in distant shadows to bring itself forward.

"What's that?" raved Kerrion. "What's going on up there?"

Oblixta stepped primly down from the podium, tired and disgusted with the body of the weak Corydian queen. She hesitated for an instant before moving around the altar to stand partially hidden behind it. She was fairly confident in what she planned to do, but once again, the lack of sorcery's weapon made her feel excruciatingly vulnerable.

"What is it?" hollered Kerrion again and Oblixta rolled her eyes in the murk.

"Be silent," she muttered. "You'll know soon enough."

True to her prediction, a loathsome behemoth made itself visible through the gaping crevice beyond. Then, even Oblixta had to draw a stunned breath at the sight of the Galwyn Crone in all her morbid splendor. With a slimy, sucking sound, she pulled her body into the chamber at last.

The Crone was larger than the hole from which she had emerged, her rancid, obese physique scraped the edges of the rock in sickening fashion, causing the pores of her bristled skin to emit a festering green sweat. She was magnificent beyond Oblixta's imaginings, her torso an undulating mass of heaving, rolling flesh that glowed a light, phosphorous yellow in the gloom of the lair. The body of the Crone was so heavy that it was bent by necessity over two stout legs as large and spiny with hair as the trunks of Moab trees. They seemed altogether incapable of supporting such heft. The fragments of what once was some sort of gown or robe now fell in shreds and tatters across the creature's jiggling flesh, failing to cover anything. One hideous, distended breast swung from a yawning tear in the ruined garment and, atop the swollen shoulders, sat the most appalling feature of all—the Crone's head.

Blind eyes of milky-blue film peered about in ghoulish fashion from the bloated face. The visage was pock-marked and rife with sharp whiskers as white as the very hair that straggled, string-like, from the top of the skull. The Crone's mouth was half open and void of all but two great incisor fangs, sucking breath in and out in lascivious gulps. Fully removed now from her crevice, the Old One sniffed the air of the chamber and swiveled her useless eyes in all directions. Her purple lips writhed around the incisor fangs, moving like two slippery, restless worms. The smell of the ancient hag made even the eyes of Oblixta begin to water. Kerrion began to retch as the scent drifted downward into the pit.

"Who hath the impertinence to summon *Us?*" yowled the Crone in a voice like sludge moving on the top of a great swamp.

Oblixta dropped the ram's horn and stood rigid behind the altar, fingernails digging in tense clutches at the surface of the stone.

"It is I who summoned you," she called, making sure to add strength to her voice, a strength she did not feel at this juncture. "I stand at the altar and beg a favor from the Great Mistress of Galwyn."

The Crone wriggled a few steps forward, seeming exhausted by the effort. She leaned at once against the chamber wall, her matted hair precariously close to the billowing flames of a torch.

"Speak, and tell Us who thou art!" demanded the Crone. "Better yet, come close so that We may touch thee, perhaps smell thee for Ourselves."

"Nay, I'll come no closer," replied Oblixta. "I know the manner of your Ancient Law, and I am aware of its boundaries."

The Crone cackled, a horrible choking sound that rattled the very filth across the floor. Rats scurried and tentacles coiled and uncoiled beneath the heaps.

"We smell arrogance!" brayed the Crone. "Dost thou think thyself wiser than We?" Oblixta did not flinch at the evaluation. Contemptible as the creature was, she knew its powers of discernment to be as great, or greater, than her own. Its wits could be as sharp as its body was slow. The Crone would sense any notable shred of fear and would try to trick her into some fateful error. Oblixta knew the legends well. She knew *all* the legends.

Once again the Crone chuckled. It gestured toward Oblixta with a fat, gelatinous arm and Oblixta beheld for the first time the staff in the Crone's stubby-fingered grasp. It was indeed the only thing of beauty in the entire depraved den. The thick, though crooked, wood gleamed as if freshly polished and, at its top, in an ornate setting of gold, was the red Delian Crystal orb that channeled its legendary power.

The Staff of Mandulis!

"Speak and speak wisely, if thou knowest Our ways," barked the Crone. "We do not suffer fools lightly, if We suffer them at all."

"Behold, I have brought an offering and I seek a favor," Oblixta asserted. Kerrion shuffled and groaned below, overcome by the Crone's bodily fumes, which seemed to coat the very lungs.

The Crone listened to the sounds of the "offering," and was as stimulated as she could get. Oblixta guessed from the hag's labored scrabble to the edge of the pit that it had indeed been some time since she had last entertained guests. Near the hole, the Crone stuck her grotesque snout outward and sniffed, almost daintily, at the air.

"A living man!" acknowledged the Crone. "Strong. Wounded."

Kerrion could only listen to the guttural voice in horror. He drew his sword, even though he had to use his left hand, as his sword-arm was the one smashed in the initial fall. Oblixta, meanwhile, demanded her favor.

"You have proof of my offering," she said. "Now fulfill your Law and grant a favor to your supplicant."

The Crone did not move from her place. "First, We shall feast, and then your request shall be considered," babbled the drooling beldam.

Oblixta did not like the sound of this proposition. "Grant my favor first," she protested, "or would you have it known that the Galwyn Crone is full of trickery? Then your pilgrims would stop coming to supply you with delicacies."

The Crone's laugh seemed to surround and crush Oblixta. "Do you really believe *We* are frequently approached by pilgrims? It has been years since We have tasted the flesh of men. Indeed, suppliants have been few and far between in the last three centuries. Perhaps We have had much to do with this, by not keeping to our Law as we ought."

"What do you mean?" hissed Oblixta, feeling a chill in her own flesh.

"We mean that such dry spells demand that We feast upon both the offering *and* the one that offers, these days," cackled the Crone. "And Thou wouldst threaten Us with telling the world that We are unfair. Let the world think what it will of Us, for I say, Thy flesh shall be mine today, as well!"

The Crone lifted her wand with the same flabby limb and panic ripped through Oblixta like a dagger.

"No, wait!" she cried out, hands lifted defensively before her. "I ... I can sweeten the offering, Great Mistress of the Canyon, if you promise to grant my favor and set me free."

"How wouldst thou sweeten what is already sweet enough?" belched the Crone, her arm still poised, the scepter still pointed at Oblixta.

"Outside your sanctuary, beyond the Gate of Sorrows, there are several strong men and a young, tender boy, all of them under my command. If you grant my favor, I will lead them back in to you and you will feast like never before. But you must promise to grant my favor by the Sacred Vow of Persullus."

The Crone paused in skeptical thought. She did not trust this bold seeker, and she was unwilling to use the Vow of Persullus, which was exceedingly ancient and magical and could sometimes trick even the treacherous. Still, the images conjured by mention of more men and a 'tender youth' were too difficult to resist after long years of hibernation and stasis. She weighed her options. In any case, she still had the offering she had smelled below in the pit. The possibility of the greater offer was well worth the risk of losing the chance to feast on the proud supplicant.

"We shall not employ the Vow of Persullus," she breathed. "Rather, We shall swear and thou shalt swear, to uphold a bargain. If We grant your favor and you lie, We have ways of punishing deception, even from afar," added the Crone in warning.

You're the one who'll be punished when I regain my form, Oblixta vowed in silence. She was warming to the idea of a good magical fight in her own skin. Even so, her voice was calm and meek as she agreed to the hag's terms.

"Excellent," burbled the Crone. "We are not the kind to let such sweets pass Our way without being savored. If it is within Our great power, we shall hear and grant Thy request." Then she gestured to the pit, exposing the foul incisors. "But first, We shall at least *prepare* the meal in hand."

With a small pass of her scepter, the body of General Kerrion came floating from the awful hole, suspended by the sudden magic that had engulfed him. He sword fell back into the pit. Now, upon sight of the captor who dangled his slowly spinning form to sniff him anew, the great warlord did not hesitate to wail in horror.

"What does it *want* with me?" he screamed. "Save me, Oblixta! Remember all my years of faithful service, I beg of you!"

His eyes met those of Oblixta for just an instant before the Crone, well-satisfied with her prize, sniffed her struggling meal, waved the scepter once more, and sent Kerrion's body flying with such force and speed that Oblixta balked at the current of wind produced. Agog, she watched as the General's flailing form was slammed and viciously impaled upon a line of spikes that protruded from the cave wall to the right of the smirking Crone. There, Kerrion's eyes were soon fixed in the hazy stare of death, his body mangled. Oblixta shrugged, felt not a shred of pity, and turned her attention swiftly back to the Crone, who was salivating at the prospect of such a dinner.

"We shall let him hang a bit. The flesh is much better once the juices dribble around for a spell. And speaking of spells … what is the nature of Thy request, woman?"

"I am bewitched," said Oblixta. "I have been changed into a form which is not my own and which is displeasing to me. I wish to return to my true form, if it is within your power to change me back, that is."

"Ha!" squawked the Crone. "We can break any transformation spell. Come closer and we shall grant thy request."

"No. Do it from where I now stand. Remember the additional offerings if you are successful."

The Crone muttered.

"*If* We are successful ... ha! What cheek!"

With a rank and putrescent sigh, the Galwyn Crone lifted her scepter once again, speaking without delay an ancient chant which enabled her to enact a change. Oblixta braced herself, still afraid of trickery but counting on the hag's slovenly hunger. She felt a surge of great power all around the magically fashioned body of Queen Adurra; it coursed through her being, from head to foot. She grimaced, knowing that the process would be as painful now as it had been in the Corydian Queen's bedchamber, but much more swift in the desired result now.

She felt a familiar boiling in her entrails and organs, along with the excruciating crack of bones as they were redirected by the Crone's spell to their former dimensions. She moaned in pain, the sound resonating in the cave like the bray of a demon. Then, a moment later, it was finished and she lay slumped against the stone altar, fighting unconsciousness with every portion of her will. It would do her no good to be transformed to her proper self only to pass-out and be eaten by the impatient Hag of the Canyon. Slowly regaining her senses, Oblixta lifted her hands to her face, recognizing the contours of her true features. She touched her hair, no longer the wavy tresses of the mincing Adurra but her own thick, black locks. Like the rest of her body, her hair was covered with a thin film of mucus. Of course, she still wore the tattered garments of the queen she had killed. They were too large for her, but that was a small nuisance, indeed.

"Excellent," she whispered in relief. She caught her breath and struggled against the stone block to stand and face the Crone. The beastly sorceress was still hunched near the foul pit, clasping her staff proudly.

"The transformation is complete, is it not?" said the Crone, sniffing. "We cannot see, but We can *smell* the success of Our spell. Now, Thou must uphold Thine own end of the bargain. Bring Us these men or We shall punish Thee beyond the darkest edge of dreams. We've put a spell upon the canyon's archway entrance, if One tries to sneak away, One *won't* get far."

Oblixta casually wiped the filmy membrane from her face with a sleeve. Then she stepped around to the front of the altar, kicking a pile of debris out of her way.

"You'll feast no more at my expense, Old One," she said, glad to hear her own voice again, even in such a disgusting place. She flexed her fingers and hands. Her body felt good.

The Crone was momentarily puzzled at the response she received. She grumbled and shifted on her pig-like haunches, rolls of fat tumbling and flopping as she moved. Rats scurried and squeaked to avoid the upheaval.

"Tell Us," ordered the Crone, "Art thou going to bring the promised men or didst Thou trick Us, woman?"

"Consider yourself well-tricked, Old One," said Oblixta, brimming with her usual confidence. "There shall be nothing added to what you have already been given."

The Crone laughed, now in genuine surprise. "Our spell hath not only transformed Thy flesh, it hath rendered Thee insane! It is no matter, lying fool. We shall feast upon Thee as We had planned from the beginning."

The hag set her warty, bristled jaw as firmly as she could and brandished the scepter with a flourish. Oblixta felt a terrible wave of power surround her at once, much more than she had anticipated. She was lifted with crushing force from the floor, just as Kerrion had been lifted from the pit.

"Thou shalt regret Thy stupidity!" gloated the Crone.

She prepared to fling Oblixta upon another, nearby legion of spikes, but something went wrong. Oblixta closed her eyes and concentrated, drawing with unholy words upon her own, restored powers to thwart her foe's intentions. It required all of her strength and craft, but in a sudden surge of resistance, she broke free from the scepter's power and fell back upon the debris-laden floor of the cave, landing off balance but on her feet.

The Crone grunted in dismay and raised her nose to smell the magically charged air.

"Thy trickery is double, woman, for We can sense now that Thou art a sorceress, plain as plain."

Oblixta stood her ground in silence, wary. "You may not find me as plain as you'd like."

"Do not think that Thy powers are a match for Our own," warned the hag. "We have fought impertinent witches before. Yes. Flesh is flesh, and We shall still consume thee."

It was then that Oblixta decided to launch an offensive of her own. Raising a talon-tipped, pale hand, she gestured toward one of the torches ensconced in the wall behind the Crone's heaving body.

"Phaerusia, balkhe, mal, wadjit!"

The burning missile flew from its place toward the Crone's head. But the hag had survived long years in the ancient dark for good reason; she sensed the coming blow and simply ducked. Instead of piercing her skull, however, the sharp end of the fiery torch buried itself in her shoulder.

"Treachery!" howled the wounded Crone as blood the color of pond scum began to bubble and flow from the wound. She slumped and tried to remove the offending stick, which was by now starting to singe her rotting strands of hair. She was much too bloated, however, to reach it.

"Give me the Staff of Mandulis and I will not destroy you!" offered Oblixta, but her offer was met with a blast from the Crone's scepter that sent her reeling and spinning madly across the floor of the cave. Rubbish flew so high into the air that it hit the unseen ceiling above and ricocheted back down. Oblixta slammed aimlessly into the base of the cave wall nearest the doorway. A last-minute, muttered incantation had softened the impact, but not enough to quell the searing pain of a broken rib. Her breath coming in gasps, she struggled to her feet.

The Crone, meanwhile, had begun a desperate retreat toward the opening of her underground labyrinth. She wanted no more part of this duel, and there would be safety in the labyrinthine darkness below.

The burning torch still protruded from the back of her shoulder. Oblixta smelled the boiling blood. Her eyes caught sight of a gnarled human thigh-bone protruding from a nearby heap. Calling out a potent charm, she sent this remnant of some ancient meal speeding at the Galwyn Crone, who was now far too bothered and disoriented to deflect it. The long bone struck her in the middle of the layered folds of the throat and the legendary hag fell against the wall of her cave with a momentous thud, the scepter flying from her grasp and clattering onto the floor.

Oblixta took an eager step forward, but was swiftly cowed by the pain in her chest. The crone whined and struggled feebly to rake her fingers at the piercing bone. Oblixta's mind blazed with agony; surely the blast against the wall had caused a rib to pierce one of her lungs. She knew several charms that would heal such an injury, but she needed the light of day to perform such reparative magic. Her mind drifted as well to the rest of the men—and Starbane—who waited outside in the grim canyon. There was no time to linger and gloat over the Galwyn Crone. Enough had been wasted as it was. They would have to return to Kelnia without delay and prepare the army for its triumphant move into Corydia. Nothing, certainly, could stop her now.

She was in her own flesh again, her powers were restored, Rowan Blaize was dead, the Prince was in her grasp, and the entire world was at her mercy. With a grimace of agony, she turned in the dark and fled the miserable cave.

V

The Staff of Mandulis

"By all the stars and planets, in this world and worlds-within! She's *dead!*"

Rowan Blaize scampered warily around the still form of the Galwyn Crone, darting first toward her feet and then around to peer at the rank blood that had pooled everywhere. Talthagar had hung well back, but was able to hear the raccoon-wizard's shocking revelation.

"Anything that smells *this* bad has got to be dead," he muttered, though with no small amount of relief. One look at the Crone's body had told him that he would have been in serious trouble, had they walked into her lair and found her alive. "I've never seen such a pathetic place, and I thought I'd seen it all. Look at the filth in here."

Rowan trotted away from the Crone's body, hissing at a couple of rats that got in his way. "She wasn't known for her cleanliness, but dead? *That* is quite the stunner! And she hasn't been dead long, either."

Talthagar moved around the stone altar, holding his nose. He barely missed falling into the awful pit.

"Whoah! Why didn't you warn me, Blaize? There's a hole here and I can't see the bottom of it."

"I'd reckon that *he* saw the bottom of it," squeaked the furry conjurer, rising on his haunches and pointing toward Kerrion, still impaled in death upon the spikes of the wretched wall. "He was a sacrifice meant for the Crone."

"Not only that, it's Oblixta's supreme warlord, Kerrion!" said Talthagar in amazement. "I'd recognize that face anywhere, much less the uniform."

"Then you were right about those tracks we saw outside this cavern when we arrived, Talthagar. Someone was here just before us. And my guess is that it was Oblixta herself."

"What?"

"She was here. There's no doubt in my mind. I can feel the remnants of her presence, and, quite honestly, mere men could not have done *that* to the Galwyn Crone. An army of men couldn't do it."

"But why would she come here? She ought to be halfway to Kelnia by now."

Blaize jumped up upon the stone block and surveyed the grim arena. "Not necessarily," he said. "My guess is that Oblixta came here because she needed the Crone's transforming powers as much as I do. What a monstrous coincidence!"

"I still don't follow," said Talthagar.

"Of course you do. I already told you—and you saw for yourself, basically—that Oblixta had taken on the form and shape of Queen Adurra. She would have had to kill Adurra to do that for any length of time like she did, and while under that self-imposed form, she would have been *without* her powers. That is why she relied upon some sort of potion to put in my wine, and to throw in the banquet hall and set the castle of King Sye afire. Something like that she would have prepared beforehand, but for whatever reason, she was either unable to make a potion to change herself *back* into her proper form, thus restoring her powers, or something else happened altogether. She came here to seek the Crone's magic. I'm certain of it. The warlord hanging above was her bargaining chip."

Talthagar gulped. "Great. That could have been me, if we'd gotten here first."

"Oh, stop your nonsense and—*wait!* If my beady little eyes are not deceiving me, I am in luck!"

"What are you talking about?"

"Impossible!" screeched Rowan Blaize as he leaped from the stone altar all the way across the pit and onto the floor near the Crone's body. "It's the Staff of Mandulis!"

"What?"

"The scepter I told you about!"

"So you found that foul thing's old walking stick. What's the big deal? We've got to get out of here and get back to Ilyssa and Skull. And probably Starbane! Oblixta is likely not far from here, if you're right about the timing."

"We'll get them in due course, warrior, but hold your tongue for a moment. This is no mere walking stick!" He managed to hold up an end of the Crone's scepter with his black paws. "Don't you recall what I told you as we were on our way to this canyon? The staff you see before you was the *real* source of most of the Galwyn Crone's power. This is it, I'm sure of it. Oblixta must have been in a terrible hurry to have forgotten to steal it. We've got to hurry ourselves, for she may wise-up and return to claim it!"

Talthagar sauntered over and reached down to pick the thing up, turning it over and over in his hands skeptically as Rowan jumped and scratched at his legs. "Are you sure? This looks like an old walking cane my granny used to have, except for the gold and this red ball on the end."

Rowan Blaize whirled in the Galwyn filth. "Enough with your comments! Place the scepter on the altar over there. It is one of the most potent magical tools known in this rat-trap of a world. I can still use it to change myself back. Put it on the altar! If we hurry, we can catch them yet."

"You pathetic little weasel."

Oblixta had fallen back on her horse to glare at her brother with the eyes he knew to be so unlike his own, yet so much like those of their father. The ragged party was now carefully maneuvering their horses through the last ridge that led northward and finally out of the dreaded Galwyn cliffs. Beside them was a dizzying drop and Starbane, still bound but now riding alone on General Kerrion's horse, thought more than once of making a quick dive over the precipice. It would be good to have it all over. To have peace at last. Oblixta's restored presence only intensified his desire to end everything.

As if sensing his thoughts as the horses made their slow trek, the Queen said, "The last of your gallant attempts at escape have been made, brother. You've nowhere left to go. I need to kill you ritually to increase my power tenfold, and thus I'm not about to let you kill yourself. Where would be the pleasure in that? For me, at least."

"No, I suppose it wouldn't be any fun, for you," said Starbane. He was pleased that Oblixta had emerged from the weird cavern and at least rendered him the privilege of speaking to her without a gag. She had not explained to any of them what had happened to General Kerrion ... had not told anyone why *he* had failed to emerge from the desolate cliffs. No one had dared to ask, but the Prince knew, just as the others did.

"You're a murderess, Oblixta. Pure and simple. You even murder those who are foolish enough to be loyal to you. Like Kerrion. Though I won't say he didn't deserve whatever fate he got, I still have to tell you that you're pathetic."

Oblixta smiled as a wind began to surge atop the ridge, raising dust and a cloud of sand that stung cheeks and bothered eyes. "Pathetic? No, dear half-wit half-brother. Merely efficient. Which is more than I can say for you. Kerrion had served his purpose. He was efficient, for a while. But expendable, as well. Everyone is."

"Everyone except you, of course."

"Clever boy."

"Let's just ride along and get it over with, Oblixta," said Starbane. His voice was hoarse, his lips cracked. They had given him only one drink of water since the previous night's disaster. "I'm not stupid and I know I can't beat you. Do whatever evil thing you wish to do to me, fast or slow. I don't really care, anymore."

"Excellent," laughed Oblixta, wincing a little at some residual pain in the rib she had healed with a swift spell after leaving the Crone's lair. "I'm glad to see that your spirit is as crushed as your body *will* be."

Starbane looked at her without the slightest halt in his gaze. "You'll never crush my soul," he said. "Even if I die."

"True, I have no power over that, unfortunately. But in terms of dying, it is no longer a question of 'if,' where you are concerned. It is a question of *when.*"

She began to laugh at him, then, along with her bedraggled henchmen, as they reached the very top of the ridge that led away from Galwyn's passes and back toward the northern side roads. None of them were prepared, however, for the sight that awaited them as they began to move down the opposite slope. There, sword drawn and gleaming in the sun, stood Talthagar. Beside him was Rowan Blaize, spiky black hair waving in the breeze, his form restored and wrapped modestly in Talthagar's cloak as if he were wearing a skimpy tunic. In the sorcerer's hand was the Staff of Mandulis. Oblixta's eyes flew wide and the Prince's jaw dropped in disbelief. This could not be real. It had to be some cruel apparition conjured by his sister to torment him. But then again ... perhaps it was not. Out of the corner of his eyes, Starbane saw Oblixta's hand fly to her mouth in uncertainty. She was speechless. The tired soldiers riding ahead turned frantically toward their mistress, awaiting her order to crush the unexpected interlopers.

"By the Gods, are you all real?" shouted Starbane as his sister's fury began to boil.

Oblixta scowled. "What manner of trick is this?" she hissed. "I finished all of you back at the castle."

"Don't worry, Prince Cadrach," said Talthagar, raising his sword high. "This is all going to end right here. She won't be hurting anyone again, I guarantee you."

Oblixta's laughter brought peals of real thunder from the cloudless noon sky. The majestic sun seemed to fade. "I don't know how any of this has come to pass, how any of you have managed this, but I promise you your deaths within the moment. Kill them at once!" she shouted to the men in her stalled party.

She swept out of the way as they leaped down from their horses and drew their swords. It was not a pretty scene, for if Talthagar ever

deserved his reputation as a master assassin and swordsman of the Corydian realm, he deserved it in that hour. Crying out with an almost
immortal howl, he hacked and smashed each of the Kelnian marauders as
they came forward, sending bodies and limbs spinning over the nearby
precipice in a bloody torrent. His anger was a wave of power as frightening as any Oblixta could conjure and, when he had made short work of
her men, the warrior turned panting to their arrogant leader. Oblixta
smiled, as if the preceding bloodbath had been little more than a trifle
in her day.

"You are about to meet *your* end, witch," said Talthagar, approaching slowly. He raised his sword again. "This is for my King, my Queen,
and for all that you've done to your parents and to your own brother,
Prince Starbane. Get ready for the trip to hell."

He sprang forward like a great vengeful cat. Just as the down-
swing of his blade would have struck its astonished target, however, the
weapon hit an invisible wall. Starbane howled as the horse he rode reared
up and threw him into the dirt, knocking the breath from his lungs.
Talthagar's sword wavered, suspended in the air for an instant, and then
it shattered in thousands of stinging pieces that pierced the surrounding
scene as needles. The warrior yelped in pain as his flesh was stung by the
remnants of his own weapon. Oblixta's sorceress fingers were poised
and, with a quick gesture and a Word of Potency, she sent him flying
onto his back in the dirt. Then she jumped from her own horse and drew
the Gragan wizard's Ritual Dagger from her ripped and worn bodice.

"It will give me the greatest pleasure to kill you once and for all,
spy," she seethed, holding Talthagar crushed and pinned to the earth
with the magic coursing through her other hand. "You've been a thorn in
my side for *far* too long."

But her fatal blow was not to find its mark. As she approached the
fallen warrior, Rowan Blaize stepped forward at last. She had forgotten
him completely in the sudden wrath of Talthagar's advance. Now, the
warlock of Shadnai Forest stood triumphantly, holding the Crone's staff
well out in front of him. With a swipe of her hand, Oblixta sent Talthagar spinning off against some nearby rocks and focused her attention

upon her more formidable foe. She recognized the Staff of Mandulis and rued the moment when, in her haste, she had left it behind in the Crone's hideaway.

"Your meddling has cost you enough already, Rowan Blaize," she said calmly. "Do you desire further punishment? These affairs do not concern you. Go back to your forest and forget these people, who are *mine* to deal with. Go back, and I'll forget our personal differences. Stay, however, and you'll face the consequences."

The sorcerer smiled and glanced, warily, first at Starbane and then at Talthagar. Both had the wind knocked out of them and the warrior was bleeding a bit from the piercing shards of his shattered sword, but they would live. He would see to it.

"I'll not move from this spot, Oblixta. You are the one who needs to conjure an escape, while you can."

"Don't let her get away, Blaize," gasped Talthagar.

"Don't worry."

"So be it!" roared Oblixta. "I'll finish you *all* at once."

She raised her hands and cried out a charm that rocked the earth beneath their feet. Stones and boulders of various sizes began to leap and roll over the lip of the ridge. A massive cyclone of sand and debris began to form behind Oblixta, whipping and whirling with menace and the promise of destruction. Rowan Blaize watched all of this and then pointed the staff with a grimace at the frantically chanting Oblixta. The resulting blast flipped her into a wildly spinning arc over the scattering horses and head-first into a briar thicket beyond the rocks. Only her feet and the hem of her gown were visible and, when the quaking had stopped, Rowan approached.

"I have the Crone's staff, Oblixta. If you are alive, I highly suggest that—"

Suddenly the entire ridge was hit with a blast of heat so intense that the Prince and Talthagar felt the tips of their eyelashes burn away immediately. The warrior flung his bloody hands to his face while Starbane buried his nose in the dust and dirt of the ground, shrieking in pain. He had just enough time to see Rowan Blaize's form engulfed in a searing ball of flame that seemed to come from the bowels of the earth. The entire thicket was reduced to ash and, from its charred midst, Oblixta levitated into the air, radiant with fury.

"She's alive," moaned Starbane into the dust. "We're done for!"

But the twisting pillar of flame that swirled around Rowan began to dissipate even as Obixta hovered. Whips and tongues of fire broke away first and, even as they sought to engulf his body again, the warlock fought against the spell. Chanting incantations that rang on the wings of the wind, he caused the blaze to explode out and away from him, where it vanished into nothingness. He was free, but the Crone's staff had been burned to a crumbling twig in his hand. Its crystal was nowhere to be seen. Snarling in annoyance, he flung the now useless magical weapon away, lifting his hands to create a new spell of his own power. Oblixta, several feet off the ground, flew forward and tumbled into him before he had a chance to complete the enchantment. Over and over the two turned, kicking and punching by this stage, until they rolled right on top of Talthagar.

Oblixta once more produced the gleaming dagger, the fateful ritual blade she had taken so long ago from the Gragan wizard and had used to kill Queen Adurra. Wedged atop both Rowan and Talthagar by a massive boulder, she raised the thing with a hoarse cry of victory and chanted a spell more ancient and dark than any she had ever uttered.

"May the noonday gods take us, Rowan Blaize," said Talthagar. "She's won."

They stared at the blade in horror as Oblixta's ululating incantation filled their ears and created another tremor along the ridge. But the knife, the dagger of ultimate doom, did not pierce them.

In a mixture of shock and horror, Prince Starbane Cadrach lifted his scorched face just in time to see his sister's head fly like a whirling orb from her shoulders, out of sight and over the very ridge of the outer canyon itself. A great fountain of blood gushed upward from her decapitated torso and spattered rock, flesh, air, and time. On the bodies of Rowan Blaize and Talthagar, it was like a burning acid as they rolled and grappled from beneath to escape. Slowly, like a falling tree, Oblixta's torso sank and collapsed in a grisly, twitching heap on the ground. What her form and the fountain of blood had obscured in those final moments was the thing that made all eyes glow with wonder, and the entire vicinity grow silent and still.

Calm and collected, with shining sword still brandished, Ilyssa, maiden of Pyr Mida, daughter of an apothecary's cowardly assistant, stood over the body. She had been hiding in a nearby thicket with Skull before the conflict had begun and, taking an extra blade from the saddlepack of Talthagar's beloved stallion, she had rushed up the hill just in time.

"You'd make *me* the wench of one of your dirty prefects?" said Ilyssa to the headless corpse. "I don't *think* so, lady." Then she glanced at her friends. "Three supposedly powerful males, and not one of you could finish the job," she mused. "Looks like that was enough to make Oblixta laugh her head off, huh?"

Starbane, Talthagar, and Rowan Blaize gazed up at her in wonder, then. Through burning, teary eyes they stared at the way the flames from the raging thicket behind were welling up to frame Ilyssa's slender figure in an image of awe that would stay with all of them … for the rest of their lives.

They stared for a long time, it seemed. And then they smiled. Finally, they laughed. At that particular moment, there was no more fitting thing that any of them could do.